SLEEPING WITH THE STRANGLER

KEITH THOMAS WALKER

For Melissa Carter +
Hope you like this one
It's not a romance, but it's
a great story. Much love
and God bless!
2/24/15

KEITHWALKERBOOKS, INC
This is a UMS production

SLEEPING WITH THE STRANGLER

KEITHWALKERBOOKS

Publishing Company
KeithWalkerBooks, Inc.
P.O. Box 331585
Fort Worth, TX 76163

For information write
KeithWalkerBooks, Inc.
P.O. Box 331585
Fort Worth, TX 76163

ISBN-13 DIGIT: 978-0-9882180-3-1
ISBN-10 DIGIT: 0988218038
Library of Congress Control Number: 2013916844
Manufactured in the United States of America

First Edition

Visit us at www.keithwalkerbooks.com

This book is for my mom. Reading her Walter Mosley books inspired me to write this mystery/thriller. And I've been dying to write something spooky ever since I raided her bookshelf and fell in love with Stephen King – I was in the fifth grade at the time.

Parents who love books have children who love books.

MORE BOOKS BY
KEITH THOMAS WALKER

Fixin' Tyrone
How to Kill Your Husband
A Good Dude
Riding the Corporate Ladder
The Finley Sisters' Oath of Romance
Blow by Blow
Jewell and the Dapper Dan
Harlot
Plan C (And More KWB Shorts)
Dripping Chocolate
The Realest Ever
Jackson Memorial

NOVELLAS

Might Be Bi Part One
Harder

POETRY COLLECTION

Poor Righteous Poet

Visit keithwalkerbooks.com for information
about these and upcoming titles from
KeithWalkerBooks

ACKNOWLEGMENTS

Of course I would like to thank God, first and foremost, for giving me the creativity and drive to pursue my dreams and the understanding that I am nothing without Him. I would like to thank my wife for being my first and most important critic, and I would like to thank my mother for always pushing me to be the best I can be. I would like to thank Janae Hampton for being the best advisor, supporter and little sister a brother could ever have. I would also like to thank (in no particular order) Jason Owens, Brandy Rees, Denise Bolds, Sabrina Scott, Dianne Guinn, Sharon Blount, BRAB Book Club, Beulah Neveu and Uncle Steven Thomas, one love. I'd like to thank everyone who purchased and enjoyed one of my books. Everything I do has always been to please you. I know there are folks who mean the world to me that I'm failing to mention. I apologize ahead of time. Rest assured I'm grateful for everything you've done for me!

SLEEPING WITH THE STRANGLER

CHAPTER ONE
ASPHYXIA

The mood was perfect.

Deja had a brand new comforter on her bed. It was soft and smooth; with nary a lent ball, loose thread or even a wrinkle.

The only source of light illuminated from a small lamp on the bedroom dresser. Deja kept a 40 watt bulb in it. Coupled with the lamp's dark chocolate shade, the room had an *easy*, earthy feel to it. It was mellow. It was pleasant and relaxing.

Deja's bed was only a queen size, but it was stylish; solid oak with strong, sturdy legs that held the mattress nearly two feet off the floor. Her dressers and nightstand matched the bed, and her camel-colored drapes pulled everything together like gift wrap.

From an unseen outlet, a Glade plug-in emanated a barely detectable scent of vanilla passion fruit. A smooth bass line from the late, great Barry White flowed from a CD player on the dresser. The music warmed Deja's soul like a security blanket. She liked a lot of the current R&B singers, but she still preferred the classics her mother used to listen to decades ago.

The setting was ideal for making love. Deja was experiencing something similar at that very moment, but it was a far cry from the passionate romance she envisioned. In fact, she didn't think what they were doing would even qualify as *getting busy*.

Her boyfriend was a big man. Jerome was big in the chest and big in his underwear. His only flaw was his heart, which Deja compared to the Grinch who stole Christmas; because she thought it was ten sizes too small. That was the only explanation she could come up with. He loved her in the beginning – Deja was sure of it.

9

But something between them changed when she got pregnant. Deja noticed the transformation the moment she gave him the news.

Back then, in the early days, Jerome was a class act. He liked to shower with Deja and cook for her. They used to snuggle on the couch and drink wine and watch movies late into the evening. Jerome would pop the hood of her car at the slightest hint of a strange sound. He'd pay some of her bills randomly. And they used to make *love*; strong and passionate, deep and mind-numbing.

But one day things became different. It was sudden and unexpected. Deja felt like the moment she told him, "I'm pregnant," the fire simply died out. Deja convinced herself it was just his nerves. She thought Jerome would come around by her third, fourth or fifth month, but that never happened. Instead there seemed to be a direct correlation between her swelling belly and the way their relationship grew more and more strained.

Jerome never came out and said he hated the child she carried, and Deja never posed the question – because to acknowledge it would ruin everything. Jerome would have no reason to stay with her after that, and Deja would have to raise their child on her own.

Instead, she chose to wait it out. She ignored the way Jerome shuddered at the sight of her new stretch marks, knowing it would all be over soon. Deja was a hopeless romantic. She truly believed Jerome would fall in love with his son the moment he laid eyes on him. And maybe that would rekindle the love he once felt for the mother of his child.

In the meantime, Deja was seven and a half months pregnant, but that didn't quell her womanly urges. She checked online for sexual positions that wouldn't harm the baby and was surprised to find a multitude of them – more than she had in rotation before she got pregnant, in fact.

The position they tried tonight was an oldie but goodie: Woman on top. According to the internet, this move was favored not only because it took pressure off the female's back and stomach, but as an added bonus it offered her partner a great view. The first part was true, but Jerome was clearly not interested in his view. With the lights on, Deja could see him well. What she saw was enough to make her lose interest as well.

Jerome was a handsome man; tall and athletic, built like a college football player. He wore his hair short; the same length all around. His eyebrows were thin, and his lips were full. He had a wide nose that Deja thought was too big when she first met him, but the more time she spent around him, the more she realized it was perfect for his face. At 220 pounds, Jerome's doctor thought he could stand to lose a few pounds. But he worked out religiously, and the weight was mostly dispersed around his arms and chest. He had small, serious eyes that looked off to the left at that moment. As Deja watched, they swam slowly to the right.

Sometimes it was better to not look at him. Jerome clearly didn't want to make eye contact, and that could be depressing after a while. He didn't look totally *disgusted* with her, but his nonchalance was nearly as bad.

Deja, on the other hand, couldn't get enough of him. She was like a starved nympho. When her stomach started to poke out, their intimacy dropped from twice a week to twice a month, and it only got worse from there. Tonight was the first time he'd been inside her in seven weeks, and Deja would be damned if she didn't get what she needed from him. She didn't need him to love it or even like it. She was cool if he just laid there.

But that wasn't true.

She leaned forward and put her hands on his chest and watched his eyes as she pumped her hips up and down. Even if his heart wasn't in it, Jerome's dick was hard. The shaft provided continuous stimulation to her clitoris, making Deja's heart flutter. She was fully nude. Her breasts were large and perky. Her dark nipples were sensitive and erect. Her stomach was big, jutting from her body and resting on Jerome like some terrible deformity – and maybe that's why he began to go limp as she grinded her hips. Deja stopped for a second, thinking she couldn't be feeling right, but there was no mistake. She lifted her hips, and his penis fell out of her like a sick snake.

Deja sighed and didn't bother putting him back in. This happened twice in their last four attempts, and she knew their session had come to an end. She didn't even reach a climax yet. She could suck him until he was hard again, but why bother, if he wasn't going to stay erect for the main event?

She climbed off of him, and Jerome rolled to his side looking for his underwear. Without speaking, Deja got out of bed

11

and went to the bathroom to shower. She didn't feel pain or embarrassment for this thing that happened to their relationship. She didn't look back at him, and Jerome didn't call out to her.

≈ ≈ ≈ ≈ ≈ ≈

She got out of the shower ten minutes later and opened the door so the fog could waft from the bathroom. She dressed in panties and a robe and stared at her reflection in the mirror when it was clear enough for her to see. Deja wore her hair back in a ponytail with a bang hanging over her left eye. She was brown-skinned, the color of cognac.

Her breast had always been B cups, but they bulged from her bras now because of the extra weight from the baby. The pregnancy also added a few pounds to Deja's hips and ass. She thought that would make her more appealing to Jerome, but that wasn't the only weight gain motherhood brought. Deja used to have a perfect stomach; so flat her belly button was nearly an outie. But now her stomach protruded from her frame at least seven inches. And then there were the stretch-marks and swollen feet and puffy face and chunky thighs.

Deja couldn't deny that she was unattractive now. She believed Jerome had just cause for his fleeting desires. But after she had the baby, things would go back to normal. Deja believed that whole-heartedly; totally oblivious to the fact that she'd given in to her boyfriend's psychological abuse.

Back in the bedroom Jerome was already dressed. For some reason, that hurt Deja more than their intimacy problems. She sat next to him on the corner of the bed. Jerome bent to lace up his shoes.

"You not staying the night?"

He shook his head. "Uh uhn. Got an early meeting."

Deja rubbed the back of his neck. "I can wake you up early," she offered.

Jerome shook his head. "I didn't bring my clothes over here."

"I have some in the closet."

"I need my briefcase, too," Jerome said. "I left it at home."

That was a good excuse, but it was also an odd one. Jerome and his briefcase were as inseparable as a preacher and his bible. Deja was sure she'd see the briefcase on his passenger seat if she followed him out to his car, but she didn't push it. If he wanted to go, he would go, regardless of how she felt about it.

"The doctor said the baby might be early," she said instead.

Jerome took the news well. He didn't look like this was the worst thing in the world for him. He tied his other shoe and sat up and looked at her. "Oh yeah?"

Deja nodded. "I'm almost eight months. He doesn't think I'll go past eight and a half."

Jerome looked down at her belly with a slight grin. "It look like he about to come right now."

Deja grinned too. "I know. I'm big, right?"

"You ain't that bad."

"I know I am," Deja said. "I'm a lot bigger than when we first met."

Jerome's smile went away, and his look was nostalgic. "Yeah..."

"I know we've been having problems," Deja said. "But it's almost over. I'll lose the weight right after the baby. I promise."

Jerome shook his head. "You think things are gonna get better *after* you have the baby?"

"Well, I know it's going to be a lot of responsibility. But at least we can get our sex life back on track."

Jerome sneered, and Deja knew she broke a cardinal rule: Never speak of your man's sexual inadequacies.

Jerome pushed off the bed. "I'm finna go."

Deja got up too and walked with him to the door. "Did you come up with any names yet?" She thought she'd change the subject, but that was just as bad.

"I don't care what you call him."

That hurt like hell, all the way down to her soul, but Deja didn't let it show. She put on a crocodile smile, much like she was accustomed to doing for the past few months.

"Don't talk like that. I know there's *something* you wouldn't mind calling him. You can only yell '*Hey boy*!' for the first month."

Either Jerome didn't get the joke, or he didn't plan on sticking around that long.

"For real, Deja. Whatever you come up with is cool."

"What about Jerome?"

13

He stopped at the front door and turned to face her. He shook his head. "Naw. I don't like that."

"Why? You don't want a junior?"

"Why don't you name him Dijon?"

Deja thought that was a terrible idea, but she was happy to engage in a conversation about their child. She stepped close to him until their stomachs touched. Back in the day, it was their hips that met first. Deja put her arms around her man, and he returned the gesture.

Jerome wore black jeans with a green button-down she bought him for Christmas. It was late March – already tee-shirt weather for most residents of Overbrook Meadows, Texas – but the shirt was thin and Jerome wasn't hot in it. He didn't have it tucked in, but he still looked very GQ. His trendy dress was the first thing that attracted Deja to him.

"What about Butters?" he asked.

"What do you mean?"

"The baby," he said. "We can name him Butters."

Deja frowned. "That might work if he's a bright yellow cat, but I'm pretty sure he's going to be human."

Jerome laughed. He had bright teeth and a big smile. It always did Deja's heart good to see him in a good mood. "Well, what about Stan?" he said with a chuckle. "Or Kyle."

Deja actually considered that until she realized he was naming characters from a television show. "Or maybe we can name him *Chef*," she said. "Or Token."

Jerome laughed again. He bent and kissed her on the mouth. His lips were sweet and warm, and they still made Deja giddy, despite all of his faults.

"Can't you go one day without your briefcase?"

"Huh?"

"I want you to spend the night," she pleaded. "Can't you go one day without your briefcase?"

He shook his head. "Oh, naw, baby. I wish I could." He kissed her again and gave her another brief hug. "I'll call you tomorrow."

"Alright." Deja walked him outside and stood on the porch until he disappeared around the corner of the building. She couldn't see the apartment's parking lot from there, but she heard his truck's big engine when he started it up. Jerome sped out of

14

the apartments like it was a race. Deja didn't close the door until he was out of earshot.

She silently wished him a safe trip, though a part of her wondered if he was headed to his home or someone else's.

≈≈≈≈≈≈

At two-thirty am Deja's eyes flashed open. She didn't lift her head off the pillow, though she fell back asleep thinking she heard something.

Fifteen minutes later, Deja woke up again. This time she definitely heard a sound; she recognized it as her mattress springs responding to the weight of someone climbing into bed with her. A dreamy smile spread across her face, and she was glad Jerome changed his mind.

"What about your briefcase?" she muttered, but he did not respond.

Deja lay on her side, curled almost in a fetal position. Jerome settled in behind her. He moved very slowly, but Deja could hear him breathing. She backed into him, and Jerome returned the favor by rolling onto his side so he could spoon her. He wrapped his arm around her, and Deja cradled his hand against her stomach. She fell asleep again, loving the way his warm breaths felt on the back of her neck.

Deja woke up again at ten minutes 'til four. This time it was because Jerome was still not asleep, and he was getting a little frisky. His left hand was no longer resting on her stomach. It was moving here and there, in an almost frantic pace. He fondled Deja's bare breasts; cupping and caressing, squeezing her nipples softly.

A curious smile parted Deja's lips, and she opened her eyes again. A knot of tension throbbed between her legs because she didn't take care of herself when Jerome left earlier. Her breath caught as her body began to respond to his advances. She couldn't remember the last time Jerome felt her up while she slept, and she liked it. His breaths were now hot and fast on the back of her head.

Deja reached back with her left hand and ran her fingers from his ear to his chin. Jerome had a sheet over his head. Deja grinned.

"Are we playing *Hide and Go Get Some*?" she asked. "Don't be shy."

She pulled the top sheet across her body until it was a wrinkled pile against her belly. She reached back again, but Jerome still had the same *condition*. Deja knitted her eyebrows and patted his face, wondering where the hell he got another sheet from. And this second sheet, it was tight. And it wasn't merely lying on his face; it was wrapped around his head somehow. Deja felt behind her, trying to make sense of things. But things didn't make sense.

She was reminded of a game she played as a child. Her teacher would put an object in a burlap sack and have the students reach in one at a time. The goal was to use your sense of touch to determine what item she had in the bag. If she had to guess now, Deja would say she felt something smooth and silky, like her panty hose.

But that was silly. And it was strange that Jerome wasn't talking to her. But then again, he wasn't making *any* sound at that moment. Deja listened closely and thought he might be holding his breath. She rolled over, thinking this was the strangest thing he'd ever done, and even when she saw that Jerome really did have her stockings on his head, Deja still thought he was trying to get a rise out of her. Her heart skipped a beat, but she managed a quivery chuckle.

"Boy, wha, what are you doing? Take that off."

She reached for it, and Jerome knocked her hand away. They lay there with their faces less than twelve inches apart. A frigid chill suddenly spread across Deja's body. Her smile slipped away, and her pupils grew large.

"Stop playing..." As she spoke, Deja's eyes registered things her mind refused to accept. Beneath the nylons, Jerome's face was distorted beyond recognition. He didn't look familiar at all. There was no way pantyhose could disguise him so completely, could they? Deja fought hard to compare Jerome's face with this current face, but she could not. It was nearly completely dark in her bedroom, but she saw enough to know that this wasn't her man. She couldn't put her finger on it, but there was something wrong with the eyes.

As that realization became a reality, Deja noticed other things that were wrong; the most obvious being the fact that the man in her bed was fully dressed. Jerome would never get into bed with pants on. And even worse; the man wasn't wearing the same colors Jerome had on earlier. Rather than black jeans, this guy had on blue pants. And instead of the green button-down, the person in her bed wore a dark-colored pullover; it was either black or dark blue.

All of these observances occurred in a split second, and when Deja looked back to the man's eyes, she saw that he was watching her eyes as well. The chill Deja felt became more frigid. Her heart shot up in her throat and pumped hard and loud. Deja's eyes were as big as silver dollars, but the man in her bed didn't respond to her change in demeanor. He just lie there and waited. Deja was so afraid she almost threw up, but she waited too, knowing the next move would reveal his intentions for her and her unborn child as well.

It didn't matter who moved first. All she knew was something was going to happen. Something had to give. Deja's whole body shuddered, and she felt a sudden cramping in her stomach. The chills she felt became an icy heat, and beads of sweat sprouted on her forehead. The man in her bed watched it all. Deja felt like they'd been watching each other for an eternity, but only three seconds passed since she first rolled over to face him.

He reached for her, and Deja made her move.

With a shriek she swung hard with her right arm. Her little fist was balled, and she had the perfect arc to pummel his ear. But the intruder blocked the blow easily with his forearm. His eyes narrowed, and Deja knew she'd made a huge mistake.

The man sat up in her bed with uncanny speed. He grabbed the arm she swung with and pushed it to the opposite side of the bed. Before Deja could come to terms with what was happening, he rolled her onto her back and straddled her legs. Deja screamed and got a hard *WHAP!* on the side of the head in return.

"*Shut up!*" His voice was deep and gravelly, more animal than human – or maybe that was just the way it sounded in the heat of the moment.

He slapped his left hand over her mouth, and Deja's whole life flashed before her eyes. She clawed desperately with both hands, and the intruder produced a knife from beneath his pillow.

17

He growled and waved it before her eyes. Deja was scared stiff. Her throat caught, cutting off her screams like someone flipped a switch. The prowler held her mouth so roughly her bottom lip split. He put the blade under her chin and pressed hard. Deja's heart thundered. She knew he sliced an artery.

He watched her eyes for a moment and then leaned very close.

"*Stop fighting,*" he ordered. "*I'll kill you! I'll kill you and the baby! If you scream again, I'll stab your stomach.*"

His voice was raspy; somewhere between a whisper and a yell. His breath was foul. His teeth were bared behind the panty hose, and there was no doubt he was telling the truth.

He took his hand away, and Deja's eyes welled with tears. She sobbed weakly, her heart thudding like a kicker box. "*Please!*" she squealed. "*Please. I'm pregnant! Please st–*"

The intruder swung quickly and delivered a vicious open-handed blow that sounded off in the room like a cap gun.

SPLACK!

Deja had never been hit like that. Her head snapped to the side, and a bright explosion of red and white completely blinded her for a moment.

"*Shut up!*" he barked. "*Get your hands down!*"

Deja didn't know she raised her arms. She fought hard to maintain consciousness as something like a freight train roared in her ears. "*Okay!*" she pleaded, a coppery taste of blood in her mouth. "*Okay, please...*" Her vision swam in and out of focus, and on some level she understood what was happening. But for the most part, none of this made sense. This was a sick dream. It was a nightmare that had somehow escaped the realm of her subconscious.

"*Turn over.*" The man spoke in a loud whisper. He shoved her shoulder roughly, and Deja submitted to him. She cried and rolled until she lay on her side.

Still straddling her, the intruder reached for her left arm. He bound her wrist with something that felt soft at first, but the more he wrapped it around her arm, the harder and tighter it became. He reached for her right hand and attempted the same motion, but Deja started to fight again.

"No." Her voice was soft and muffled like she was speaking through a mouthful of cotton. Her heart still raced, but the blow to her head made everything slow and disconnected. She knew she couldn't get him off of her, but she twisted her wrist to and fro to make his job harder. He eventually did get her right arm bound, but it wasn't as tight as the left wrist. Deja thought she could probably free herself if she fought really hard.

The thought went away when the man rolled her over again. The room spun, and Deja didn't know which way was up anymore. Her left eye was partially swollen closed. She felt blood on her cheek. She'd never been raped before, and so far it was as horrifying as she imagined. She wondered what kind of sicko would want a woman so far along in her pregnancy. She wondered if he looked on the internet for safe positions that wouldn't harm the baby.

The rapist was speaking, but she couldn't understand him until she watched his mouth.

He sat on her legs, leaning over her stomach. "Why don't you like me?" he asked. "Why you don't love me?"

Deja was close to blacking out. In her delirium, she again thought it was Jerome in bed with her. "I do," she whispered. "I do love you."

"*Stop lying!*"

He punched with his fist this time, and Deja's head rocked like a bobblehead doll. Her eyes rolled to the back of her head, and sleep fell upon her like heavy rain. Rather than fight it, Deja ran to the darkness. She wanted to go to sleep. She needed it. Sleep was her only respite, and this would all be over when she woke up.

Except, she couldn't sleep.

Because she couldn't breathe.

Deja gasped for air and her eyes fluttered open. What she saw vanquished all vestiges of drowsiness from her head. The rapist had both hands on her throat, and this was definitely not a dream. She could see the fire burning in his eyes. She could see the muscles and tendons straining in his arms.

Deja's mouth fell open. She gagged but could only squeeze a teaspoon of air down her windpipe. Her tongue rolled sickly, and her eyes darted like hockey pucks. She gagged again, horrified to learn that rape wasn't on his agenda after all. He stared into her eyes, and Deja watched his in a panic. And she knew she was going to die. This man was the epitome of evil. This was the devil himself.

Refusing to accept her impending doom, Deja's struggles increased to a wild and rabid frenzy. But it was no use. The intruder was nearly twice her size, and she didn't have her arms to fight with. She kicked out anyway, but the killer sat firmly on her thighs. Her wild legs were barely a distraction. She pushed against the bed and tried to buck him off. He rode her like a cowboy, and Deja knew that each buck did more harm to her child than to the intruder.

That sick understanding pushed Deja into a survival mode that was primed with maternal instincts. She didn't know what hypoxic meant. She couldn't define asphyxia or cerebral ischemia either. But one thing Deja did know was that if she couldn't breathe, her baby couldn't breathe, either.

He wasn't just killing her.

He was killing the baby!

Deja's head started to drum at the same pace as her frantic heartbeats. Her face was beet red. Her jugular veins and carotid artery bulged as blood rich with life-saving oxygen stalled beneath the attacker's grip. And even as her hyoid bone cracked in two, Deja forced herself to remain focused. Tears streamed down her face. Her lungs were on fire, but she finally found the advantage she sought: The assailant moaned with pleasure. Through the stocking, Deja saw ecstasy in his eyes. This was the moment he lived for. His delight was real. It was euphoric, and the killer was nearly lost in the sensation.

At that second, Deja fought her hardest against the bindings on her wrists. Her left arm held secure, but her right arm was still a little loose. She yanked against the restraints and was greeted with a searing pain deep in her wrist and thumb joint. She ignored the anguish and jerked harder, wondering how long it had been already. Three seconds? Four? Maybe ten? How long before her brain became oxygen starved and useless? She wondered if her baby had already suffered irreparable injuries.

The pain in her wrist somehow rivaled the pain in her throat, and Deja heard a slight **POP** as something came out of its socket. But her arm pulled free from the binding, and that was all that mattered. The killer saw it, too. His eyes narrowed and his grip on her throat intensified. But Deja was already on the attack.

20

She didn't think she had any energy left, but her first punch was heavy and hard, landing squarely on the killer's chin. He grunted and tried to shake it off, but her follow up blow caught him flush on the Adam's apple.

His hands slipped from her neck. It was rewarding to see the look of shock as he reached for his own throat, but Deja didn't have time to enjoy his suffering. She frantically used her free hand to remove the restraints on the other. She rolled to her side and gulped air like a fish out of water as she slithered across the mattress. Her first breath was rough and choppy. Her lungs all but rejected the oxygen it craved so much. But still, that was the best air Deja ever tasted.

She squeezed another breath down her collapsed esophagus and sucked in another and another. Her body forced most of the oxygen back out in harsh coughs, but some got in. Deja felt nauseous and was on the verge of passing out again. She fell off the bed, and a sharp pain in her stomach jolted her back to awareness.

She looked back and screamed when she saw him coming for her. But she was next to her nightstand now, and salvation was only inches away. Deja clawed at the small drawer and saw that it was a telephone cord wrapped around her left wrist. She reached into the drawer with her right hand as the killer fell onto the floor behind her. He clawed at her legs. Deja's hand came in contact first with her bible and then with cold steel. Her thumb did not want to close around the handle of the pistol. She forced her hand to work, ignoring the agonizing pain that radiated up her arm.

The intruder was already retreating when she turned in his direction again, but Deja fired anyway.

BLAM!

The gunfire was deafening. A flash of lightening illuminated the room. She saw a dark figure duck into the hallway. Deja pointed her gun at the thin wall. She aimed five feet ahead of him, trying to calculate his movements.

BLAM!
BLAM!
BLAM!

Her ears were ringing in the wake of the gunshots, but Deja didn't hear anyone screaming. Eventually she did hear a scratchy, wheezing sound that terrified her until she realized she was making the noise. She coughed and cried and hurried to wipe the tears and snot from her face. She steadied the gun with both hands and trained it on the only entrance to her bedroom. There was no one there, but her brain would not accept that he was really gone.

Her arms trembled. She refused to lower them. Her breathing became so bad she could've sucked more air through a straw, but she did not lower the gun. Even when her panties became wet with what she assumed was blood, Deja wouldn't look away from the doorway.

She dared not.

She sat and waited and cried for an eternity. The police announced their presence when they entered her apartment, but Deja didn't lower the gun until a uniformed officer appeared in the bedroom doorway.

"**DROP YOUR WEAPON!**" he screamed.

Deja did as she was told. Her gratitude came in the form of a spine-tingling wail that was wrought with agony. Before the officer could reach her, Deja's mind flooded the room with sweet darkness once again.

This time she had no choice but to succumb to it.

CHAPTER TWO
ASAD

shhhhhhhhhlllaaaarrrrrrrrrrrrrrmmmmmmmmm
shhlllaarrmm
shhhhhhhhh

White light sped towards her. Through a haze. Like a big truck's headlights rushing out of a fog. She knew it was wrong to stand in the middle of the street. It made even less sense to wait for a light that was affixed to the front of an 18-wheeler, but she stood and waited anyway.

She waited with pinpricks rolling up and down her thighs. She shifted her weight from one leg to the other and then back again. She waited and watched, and the headlights drew closer and closer. The truck's engine was loud. And as it advanced, she could hear the driver laying on the horn; trying to warn her.

shhhhhhhhhlllaaaarrrrrrrrrrrrrrmmmmmmmmm

The sound didn't quite fit an 18-wheeler, but she knew that's what it was. She knew it because the sound got louder as the lights grew brighter and the truck got closer. When it was within a mile, the brightness was much more than she expected. She was bathed in the radiance. And she felt fearful and exposed.

She tried to run then. But the pinpricks she felt on her thighs were now fiery hot. They were glowing fireplace pokers that pierced her skin and dug into her muscles. They burned so badly. They hurt more than anything she ever felt before. And it wasn't just her thighs anymore. The pokers stabbed between her legs and in her belly and in her uterus.

Deja's heart froze and then hammered in her chest like a rain song on a hoop drum. Her immediate concern was for her unborn child. She tried to throw her arms over her stomach to protect her baby. But she couldn't move.

She screamed, but it was too late. At that moment the truck was upon her. The collision was not what she expected, but it was still devastating. Deja felt herself falling backwards.

She fell for a long time. She braced herself for the impact of the hard, cold street. But once again things were not as they seemed. Deja fell onto the soft mattress of a bed instead. And with that realization, she understood that the bed had been there all along.

The bright headlights faded and settled into the dull illumination of florescent bulbs. Deja fought to open her eyes, but her eyelids disobeyed her. They held fast as if stitched together. The fiery pokers continued to stab her like a king crab tearing into a fish's soft underside.

Deja tried to get up, but she couldn't do that either. Something held her down. The more she struggled against it, the stronger her restraints became. To make matters worse, Deja realized she could no longer breathe. She felt hands on her throat again. She fought against them with all her might. Fat tears welled in her eyes and rolled down her cheeks.

She tried her hardest and somehow managed to fill her lungs with oxygen. With all of her remaining strength, she belted another scream. This one was ten times louder and more forceful than the first. It exploded from her body like an erupting volcano. ***STOP!***

≈ ≈ ≈ ≈ ≈ ≈

Deja's eyes flashed open. She sat up in the bed with sweat and blood glistening on her cheeks. She had a huge contusion on her forehead, but it was almost unnoticeable compared to her split and swollen lower lip. She recognized her surroundings as a hospital room, but that understanding did not immediately ease her apprehension.

There were six people in the room with Deja, and they all had on gowns and masks. Most of their attention was between her legs where a doctor crouched with both hands inside her. To his left a female in dark blue scrubs held Deja's right leg steady. To the doctor's right another female nurse struggled to keep her other leg still.

Deja looked around frantically and saw that her wrists were not bound with telephone cords. She couldn't move her arms because each one was in the grip of a medical assistant. Everyone watched her with more compassion than anger at the way she was fighting them.

The last person in the room stood at the head of the bed. She was a brunette with large, comforting eyes. She leaned over Deja and dotted her forehead with a soft, damp towel.

"She's awake," the woman announced when her patient's eyes fluttered open. "Hey, honey. Are you okay?" Her voice was soft. Her smile was gentle. She ran a gloved hand through Deja's sweat-drenched hair. Her touch was surprisingly calming. Deja's expression became less and less like a wounded animal as memories slowly came back to her.

"Where, what?" Her throat rattled painfully. It was not possible to speak. Deja felt like she had a thorny, petrified meatball stuck in her trachea. She tried to reach for her throat, but she still couldn't move her arm. She gazed curiously at the girls holding her and then looked back to the woman with the towel. "What..."

"It's okay," the nurse assured her. "You're safe now." She reached for Deja's shoulders and gently pushed her back to the bed. "Calm down. You can let her go," she told the orderlies.

When her arms were free, Deja's hands immediately flew to her throat. She felt soreness and swelling, but thankfully there were no murderous hands squeezing the life out of her.

The doctor looked up over her belly with a half-smile. He was black and clean-shaven. His hair was short and mostly gray. He wore big glasses with thick lenses that made his eyeballs look very small. "You're doing great," he told Deja. "We've got the head."

Deja had only half a second to make sense of that before the fiery poker pierced her abdomen again. She threw her head back and screamed like a banshee as something like a watermelon stretched and squeezed and tore itself from her body. It was the most pain she ever felt, but it soon subsided into a mellow throbbing. The doctor looked up again with a full smile this time.

"Got him," he said and handed a grayish, wrinkly baby to one of the nurses.

Deja stared in astonishment and forgot about all else for a moment. The doctor cut the umbilical cord while the nurse sucked mucus from the baby's mouth and nose with a bulb syringe. There was another brief tug when Deja delivered the afterbirth, but she was in a state of shock and fantasy by then, and she barely felt it.

She watched her baby with her head cocked and her mouth ajar. For so many months she dreaded labor and delivery. It didn't seem possible that she got through it with hardly any dread or recognition. But her eyes were not deceiving her and neither were her ears. The baby started to cry. The sound filled Deja's heart with relief and wonderment.

They wrapped the infant in a blanket but didn't bring him to his mother as expected. Instead they headed in the opposite direction. Deja nearly leapt from the bed in an attempt to follow them.

"Wait!"

The shout caused a huge explosion of pain in her throat that rivaled the soreness in her lower abdomen. The many hands were on her again; pushing her back to a lying position. Deja didn't fight them this time.

"It's okay," the doctor said.

Deja's eyes were wide and panicked. Her breaths were quick and painful.

"You must go to surgery," the doctor explained, and Deja noticed his African accent for the first time.

"*Why?*" she pleaded. "*My baby...*"

"It's okay. Let her go," the physician ordered.

They unhanded her, and Deja did not try to get up.

"You must have surgery," the doctor said again. He approached the side of the bed and stared down at her woefully. "You were attacked. Very badly. You have a broken bone in your neck, and they must repair it. It is a simple procedure. You will be fine."

The horrors of surgery meant nothing at that point. "But, my baby..."

"Your baby is fine," the doctor assured her. "It is you who is hurt. Now, they will take you to surgery. They are waiting for you." He nodded to the medical assistants, and they prepped her bed and IV line for travel.

Deja watched the doctor until he nodded and walked away. A nurse stepped between her legs and began to clean her, and Deja decided she didn't feel good about her labor and delivery at all. This was a special moment. It was supposed to be magical. There wasn't even a familiar face there to support her.

She closed her eyes and wept quietly. It was impossible to swallow, and with this realization her mouth quickly filled with saliva.

≈≈≈≈≈≈

Deja only remembered two things about her surgery. She remembered when the anesthesiologist told her to count backwards from ten to one, and she remembered waking up in a surgical recover unit.

As soon as she had enough strength, she raised her hand and summoned a nurse to her bedside. She couldn't talk, so she whispered her request. *"Can I see my baby?"*

"Uh, no. Not on this unit."

Deja started to cry again, and the older woman melted.

"Uh, let me see what I can do," she said.

It took twenty-four minutes, but they finally brought the baby to her. They rolled him in on a small bassinet. Deja couldn't get up, but she could watch him from her vantage point, and she was content with that. Her son was beautiful and healthy. He had vanilla-colored skin and a head full of hair.

"You early," she whispered with a weak smile.

The baby was fast asleep, and soon Deja was too.

≈≈≈≈≈≈

She couldn't get any visits until they moved her to a private room, and that didn't happen until two hours after the surgery. Deja didn't think anyone knew she was in the hospital, but when they got her to the sixth floor, there were four people waiting on her.

Her parents, Bernard and Shirley Franklin, were as forlorn as she'd ever seen them. The sight of their battered and bruised

27

daughter didn't brighten their moods at all. Deja's appearance actually made them feel worse. Her mom's legs weakened and wobbled, and she dropped like a sack of potatoes.

"*Oh my Jesus!*"

Her husband caught her before she hit the floor, with the help of Deja's big brother Vincent.

"Mama!"

With four strong hands on her, Shirley was no longer in danger of falling. But she still looked sick and frail. They helped her to a chair, where she slouched and began to sob loudly.

"*Oh, Jesus, what they do to my baby?*"

"*I'm alright,*" Deja whispered, but the sound of her voice said otherwise.

"*I can't believe this happened to my baby!*" Shirley wailed. "*Why, Jesus? Why they do this?*"

Deja's mom was a large, dark-skinned woman with strong arms and a jet black wig that wasn't on straight this morning. She wore green slacks with a gray sweater and white tennis. Shirley was usually a good dresser. But no one could blame her for today's fashion faux pas, given the dire circumstances.

Deja's brother approached the bed once they got Mama settled. Deja's sister Julie stood demurely at his side. As twins, they were physically similar, but their emotions couldn't have been more different.

"Are, are you okay?" Julie spoke softly. Her voice was almost childlike. "You had your baby already?"

Deja nodded. "Yeah."

"Man, I can't believe somebody fucked with my sister," Vincent spat.

"I'm okay," Deja whispered.

Julie reached down and touched the knot on her sister's forehead. She brushed her cheek softly, and then Julie's face contorted in sorrow. "Oh my God, Deja..."

"Stop it," Deja said, on the verge of tears herself. "It's okay. I'm okay now."

Her father, Bernard, offered his arm as a cane, and Shirley was able to make it to a standing position. They shuffled to the other side of the bed like a much older couple. With so many eyes staring down at her, Deja never felt so vulnerable and so loved.

"You doing okay, sweat pea?" her father asked.

Deja nodded, but even that hurt her neck. "Yeah," she whispered. Her mouth was dry, her lips chapped.

"Who did it?" Vincent wanted to know. "Who did this to you?"

Deja shook her head and tears rolled down her cheeks. "I don't know."

"Where was yo punk ass boyfriend?" Vincent asked. "How come Jerome wasn't with you?"

Deja's brother was a 34 year old self-proclaimed goon. Deja had no doubt he would track down and physically harm her assailant if she could provide a name. For that reason, she was almost glad she didn't know who it was. Vincent was already on probation. His vigilante justice would only make things worse.

"Jerome had to go home," Deja whispered. "I don't know who did this. I really don't." Her voice was rusty and squeaky, like an old hinge. Listening to it made her mother cringe.

"*Oh, what they do to my baby*?" Shirley cried. She leaned on the bedrail with hands that shook uncontrollably.

Deja's dad put a strong arm around her waist. "It's gonna be alright, sugar."

Bernard wore denim overalls with a short-sleeved button down. At six-foot-five and 280 pounds, he was the biggest man Deja knew personally. He wore a salt-and-pepper afro with a short beard. Contrary to his propensity to dress like a farmer, Deja's father had a bachelor's degree and had worked behind a desk his whole life.

"Where yo punk ass boyfriend at *now*?" Vincent asked.

"Chill with all of that," Julie told him. She took his hand and held it tightly. Julie was one of few people who could calm Vincent once he got riled up.

Deja's brother and sister were brown-skinned. They were both five-foot-nine inches, which made Julie tall for a girl and Vincent short for a boy. They both wore their hair short and had the same beady eyes and small noses. Julie was more handsome than pretty, and Vincent had long eyelashes and thin lips that made him more pretty than handsome. Deja loved them dearly.

"Can you tell us what happened?" her father asked.

"I don't know," Deja whispered. "I woke up and there was, there was this man in my bed. He punched me and tried to kill me."

Her mother brought a hand to her mouth. Fresh tears squirted from her eyes.

"What happened to your neck?" Julie asked.

"He choked me. He broke my, my..." Deja trailed off because she forgot the technical term for the broken bone.

"*He broke your neck?*" Vincent was so upset, Deja thought steam might shoot from his ears.

She shook her head. "No, my..."

A nurse walked into the room then, and she wasn't too happy about the scene around her patient.

"Hey, hey... I'm glad all of you could make it, but can you please back away from the bed. You're crowding her. She can't talk too much right now."

The nurse had a thick, Caribbean accent that reminded Deja of Miss Cleo from the infamous psychic hotline. She had beautiful dark skin and the tall, thin figure of a runway model.

Everyone took a few steps away from the bed to give her space to check Deja's vitals.

"You look a lot better," she said with a friendly smile.

"I'm okay," Deja croaked.

"What's, what they say wrong with her neck?" Vincent asked.

"She has a broken hyoid," the nurse said without looking back. "It's a bone in the front of the neck. The hyoid is almost always broken when someone is choked this severely."

"She don't have to wear no neck brace?" Vincent asked.

"No," the nurse replied. "The doctors used a procedure called *tension band wiring pin*. It will heal soon. She had a dislocated thumb as well, but we popped it back in. She'll be fine."

"They don't know who did it?" Shirley asked.

The nurse didn't answer because she was listening to her stethoscope. She looked up when she was done. "What was that?"

"Do they know who did it?" Deja's father asked.

The nurse shook her head. "I am not sure, sir. But I am not a police officer. There is a policeman here, and he has – ah, here he is."

Everyone followed her gaze to the doorway where a neatly dressed detective stood. He wore khaki slacks with a dark green button down. He did not have a visible badge anywhere Deja could see. He was handsome, in his late thirties. He stepped into the room carrying a manila folder.

"Hi," he said. "Is she awake?"

Deja's family remained mute, but the nurse responded. "Yes. She's doing well. But she can barely speak. Do you need to talk to her now?"

"I'd like to ask her a few questions," the policeman confirmed. "I can wait 'til later for the formal interview, but I have a couple of things..."

The nurse nodded. "Okay. But don't stress her. Come on," she said to the visitors. "Let's leave them alone for a moment."

Deja's family reluctantly followed the nurse out, and the policeman came and stood at the side of the bed.

"Hello," he said. "I'm Detective Rudy Cervantes."

"Hi," Deja squeaked.

The officer studied her closely and then removed a small digital camera from his pocket. He turned it on and asked, "Do you mind?"

Deja shook her head, and Mr. Cervantes snapped a dozen pictures of her injuries.

"How are you feeling?" he asked when he was done.

"I'm okay," Deja whispered.

"I'm a homicide detective," the policeman said.

That was a shock, and it showed in Deja's eyes.

"I don't normally handle cases where the victim is still alive," Mr. Cervantes said. "But I believe your case is related to others I've been working on. I know you can't speak well, but do you think you can answer a few questions?"

Deja nodded, and the detective produced a small tape recorder.

"Do you remember what happened to you?"

Deja nodded. "I woke up and somebody was in my bed." It hurt to get the sentence out. She winced after every few words.

"He was already in bed with you when you woke up?"

Deja nodded and then whispered, "Yes," for the recorder.

"And then what happened?" the detective asked.

"He tied me up and tried to choke me," Deja said. The memory of the attack flooded her mind. She frowned and shuddered unconsciously.

"How did you get away?" Mr. Cervantes asked.

31

"The ropes," Deja said. "The phone cord, it wasn't tight. I got my arm out and hit him. I made it to my gun."

The detective nodded and scribbled in his notebook. "Did you get a good look at the intruder?"

Deja shook her head. "No. He had a mask."

"What kind of mask?"

"It was, panty hose."

More scribbling. "I'll come back and talk to you later, in more detail," the policeman said. "When you feel a little better."

Deja nodded.

"There was no sexual assault?"

Deja shook her head. Something tugged at the back of her mind, but she couldn't figure out what it was.

"Are you familiar with the South Side Strangler?" the detective asked, and Deja's body was suddenly enveloped in chills.

She nodded hesitantly, though she didn't know much. She heard there was a murder or two a couple of months ago, both on the south side of town. But she thought they caught that guy. Either way, those stories were like urban legends. Stuff like that always happened to *other people*.

"We believe you were assaulted by the same individual," Mr. Cervantes said, and the ground fell from beneath Deja.

As she swooned, her mind went back to the attack, and she could see everything vividly. She remembered rolling over, thinking it was Jerome in bed with her. She remembered the intruder hitting her, tying her up. She remembered when he asked how come she didn't love him.

Deja knew he was a weirdo, but she never imagined he killed before. She certainly didn't think she was in the presence of a *serial killer*. Now it was even more astonishing she made it through the ordeal. The detective read her expression perfectly.

"You're very lucky to be here," he said. "To my knowledge, you're the only one to live through his attack."

Deja's heart began to knock in her chest. She could still see those eyes behind the pantyhose. She could smell his breath again. She looked around fretfully, as if he might be lurking in the hospital somewhere, waiting for his chance to finish her off.

"Everything's okay," the detective said. "We caught the guy. He's in jail right now."

His words hit Deja like an unexpected summer rain. She never felt so relieved.

"You, you got him?"

"Yes," Mr. Cervantes said with a smile. She could see the pride in his eyes. "He's not going to hurt anyone else."

Deja smiled hesitantly. Her breaths gradually became slow and steady. "What does, he look like?" she asked.

"I'll bring the file with me when I come back," the detective promised. "I'll tell you anything you want to know about him. For now, I can tell you his name is Gilbert Reynolds, and he's been locked up before. He did ten years for rape and kidnapping back in '94. While in prison, he choked a man nearly to death. He's a real bad apple. We're glad to get him off the streets."

Deja was glad, too. She might actually be able to sleep at night.

"Everyone's very proud of you." The detective stood and patted her shoulder softly. "We'll talk more tomorrow. I'll send your family back in."

"Thanks," Deja whispered. "Thank you so much."

≈ ≈ ≈ ≈ ≈ ≈

Her family returned with Jerome in tow. Deja was very happy to see her boyfriend. He said he got there as soon as he could, and she believed him. Vincent continued to give him dirty looks, but he didn't know Jerome like Deja did. No one did. It didn't matter how long it took him to get there. Jerome was there now, and that's all that mattered.

Later they brought the baby to the room, and it finally started to feel like a special day. Deja's parents doted on their brand new grandchild, and no one talked about the strangler for a while.

Jerome even held his son for a few minutes. Deja didn't think he fell head over heels in love with the baby, as she hoped he would, but she did believe the magic was starting to work on him. It was only a matter of time before his fatherly love blossomed.

≈ ≈ ≈ ≈ ≈ ≈

When they brought the birth certificate, Deja didn't have to think too hard about what she wanted to call her baby. She named him Adrian Asad Beckett. *Adrian* came from her favorite grandfather; on her father's side. *Beckett* was Jerome's last name. Deja got *Asad* from the chubby medical assistant who took her vitals that night.

Asad was Arabic for *lucky*. Deja couldn't think of a better way to describe her precious baby.

CHAPTER THREE
MURDERER!

"Alright..." the news anchor said. He was a handsome man with dazzling blonde hair and piercing blue eyes. "For more information on the victim, let's go to our reporter on the scene."

The view changed to a split screen of Chad Collins in the newsroom and a female reporter who was standing outside, somewhere sunny.

"Jessica, what can you tell us about the survivor?" Chad asked. "I know the police aren't giving much information."

"That's right, Chad," the female reporter said. The producers dropped Chad's camera, and the screen filled with just the shot of Jessica. The reporter stood next to the main entrance of a red brick building. There was a placard and revolving doors, and the cameraman made sure to get the whole sign view so there was no doubt about where they were filming. The sign read: JACKSON MEMORIAL HOSPITAL.

"The police will not release the name of the victim," Jessica went on. She was a short woman with long, curly hair and an unusually strong jaw line. She wore a short-sleeved blouse because the temperatures in March were always pleasant in Overbrook Meadows, Texas. A soft breeze ruffled her hair and shirt collar.

"But we do have *some* information." Jessica produced a clipboard and read directly from it: "We do know that the victim is 32 years old. She checked in with several contusions on her face and head, and she also had a broken bone in her neck. She was seven and a half months pregnant when they brought her in, and she did deliver the baby last night. I'm told the baby is doing fine."

Deja shot her nurse a look, and the nurse shook her head. During the evening shift, Deja's caregiver was Nathalie, from Jamaica. During the day she had Gisela from Oregon. Gisela was fair-skinned and attractive. She was a big girl, but she carried herself well.

"There are crooks everywhere," Gisela said in response to Deja's look. "The admissions department makes ten-fifty an hour. Those reporters will pay a thousand or more for that kind of information. You should be glad they didn't give them your name."

Deja was glad they didn't say her name on TV, but she didn't think it was right that her privacy was for sale. Her nurse's nonchalance made Deja wonder if *she* was the one who leaked the information.

It was eight o'clock am. Deja watched the sun rise in the eastern skies an hour ago. Gisela came in to change the bandage on her neck, and both women stopped to watch the news when Deja's story came on.

"Tell us more about that broken bone," Chad prompted.

"The hyoid bone often gets broken during strangulation," Jessica said. "Most of the time death quickly follows, so we know this woman was very fortunate last night. She's the first woman to survive an encounter with the South Side Strangler."

"How did she get away from him?" Chad asked off camera.

"The police aren't saying right now," Jessica reported. "But we do know there were shots fired at her residence last night. It was these gunshots that prompted several neighbors to call 911. And since the strangler never uses a gun, we can speculate it was the victim who fired those shots, Chad."

"Was the strangler injured?" Chad asked.

"No," Jessica said. "He was briefly taken to the hospital for scrapes he received during a minor scuffle with police during his arrest. He was treated and sent to jail. He did not have any gunshot wounds."

"*Damn*," Deja muttered. She thought she was a better shot than that.

"Were you able to speak with the victim at all?" Chad wanted to know.

Jessica shook her head. "No. Not at this time. The police are not done questioning her, and the hospital is not allowing any contact at this time. But we do know her injuries are not life-threatening. She will probably be released within the next day or so."

That was news to Deja. "Really?" she asked her nurse.

"Yes, probably," Gisela said, her eyes still glued to the television.

"Well, I'm glad she's okay," Chad said. The view switched back to a split screen with him and Jessica. "This is a very troubling story."

"Yes, it is," Jessica agreed. "But there is a bright side: The strangler did not claim his fifth victim last night, and a suspect is now in custody. I'll keep you posted as soon as we get more developments."

"Thank you, Jessica," Chad said, and they went back to a full shot of him. "Alright. We were just talking to Jessica Serrano, who is at Jackson Memorial Hospital where the South Side Strangler's fifth victim is recovering from wounds she received during an attempted murder. We're told the victim is doing well after delivering a baby and neck surgery earlier this morning.

"Now, we've already had quite a few viewers calling in, asking what kind of sicko would attack a pregnant woman. And we now have breaking news on that matter."

To emphasize the importance of his bulletin, the words **BREAKING NEWS**! Scrolled across the top of the screen.

"This just in," Chad said. "We not only have the name, but we also have a picture of the man police arrested in connection with the four strangulation murders..."

Deja couldn't believe it. Channel Six was definitely on top of things. Chad's handsome mug went away and was replaced with a photo of a far less attractive man. The new guy was black and angry in what appeared to be a recent mug shot.

Deja's heart froze, and she almost screamed. Her eyes bulged as she stared at the screen. Her jaw went slack.

"Oh my God..."

"Here he is," Chad said. "His name is Gilbert Reynolds, and he's no stranger to the police..."

Gilbert had short hair, thin eyebrows and small eyes. He had thick lips, a struggling moustache and a flat nose. His skin was as dark as the shadows he chose to lurk in. His expression was fierce. He was about forty years old. He definitely looked like the kind of person who would commit such heinous crimes –and not just because of the way the anchorman introduced him.

Deja imagined that face squeezed behind nylon pantyhose, and it fit perfectly. His nose, eyes and lips were all a match for the man who crept into her bed and tried to take her life as well as the life of her unborn child. Deja was overcome with chills, and she couldn't look away. She studied every inch of her attackers face. She memorized each contour. She immediately hated him more than she'd ever hated anyone or anything.

"That's him?" the nurse asked.

"Yeah," Deja said definitively. "That's him."

"I'm glad he's off the streets," the nurse said. "He *looks* like a monster."

Deja shook her head vaguely. "You have no idea."

≈≈≈≈≈≈≈

After breakfast they brought Deja's baby so he could spend the day with his mama.

At 8:35 a reporter made it all the way up to Deja's room. Her nurse turned him away at the door, but he looked over her shoulder and made eye contact with the strangler's fifth victim before he took off.

At 8:45 they moved Deja to another room on a different floor.

Fifteen minutes after that, it was officially visiting time. But because of her confidential status, not too many well-wishers made it past the hospital's security. Deja's parents were the only ones who showed up, but they said everyone had asked about her.

"Them peoples downstairs is going crazy," her mother reported, taking a seat next to Deja's bed. She sighed heavily and immediately took off her shoes.

"What you mean?" Deja asked.

"They asking everybody that comes through there if they're coming to see *you*," Shirley said. "They not even shy about it. They wanna talk to anyone who knows you."

"You got yourself a *media circus*," her dad agreed.

Deja found that amusing. Of all the things she thought she might do in life, creating a media circus wasn't even on the radar.

Her pastor showed up at ten with balloons and flowers. And Jerome took off from his job at lunchtime to pay his baby-mama a visit. Deja was already feeling better by then. Her spirits shot to the roof when her man walked through the door.

"*Hey baby.*"

"Hey." He smiled hesitantly and slowly made his way to the bed.

Deja's parents discreetly left the room, to give them some privacy.

"Your voice sounds better," Jerome noticed.

Deja still had bruises on her neck as well as a small bandage to cover the wound from her surgery. The whites of her eyes had small clots of blood. But her positive attitude slightly diminished her physical trauma.

"I know." Deja beamed. She was still hoarse and raspy, but it sounded like someone gave her rusty hinge throat a few drops of oil. It still hurt when she swallowed but not that badly when she talked.

Jerome wore a beige golf shirt with wind pants and sneakers; typical attire for his job as a P.E. teacher.

"I brought you something." He offered half a dozen roses he was carrying. The flowers were beautiful, but they weren't in a vase and Deja didn't think they would last long. She took them with a grateful smile.

"Thanks." She gestured to the bassinet on the other side of her bed. "They said I can keep him all day."

Jerome looked in that direction but didn't move. "Cool."

"Go pick him up," Deja said. She grinned wistfully and rubbed her hair back with her hands. She wished she had a brush and some cosmetics. There was no telling how bad she looked.

Jerome walked around the bed and stared at his little boy for a while. It didn't look like he wanted to touch him, but he eventually bent and reached for the infant. As soon as he picked him up, Adrian started to cry. That was enough for Jerome.

"See. I knew he was gon' do that." He held the baby out at arm's length. "Here."

Deja reluctantly took her child. Adrian stopped crying as soon as she laid him on her chest. Within a few seconds, the baby was asleep again.

"I shouldn't have took him," Deja said. "You have to get used to your son sooner or later."

"I told you I'm no good with babies," Jerome said, and that must have been the truth. He told her that so often, Deja couldn't count the times.

"Is it the poopy diapers you don't like?" she asked. "Or is it something else?"

Jerome avoided the question altogether. "They was talking about you on the news this morning. Did you see it? They say they caught that guy."

"Yeah," Deja said. "I saw it. It was creepy; to see him again – without the mask."

"You didn't talk to the police yet?"

"Not really," Deja said. "I talked to them for a minute yesterday, but they said they were going to come back and do a formal interview. It's crazy. I can't believe I'm involved in this. You know that guy killed *four* women? He really was trying to kill me. I, I didn't know that, at first."

"What you mean?"

"I mean, when I felt someone get in my bed, I thought it was you."

Jerome frowned.

Deja did too. "That was the first thought in my mind. You were the only person who had a key to my apartment. I thought you came back to spend the night."

Jerome's frown intensified. "Are you serious?"

Deja nodded. "Yeah. Even when I saw that he had pantyhose over his head, I still thought it was you. Until he hit me. That's when, that's when I knew I was in trouble."

Jerome's eyes watered, and he sighed heavily. "I been feeling guilty," he said. "You asked me to stay the night, and I didn't. I keep feeling like–"

"Don't even go there," Deja said. "You can guess and *what if* yourself all the way to the crazy house. What happened happened. None of it's your fault. That man who did this, he's *crazy*, Jerome. And he's *evil*. If he wouldn't have got me that night, he would've got somebody else. In a way I'm kinda glad it was me, because now *they got him*. He's in jail, and he can't hurt nobody else."

Jerome sniffled and reached to caress her shoulder. It was the most affection he had initiated in recent memory. His touch made Deja feel safe and loved.

≈≈≈≈≈≈≈

"So where his punk ass at now?" Vincent lounged in a recliner a tech brought in for the comfort of Deja's visitors. He sucked on a barbecued rib he got from Lord knew where. Deja was still on a liquid diet. The sight and smell of real meat had her stomach growling.

"Alright," she said. "You don't like him. I get it. Let's move on."

Deja sat up in bed with her precious baby in her arms. She fed him a bottle of her very own breast milk. It was three o'clock in the afternoon, and the twins were her only visitors at the moment.

"I *will* get over it," Vincent said, "as soon as *you* get over it. Tell that fool to stop coming 'round, and I won't say nothing else about him." Vincent had on the one piece jumpsuit he wore for his job at an auto shop. His uniform was so stained, Deja knew he'd soil the recliner. Thankfully this wasn't her house.

Her sister sat on a less comfortable wooden chair at the foot of the bed. The television was tuned in to another news story about the strangler. Julie watched quietly, shaking her head in disbelief every now and again.

"Why do you hate Jerome so much?" Deja pondered. "And I know it's not because he wasn't with me last night."

"I never liked that punk," Vincent said, his nose wrinkled. "That nigga had seven and a half months to marry you. The baby here, and you still don't got no ring on your finger. That's disrespectful."

That was laughable, but Deja knew it would hurt her neck something serious if she gave in. She chuckled, and that hurt too. "Ouch, boy quit making me laugh."

"Ain't nothing funny."

"You got *four kids*, and you're not married to any of their mothers," Deja pointed out.

"Yeah, but you my sister."

41

Deja shook her head. "Maybe you should treat every woman like she's your sister."

Vincent was perplexed. "How I'ma do that? I won't never get none!"

Deja burst into laughter, and the pain made her regret it instantly. "Boy, stop!"

Her nurse stepped into the room with an easy smile spread across her face. "Hey, y'all. What's so funny?"

"Nothing," Deja said. "Just laughing at this fool." She nodded towards Vincent.

Gisela gave him a grin. "Is this your brother?"

"Yeah."

"I came to get the baby," Gisela said and proceeded to do just that. "We're going to give him a bath and weigh him again. Oh, and that detective is here to see you."

She left cradling Adrian. Vincent turned to watch her booty until it was out of sight.

"Say, lil sis, you need to–"

"Ugh!" Deja said. "Don't go there."

"What?"

"I'm not gonna hook you up with that nurse."

Vincent turned back to her, his eyes devilish. "You know me so good."

"I know you *ain't* no good," Deja said. "Don't you have enough babies?"

"Who said anything about babies?" Vincent grinned. "I wears a condom *every* time now. I learned my lesson. Shit, I got a condom on right now – just in case."

"Eww!" Deja said, and there was a chuckle in the doorway. All eyes went in that direction. The detective from yesterday was back.

"Excuse me. How you guys doing?"

"Fine," everyone said.

Vincent gathered his Styrofoam box of sucked-clean rib bones and stood quickly.

"Y'all, uh, y'all need to talk? You want us to leave, right?"

"If you don't mind," the policeman said. He walked in with a much bigger folder than he had last night.

Vincent and Julie headed for the door, and the detective pulled the wooden chair next to Deja's bed.

"We'll see you later," Julie said and closed the door behind them.

Deja smiled after her and then gave the detective her attention. "I know you have a bunch of questions…"

He nodded. "That's right. My name is Rudy Cervantes, if you don't remember."

"I remember. I've been waiting for you."

≈≈≈≈≈≈

Mr. Cervantes took a seat very close to her and produced the recorder from yesterday. "Did you see the news this morning?" he asked before he turned it on.

"I did," Deja said. "They had a picture of that man…"

The cop nodded. "Yeah. We've been under a lot of pressure to catch this guy. It was, it was a great day down at the precinct. I didn't want you to see that picture until I showed it to you first, but it really couldn't be avoided."

"It's alright," Deja said. "I understand."

"What'd you think of him," the detective asked, "that picture?"

"It freaked me out," Deja admitted. "I got scared all over again."

Mr. Cervantes nodded. "I'm sorry about that. But we got him, and there's nothing to be afraid of."

"I know."

The detective turned the recorder on and asked Deja to state her name and address. He indicated the date and time before he started the interview.

"Could you tell me what happened to you on the evening of Tuesday, March the 20th?"

Deja told the whole story, starting with Jerome leaving for the evening and ending with her shooting at the intruder as he fled her home. The detective didn't interrupt, but when she finished he wanted to go over a few things in more detail. He wanted specifics about how the strangler got her submissive enough to tie her up, how he hit her and what he said to her during the attack.

It was hard to take herself back to that horrible place and time, but Deja told him everything he needed to build his case against the boogeyman.

"Did he touch you or fondle you, or attempt anything sexual at any point?"

Yesterday something tugged at the back of Deja's mind when he asked this question. Today she had the same hesitance.

"No. I mean, yes."

"What do you mean?"

"He..." Deja sighed. "He touched me, on my chest. That's what woke me up. He didn't try to rape me. But when he was choking me, right before I was going to pass out, I saw something in his face. His eyes, rolled back in his head. He started grunting, and, and I thought he was, having an orgasm. I mean, he didn't take off his clothes or nothing, but... I don't have no way of knowing for sure, but that's what I thought. If I had to swear to it, I'd have to say yeah, he did have an orgasm."

The detective didn't dwell on that anymore while the tape was rolling. But he went back to it when they completed the interview forty minutes later.

"That, was uh, what you said about him having an orgasm. That was interesting."

Deja thought so too, and she was eager to hear his take. "How come?"

"Because when we were working the other cases, we had the FBI do a profile on this guy. That was one of the biggest mysteries. They said there should be semen, but we never found any. It stalled the case a little. We went back to all of the crime scenes looking for semen we missed." He sighed. "I can't tell you how much time we spent on that semen – or lack thereof..."

Deja nodded. "Were you, can you tell me about the other cases?"

The detective looked up from his papers. "Oh, um, yeah." He opened his folder and flipped a few pages. "Understand that some of the information I give you is confidential. When you do your interview with the press, you can tell them the basics about your attack. But don't tell them about the orgasm. And don't tell them anything about these other cases."

"I'm not doing an interview."

Mr. Cervantes smiled. "Deja, there are at least six media vans downstairs. At some point you're going to leave this hospital. And when you do, they'll be all over you. You'll either do an interview or feel like Britney Spears for the next six months.

"The good thing is none of them really care about you. They just want to be the first one to get your story. After you do one interview, the rest of them will lose interest in you pretty quickly."

Deja was surprised by his candor, but she still didn't think she'd do an interview.

The detective removed a photograph from his files. It was a color photo, an eight by ten. He handed it to her, and Deja took it, almost reluctantly.

The picture was an enlarged mug shot of a black female in her late twenties or early thirties. She was very thin, with sunken jaws and bug eyes. Her hair was unkempt, and she had a few old scars on her cheeks and forehead. Her ghoulish stare spoke volumes about her frustration, heartache and suffering. It was clear from the mug shot that she'd had a rough life up to that point. Deja knew it got rougher sometime after the photo was taken.

"Tawanda Murphy," the detective said. "She was twenty-four years old. A crack addict and prostitute. She was the strangler's first victim."

Deja felt goose bumps sprout on her arms. She had a hard lump in her throat, and then she felt the hands squeezing her windpipe again. The more she stared at the picture, the more Tawanda seemed to stare back at her.

"She was found in a motel room," the detective said. "She was a regular at the motel, due to her profession. We found her in bed; strangled, with the sheets pulled over her body. She was fully clothed, and she was not tied up. This is the scene we got the most evidence from."

He looked down at a crime scene photo but did not hand it to Deja. She was glad for that.

"Killers always start off sloppy," the policeman explained. "As with any job or hobby, you're not going to be your best at it the first time you try. Tawanda fought like hell. There was a big struggle.

"Strangulation is probably the hardest way to kill someone. You have to be in their presence. You have to get very close. You have to be strong enough to hold your hands on their throat while they fight their hardest to stop you. The killer might have an adrenaline rush, but the victim does, too – which can make even a small woman very strong."

That was all very familiar. A cold shiver rolled down Deja's back.

"We got fiber evidence from beneath Tawanda's fingernails," the detective said. "We would have preferred skin, but the fibers were pretty good, too. We matched them to a pullover sold exclusively at Walmart. The problem is there are Walmarts all over the country. But we did get our first clue: The killer wore pullovers."

Deja handed the picture back without speaking, and the detective traded it for another. The second photo was also from a mug shot. Before the cop spoke, Deja knew this woman was a drug addict as well. The victim was fair-skinned and skinny, about forty years old. She had huge eyes with dark pupils that were still dilated from whatever toxins she'd ingested prior to her arrest.

"Danielle Struthers," Mr. Cervantes said. "We found her in a vacant house."

Deja's breaths became hot and slightly labored. Her fingers trembled, and the photo shook visibly. She placed it carefully on the bed but couldn't stop looking at it.

"With this murder, we saw the killer's evolution in a few ways," the detective said. "He didn't take her to a motel, where the manager might get suspicious of him. We believe Danielle accompanied him to the vacant house willingly. She was a prostitute and a drug addict, so spending time in a vacant house or apartment was not something new to her."

The policeman looked through his files, and again he didn't offer the crime scene photo to Deja. "He beat her," he said after a while. "That's what the killer learned from Tawanda: The more you hit her, the less she'll fight back. He beat her..." The detective put a finger to his mouth and wiped his nose. "He beat her, pretty bad."

When he produced the third photograph, Deja was almost ready to stop this. What did she need to know all of this for? She was already spooked enough. But she couldn't stop him anymore than she could stop her next breath. She was connected to all of these women, whether she liked it or not.

The third picture was probably the worst, but not for the obvious reasons. This one wasn't a mug shot. It was a portrait taken at a studio. The woman was young, possibly a teenager. She was beautiful. She smiled at the camera with a laughing toddler on her lap. Deja stared at the picture so long her eyes blurred and filled with tears.

"That's Sheila Montgomery," the cop said. "She was twenty-one. This one was so different, it almost got attributed to another killer. But there were a lot of similarities also. The killer broke into her home this time, and he tied her up before the strangulation. Both of these were firsts for him. The main thing that linked this case to the others was the fiber evidence. The killer always wears the same type of pullover. The fibers he left at this scene matched the other murders perfectly.

"Sheila's son was at home during the attack, and he was the one who called 911 the next morning, when his mama didn't get up for work."

Tears rolled down Deja's cheeks. The detective took Sheila's picture back.

"We don't have to do this," he said.

Deja shook her head. "No. I want to finish."

Mr. Cervantes gave her the last picture. Deja wiped her eyes so she could see it. Again the strangler's final victim was pretty and young. She was of medium build and brown-skinned, and her photo was also from a studio.

"Tracy Fielder," the policeman said. "The killer broke into her home on the west side of town. The papers started calling him the *South Side Strangler* because of the first three murders. This one let us know he was getting bolder and more confident. Tracy was bound and beaten. She lived alone.

"All of the victims were black, so we knew we were looking for a black male, most likely between the ages of 30 and 40. We knew he'd be a relatively strong guy; at least 200 pounds. We knew he'd be an Overbrook Meadows native – or at least someone who has lived here for the past ten years. And we suspected he'd have an arrest history for rape or burglary – or both. All of that fits our suspect, Gilbert Reynolds, perfectly.

"We picked him up a mile and a half away from your house. He didn't have the pullover or pantyhose anymore, but he had a burglary kit in his pocket. He was drenched with sweat. He didn't have an excuse for walking the streets at three in the morning."

Deja nodded vaguely, the deaths of those four women swirling in her head. She marveled at how close she got to becoming victim number five. The strangler beat her and tied her up. He had his fingers clamped around her neck. Deja knew she should be dead, but she didn't feel relief at that moment. She was completely overwhelmed with empathy for the fallen four.

Nobody deserved to die like that.

The detective gathered his things and gave Deja a long, hard look before standing.

"What you did is outstanding. If you didn't stop him, there's no telling how long this would have gone on. The whole city is in your debt." He fished a card from his breast pocket and handed it to her. "This is a group, a support group for victims... They meet every week. It might be helpful for you to go, talk to other women."

Deja didn't think she would meet with such a group, but she took the card anyway. She knew her life would never be the same. She had no way of knowing where her new path may lead.

CHAPTER FOUR
THE SLEEPING STRANGLER

On Friday, March 23rd Deja got discharge orders from her OB/GYN as well as her trauma doctor. It was a beautiful spring morning. She couldn't wait for Adrian to get his first splash of sunlight. Deja was eager to feel the warmth on her skin as well. She'd been in the hospital for four days. She was sick of living in one room, smelling the same disinfectants and getting poked and prodded by so many strangers.

Deja sat on the corner of the bed wearing sweat pants with a blue pullover her sister brought for her. She cradled her baby against her bosom while her nurse, Gisela, went over the discharge orders. Her family waited anxiously.

"I already called transport," Gisela said. "They won't take you down until you have the baby strapped in the car seat."

"Got it," Julie said. She hefted a baby seat onto the bed and carefully took Adrian from his mother's arms. She placed the baby in the seat ever so gently. Everyone watched while she buckled him in. Deja was surprised to see tears in her father's eyes.

"If you experience any dizziness or severe pain," Gisela went on, "don't hesitate to call us. Or you can go to your regular doctor, if it's non-emergent. Um..." She flipped the page. "Dr. Ellis said your thumb should be fine. It will be tender for another week, but you don't have to avoid using that hand. It will actually heal quicker if you use it more. The contusions on your head have mostly gone away, but you can still use ice on them if you like.

"Dr. Ellis wants you to follow up with him in a week so he can look at your neck again. I'll leave his card with your paperwork, so you can make an appointment. And, yeah, looks like that's it. You ready to go home?"

Deja nodded. "Yes, I am." Her throat didn't hurt at all, but she was still a little hoarse and raspy. She still felt a noticeable *click* when she swallowed, but the doctor said that too would go away soon.

Gisela approached and gave her a side-to-side hug. "Well, it was great working with you. I hope everything goes well, Deja. Everybody here wishes you the best of luck. You gave a lot of women hope and strength. We're all very proud of you."

"Thanks," Deja said. She smiled and looked away nervously. She wasn't normally a shy person, but it was hard to accept praise of that magnitude. What she did to the strangler was to save her own life. She didn't believe she was special.

The nurse walked out, and the family was left with a big decision they should have worked out beforehand: Where was Deja going when she left the hospital? The crime scene investigators were done with her apartment, but Deja didn't want to go there right away.

"Are you going to come with me?" Julie asked. "I talked to Leonard, and he's cool with it." Deja's sister had a nice, two-story home on the north side of town. Her husband was a contractor, and Julie worked full time herself. They had three kids; one in grade school, one on the bottle, and another who just finished potty-training.

"You got too much going on over there," Shirley said. "Deja, you should come home with us."

Deja's mom was retired, and her father worked part time. Deja would have a peaceful environment at her mother's house and plenty of help with the baby. But she didn't really want her mother's help – not right away at least.

"You can stay with me and Meesha," Vincent offered. Deja shook her head at that.

"Maybe if you had your own place," she said. "I don't want to live with your girlfriend."

"It's cool," Vincent assured her. "She ain't gon' say nothing."

"That's alright," Deja said, and all eyes went to the only person in the room who hadn't offered his space. Jerome cleared his throat and took a manly step forward.

"I, uh, I think you should come live with me for a few days – until you're ready to go back to your apartment."

That's what Deja wanted all along. But not everyone was pleased. Vincent frowned and scoffed at the idea.

"No, she don't need to go over there. She need to be with her *family*. I think you should go with Mama."

Jerome took a step back without sticking up for himself. Deja had to come to his defense once again.

"I think Jerome is right. Adrian should be with his parents. I appreciate everyone's help. I really do. But I think me and Jerome need some time alone; just us and the baby."

Everyone knew Deja wanted to be married. She wanted a loving husband who would pass out cigars and transform the spare bedroom into a beautiful place for their child. She didn't have any of that, but at least she could go home with her man. If Jerome had any intentions of being a good father and boyfriend, this is how Deja would find out.

"Alright," her mother said. "If that's what you want, then you gotta follow your heart. If you need any help, you know we're here for you. But you're right: This time is for the baby to be with his parents."

Jerome looked around sheepishly, but he didn't withdraw his offer. He approached the bed and hefted the car seat with two hands.

"Okay. We ready?"

"We have to wait for transport," Julie said – just as another hospital employee appeared in the doorway.

"Deja Franklin? Are y'all ready to go?"

"Yes." Deja rose to her feet with a big grin spreading her cheeks. She paid no mind to the mean look her brother wore in the background.

≈ ≈ ≈ ≈ ≈ ≈

Over the past few days Deja heard quite a bit about the reporters waiting for her downstairs. But she was still ill-prepared for the onslaught. With her family encircling her, she was somewhat protected, but it's hard to force your way through a crowd that doesn't want to make way. She could barely hear

51

Jerome's directions, with so many reporters yelling at her at the same time.

"Deja!"

"Deja! Over here!"

"Do you have anything to say about the strangler?"

"How did you get away from him?"

"Did you have a gun?"

"Do you have any comments about the other victims?"

"Deja!"

"This way!"

"Just one question!"

"Deja, over here!"

"Deja!"

"Where are you going?"

"Are you going back to your apartment?"

"Deja, this way!"

"Deja! How's your baby?"

"Where you parked?" Vincent growled from somewhere behind her.

"Right up here!" Jerome shouted. *"On the right."*

Deja looked in that direction, but she couldn't make out anything past the reporters and flashing cameras. Microphones pushed through the crowd like heavyweight jabs. Deja shied away from them. She grabbed the back of Jerome's shirt and held on for dear life.

"Keep moving!" Julie shouted. But there wasn't always forward progress. Deja was mystified. She had a hospital employee pushing her wheelchair and security leading the charge, but the press was incessant. Even with a hoodie pulled over her head, Deja felt wide open.

"Man, get your ass on!"

Deja looked to the left and was horrified to see her brother respond (as usual) with violence. He shoved a portly cameraman, sending him stumbling into his cohorts. The cameraman landed hard on his butt, taking three more reporters down with him.

"Hey!"

"Where's the car?" Shirley yelled.

"We're here! Right here!"

Jerome raced to his Tahoe, and the reporters did too. They encircled the car like bees protecting their queen. Flashes went off in all directions. Deja pulled her hood tighter and kept her head down.

Jerome got the passenger door open, and she quickly climbed inside. The reporters knew their story was getting away, so they crowded the windows; each fighting for the best shot of the strangler's fifth victim. Deja felt like she was in a kooky carwash with human arms and yelling faces instead of soap and scrub brushes. Her heart hammered. The detective was right: These people wouldn't stop until she submitted to them. If they could, they would push the truck over and force her to climb out and face them.

Jerome pushed the baby through the side door. Deja grabbed hold of the car seat and held it tightly. She didn't even think about strapping it down properly as her nurse instructed. Jerome jumped in and scrambled to the driver's seat. Vincent slammed the door closed behind him, and he stood guard until Jerome got the car started.

Deja didn't think they would get out of there, but once Jerome got rolling, the crowd was forced to move – or grow bumpers. Deja turned in her seat to watch them when they pulled away. They were like an angry mob with their bloodlust unfulfilled. Deja knew they were only doing their job, but when it came to paparazzi, she sided with Kanye West. No way could anyone with a conscious do that on a daily basis.

≈≈≈≈≈≈≈

Jerome lived in a one story house on the south side of Overbrook Meadows. Deja had been there plenty of times. But they had a baby now, and there was a strong sense of *togetherness* when she crossed the threshold that morning. Adrian was asleep, so she took him to the bedroom and made a place for him on Jerome's king size mattress.

When she got back to the living room, Jerome was sitting on the couch watching a report from Channel Six News. They had footage of Deja leaving the hospital. It was weird to see the chaos from a different perspective. They were using her full name now, so Deja knew it was only a matter of time before someone she knew did an interview. She sat next to her boyfriend and watched for five minutes without saying a word.

53

"Don't they have a life?" she asked when they cut to commercials.

Jerome shrugged. He turned and gave her a caring look. Deja wrapped her arms around his torso and laid her head on his shoulder.

"You doing alright?" he asked.

"I feel better. Now that I'm here. What made you come up with this idea? You never said anything about it before."

"I know," Jerome said. "But I've been thinking, and I know it's the right thing to do. You gave me my first child, and we need to be closer. I know your brother hates me, but I want to do right by you."

Deja's heart fluttered. Her whole body grew five degrees warmer. She'd been waiting eight months to hear those words. "My brother doesn't hate you."

"Yeah, he does." Jerome sighed. "I see it in his eyes. He doesn't think I've done enough for you, and he's right. I haven't. But that's all going to change now. I want to work on strengthening our relationship."

Deja was floored by this declaration, and she couldn't have been more pleased. "I think that's a great idea."

"You know," Jerome said, "as far as those reporters, I don't think we can avoid them every day. Pretty soon they're going to find out where I live. When they do, they'll bring all of their vans and cameras over here."

Deja was surprised by his change of direction, but she agreed with him. "I hope they don't find us."

"I'm pretty sure they will," Jerome said. "I think we should go ahead and do an interview, so they won't mess with us no more. I think they'll leave us alone, after they get what they want."

"Yeah," Deja said. She let go of him so she could look him in the eyes. "Someone else told me that."

"Channel Six will pay you three thousand dollars," Jerome reported. "I think you should take it."

"How do you know that?"

"They called me," he said with a straight face. "I don't know how they got my number, but they called me yesterday."

Deja found that odd. "What did you tell them?"

"I told them I would ask you," Jerome said.

"And, you think I should do it?"

"You're going to have to talk to somebody sooner or later," Jerome reasoned. "You might as well get paid."

Deja gave it a few moments thought and decided he made sense. She didn't want to be hounded every time she walked outside. And who wouldn't want three thousand dollars?

"Okay," she said. "If you think I should do it, I'll do it."

"Cool," Jerome said and shot to his feet. "I'll call them and set everything up for you. You ain't gotta do nothing, baby. Wait here. I'll be right back."

≈≈≈≈≈≈≈

Jerome set her interview up for ten a.m. that same day. Deja didn't think they could assemble a news crew in just one hour, but again she was underestimating the scavengers she was dealing with. Of course they could be there in an hour. If all went well, they would do a quickie edit on her segment and have it ready for the news at noon. And then they could run it again at five and one more time at ten p.m. – in case anyone missed it.

A van showed up at 9:45, and a team of six jumped out like a police raid. They rushed inside and went to work setting up lights and cameras in Jerome's living room. Deja thought she was in the presence of royalty when Channel Six's award-winning reporter Jessica Serrano walked in, but the mystique quickly faded when Jessica unleashed the bitch within. She yelled at her crew about everything from moving a light out of her shot to getting that *goddamned blueberry muffin* she requested three times already.

For her first time on television, Deja wore an olive colored blouse with dark green slacks. She wore her hair up in a bun and got her make up done by a professional for the first time ever.

≈≈≈≈≈≈≈

Twenty minutes later, everything was all set and ready to go. Deja and Jessica sat on the couch facing each other while most of her crew stood quietly against the walls. The room was dimly lit except for the boom lights facing the couch. The lights were much brighter and warmer than Deja expected, and she feared she'd start to sweat soon.

Jessica gave her a brief walkthrough of what the interview would entail. It didn't seem too bad.

"If I ask you anything you can't answer because of the police or whatever reason, just say, *'I'm sorry, but I cannot comment on that.'* I won't ask about it anymore, okay?"

That sounded fair. "Okay," Deja said.

"Are you ready?" Jessica Serrano had a bright smile, and she didn't look evil at all now.

Deja found her boyfriend in the crowd, and Jerome gave her a reassuring nod.

"Yeah, I'm ready," Deja said.

"Great," Jessica said. "Alright, let's roll," she told her crew.

After a few seconds the cameraman held up five fingers and slowly counted them down to one. When his hand became a fist, a red light glowed on the camera and they were hot.

"Good afternoon," Jessica said. She stared into the camera like it was a long, lost friend. "My name is Jessica Serrano, and this is a Channel Six News exclusive. I'm sitting here with Deja Franklin. Deja made headlines recently when she went up against the notorious South Side Strangler and survived a brutal assault that left her with head contusions, a split lip, a dislocated thumb and a broken bone in her neck.

"The first four women who were attacked by the strangler, who the police suspect is Gilbert Reynolds, did not survive the ordeal. Deja is the first to live through his assault, and we're honored to speak with her today. Deja, how are you doing?"

"I'm, I'm okay." *Damn!* Her first words on TV were shaky and stuttered. She took a deep breath and willed herself to do better.

"Deja, you just got out of the hospital today, is that correct."

"Yes," she said, and then kept talking when it was clear Jessica wanted her to elaborate. "I was there for four days. I had my baby, and I couldn't wait to get discharged so I could go home."

"You survived a horrific ordeal," Jessica stated. "Were you ever fearful while you were in the hospital?"

"No," Deja said. "They told me they arrested him on the first day, so I wasn't afraid anymore. The scariest thing at the hospital was probably the reporters."

Jessica took the jab well. "What you did is an inspiration to women all over the world. I think the main thing our viewers want to know is exactly *how* you did it. Could you tell us what happened the night you were attacked?"

"Yes," Deja said. "It all started when my boyfriend left for the night…" She told the whole story again and was interrupted more than a dozen times. Jessica wanted details on everything from the set-up of her bedroom to what she wore to bed that evening. Were there any strange people in her neighborhood? Had she ever seen Gilbert stalking her previously?

The reporter was genuinely interested when Deja recalled how she fell back asleep with the killer in her bed – twice. That was a monumental revelation. Jessica's acting got a little cheesy then.

"Are you serious?" The reporter's eyes were big like moon pies. "You went back to sleep?"

"Yes," Deja said. "I thought it was my boyfriend. I never imagined it was an intruder."

"You woke up and then went back to sleep a second time?"

"Yes," Deja said. "I think I slept with him in bed with me for about two hours."

Jessica shook her head. "That's amazing. I'm getting chills just thinking about it."

"Me too," Deja said.

They talked for another twenty minutes, and Deja explained the most crucial part of her story; how she escaped the clutches of a cold-blooded killer. While talking, Deja couldn't help but wonder where Gilbert Reynolds was right then. If he had access to a television, he'd surely be glued to the screen when this story aired. Deja wondered if she should tell about her improperly tied right arm. She decided it didn't matter. It wasn't like Gilbert would ever have an opportunity to improve on his technique.

When she was done talking, forty-five minutes had passed, and Jessica was supremely pleased. She now had one of those coveted *scoops*. She might even win a Peabody with Deja's story. She gave Deja a handshake and a hug before they packed up and rushed back to the news room.

"Thank you," Jessica said. "Thank you so much. You're an inspiration to women everywhere."

Deja still had a hard time believing that. She accepted the praise modestly.

"Thank you. I really appreciate it."

≈≈≈≈≈≈

As predicted, they broadcasted an abridged version of Deja's interview at noon and promised to air the rest during their five o'clock show. Deja thought she looked pretty on TV. Her cellphone started to explode with friends and family who felt the same way.

The only unexpected part of the news was the emphasis the reporters placed on the fact that Deja slept with the killer in her bed for hours. Considering Deja lived on the west side of town, as well as the killer's fourth victim, one reporter thought they were premature in calling Gilbert Reynolds the *South Side Strangler*.

"I think we should've called him the *Sleeping Strangler*," the anchorman joked, and apparently everyone agreed. From that moment forward, every journalist, author, and average Joe on the streets referred to the serial killer as the *Sleeping* rather than *South Side* Strangler.

After the news Jerome took a shower. Deja was stunned to see him get dressed for work when he got out.

"Where are you going?"

"I gotta go to work, baby."

"I thought you were going to stay here with me."

"I only took a half-day off," Jerome explained. "I still have to be there for the after-lunch classes. Plus I have to coach the boys after school."

Deja didn't like to nag, but, "I could've gone to my Mama's house, if you weren't going to be here."

"I can take you over there, if you want."

"No, I don't want to go over there."

"Then chill, baby. I'll be back." He went to the dresser and snatched an envelope from on top. "Here."

Deja opened it and was surprised to find a $3,000 check made out to her. It was from Channel Six News. "Where'd you get this?"

"From the news crew." Jerome looked confused that she would ask.

58

"I didn't know they gave it to you already."

Jerome shrugged slightly.

"When?" Deja asked.

"While you were getting your make-up, baby. What's wrong?"

"Um, nothing," she said. "You, um, thanks, I guess. You, you didn't want any of this?"

"Nah, baby. I'm okay. You keep it."

Jerome grabbed his keys and was out of the door without so much as a kiss on the cheek – for Deja or the baby. She took Adrian to the living room and called her mother while she fed him. Deja thought there was something fishy about her boyfriend's behavior, but her mom liked to take things at face value.

"Child, you just got three thousand dollars? For talking? Hmph. I don't know what your problem is. You got so much to be grateful for. You should be happy."

"Yeah, you're right," Deja said, and she gradually allowed her suspicious thoughts to fade away.

CHAPTER FIVE
WAAR

The killer used the trees.

That's what the police got wrong. That's why they couldn't catch him. The killer liked to use the trees, and they never checked the trees.

If they had checked, they would've found evidence of his stalking. He didn't kill women at random, and he didn't kill spontaneously either. He stalked them, for weeks sometimes. He waited high above, amongst the branches. Sometimes he got bored and chipped the bark with his pocket knife.

Sometimes he got hungry and had a snack up there. He stuffed a Slim Jim wrapper in a small hole pecked out by a woodpecker as he waited for Sheila Montgomery to go to sleep. He always knew when his victims were asleep, just as he always knew there was no man in the house.

He knew this because he waited

in the trees.

When there was a full moon, he was camouflaged perfectly in his black pullover and dark pants. Deja's apartment had a lot of oak trees, and she knew exactly which one the killer waited in. It was the one standing at the corner of her building. It was the tallest tree on the property.

One of the lower limbs was only four feet from the ground, which made it easily accessible, and the branches didn't get small until close to the top. The killer climbed high in that tree, and he had an excellent view of Deja's front door as well as her bedroom window.

He waited patiently until he saw Jerome leave. He saw all
of the lights in the building go off one at a time. And when the
neighborhood was at its quietest, he climbed down the tree and
crept like a demon in the night. He made it inside Deja's
apartment with hardly a sound. He stopped in the kitchen to find
a knife on his way to her bedroom.

≈ ≈ ≈ ≈ ≈ ≈ ≈

Deja sat up with a start. Her breaths were quick, her
nostrils flared. Her eyes scanned the darkened bedroom; darting
to and fro like hummingbirds. For a moment she didn't
understand why she was alarmed, but then it came to her: The
trees.
        She looked to her left and saw Jerome sound asleep,
snoring lightly. Jerome slept in boxers only. He had the sheets
pulled up to his shoulders. Deja looked to the other side of the bed
and saw her baby curled in the fetal position. He too was fast
asleep.
        As her eyes adjusted to the darkness, Deja saw that
Jerome's blinds weren't completely closed. A nearby street lamp
produced a scant amount of light in the bedroom. With this light
came shadows. Deja was alarmed to see the shadows of a weeping
willow swaying on the opposite wall.
        She got out of bed with pinpricks stabbing her legs and the
bottom of her feet. She went to the window and peeked out into
the gloomy neighborhood. Most of the trees were well lit because
of the street lights, and the weeping willow wasn't strong enough
to support a man's weight. But still...
        Deja closed the blinds, and then she heard a sound behind
her. Her heart stopped cold as she spun like a cornered animal.
The bed was still the same and Jerome hadn't moved. Adrian
didn't move either. Deja had no idea what sound she heard, but
she knew it was real and it must have come from beyond the
bedroom.
        She exhaled loudly and crept on the balls of her feet. She
knelt at the head of the bed and tapped Jerome on the shoulder.
He grunted but did not open his eyes. She pushed harder, and his
head jerked up from the pillow. He looked around groggily until
his eyes focused on Deja.

"What?"

"I heard something," she whispered.

Jerome sighed and blew hard from his nostrils. He wrinkled his nose in frustration.

"*What?*"

"Can you go check?" Deja pleaded. "I heard a noise."

Jerome rolled and turned his back to her. Deja couldn't believe it.

"You didn't hear nothing," he grumbled. "Go back to sleep."

"I can't," Deja whined, but Jerome didn't look back in her direction.

Deja stood, feeling angry now in addition to fearful. She went to the bedroom door and leaned into the hallway with both hands on the door frame. The house was eerily quiet, but it was also dark and spooky. She dared not leave the bedroom, but with that thought, she suddenly had to go to the bathroom. *Give me a break*, she thought as her bladder began to scream its urgency. Deja went back to the side of the bed and woke Jerome again.

"Baby, please. I gotta go to the bathroom. Go check for me."

Jerome's eyes flashed open. He rolled to face her. And for a moment, Deja would swear she saw pure hate behind his dark pupils.

"Woman, what do you want?" He spoke slowly, as if she might be simple-minded in addition to a pain in the ass.

"I'm scared," Deja breathed. "I have to go to the bathroom, and I think I heard somebody in the house."

Jerome yanked his sheets off so quickly, Deja thought he was taking a swing at her. He got out of bed, stomping hard and fast. He left the bedroom and came back five seconds later. He got back into bed without a word and rolled his back to her again.

Deja was still frightful, but she summoned the strength to leave the bedroom so she could relieve herself.

≈ ≈ ≈ ≈ ≈ ≈

The sun was high in the sky at seven a.m. the next morning. With the sun came light, and with light came peace.

Deja didn't feel frightened at all when she woke up. Instead she felt silly for the drama she caused last night.

The killer was in the trees? How ridiculous was that? And the idea that Gilbert might be out of jail with nothing better to do than finish off his last victim was just as impractical. Deja understood that the mind is a powerful thing, and if you don't have control over it, it can easily take control over you.

She didn't blame Jerome for getting upset with her last night. In fact, Deja understood that she was at fault. She made her man a big breakfast as a form of apology.

Lured by the smell of bacon, Jerome woke up at seven-thirty. He stepped into the kitchen wearing his boxers. Deja was captivated by his physique. She left the stove and hugged him with one arm because she held the baby in the other.

"Morning, baby."

"Hey. What you making?" Jerome wiped the sleep from his eyes and walked to the counter for a better look.

"Bacon," Deja said with a smile. "And pancakes. I got some biscuits and gravy, too."

Jerome took a hearty sniff and shook his head. "Sounds good, but I don't have time for breakfast."

Deja's heart sank all the way to her ankles. "Why not?"

"I got a track meet today in Midlothian. I'm supposed to be at the school at eight. I'm running late as it is." He turned and headed for the bedroom with Deja right behind him.

"Why didn't you tell me about your track meet? I thought we'd get a crib today. You never tell me anything about what's going on with you."

"I'm not used to you spending the night," he said. "I'm sorry." He slipped out of his drawers on the way to the bathroom. Despite her frustration, Deja was momentarily sidetracked by how nice his naked ass looked.

"Jerome, you said you wanted me to come home with you so we could work on our relationship. But you haven't spent any time with me since I got here. *Why'd you bring me here*?"

Jerome started the water and pulled the shower curtain closed. "Baby, I'm sorry I can't stay home from work for you. I'm the only one paying bills in this house, and nobody's going to help me if I don't have the money."

63

"*I'll* give you the money," Deja said, thinking about her three grand.

"I'm not living off no woman," Jerome countered, and soon the bathroom was filled with steam.

≈ ≈ ≈ ≈ ≈ ≈

Jerome got out of the tub at 7:36 and rushed out of the house at 7:48.

Deja was so upset, she threw all of the food away without thinking about her own growling tummy. She called her mom when her tears flowed so hard they threatened to never stop.

"Hello?"

"*Mama.*"

"Deja? Child, what's wrong?"

"*He don't love me.*"

"Wha, what?"

"*He don't love me, Mama.* I don't know why he brought me here. *He hates me!*"

"Calm down, child. Wha, what are you talking about?"

"*Jerome!*" Deja wailed. "He left me. He, he had to go to work yesterday, and then he went to work this morning, too. He said he wanted to spend time with me, but he doesn't. He's a–"

"Hol, hold on, girl. He went to work? Is that what you mean when you say he left you?"

"Yea – yes." Deja had the hiccups now. She felt like a fool.

"Now, Deja, you know a man has to work. That don't mean he doesn't want to be with you."

"But, but last night I told him I was scared, and he didn't want to go look around for me. He gave me a real mean look."

Her mother chuckled. "Girl, do you know how many times Bernard gives me mean looks? The last time I told him I heard a noise in the house, he gave me the bat and said go check it out."

Deja smiled. That was her daddy alright.

"Did Jerome say he doesn't want to be with you?" Shirley asked.

"Nuh, no."

"I think you need to calm down and stop jumping to conclusions, child. I know it's hard. But you got to understand that Jerome is a new parent, too. He's probably scared and worried just like you. You have no idea what goes through a man's head at a time like this.

"Maybe he *does* want to get away from you for a while, but that don't mean he's through with you. If he didn't want you around, he wouldn't have taken you from that hospital. Plus, baby, your hormones are going crazy right now. That's why you're so upset."

Her mother made sense, but Shirley was the type of woman who would stick with her man through thick and thin, fire and brimstones. Deja took a deep breath and tried to get herself together.

"You're probably right, Mama. But I don't know. I don't feel like he loves me no more."

"Well, if that's the case, sweetie, I'm sorry to hear that. But until you talk to that man and hear it from his mouth, don't believe it."

That was good advice and Deja knew it. "Okay."

"Good," Shirley said. "Now I'm glad you called, 'cause I got some bad news..."

Deja put a hand to her head and rubbed her temple. "What happened?"

"Do you still got that three thousand?"

Deja groaned. "You know I do."

"Hold on to it," her mother said. "We might need it for bail. Vincent got arrested this morning."

"What? What for?"

"You remember that man he pushed yesterday, at the hospital?"

Deja shook her head. "The reporter?"

"Yeah. The police hemmed him up after you and Jerome left. They didn't arrest him then, but they came and got him this morning. They said that cameraman wants to press charges for assault."

"How much is the bond?"

"Ten thousand."

Deja sighed. The most they'd need was a thousand to get him out. "Well, let me know what you want me to do."

"Alright," her mom said. "I will, baby. And you need to try to keep your head up. What are you doing today?"

"I don't have anything to do," Deja said. "I guess that's why I got mad when Jerome left."

"Are you going to meet with that group you was telling me about?"

"What group? Are you talking about those *victims*?" She said it like they were lepers.

"Yes. You say you was scared last night. You should probably go."

"Yeah, I guess I could. Will you go with me?"

"No, child. You know I don't want to be up in there, hearing all those sad stories. I don't like to hear about no woman getting hurt. I can't stand it."

"I'll call Julie," Deja said. "She doesn't work Saturdays."

≈≈≈≈≈≈≈

Not only was Julie gung-ho about going to the women's group, but she also had strong opinions about Adrian's sorry-ass daddy. She showed up at Jerome's house at three o'clock to take Deja to a WAAR (Women Against Abuse and Rape) meeting at four.

"How the hell he say he wants to be there for you, when he won't even take a day off work?"

"That's what I told Mama."

"I don't know why you bothered talking to her," Julie said. "You know Mama wants you to stay with your man *regardless*. That's good when you got somebody like Daddy, but not for dumb asses like Jerome."

The ladies sat in the kitchen munching leftover casserole Deja made for lunch. Julie had on white shorts and a green camisole. Deja assumed the women at the meeting would recognize her, so she dressed more conservatively in a black skirt with an expensive blouse. Both ladies were beautiful, and Deja was a stronger and more radiant woman around her sister.

"I don't know why you stayed with him this long," Julie said. "I hope it's not so your baby can have a daddy."

"You don't think that's important?"

"It ain't important enough to put up with a bunch of bullshit. You can't make that man love his child, and you can't make him love you, either."

"I know," Deja said. "And if that's what it ends up being, then I will leave him."

"You still on that, '*He'll come around,*' shit, ain't you?"

"I think I should give him a chance."

Julie rolled her eyes. "Alright, girl. Go on and give him a chance. How long are you going to give him? A month? A couple of years?"

"No, and stop talking to me like that."

"You're the one who wanted to talk about it."

Deja gave her a mean look before she got up to get the baby ready. "You ready to go?"

≈≈≈≈≈≈

The WAAR meetings were held at the downtown YMCA. It was a beautiful facility with two swimming pools, a state of the art fitness area as well as multiple conference rooms. The building hosted events for everything from weddings to banquets. The WAAR group met twice a week for what Deja assumed would be a bunch of crying and complaining and sad stories about bad men.

She certainly didn't expect any laughing or happy faces, but that's the first thing Deja and Julie encountered upon entering. The room was packed with forty chairs, an equal number of women and long tables in the back where guests snacked on coffee, Oreo's, and little sandwiches made with ham or tuna.

When they walked in, a short woman approached Deja and Julie and ushered them to a sign-in table.

"Hi!" She stuck out a pudgy hand for them to shake. "Can I get you guys to sign in over here, so we can get your nametags? Sorry, but we have to keep track of our attendance or they'll cut our funding."

They followed her and signed in as the 37th and 38th guests.

"Are y'all new here?" The host was a round woman with bright eyes, blonde hair and rosy cheeks. She had perfect teeth, but they were too small for her face.

"Yes, this is our first time," Deja said.

"Well, we're glad to have you," the woman said. "My name is Marjorie. I'm the coordinator for this group. And you, you look really familiar..." She frowned and rubbed her chin while she tried to figure it out.

67

"I'm Deja Franklin. I was on the news this week for–"

Marjorie's face lit up. "The Sleeping Strangler! Oh my goodness! We were just talking about you the other day!" She stared in awe. "Everyone's so happy for you! I am so sorry for what you went through. We, you're just... Aww! *Give me a hug!*"

She threw her arms around her as Deja stood stiffly. She looked over at her sister who thought it was hilarious.

"Are you going to speak today?" Marjorie asked when she let her go.

"No. I don't think so."

"That's fine," Marjorie said. "There's no pressure. Whenever you're ready to share, it's fine." She wrote Deja and Julie's names on HI, MY NAME IS stickers and handed them over.

"Thanks," Deja said.

"No, thank *you.*" Marjorie smiled and shook her head slowly.

"I hope she doesn't make a big deal out of it," Deja said to her sister when she walked away.

"Stop playing," Julie replied with a chuckle. "You *know* she's going to make a big deal out of it!"

≈ ≈ ≈ ≈ ≈ ≈

The meeting started ten minutes later after Marjorie got everyone to take a seat. She stood behind a podium that was nearly chest high, grinning mischievously like she had the most delectable secret.

"Good afternoon, ladies. How is everyone?"

She got patchy responses from the crowd. Everyone was good.

"That's great," Marjorie said. "For anyone who might be new, this is a meeting for WAAR (Women Against Abuse and Rape). So if you're looking for the Taekwondo class, you're in the wrong place."

That brought chuckles from the group. Deja and Julie sat near the back. Deja hoped the host wouldn't mention her right away, but she sensed it wouldn't take long.

"For those of you who are not familiar with us," Marjorie went on, "Our goal here is not to bash men. We do not want you to relive your traumatic experiences every time. And we do not want you to *ever* leave here depressed.

"This is a place for healing, a place for communion. This is a place for understanding, love and compassion. Everyone here has been through something similar to your experience, so you never have to be ashamed or embarrassed about anything."

Deja felt good about that introduction.

"Before we get started," Marjorie went on, "I'd like to talk about a very special guest we have today. I'm sure you all know we've had a terrible, terrible person on the streets lately. He killed four women, all by strangulation, and we're so happy the police made an arrest last week."

Most of the audience agreed with nods or applause.

"The main reason for his capture," Marjorie said, "was because his fifth victim stood up to him and refused to be victimized. Her name is Deja, and I'm very excited to have her here today."

A lot of faces looked around. Marjorie kept talking.

"Deja doesn't want to talk this afternoon, and that's fine. She can share anytime she wants. Anyone can. As most of you know, I was once a victim myself. A lot of people think you can't be raped by your husband, but that's not true, and I'm a perfect example.

"I put up with the abuse for twelve long years. I stayed for the children. I stayed because I made a vow. I stayed because I was afraid. I stayed for a lot of reasons, but none of them were good reasons.

"I submitted to my husband whenever he wanted, and he did things to me that I never even knew existed. I was scared to death most of the time. I now know that I was being raped. Every time he touched me and I didn't want it, it was rape. Every time he hit me and forced me to use my mouth on him, every time he shoved foreign objects into me – it was rape.

"So, Deja, please understand that there is nothing you can tell us that's too horrible. There's no emotion you can show us that we're not familiar with in some way. We all love you, and we're here to help you. Anytime you want to share with us, we're ready. Okay?"

Deja nodded. Julie put an arm around her shoulder and pulled her closer.

"Alright," Marjorie said. "Let's get started."

≈≈≈≈≈≈≈

The meeting lasted two hours, during which time the ladies talked about their topic for the day: What are the effects of rape? Deja was never penetrated by the strangler, but she gradually understood that his attack was mainly sexual. The way he lay with her and maybe slept with her, and the way he fondled her said a lot about his motives. And Deja found that she did suffer from a lot of the effects of rape; like fear, worry, anger, shame, regret, self-blame, depression, nightmares and flashbacks.

When they were done, Deja decided she learned a lot about the cycle of abuse. She definitely wanted to come back for another meeting.

Quite a few women approached her on the way out. There was one Deja remembered more than the others.

"Hi," she said. "My name is Tamara." Tamara was dark-skinned, like coffee with just a dash of cream. She had long hair and beautiful eyes. She had the figure of a high-end fashion model; thin with hardly any boobs or curves.

"Hi," Deja said.

"I really wanted to meet you," Tamara replied. "Your story is awesome. You should travel the country and talk to groups like this. A lot of people are inspired by you." Tamara had a New York accent. She had a big smile and nice teeth.

"Thanks," Deja said. "But I don't feel like I deserve all of this praise. All I did was fight back."

"That's the key," Tamara said with a grin. "Whatever it is in you that made you fight rather than give in to it, that's what women need to know. They need to know that they have a choice."

Deja shook her head. "I was just scared. I'm still scared. Last night I almost had a heart attack when I thought I heard a noise in the house."

Tamara nodded and dug in her purse for a business card. "Here," she said. "My cell number is on the bottom."

Deja studied the card and saw that her new friend was an inspector for General Motors.

"If you ever get scared again, call me," Tamara offered. "It doesn't matter if it's three in the morning. We can talk. I can help you through it."

Deja was dumbstruck. That was one of the nicest things anyone had ever offered her. "Really?"

"Sure," Tamara said. "I'm an insomniac, so I'll probably be awake anyway."

"Okay," Deja said. "I appreciate that."

She watched Tamara as she walked away. She wondered what a woman as beautiful as her was doing at a meeting like this. She was afraid to ask.

≈≈≈≈≈≈≈

When Julie took her back to Jerome's house, Deja gave her the thousand dollars it would cost to get her brother out of jail. A part of her resisted, thinking he would never learn his lesson if there was always someone there to bail him out. But Vincent got arrested for defending his sister this time, so she felt somewhat responsible.

CHAPTER SIX
PRE-TRIAL HEARING

Jerome was exhausted when he returned from the track meet. He didn't talk much during dinner, but he did spend a little time with the baby when Deja took her shower before bed. When she got out of the tub, Jerome had Adrian on his lap; teaching him how to knock back a six-pack. Jerome went to sleep drunk at ten o'clock. Deja wasn't sleepy, but she went to bed too because she didn't want to be up alone in the big house.

On Sunday Jerome didn't want to go to church. That was nothing new, so Deja didn't nag him. Her sister picked her up at nine, and Deja went out to eat with Julie's family after the service. When she got home, Jerome was out and about with friends. She didn't see him again until after dinnertime.

"Do you love me?" she asked while he undressed for bed.

"Yeah, baby. Why you ask me that?"

"Do you love your son?"

He frowned. "You know I do, Deja. What's up with the questions?"

"It seems like you don't want to be around either of us."

"I told you I'm not good with babies."

"Stop saying that. The only way to get better at it is to spend more time around them – starting with your own baby."

"Just give me some time, okay?"

"How much time? I don't want my son to start school before you finally give him the time of day."

"You nagging me ain't gon' make it no better," Jerome warned. He got up and went to the bathroom and closed the door.

≈ ≈ ≈ ≈ ≈ ≈ ≈

On Monday Jerome left for work bright and early. Deja fumed the whole time he was gone. She felt like a fool for loving him and putting up with his shit. He said he loved her, but his words and actions were going in opposite directions. When he got home, Deja told him to drop her off at her mother's house.

"Why you wanna do that?"

"'Cause I'm sick of waiting on you to be here for me. You don't want me here, and you know it."

"I do want you here." He wrapped both arms around her and kissed behind her ear.

His touch made Deja's flesh tingle, despite her anger. "I know you don't want anything to do with our baby."

"Yes I do, baby, and today I'm gonna show you. I'll take care of him for the rest of the day."

Deja doubted that very seriously, but Jerome kept his word. He took Adrian when he woke up from his nap. He fed him and changed his diaper with no assistance from Deja. He bonded with the baby while Deja cooked dinner, and he changed Adrian's diaper again after they ate. It was all very beautiful. It was exactly what Deja wanted, but she wouldn't be fooled by one day's worth of affection. Jerome would have to behave this way for a whole month before she totally forgave him.

On Tuesday Deja decided it was time for her to go home. She had her things packed and stacked in the living room by the time Jerome finished his breakfast. He went to the front room and watched her for a moment before speaking.

"Hey, baby. What, what's going on?"

"I'm ready to go back to my apartment."

"I thought you wanted to stay with me."

"What for? So I can clean the house while you're at work?"

"You know it ain't even like that."

Deja swallowed down the many bitter comments that were itching to roll off her tongue. "Can you drop me off on your way to work?"

"I can't. I'll be late."

"You haven't taken a day off since I went to the hospital. I'm sure you can make this *major* sacrifice for me," she said sarcastically. "Besides, you don't even have a first period class."

73

"Alright," Jerome said. "So what does this mean? You don't want to see me no more?"

"The better question is do you want to see *me*, Jerome? If so, you can come to my apartment, 'cause I'm sick of being here."

"Alright. I'll come over there," Jerome promised.

"Yeah, right."

"Naw, for real. I'm going to spend the night."

"Whatever. Just take me home."

≈ ≈ ≈ ≈ ≈ ≈

After what had to be the most bizarre week ever, Deja finally returned to her apartment on a sunny Tuesday morning. She walked in expecting police tape and fingerprint dust all over the place, but her home was clean and neat; just as she left it.

Deja felt a prick of spooky nostalgia when she walked into her bedroom, but it wasn't so bad in the daylight. She knew the shadows would stretch towards her pillow like phantom fingers tonight, but she would cross that bridge when she came to it.

After she got her things unpacked, the first thing Deja did was leave to get a crib for Adrian. She didn't need a man's help with that. She took her baby to the Walmart up the street and came back with a huge box that didn't require much assembly. There was no way she could lug the box into her apartment, but Lady Luck was on her side that morning. Deja looked around and spotted one of her good friends crossing the parking lot.

"Shannon!" She threw a hand in the air and waved. "Hey, Shannon!"

Shannon was tall for a girl; over six feet, and she was thin, almost to the point of boniness. She wore denim Capris with white Keds and no socks. Shannon was pretty and very feminine, despite her strong jaw line, unmistakable Adam's apple, and her big, manly hands. Scientifically, Shannon was definitely a *male*, but acknowledging that was the easiest and quickest way to get on her bad side.

"Deja!" She threw her hands up and rushed to her. "Oh my God! Is it really you?"

"Yeah," Deja said. "It's me." The ladies embraced for a full five seconds.

"Girl, I'm so glad to see you!"

Shannon backed up and held her at arm's length. "Damn, girl! I saw your little story on the news! I am so sorry that happened to you! Where you been? Didn't nobody know if you was ever coming back."

"I been with Jerome," Deja said.

Shannon's face fell slightly. "Jerome?"

"Don't worry. I'm starting to see him for what he really is."

"He a goddamned fool," Shannon said and hugged her friend again. "Girl, I missed you so much. I can't believe that man tried to *kill* you! Where's your baby?"

"He's in the back seat." Deja grinned pleasantly.

Shannon ran around the Sentra and stuck her head in the window. "Ooh, girl, he's so cute! So, are you back now? You're not going to move?"

"Why would I move?"

"I don't know. You know how some people be scared to go back, if somebody got killed in their house."

"Nobody got killed," Deja said with a smirk.

"I know. But some people are scary. Mrs. Whitley moved out."

"Really?" Mrs. Whitley resided in the complex for over fifteen years. Deja lived in the unit across from her for the past three.

"She went to stay with her son," Shannon informed her. "Said she couldn't live by herself no more. The world is too crazy."

"It is," Deja agreed. "Hey, can you bring this crib in for me?"

Shannon eyed the box hanging out of Deja's trunk and frowned. "*That's* a crib?"

"Yeah. I have to put it together."

"Don't they make cribs already put together?"

"For, like, two hundred dollars more!" Deja said. "I got a real good deal. I only have to unfold it and put in twelve screws."

Shannon shook her head. "Girl, you know I don't like no manual labor." She admired her freshly painted nails.

"I just had a baby," Deja reminded. "Plus, I thought since I was a victim and all..."

Shannon rolled her eyes. "You ain't gotta throw that in my face. I'll help with your little crib."

"Thanks." Deja went around to retrieve her baby.

75

"You looked good on TV," Shannon said. "Who did your make up?"

"I forget her name," Deja said. "It was a make-up artist from the news."

Shannon's eyes widened. *"A real-live make-up artist?* Shit, I wish somebody would try to kill me one day."

"You're making me want to give it a shot right now," Deja told her.

≈ ≈ ≈ ≈ ≈ ≈

Putting the crib together looked a lot easier on the box. Deja thought she might have a better go at it if her guest got involved, but Shannon sat on the bed talking her ass off, for the most part.

"Girl, they was walking in your apartment, back and forth, all day and all night. They took some stuff, too."

"Some stuff like what?"

"I don't know. They had it in a paper bag – one of the big ones."

Deja wondered what it could've been. She sat in a corner of her bedroom with parts of the crib scattered about her. "Can you hold this?" she asked.

Shannon sighed and pushed off the bed lazily. She knelt and held the railing like it was made of boogers.

"It's not going to bite you," Deja said with a grin.

"I don't want no splinters," Shannon said and started to get up. "I need to get some gloves."

"No you don't. There are no splinters on a baby crib, goofball." Deja shook her head, and then she heard her cell phone ringing. She looked around for her purse, but it was somewhere in the living room. She shot to her feet. "Hold that. I'll be right back."

"I'm not holding this."

"Just hold it."

Deja found her phone on the couch. She didn't recognize the incoming number. "Hello?"

"Hi, Deja?"

"Yes, who's this?"

"This is Detective Cervantes. I met with you at the hospital."

The memory of the cop brought the vision of four dead girls.

"Hi. What's going on?"

"Not too much. I was calling because our guy is having a pre-trial hearing tomorrow. It's open to the public. I didn't know if you'd be interested in going, or what..."

The thought of seeing the strangler again gave her a fierce chill. "What's a pre-trial hearing?"

"They'll drag him out of jail, so he can go before a judge," Mr. Cervantes explained. "He'll say whether he's innocent or guilty, and they'll set up a jury trial or a trial with just a judge. You don't have to come. But if you want to see him—"

"I do," Deja said. "I do want to see him."

"It's going to be at nine o'clock, at the main courthouse on Lamar. You may want to get there early. I'm sure a lot of people will show up."

"Okay," Deja said. "Thanks."

Back in the bedroom, Shannon noticed her change in demeanor.

"What's wrong? Jerome broke up with you?"

"No. Why would you say that?"

"Just wishful thinking, I guess."

"The strangler has a hearing tomorrow morning," Deja reported. "They asked me if I wanted to go, and I said yes."

Shannon shook her head. "Uh-uhn, I couldn't do it."

"Why not? You wouldn't want to see him?"

"Yeah, I would," Shannon said. "But I'm scared I'd get arrested for jumping on him. If somebody tried to kill me while I was pregnant, I'd snatch his eye out, girl. I'd run around the courtroom with it, screaming."

Deja laughed. "Snatch his eye out?"

"Hell yeah. How he gon' stop me with his hands cuffed?"

≈≈≈≈≈≈≈

Deja got her crib assembled by lunchtime. It wasn't that big of a deal, but she was filled with a sense of accomplishment. Adrian's new bed was sturdy and beautiful; cherry wood with sleek bars and storage drawers at the bottom. Deja didn't have any screws or washers leftover, so she was confident the crib wouldn't collapse late in the night.

She still had seventeen hundred dollars left from her interview money, so Deja took Shannon out to eat and deposited the rest in the bank. The girls were in good spirits when they returned to the apartments. They lounged in Deja's living room for a couple of hours talking about anything and everything that *wasn't* related to the strangler.

When someone approached her door at five-thirty, Deja thought it was her landlord or another one of her neighbors wanting to check on her. When the visitor inserted a key and attempted to gain entry on his own, Deja knew exactly who it was. Shannon knew too, and her features were suddenly downcast.

"Oh, Lord, it's *that man.*"

"You don't have to say it like that," Deja said, but her friend's dread was warranted. Deja had to unlock the door for her boyfriend, and Jerome didn't look pleased when she swung it open.

"How come my key doesn't work?" he asked. Jerome gripped his briefcase in one hand and clutched half a dozen roses wrapped in tissue paper in the other. Once again he showed his frugality by not getting her a vase, but it didn't take a lot to please Deja.

"Thanks, baby." She took the flowers and attempted a hug.

Jerome stepped out of her embrace and walked inside. "Why doesn't my key work?" he asked again.

"The manager changed the locks," Deja said. "I have to get you another one. Me and Shannon have just been in here..." Deja trailed off because of the looks Jerome and Shannon fixed on each other.

Jerome was openly anti-gay, and Shannon was 100% out of the closet. The malice between the two was as old as time, but they usually managed to be civil.

Shannon smacked her lips. "Hello, Jerome."

Even if she hadn't rolled her eyes during the greeting, her attitude was unmistakable. For whatever reason, Jerome wasn't in the mood for her today. He dropped his briefcase by the door and stepped to the center of the room.

"Nigga, don't say shit to me."

Deja's mouth fell open. Shannon flinched like she got slapped. Her eyes widened, and she rolled her neck like an Egyptian.

"Uh, *excuse me*?"

"Boy, you heard what I said." Jerome took a few more steps until he acquired a more dominant stance, no more than three feet away from Deja's guest. He stood with his arms folded and his eyes dark and threatening. He looked down on Shannon like she was the scum of the earth.

Never one to back down, Shannon stood and put her hands on her hips. She matched Jerome's glare and attitude.

"I don't know what your problem is, but you need to back the hell out my face!" Shannon's voice barely rattled.

"Or what?"

"I ain't scared of you."

Jerome's lip curled. "Nigga, I will–"

Deja jumped between them, shocked at how quickly things went from zero to a hundred. "Hey! Stop that! What is wrong with y'all?" She pushed Jerome away.

"You don't know me," Shannon spat, pointing a finger now. "I ain't never did nothing to you, *Jerome*! Don't get in my face like that!"

"Fuck you!" Jerome shouted over Deja's shoulder. "I'll whoop your ass, homey. You not a girl! You a *dude*! You need to take that goddamned lip gloss off and stay away from my son with that gay shit!"

"*Jerome, stop*!" Deja pushed him towards the couch. Jerome responded by turning his anger on her. He grabbed her shoulders in a vice-like grip and spun her towards the sofa instead. He pushed her backwards, and Deja went flying. She landed on the soft cushions, but it was still a hair-raising experience.

Before Jerome could go after Shannon again, she scooted past him and made it out of the front door. Rather than head for the hills, Shannon turned to face them when she was safely on the breezeway.

"*You ain't no real man; putting your hands on her like that!*"

"Shut up!" Jerome growled. "*Shut your punk ass up!*"

"*You a punk!*" Shannon taunted. "*You a punk ass nigga, Jerome!* You gon' get yours sooner or later. Niggas like you–"

Jerome charged and Shannon turned tail; squealing like a frightened mouse.

"*Stop!*"

But Jerome slammed the door closed rather than go after her.

"*You a bitch!*" Shannon yelled from the other side. She gave the door a hefty kick before heading off. "*Deja, your man a bitch ass nigga!*"

Jerome fumed. His big shoulders rose and fell like a dark tide. When he turned back to his girlfriend, his eyes didn't immediately express regret for what he did. He walked slowly and took a seat on the couch next to her. Deja sat up and regarded him like he sprouted a horn in the middle of his forehead.

After a while Jerome sighed and the tension dissipated like smoke in a breeze. "I'm sorry."

Deja figured as much, but, "What the hell is wrong with you?"

"Nothing," he said. "I..." He sighed. "I had a bad day at work. Then I come up in here and see this he/she nigga chilling. I guess I..." He rubbed his forehead. "My temper got the best of me. I can't stand that lazy faggot. You know that."

"This is not your house," Deja informed him. "You have no right to tell me who can or cannot come over here. And you don't have no right to put your hands on me. If Vincent ever saw that..."

"I didn't hit you," Jerome said. "I just pushed you down on the couch. I'm sorry about that, but I didn't hurt you."

Deja found it interesting that he should be the one to decide what did or did not harm her. But she wasn't hurt, and she didn't think Jerome had ever shoved her like that, so she didn't push the issue.

"I don't want you talking to my friend like that," she said. "If you want to marry me and move me into a nice, big house, then *maybe* you can have a say over who can come over. But this is *my* house. You can't tell me who I can be friends with."

"Alright," Jerome said. "I'm sorry. I just, I don't like that fag shit. It's disgusting."

Deja thought Jerome's behavior was the only thing that was disgusting. "What went so bad at work?"

"Nothing a swift kick in the ass wouldn't have fixed," Jerome complained. "I tell you; whoever outlawed corporal punishment in school is a goddamned fool. If you spare the rod, you spoil the child. Everybody knows that."

≈ ≈ ≈ ≈ ≈ ≈ ≈

Jerome made a clear effort to spend time with his son that evening, and Deja gradually forgave him for the incident with Shannon. His presence also made Deja's return to the crime scene a lot more tolerable.

She woke up at three a.m., thinking the man in her bed surely had pantyhose stretched over his head. But when she forced herself to roll over and look, it was still Jerome. He put a comforting arm around her mid-section, and Deja slept peacefully for the rest of the night.

≈ ≈ ≈ ≈ ≈ ≈ ≈

In the morning she made Jerome a quick breakfast of grits and toast and gave her parents a call when he left for work. Her mom was definitely not interested in going to Gilbert Reynolds' pre-trial hearing, but she offered to watch the baby while Deja went with her dad.

The hearing lasted only ten minutes, which was a lot shorter than Deja anticipated. There were two high points that would remain in her psyche forever. The first was when they marched the Sleeping Strangler into the courtroom. Gilbert wore a bright orange jumpsuit with wrist as well as ankle shackles.

From Deja's vantage point, she could only see the side and then the back of his head. But that was enough to give her a temporary case of AFib. The strangler was just as ugly as his mug shot picture. Even with policemen escorting him, he was still just as scary.

The second high point came when Gilbert and his lawyer stood to enter a not guilty plea and request a jury trial. Deja hoped the killer would speak, so she could compare his voice to the voice in her nightmares.

I'll kill you! I'll kill you and the baby!
If you scream again, I'll stab your stomach.
But Gilbert wisely let his lawyer enter the plea.

And that was okay. Deja didn't need to hear his voice to further her disgust. She hated this man more than Satan himself. She couldn't wait for him to be found guilty.

She couldn't wait for the day she could stand in court and look him dead in the eyes and tell him he was going to hell for what he did to her and the other women. She ached to tell him that he was going to rot in prison and get attacked and persecuted until the day came for the state to take his life away.

This was Texas, so there was no doubt they would execute him. The crowd would cheer at five minutes after midnight when the doctor declared his murdering ass no longer had a pulse.

Deja would have a front row seat for his death, and she wouldn't feel one bit guilty.

CHAPTER SEVEN
STREET WOMEN

"They just, they see us on the corner, and they think it's like, *whatever*, you know? Whatever they want to go down can go down. Sometimes they want you to call them *Daddy*, or Mr. Smith or whatever. Sometimes they want you to hit them. They get a rush out of that. I had this one guy who liked me to knee him in the balls. He was a creep. That's all he wanted."

The speaker was Juliette Moss. Juliette was no longer a junkie or a prostitute, but she wasn't far removed. She got out of rehab two days ago. Three months before rehab, she was heavy in the streets; selling her body for drugs, stealing from people for drugs, and apparently getting raped repeatedly for drugs.

It was Saturday evening, April Fools' Day. This was Deja's second meeting with the WAAR group. Juliette's story was mind-blowing. Deja was not prepared for the sheer rawness and ugliness of it. She knew people like Juliette existed. She knew what they did and why they did it. But other than cursory information, Deja didn't know anything about crack addict prostitutes.

"I got raped my first time out," Juliette said. Her voice was deep and raspy from decades of dope and cigarettes. Juliette was a thin woman with short blonde hair and dark, serious eyes. She looked fifty, but when she first started talking, she said she was thirty-seven. She had small, bony hands and dark, leathery skin like Edward James Olmos.

"It was a young white guy," she said, "my first trick ever. He was tall and cute. I thought he was a college kid. His truck was so neat. He didn't *look* like the kind of guy who would hurt somebody. But that's when I learned my first lesson about the streets: Never trust the way a man looks. He can always hurt you, if you're not prepared.

"But my first date, I wasn't prepared for him at all. I didn't know nothing. He took me to Sycamore Creek. I thought it was because he wanted a more secluded spot. He did, but it wasn't for good reasons. As soon as he parked, he reared back and knocked the shit out of me. He hit me harder than anyone ever has.

"I almost passed out. I wish I had, but I stayed awake, barely. I saw everything he was doing to me. Worse than that, I understood it. He put a knife to my throat and made me, suck him. He said he'd cut me if I bit him, so I didn't. When I was done, he made me take my clothes off. All of them. He had his way with me every way he wanted, and then he kicked me out of the truck and called me a whore and a slut. He said I liked it, and he wasn't going to pay me because I liked it."

Juliette lowered her head. The ladies in the group were quick to offer her affection. The woman seated on her right put a comforting hand on her back and rubbed between her shoulder blades. The stranger on her left reached for her hand and held it tightly.

"I was so strung out," Juliette said, "I went right back to the same corner where he picked me up, and I got in the very next car that stopped for me. I had no job, no friends, no family. I chased the dragon for nine more years after that. I can't tell you how many times I've been brutalized since then. I lost every–"

Her voice cracked and then faded completely. Fat tears welled and spilled from her eyes. Half a dozen more women were crying by then. Tissues were plucked from boxes in all directions.

"I lost everything I ever had," Juliette continued. "I don't care about the material things. But I lost my kids to CPS. I lost my mom and dad, my brothers and sisters. I lost every photo album, every sentimental gift.

"At the time, it didn't matter. I felt like since I couldn't stop smoking crack, I deserved to be on the streets. I deserved it every time a trick hit me, or raped me or ran off with my money."

Heads started to shake all over the room. But Juliette already learned the truth when she was in rehab.

"But I didn't deserve it," she said. "No matter what I did, and no matter how bad I was, that didn't give nobody the right to abuse me. I am a human being," she declared. "I'm a woman, and I deserve to be treated with kindness and respect. I didn't know it then, but I know it now. And I'll tell you, I am *never* going back to the way I was!"

The place erupted in cheers. Nearly everyone was misty-eyed. Everyone wanted to hug the new Juliette. Deja was on the far side of the room, so she had to wait a few minutes before she got her turn.

The meeting lasted another forty minutes. The women discussed how to find their identity in Jesus and how God could help them with any struggle.

When they dismissed, Deja hung around for a while, looking through self-help pamphlets provided by the host. A woman she recognized from last week approached with a friendly smile.

"Hi, Deja. Did you come alone today?" It was Tamara, the one who offered her business card at the last meeting.

"Yeah, my sister had to watch her kids tonight," Deja said. "But I'm okay. I just wanted someone with me that first time, in case it was..."

"In case it was like today?" Tamara wore a one piece jumpsuit. It was tan and fashionable, with shorts and short sleeves. Her long hair was flawless. She was very pretty, one of the most beautiful women Deja had ever met in person.

"Yeah, I wish she was here today," Deja admitted.

"What'd you think about Juliette's story?"

"It was, bad," Deja said. "It reminded me of the strangler's first two victims. They were both drug addicts and prostitutes."

"That's typical," Tamara said. "Those women are invisible. Society wants to sweep them under the rug. If one or two gets killed, who cares? Just one less eyesore in the community. Almost all serial killers start with drifters, prostitutes or runaways."

"I didn't know that."

"It's true. And a lot of serial killers know their first victim. They won't attack a stranger until they're comfortable with murder."

Deja nodded. "I think I heard that somewhere before."

"Probably *Silence of the Lambs*," Tamara said, and then she embarked on a game of movie trivia. "*'Clarice, what does he do, this man you seek?'"* she asked in a pretty good Hannibal Lecter voice.

That was one of Deja's favorite movies, so she didn't skip a beat. *"'He kills women...'"*

"'No,'" Tamara said with the chilling accent. *"'He covets. And how do we begin to covet?'"*

"'We covet what we see every day,'" Deja said, and an icy chill rolled down her spine.

"That's my line," Tamara said. She looked a little spooked, too.

"Let's do a scene from *Good Times*," Deja suggested with a half-smile. "I'm getting creeped out."

"Okay," Tamara said. "Tell me if you remember this one: *'She has a figure that makes the number eight look like the number one and a smile that lights up the night. And it all belongs to...'"*

Deja chuckled. *"'Kid Dy-no-mite!'"* she said, and they both laughed.

≈ ≈ ≈ ≈ ≈ ≈ ≈

Outside the sun had all but faded from the horizon, leaving a beautiful violet hue in the skies above Overbrook Meadows. Tamara walked with Deja to her car.

"So, you never called," she said. "Does that mean you don't have any problems sleeping?"

"I did have a few bad nights," Deja said. "But my boyfriend's been staying with me."

"That's good."

"It's not as good as it sounds," Deja confided. "Sometimes I feel like any day could be our last. I guess it all boils down to how much I can put up with."

"You shouldn't have to put up with anything," Tamara said, her smile completely gone now. "You shouldn't have to settle in a relationship. If he's not everything you need in a man, then move on. I don't want you to have another sad story for the women in the group."

"He's not like that," Deja said, but she remembered the way he pushed her the other day.

"Mmm hmm," Tamara said. "If you say so."

Deja changed the subject. "I've been thinking about what Marjorie said about getting involved in my community."

"That's a good idea."

"Yeah, except there's nothing to get involved in," Deja said. "We don't have one single program."

"Then start one," Tamara suggested.

"Yeah right."

"I started a neighborhood watch in my neighborhood," Tamara said. "It was very fulfilling. I don't feel scared anymore, knowing people are looking out for me when I sleep."

"Sounds great, but I don't think I could do that. It's a lot of work, right?"

"How many jobs do you have?"

Deja's eyebrows knitted in confusion. "Just one."

"Then you have time," Tamara decided. "Every neighborhood needs a watch program. I hate to say it, but if you had one set up already, that guy might not have broken into your apartment. And who's looking out for the next girl? It has to start somewhere, so why not with you? If you need help, I'll give you whatever you need."

Deja was surprised by her friend's support. "I do want to feel safe," she said. "If you're willing to help me, I'll give it a shot."

"You can count on me," Tamara said. She gave Deja's hand a quick squeeze before walking off to her own car. "See you later."

Deja watched her go, wondering again why Tamara came to the WAAR meetings. She was still not comfortable enough to ask.

≈≈≈≈≈≈

Jerome wasn't home when Deja got there. He didn't show up until nine o'clock. He stopped in the kitchen and gave Deja a hug while she washed dishes.

"Hey, baby."

"Hey," she said. "Where you been?"

"Kicking it with the homies." He opened the refrigerator.

"I got your plate in the microwave."

"What is it?" Jerome asked on his way to retrieve it.

"Chicken fried steak."

"Damn, baby, you the best." He gave her a pat on the bottom. He checked out his meal and set the timer to reheat it. "You be cooking your ass off."

"How come you don't come to the meetings with me?" Deja asked.

"I thought they was for women."

"There are a few men there. Some husbands come to support their wives."

"How come you didn't go with Julie?"

"She didn't have anyone to watch her kids."

"Your mama can't go with you?"

"You can't go with me?"

Jerome shook his head. "Uhn-uhn. That's like a bartender going to an AA meeting. I ain't got nothing to contribute. Those broads would be looking at me crazy, like I'm the one who hurt them. Most of them wouldn't even be there if they would've put on pants instead of showing their ass and titties all the goddamned time. They dress like hoes and get mad when somebody wanna fuck."

Deja was shocked. She dried her hands and turned to face him. "Don't talk about women like that. No woman deserves to be raped."

Jerome grinned. "See, you already sound just like them. What about those skeezers at the club, be coming in with their ass out, getting drunk and following niggas to their cars? Then they wanna holler '*No!*' at the last minute. Cock teasing ain't cool."

The microwave dinged.

Deja narrowed her eyes and headed the other way. "I don't even know you."

"Baby, quit getting mad," Jerome said. "I'm just giving my opinion. See, that's why I shouldn't go to your meeting with you."

"Shut up."

Jerome took a seat at the table. "Are you gonna get my food?"

"Get it yourself," Deja shouted from the hallway. "I'm going back to work on Monday."

"Why, baby? You supposed to have six weeks off."

"I don't need six weeks. I just need to get away from you."

"Oh, okay," Jerome said with a chuckle. "You know, you said the same thing when we were at my house?"

Deja was aware of that, but she didn't respond.

"Oh, I see how it is," Jerome said and got up to retrieve his own meal.

≈≈≈≈≈≈≈

Deja didn't think he truly saw how it was until she awakened at two-thirty a.m., and there was no one in bed with her. She sat up and patted the crumpled sheets next to her, just to be sure. There definitely wasn't a body resting beneath them.

Ain't this a bitch, she thought. Why would he go to bed with her if he wasn't going to stay the night? And why didn't he tell her he was leaving? Deja sighed because none of that really mattered when dealing with someone like Jerome. He was a dick, and nothing a dick did had to make sense because dicks were brainless.

The bathroom.

The thought struck Deja like inspiration, and she felt guilty for bad-mouthing her man without checking the most obvious explanation. She turned towards the hallway to see if there was any light shining under the bathroom door. And that's when she saw him.

A darkly clad man stood stiffly next to her dresser. Deja first thought it was Jerome, because the height and size matched perfectly. But there were a few major discrepancies that could not be ignored.

First, the man in her room was fully dressed – which would not have been the case for Jerome at two o'clock in the morning. Second, the man wore a pullover. It was black and basic, the kind you might find anywhere, like your neighborhood Walmart. Finally, and most significantly, the man in her room had pantyhose stretched over his face. He was as dark as the night, and Deja couldn't make out his features at all. But she saw all she needed to see.

Again?!

She screamed so loudly the neighbors on the far end of the complex would surely hear. The man advanced then, and Deja rolled to her knees and scrambled towards her nightstand. Her whole body was energized from a sudden rush of adrenaline.

89

Halfway across the bed, she remembered her gun wasn't there anymore! The police took it for evidence and had yet to return it.

Her only other option was a screwdriver on the floor next to the crib. But that was in the opposite direction. Deja didn't have time to get to it. Before she could reverse direction, the intruder was on her back. He was heavy. So heavy. Deja couldn't support him on her hands and knees. She screamed again. The intruder rested all of his weight on her and flattened her out on the mattress. He slid one arm under her neck.

Before Deja recognized the choke hold, her trachea was in the crook of his arm. The masked man squeezed expertly. His bicep and forearm began to cut off the blood flow to her brain. He clamped his free arm on the back of her neck and applied more pressure. Within a matter of seconds, Deja couldn't scream or breathe. She kicked her legs ferociously, but his hold was secure. She reached back wildly, punching and clawing. The strangler burrowed his head next to hers, so she couldn't get at his face.

Deja's chest burned. Her head throbbed. Her heart kicked like a mule, but without oxygen, it became weaker and weaker. Gray and blue dots swam in her field of view. Deja's mouth hung open. Her tongue poked past her bared teeth. In a last ditch effort, she used her arms and legs to push off the bed, and she managed to catch the killer off guard. She rolled to her side, but he rolled with her. The grip on her neck remained anaconda tight.

Oh, God, please! Not again!

Don't let him hurt my baby!

With all remaining strength, Deja lashed out with a flurry of hard, sharp elbows. The killer couldn't maintain his choke hold unless he was very close, so each blow found its mark. Deja connected repeatedly with his ribs and stomach.

But she still felt the world slipping away from her. She fought harder and faster, and she was eventually rewarded with a satisfying grunt of pain behind her ear. The arm around her neck loosened slightly. But it was too late.

Deja felt herself falling, descending into a deep, dark pit. The whole house tilted to the left and spun like a merry-go-round. She punched over her shoulder one last time and managed to catch his face. It was a weak blow, but she felt the satisfying squish of nose and lips, and the hands around her neck disappeared. They grabbed her arms instead. The moment Deja realized she could breathe again, she awakened from her dream.

Jerome let go of her and pushed her forward so hard it felt like a car accident. Deja rolled over quickly, just in time to see him advancing on her. Jerome's face was a mask of darkness and fury. His nostrils flared. He grabbed her shoulders and shook her angrily.

"What the fuck is wrong with you?!"

Deja stared at him, gasping, her eyes huge with fright. She gulped air like she just ran a mile, and it occurred to her that she could breathe all along. Her neck wasn't hurting, and Jerome never left the bed. He'd been with her the whole time. Her head gradually stopped spinning, and Deja forced her eyes to focus. She saw a cut on Jerome's lip. He felt it at the same moment. He rubbed his mouth tenderly and then looked down at his fingers.

"Bitch, what the fuck is wrong with you?" He wore a look of shock that was quickly giving way to anger.

"I'm sorry!" Deja wailed. "I, I thought..." She shivered and shied away from him. Jerome let her go and sat up in the bed.

"You fucking crazy!"

He made it to his feet and stomped to the bathroom. Deja got up too, her heart still pounding. Jerome was leaning over the sink by the time she got there. He had the light on and was inspecting a rapidly growing bruise on his lower lip. It wasn't bleeding much, but the swelling was already noticeable.

"Oh, my God. Baby I'm so sorry!" She put her hand on his shoulder, and Jerome jerked away roughly.

"Don't touch me!"

The pain and rejection made Deja's face crumple. *"Baby, it was an accident! I had a dream. I thought–"*

"Get away from me!" Jerome spun on her. The look in his eyes was animalistic. *"Get away from me!"* he roared.

Deja bawled as she backed out of the bathroom.

Jerome slammed the door so hard the whole house shook.

He wasn't interested in her apology when he left the restroom ten minutes later. He was so upset, Deja didn't follow him back to the bedroom. She went to the living room instead and sat on the couch and cried and listened to the quietness of her neighborhood.

SLEEPING WITH THE STRANGLER

She was still there four hours later, when the sun ushered in a bright new day.

CHAPTER EIGHT
MIDNIGHT RIDE

It was hard to come to terms with Jerome's behavior last night. Deja had never been in a relationship like this before, and she had never been in one where there was a child involved. She knew Jerome was in the wrong most of the time, but he always left room to weasel his way out of trouble.

She knew he'd come up with a perfectly rational explanation for the way he responded to her dream. Jerome was historically grouchy when he slept, and surely (he'd say) she couldn't condemn him for something he did while half-sleep. He would apologize and swear he didn't know what was going on.

Or he might tell her she deserved it for busting his lip. Deja definitely didn't want to hear that, so she avoided the conversation entirely. At seven o'clock she showered and got dressed for church. She packed up the baby and left the house at eight. Jerome remained asleep the whole time.

Deja arrived at church an hour early for prayer. Noticing her state of distress, an elder asked if he could pray for anything in particular.

"My family," she said. "I just had a baby, and I'm starting a new family. It's not going good."

The deacon laid healing hands on her and her child. He prayed his best, but Deja didn't think God blessed her and Jerome's union. As she knelt at the altar, she understood that she'd been fighting for a long time for something that was not meant to be.

≈≈≈≈≈≈≈

But when she got home, Jerome was different again. Upon entering, Deja was greeted with the wonderful scent of garlic and tomatoes. She found her boyfriend in the kitchen toiling over a spaghetti and meatballs dinner.

"Hey," he called. "Why you didn't wake me up before you left this morning?"

Deja went around the stove to see how things were coming along. Everything looked good. "I knew you didn't want to come to church."

Jerome put both hands on her sides and bent to kiss the baby in her arms. "Yeah, but I did want to talk to you before you left," he said. "I wanted to apologize for last night. I didn't mean to grab you like that. It was just, a reaction. It was subconscious. I didn't know what I was doing. I should've apologized last night, but I was mad. And I know that was wrong of me. I got a bad temper. I shouldn't have treated you like that. I love you."

Two months ago Deja's heart would've soared at such thoughtful words, but she now believed that most of what Jerome said was game. Sweet talking her was easy for him. Deja had been complacent for much too long.

"It's alright," she said. "I understand." She turned to walk away, but he grabbed her hand.

"Hey, you're not mad at me, are you? I know it's not much, but I made dinner for us. I really want you to accept my apology."

"Alright," Deja said and forced a smile.

"Cool," Jerome said. He kissed her on the mouth and got back to his cooking.

Deja went to the bedroom to change out of her church clothes.

≈≈≈≈≈≈≈

On Monday morning Deja returned to work at the Seminary Animal Clinic. Ever since she was a child, helping animals was a passion. Ten years ago Deja got closer to her dream by taking classes at the community college. She graduated with an associate's degree in veterinarian assistance and now worked as a tech for one of the best vets in Overbrook Meadows.

At the clinic, Deja snipped the tails off cute little puppies, declawed boorish tom cats and spayed and neutered big and little critters on a daily basis. She didn't perform the actual surgeries, but she had eight years of experience, so Dr. Fogerty gave her a lot of leeway in the office. Deja did all of the pre-surgery anesthesia, and she stitched up the animals after their procedures.

Deja wasn't due back to work for another two weeks, but Dr. Fogerty welcomed her early return. The small staff at the clinic put up a WELCOME BACK sign and had a beautiful cake waiting for her. She walked in at eight-thirty and almost cried when she saw how much they cared.

"Oh, wow."

"Deja!" Beatrice jumped from her desk and ran around the counter to give her a hug. Beatrice (who preferred to be called Bea) was the clinic's secretary, cashier and office manager. She was fair-skinned and pleasingly plump. Bea wore her hair short, about an inch all over. She was in her early fifties.

"Are you okay?" she asked. "We saw your story on the news. I'm so glad they got that man! I hope he gets the death penalty."

"I'm fine," Deja said. "How's everything been going?"

"Nothing's changed," Bea said. "Except the doc has really been missing you in surgery. Every one of them takes him twice as long without you."

Deja smiled. She didn't like to hear about Dr. Fogerty's trouble, but it did feel good to know that she was appreciated.

"Why'd you come back so early?" Bea asked.

"I didn't want six weeks off," Deja said. "I feel good. Plus I needed something to occupy my mind other than Jerome every day."

"How's it going with y'all?" Bea asked. "Any better?"

Deja sighed, and her expression said it all.

Bea shook her head. "I'm sorry to hear that. Do you want to talk about it?"

"I–"

"Deja!"

They looked up as their boss entered the lobby. Dr. Fogerty was a tall man with a head full of silver hair. He wore a big handlebar moustache that curled up at the ends. He was as

Texan as you could get, but he was a democrat and more compassionate than the average cowboy.

"Hi," Deja said.

Dr. Fogerty gave her a big, side-to-side hug. "You doing alright? We saw you in the papers. I know it was hell to go through that."

"It's alright. I'm better now."

"How's your baby?"

Deja's smile was beautiful. "He's great. Thanks."

"You didn't bring lunch today, did you?"

"Um..." Deja actually had a Tupperware bowl stuffed with Jerome's leftover spaghetti. It was a little bland, but still good.

"Throw it away," Dr. Fogerty said. "We're all going out for lunch today – my treat."

Deja's eyes widened. "Really?"

"Wherever you want to go," he said. "I'm happy to have you back. It's not the same here without you."

≈≈≈≈≈≈

Deja didn't want to be an expensive date, so she selected the Cousin's Barbecue on McCart for her celebratory lunch. In addition to Deja and Bea, Dr. Fogerty had to buy a meal for two more techs, a groomer, and a part time custodian.

After lunch Deja got back into her regular routine of cleaning wounds and bathing and shaving animals in preparation for surgery. She didn't get a chance to talk to Bea again until quitting time. The secretary met her at the time clock, and they exited the building together.

"You found a good daycare for your baby?"

"Yeah, my mom," Deja said. "She doesn't even want to charge me."

"That's good."

"Yeah, I definitely needed a blessing to come from somewhere."

"That man of yours," Bea said, "it's pretty much over between you two?"

"Yes," Deja said quickly. "But he'll never break up with me."

"Why not?"

"Why should he?" Deja pondered. "He has everything the way he wants it. He comes and goes as he pleases. He doesn't have to change or follow through with his promises because my dumb ass will be there for him regardless. He thinks he can just bring me flowers and hold his son every now and then, and I'll be okay with it."

Bea frowned. "You telling me you know what he's doing, and you still let him?"

"I didn't always know," Deja said. "But I'm learning. Every day I learn a little more."

"Sounds like you know what you need to do." They stopped at Bea's car. She dug in her purse for the keys.

It was April now. Overbrook Meadows' daily highs were up to 85 degrees. It still felt good though, tons better than it would three months from now. Petals from a nearby dogwood tree floated and twisted in the air like miniscule acrobats.

"Actually I don't know what to do," Deja said. "I still love him, and he's my child's father. I keep thinking about the way things were, before I got pregnant."

"Then give him one more chance," Bea suggested.

"I already—"

"No, you need to give him *an ultimatum*. When he comes home tonight, treat him good. Cook for him like you always do. While he's eating, let him know how you feel. When he starts saying, *I'll do this, or I'll do that*, tell him, *That's good, because this is your last chance*. Give him a timeline for when you expect to see changes. If he doesn't do right, then you have to leave him. The time for him to get his act together is right now."

Deja thought about it and decided it was worth a shot. There was nothing to lose and so much to gain.

"Alright," she said. "I guess I'll tell you how it went tomorrow."

≈≈≈≈≈≈

On the way home, Deja stopped at the grocery store and bought everything she needed to make chicken enchiladas. The meal would take an hour to prepare, but she had plenty of time. Jerome coached the track team on Mondays, and he wouldn't leave school until after six.

When she got home, Deja put a whole chicken on the stove. She showered while it boiled and found a nice outfit for the evening. She hadn't worn a dress for Jerome in a while. She pulled one of her sexiest gowns from the closet.

An hour later she had the chicken shredded and the tortillas stuffed and simmering in the oven. Of all of her home-cooked dishes, this was Jerome's favorite. Deja got dressed and put on a little make-up while the enchiladas baked. Everything was perfect by six-thirty. Deja expected her man at any minute, but he still wasn't home by seven.

Jerome wasn't there by seven-thirty, either.

Deja called him. The call went to voicemail after a few rings.

"Hey, baby. I thought you were coming here after school. I made you something nice for dinner. It's getting cold. I hope you're not working this late. Call me when you get this message..."

By eight o'clock Deja was sure Jerome wasn't at school anymore, but no one answered his home phone or his cell. By nine o'clock Deja figured he wasn't coming, and by ten o'clock she was positive. She left her apartment and climbed the steps of another building twenty yards away. She knocked on her friend's door. Shannon answered wearing tight jeans with a small tee shirt.

"You want some enchiladas?" Deja asked.

"Hell yeah," Shannon said. "Where your punk ass boyfriend at?"

"I don't know," Deja said, fighting back tears.

"Okay," Shannon said. "Let me get my shoes."

≈≈≈≈≈≈

Ten minutes later the girls sat at the dining table eating what would have been a great meal if Jerome had brought his sorry ass home. Shannon had much more of an appetite than Deja, even though their conversation upset both of them.

"I'm lazy? How the hell he gon' say I'm lazy?" Shannon used a fork while she ate, but she still licked her fingers a lot.

"He probably thinks that because you don't work."

"I don't have to work."

"I know," Deja said. "You live off of your dad's allowance."

"It's not my fault my family got money."

"I never said it was."

"Why does he care how I live my life?"

"I don't know," Deja said. "You asked why he called you lazy, and I'm telling you. I never said it was right."

"That's just an excuse." Shannon frowned. "Even if I had ten jobs, he still wouldn't like me."

"You're probably right."

"That gets on my nerves," Shannon said. "You know, white people ain't like that. If they don't like gay people, they'll probably roll they eyes and go on about their business. Black men can't stand gay blacks. And they feel like it's their personal duty to do something about it."

"Well, you don't have to worry about him anymore," Deja said.

"Why? Y'all breaking up?"

"I'm pretty sure we will."

"Good. You know he cheating on you."

That was a news flash. "How you figure?"

"Where you think he is?" Shannon pondered. "What kind of man don't answer his cell phone or his home phone?"

"That don't mean—"

"And how come he stopped giving you some when you was pregnant?" Shannon reminded. "What kind of man can stop having sex – for five months? When was the last time y'all did something?"

Not counting the time Jerome went limp on her the night of the attack, it had been four and a half months. "That doesn't mean he's cheating."

"Go over there then," Shannon suggested. "If you got so much faith in him, go over his house – right now."

"I'm not going over there."

"'Cause you don't want to know."

"No, because it's after ten, and I have to work tomorrow. And I don't want to waste my time."

"He stole your interview money, too."

Deja was getting dizzy trying to keep up with all of these accusations. "What are you talking about now?"

"You said Jerome gave you three thousand dollars," Shannon recalled. "Why they give *him* the money. And how much you think his check was? You said you offered him some of your money, and he wouldn't take it. What kind of nigga don't want free money? I'll tell you what kind: The kind that already *got* your money."

Deja didn't comment because she had suspicions about that one herself. How much did Channel Six pay Jerome for setting up the interview? Another three thousand? Deja hated to admit it, but she had no idea how much her interview was worth to them.

"And I'll tell you something else," Shannon said. She lowered her voice and leaned in for this one: "Jerome is the one who tried to kill you."

Deja frowned and cocked her head. "Why you say that?"

"He didn't want that baby," Shannon said in a hushed voice. "He would've done *anything* to stop you from having him. And he was the only one with a key to your apartment. I think it was him, girl: Jerome's the strangler."

Deja couldn't say she never thought about it. During the attack, the first thought in her mind was that it was Jerome in bed with her. And the way he manhandled her (twice in the past week) showed he had a violent side. But could she accuse him of murder?

"So, so you think he killed all of those women, or did he only attack me?"

"I don't know about the other ones," Shannon said. "But you for sure."

"For sure? Why are you so sure? They already arrested the strangler."

"I know."

"Gilbert Reynolds has a history of sexual assault, and he went to prison for rape. He got in trouble for strangling a guy nearly to death when he was locked up. They caught him about a mile away from my house, and he was dripping wet with sweat, like he'd been running. *And* he had a burglary kit in his pocket – at three in the morning. Now you tell me how he's not the guy."

"He didn't have a pullover," Shannon said. "Or pantyhose on his head."

"He had a whole mile to get rid of that."

"They had dogs," Shannon countered. "They went through the whole neighborhood with dogs, and they didn't find no pullover."

"There's about twenty manholes in a one mile radius," Deja said. "The dogs didn't go down in the sewers."

Shannon smacked her lips. "I'm just saying. That sounds like some shit Jerome would do."

"Well, you don't know Jerome like I do. He's an asshole. He's a liar. He's an all-around *bad boyfriend*, but he doesn't want to kill me – or anyone else. He could never do that."

"You sure about that?"

"Yeah," Deja said. "I'm sure."

"You better be."

≈ ≈ ≈ ≈ ≈ ≈ ≈

Shannon left at eleven-thirty, and Deja went right to bed. She got up five minutes later and got dressed for a midnight ride. It wasn't like her to show up at her boyfriend's house unannounced, and it was out of character for Deja to check on a man, but tonight she had to do both. Jerome wasn't the strangler, but whether he was cheating on her or not was still up for debate.

Deja strapped Adrian in his car seat and started her Sentra up at 11:47 p.m. Jerome would be shocked to see her. Deja hoped that was the only surprise they had that night.

CHAPTER NINE
PLAYING THE FOOL

Jerome lived on the south side of town.

That never meant much before, but Deja thought about it when she exited the freeway on Rosedale. She considered it now because of what Shannon said about her boyfriend being the strangler. Deja thought about the conversation with her friend from WAAR. Tamara said a serial killer always starts near his home.

We covet what we see every day.

The words permeated Deja's consciousness as she drove past the many seedy motels in Jerome's neighborhood. She rarely cruised the south side this late. Deja was surprised by the abundant night life. Overbrook Meadows wasn't a high crime city, but they had their fair share of murders and violent offenses. Drugs were at the root of the problem half the time. These run-down motels catered to hookers and johns, dealers and users.

This is where the strangler found his first victim. He would have fit right in because the drug culture is notoriously anonymous. Deja imagined Jerome checking into one of those disgusting motels. Try as she might, she couldn't see her boyfriend in the midst of those lowlifes. Jerome was college-educated and clean cut. He was a teacher, for Christ's sake. As far as Deja knew, he never committed a crime other than speeding.

Deja shook her head and cleared her mind of the thought. Shannon was intuitive, but she was speaking out of anger. Her theory was way off track. The idea that Jerome was somehow hateful enough to strangle people to death was preposterous.

But he was a bad boyfriend.

Deja got more evidence of this when she made the last turn onto his street. Jerome's driveway was big enough for two vehicles, but tonight Deja's Sentra wouldn't fit. There was already another car parked next to Jerome's Tahoe. The sight of it made Deja's heart turn hard and heavy in her chest. She pulled to a stop along the curb and stared at the new car for a couple of minutes.

Her breathing became labored. Her enchilada dinner suddenly felt like cold rocks in her belly. She tried to remain calm, even as her vision blurred with tears.

She wondered how long Jerome had been home. Was he there all along? Whose car was parked next to his, and how long had they been there? Were they spending the night? Deja checked her watch: It was fifteen minutes after midnight. It was too late for a casual visit, and the lights were not on the in front room.

The suspicious vehicle was a Chrysler Sebring. It was champagne colored and clean; glistening under the soft moonlight. Deja scanned it slowly, trying to convince herself it wasn't a woman's car. That wasn't too hard. There was no calligraphy on the back windshield reading *Peaches*, *Keisha* or *Tasha*. There was no stuffed animal hanging from the rearview mirror, and there was no girly license plate frame.

The car could belong to anyone, but Deja girded her soul for the worst. She exited her vehicle quietly and wiped the tears from her eyes while she extracted Adrian from his car seat. The baby was so innocent; totally oblivious to the hell about to erupt around him. Deja gave him a kiss and held him close to her heart.

She had her emotions mostly under control when she mounted the steps to Jerome's door. She didn't think he would answer. Why should he? It was easier to wait until tomorrow and tell her he was fast asleep.

I didn't hear anyone knocking, baby. Sorry.

By then he would have concocted an unshakable defense for the car in his driveway.

But Jerome fooled her so many times, he was now a cocky sonofabitch. Three minutes after Deja's first knock, he answered the door. He wore a pair of boxers and unconcealed irritation. He yawned and rubbed his eyes to further the impression that she had awakened him from a deep sleep.

"What, girl, what you doing here?" His voice was gruff. He did not step aside to allow her entry.

Deja's eyes glistened under the porch light. Her baby slept soundly against her chest. She shifted her weight from one leg to the other and felt foolish under his hard glare. "Where, where were you today?"

Jerome frowned. "What you mean, coming over here asking me some shit like that? Do you know what time it is?"

"How come you haven't answered your phone?"

Jerome shook his head. "You need to quit tripping."

"Who's car is that?"

"Look, I'll talk to you tomorrow," he said. "You got to be out of your mind, coming over here like this."

He tried to shut the door, but he already made a crucial mistake by answering it. Deja didn't come halfway across town for nothing. She put her foot in the way, daring him to close it on her. Jerome looked down at her sneaker, and Deja saw that he wasn't sleepy at all.

"Move your foot," he ordered. "I'm not going to argue with you. It's too late for this shit."

He continued to push the door, and it started to hurt. Deja stepped forward and pushed her shoulders through the opening. Jerome would have to hurt the baby if he wanted her out, and it looked like he might do just that.

"Move out the way," he said calmly.

"Whose car is that?" Deja asked again. She tried to force her way inside, but Jerome stepped in front of her and put a hand on her chest. He pushed gingerly at first and then harder when she wouldn't back up.

"You can't be running up in my house."

But the more he fought her, the more Deja knew her fears were valid.

"Stop," she said, pushing his arm away. "Stop. You're hurting me."

"Then get back."

"Stop!" she shouted. *"You're hurting me!"*

Jerome looked around to make sure none of his neighbors were up at that hour. Deja used the momentary distraction to duck under his arm and squeeze by him. She made it into the living room with her heart pounding, all of the hairs on her arms standing erect. She flipped the light switch and squinted a little while her eyes adjusted to the brightness.

"Who you got in here? Where that ho at?"

Jerome followed her. "Quit tripping!"

"*Who's in here*?!"

"*Nobody*! You need to quit tripping!"

"Mmm hmmm." Deja turned away from him, her eyes wide and wild. "Where she at, Jerome?" She headed for the bedroom. Jerome was right behind her.

"Stop, girl!" He grabbed her shoulder. Deja yanked away from him. The move jostled Adrian, and he woke up with a mighty wail.

"*You're hurting the baby*!" Deja yelled and kept walking.

"That's *you*!" Jerome shouted.

"*Where she at*?" Deja screamed. She flipped the light in the bedroom. It was empty. She checked the closet and knelt to look under the bed but found nothing. When she stood again, Jerome got in her face.

"I told you there wasn't nobody here! Now can you please get out of my house? You pissing me off, Deja. You know I don't like this crazy shit."

"Whose car is that?"

"It's my, brother's!"

The hesitation was slight, but Deja caught it. "You're lying, Jerome. Where he at then? Huh? Where he at?"

"He left it so I can take – You know what, I ain't gotta explain myself to you. You're crazy, and I'm not arguing with no crazy woman! You need to get out my house. I'll call you tomorrow, and we can..."

He trailed off because Deja wasn't standing there anymore. She stomped past him and searched the hallway bathroom and the linen closet. Jerome didn't try to stop her again until she headed for the guest room.

"Hold on!"

He tried to get around her in the hallway, but Deja walked quickly and lunged from side to side each time he tried to pass.

"Stop!"

"Move, Jerome!"

"Get, come here!"

"*Leave me alone*!"

The baby screamed the whole time. Deja knew things between her and Jerome would never be the same if she was wrong. But she wasn't wrong, and she knew it. And as soon as she entered the guest bedroom, she could prove it. Rather than hide under the bed or make a run for the closet, Jerome's other girlfriend stood stiffly, like a deer stuck in bright headlights.

The interloper had long, curly hair. She wore a frilly, pink nightie. If not for the baby in her arms, Deja would have charged her, clawing and kicking. But one of Adrian's parents had to be responsible. Deja reached calmly for the light switch and turned it on. She watched the stranger for a few seconds, and the stranger watched her back. Jerome stood quietly in the background while Adrian screamed.

Jerome's new friend was tall and pretty; a Hispanic woman with large eyes and full lips. She was thin but curvaceous, with dark skin like an Apache. Her breasts were large and perky. The bitch had legs for days.

Deja took a deep, slow breath, and everything suddenly made sense. Of course Jerome didn't want to sleep with his baby's mother anymore. Who would if they could be with someone as beautiful and exotic as this?

Deja was beyond furious, but before she could vent, she needed Jerome to reject the tramp. She looked over her shoulder with fire in her eyes. Her eyebrows were bunched together in anger. Her voice was gravelly.

"Get this bitch out of here."

Jerome's other woman flinched and trembled visibly. Her eyes darted from Deja to Jerome. Her voice quavered when she spoke.

"I, I, I didn't know he had a—"

"*Get this bitch out!*" Deja ordered.

The floozy shrieked and backed away until she bumped the bed. Jerome knew he had to comply.

"You need to leave," he said.

When the hussy didn't budge, Deja turned to her man. She was shocked to see him staring at her.

"You, *you* need to leave, Deja."

That felt like a slap in the face from God Himself. Deja's knees buckled. She studied Jerome's eyes. It was clear who he was talking to, but still she had to ask...

"What?"

It was wrong to think things couldn't get any worse, just as it was foolish to expect Jerome to man up one day. Deja had no idea how absurd her faith in him was until she saw it with her own eyes that night. She saw that his cruelty knew no bounds, and Adrian was already a bigger man than his father. Jerome looked her dead in the eyes and didn't look one bit regretful.

"I already told you; we're through. I don't want to be with you anymore. Now get out of my house, please. You know that baby ain't mine."

Deja was literally stunned silent. She knew he was saying that for the benefit of his new girlfriend, but his words pierced her soul like bullets. Her heart ruptured. Sick blood flowed through her veins, and her whole body became weak and slow. She didn't want to cry in front of Jerome or his woman, but she felt the tears rolling down her cheeks.

"Why are you saying that?"

Jerome stuck to his story. "I already told you I don't want to be with you. I told you that baby ain't mine, and I told you I'm with Melinda now. You need to leave and go on about your life. I don't want you no more, Deja! Can't you get the picture?"

Deja finally did get the picture. It was crystal clear. She thought about putting the baby down for a second, so she could go after Melinda, but what good would that do? Maybe she should attack Jerome instead. But again, what would it solve? Could she exact her animalistic vengeance while her baby rolled around crying on the floor?

The Christian thing to do was simply leave, so she chose that route. But not until she spoke her mind. She returned her attention to the new girlfriend, and tried to push back the pain.

"You're making a mistake," Deja warned. "Jerome is a liar. He never, he never told me anything about you. He *knows* this is his baby. He was at the hospital, and, and he, he signed the birth certificate, and–"

"That's because–"

"Shut the hell up!" Deja spun on him like a mad dog. She cocked her head and shook it slowly. "You're going to pay for what you did to me. If you didn't want to stay together, all you had to do was say it. I never forced you to be with me!"

"I did tell you! And I told you that's not my bab–"

SPLACK!

She slapped him hard and fast. Jerome's head snapped to the side. It took his face a second to catch up with it. Deja didn't think violence would help, but it did. It helped a whole bunch. She felt an immediate release of tension.

"Don't you *ever* deny your son again," she growled. Her lip was curled, her teeth bared. She pointed a trembling finger no more than a foot from his nose. "All this other shit you're doing, that's fine. I can deal with it. But don't you deny him. You're a sorry piece of shit, Jerome, and you're gonna get yours. Mark my words." She turned back to Melinda. "And you're a fool if you stay with him. That'll be one of the worst mistakes you *ever* make."

Deja paused a few moments to let her words sink in and then turned back towards the hallway.

"Move!"

She gave Jerome a mean stiff-arm, and he took a stumbled step backwards. Adrian's cries were ear-splitting by now. Deja put a hand on his back and comforted him as she walked. She kissed him on the cheek, and he quieted down right away.

As soon as she stepped outside, Jerome slammed the door closed so hard the wind ruffled Deja's hair. A cool breeze from the north chilled the sweat on her neck and face, but it didn't diminish her fury.

She stood there for a moment, thinking she should have a more dramatic exit. Jerome had a few potted plants on his porch. Deja thought about using one of those. She could send it flying through the living room window, or even better she could throw it at Melinda's pretty car. Just as quickly as the thought came to her, Deja decided against it.

She was a thirty-two year old single mother, not some eighteen-year-old with a crush. Contrary to the language she used in Jerome's house, Deja considered herself a respectful woman. And the Bible said vengeance belonged to the Lord. Jerome would get what was coming to him sooner or later. When that time came, Deja wouldn't have to lift a finger.

That faith gave her the strength to hold her head high and leave the house without further incident. It took her a while to calm down, but she eventually did. And she also came up with two bright sides to this horrible night.

First, Deja knew that was the last tear she would shed for her child's father. And second, she no longer had to waste her time giving Jerome an ultimatum he never would've fulfilled. She was free to move on with her life now. It was a weak victory, but it was all she had, so she embraced it.

CHAPTER TEN
MOVING ON

The next morning started off terribly.

Deja didn't get much sleep after the debacle at Jerome's house. When the alarm went off at six forty-five, she prayed it wasn't so. But Mickey Mouse never lied, and his hands were indeed pointing at the six and the nine.

Deja didn't say her prayers every morning, but she knew it was going to be a bad day, so she immediately acknowledged God.

Lord, you know I didn't mean to hit that boy. Forgive me for having such a bad temper. I'm going to need your help getting through this day. I don't feel like I got any sleep at all. Peace and energy, Lord. That's what I need...

Deja felt good about her prayer, but Adrian fussed the whole time she got ready for work, so peace was elusive. He didn't quiet down until they got in the car. By then Deja was frustrated and reminded that she was completely alone in this thing called *parenthood*. That unfortunate fact served to depress her all over again.

She dropped Adrian off at her mom's house at eight, and at work Deja finally found serenity with the animals she cared for. Most of the pets that spent the night at the clinic were recovering from surgery. They were anxious and upset about the whole ordeal. A two minute cuddle did wonders for their state of mind and Deja's as well.

When Bea summoned her to the front at twelve o'clock, Deja strolled to her desk wearing her first smile of the day. Unfortunately the devil is always waiting for such an opportunity to knock you down a peg. Deja saw Jerome waiting for her in the lobby. Of course he was the absolute last thing she wanted to see.

Her baby-daddy stood near the front window flipping through a pamphlet on heart worms. He looked up at Deja with a blank expression. He didn't have flowers, so she knew he didn't come to apologize.

"What do you want?"

"I came to see you," Jerome said and returned the pamphlet to its slot. "Can I take you to lunch?"

Deja thought he had some nerve. Bea realized what was going on right away.

"Is there a problem?" she asked Deja. "Do you want me to call Dr. Fogerty?"

"This is my *ex*-boyfriend," Deja announced. Her eyes were cold and unforgiving. "And yes, there is a problem if he thinks I'm going anywhere with him."

"Sounds like you need to leave," Bea told him.

"I don't want no trouble," Jerome said. He held his hands up to show how innocent he was. "I just want to talk."

"About what?" Deja asked.

"Can we talk in private?"

"Uh-uhn," Bea said, but Deja was willing to hear him out.

"I'll be right back."

Bea started to rise from her seat. "Uh-uhn, girl. Where you going?"

"Outside," Deja said and placed a reassuring hand on her shoulder. "I'll be right back."

Jerome went to the door and opened it for her.

"You go first," Deja instructed. She was 90 percent sure Jerome had no plans of harming her, but she wasn't going to have her back to him if it turned out she was wrong.

He *hmphed* under his breath and grinned. "Yes ma'am."

≈ ≈ ≈ ≈ ≈ ≈ ≈

It was April 3rd. The sun was barely visible in the sky, obscured by a curtain of storm clouds that were dark and full, threatening to burst at any minute. It was windy, too. The air was thick and humid, laced with static electricity. All around them the power lines were packed with blackbirds that didn't want to exert too much energy flying in those conditions.

Deja was a lover of nature, but she got chills when she saw the birds grouped together like that, like they were plotting. All it took was for one of them to attack. Once the first human eyeball got pecked out, it was on. The whole congregation would swoop down and make Alfred Hitchcock's tale a reality.

Jerome took a few steps into the parking lot and turned back when Deja didn't follow.

"Why you standing way over there?"

"Hurry up and tell me what you want."

He took a couple of steps towards her. "I want to talk about what happened last night."

"Which one of your lies do you want to talk about?"

He stopped and rubbed his chin. "You getting a little feisty, ain't you?"

Deja reached back for the door handle. "Is that it?"

"Naw," Jerome said. "I, uh, I want to apologize for—"

"Man, don't apologize to me for *nothing*. I'm sick of your apologies, empty promises. Everything went down exactly how you wanted it to."

"Naw," he said. "It didn't. I didn't want you to find out like that."

"Then maybe you shouldn't have did it."

"I know. I was, it was wrong. I thought—"

"And you got the nerve to deny your son," Deja said. "That's *despicable*, Jerome. You're not a man. You ain't nothing at all." She sneered. Her contempt was searing.

Jerome looked away. "I didn't want to do that. But the way you ran up in there... I didn't have time to talk to her yet."

"So you lied," Deja said coldly. "That's your favorite way to get out of everything. You could've told me you wanted to break up, Jerome. I didn't have no handcuffs on you."

"I know." He looked truly remorseful. "I didn't mean to hurt nobody. I didn't want to break up with you. You got my son, and you, you was a good woman to me, Deja."

"You just wanted something skinnier and prettier," she interrupted. Her eyes watered, but she swore she would never cry for him again and she meant it. "One day you'll see," she said. "One day you'll see what you had."

"I know," Jerome said. "I already know."

Deja looked back through the glass doors. Bea stood right behind her, watching them openly.

"I'm going back to work," Deja told Jerome. "What'd you come over here for?"

"The baby," he said. "I came to talk about my son."

"Then talk." Deja thought Jerome *finally* wanted to man up, but no such luck.

"I wanna pay you child support," he said. "One fifty a month."

Deja didn't think he could disappoint her further, but there it was.

"Okay, two hundred," he said.

Deja put a hand to her head and rubbed between her eyes. She looked up at the birds wondering why the hell they weren't attacking him yet. "I was so weak behind you," she said finally.

Jerome knitted his eyebrows. "Wh, what?"

"Anything you said..." Deja reminisced, staring at the storm clouds. "All you had to do was snap your fingers, and I was there."

"You, uh..."

"Not anymore." She met his eyes and saw him for the coward he was. "Never again, Jerome. I can do it by myself. I don't need you. Even when you were there, I was still doing it by myself. I just didn't realize it."

Jerome nodded and then shrugged. "So, two hundred is cool?" He reached in his pocket and produced two bills. "I brought, um..." He trailed off because Deja was chuckling.

"You giving me my money back?" she asked.

"What?"

"That's my money from the interview, right?"

"Huh?"

"Huh? What? Who? You heard me, boy. I wanna know if that's my money from Channel Six?"

He shook his head. "I don't know what—"

"Save it," Deja said. "I don't want you to have to lie again. Go ahead and keep that money, Jerome. We'll work it out in court. If you're offering me two, that must mean I can get four, if we see a judge. You think you're two steps ahead of me? Not anymore. From now on, I'm going to be *five* steps ahead of your lying ass."

She went back to work and left him to mull that over. Deja didn't watch, but later Bea told her Jerome sat in his car for five minutes after she came inside. She thought he was going to kill himself in the parking lot, but he eventually drove away with his music up loud.

≈≈≈≈≈≈

With so much drama in her last relationship, it wasn't hard to decide what changes Deja needed to make in life. She understood that she could never give another man so much control over her. It was easy to feel depressed because of Jerome's rejection, but Deja wouldn't allow that either. Even at his best, Jerome was an asshole. Losing him was nothing to cry about.

He did make a good security blanket though. On the way home from work, Deja wondered if the lonely nights would find her fearful of the strangler again. She decided to be proactive with that, too. Fear was another form of weakness. She knew that she could never be independent if she was afraid to be in an empty home.

When she got to her complex, Deja stopped at the front office. Her apartment manager was a thin woman with blonde hair and strong features. She had a nice figure, but she played it down with long, oversized dresses. She looked up from papers on her desk and eyed Deja peculiarly when she entered her office.

"Hi. Can I help you?"

"Hi," Deja said. She moved her baby to the other hip and pulled out a chair. "Can I sit down?"

"Sure." The landlord leaned forward in her seat. "I'm Stephanie. What can I do for you?"

"I'm Deja. I came by to ask–"

"*Oh my goodness!*" Stephanie's eyes widened. "It's you."

"Yeah. I'm me."

"I'm so sorry for what happened to you!"

"I know. It's okay."

"How's everything going?" Stephanie asked. "I got your locks changed. Is everything okay?"

"It's fine," Deja said. "Thank you."

"Nothing like that has ever happened here before," the manager said. "I'm glad you got through that, somehow. It must have been horrible. What can I do for you?"

"I, uh, I joined this group," Deja said. "It's a support group for women."

The manager nodded.

"They were telling me," Deja went on, "that it might be good to join a neighborhood watch in my area, to feel safer. I was looking around, and I don't see any stickers anywhere. Do y'all have a neighborhood watch?"

Stephanie looked like she was admitting to a felony. "No. We don't. I'm sorry. I wish we did."

"Well," Deja said, "I have a friend who said she'll help me start one here, if you don't mind. She's done this before, in her own neighborhood. I probably won't need much help from you, but—"

"Anything you want," the manager said, suddenly happy again. "It would be so nice if you'd like to spearhead something like that. I can get you walkie-talkies and tee shirts, if you want. Anything you need."

Deja hadn't thought about radios and tee shirts but, "That's a great idea."

"There are a bunch of knuckleheads around here," the manager confided. "But the majority of our residents are honest, hardworking people. They'll be happy to know you're starting this up. I can put a bulletin in our newsletter to announce your meetings."

Deja was surprised she was so helpful. "Thanks. I probably will need that. But I have to talk to my friend first, to find out where to start."

"Okay," Stephanie said. "Let me know when you're ready. I'm really excited."

"Alright. I will." Deja left the office smiling from ear to ear. *Spearhead.* Ha! She bet Jerome never thought she had the initiative to spearhead anything bigger than Sunday dinner. Come to think of it, Deja never thought she did either.

≈≈≈≈≈≈≈

115

The WAAR women met twice a week. The group was much smaller on Tuesdays than it was on Saturdays. Because of this, or maybe because of the incident with Jerome, Deja was finally ready to share her testimony and bare her soul to the other victims of abuse.

Her story was a little different today than it was on the Channel Six interview, mainly because the women in her group didn't ask questions. They didn't care about the timeline of events. They were more interested in Deja's thought process during the attack and how she found the will and courage to fight back and survive.

Deja wasn't comfortable with public speaking, but she stood at the front of the room to build her confidence. In the wake of Jerome, she felt like she had a unique opportunity to create a new persona for herself. She wanted the new Deja to be strong and charismatic.

She didn't tell her story for shock value or for kudos from her peers. She wanted to help every woman in attendance, though she was still not sure how to accomplish that.

"I um..." Deja paused halfway through, looking for the right words. The women waited quietly. There were nineteen people in attendance. All eyes were focused on Deja. A few women were crying already, but Deja didn't want her story to be a sad one.

"I swung at him first," she said. "Not because I'm a strong woman. I'm really not. I was even weaker back then. I was in a bad relationship. My boyfriend had so much power over me... I never stood up for myself. But right then, when I saw that man in my bed..." She looked away. All of her emotions from that night rushed back like a tide, and she tried to describe them.

"That's *my* bed," she said, "and my house. All of the stuff I let my boyfriend put me through... That was different because I loved that man. I gave him my heart and I invited him into my life. But the man in my bed..." She pursed her lips. "I never gave him permission to do anything. The thought that he would come to me, break in my house and lie down in *my* bed... That was so disrespectful.

"I was scared. I was real scared. But beneath that, I was mad too. How could this man come into my home – and sleep with me? I hadn't had a fight since grade school, but I took a swing at him. I wanted to knock his head off. I wanted him to regret ever coming to my apartment."

The women nodded their approval. Deja sighed.

"But he got the upper hand," she said. "He hit me so hard, I saw stars. And then I did exactly what he wanted me to do. I stopped fighting, and he turned me over and tied me up. I knew what he was doing the whole time. I felt like I should fight back, but the only thing on my mind at that point was how hard he hit me. It was like, I was willing to accept whatever he wanted to do to me, so long as he didn't hit me again. I never wanted to be hit like that again."

Deja looked around and saw familiarity in the eyes watching her. These women knew what it was like to submit and suffer. Some of them were still living under those circumstances.

"But then," Deja said, "then something happened that made me forget about his punches. He put his hands on my neck, and, and he started squeezing. At first I was shocked. I asked myself, *What the hell is he doing now*? But then I understood, and the anger came back.

"Not only did he have the audacity to break into my home, but he wanted to *kill* me – for no reason. He wanted to kill my baby, too. I, I couldn't allow it." She shook her head. "No matter what else happened, I made a decision that he would not kill me. He would not rape me. Nobody else could stop it, so I had to. I vowed to fight 'til my last breath to make him stop."

Deja paused and slowed her breathing. "And that's what I did. I fought him with everything I had. I fought so hard, I pulled my thumb out of the socket. And as bad as that hurt, I kept fighting until I got my hands loose. Once I was free..." She frowned. "You'd better believe I let that asshole have it. I didn't do it just for me. I fought for my baby. I fought for every woman that came before me and every woman he might think about going for after me.

"I'm not a saint or a hero. But that night... That night I stood up for the so-called *weaker sex*, and I understand that now." Deja scanned the audience until she found Tamara. "A friend once told me I should tell my story to inspire others. If that's possible, I guess this is what I want you to remember about me: I'm not a strong woman, and I'm not a special woman.

"I'm a scared little girl who, one day, decided enough is enough. I made a decision to stand up for myself, and that was something I was willing to die for. Every woman has the same well of strength I have. It just needs to be tapped into. It all starts when you say *No*. When you decide you're not going to take it anymore, you have the power to do anything you want. Even if the odds are against you, you have the strength, deep inside. All of you do. Thank you for your time."

Deja returned to her seat amidst a barrage of applause from the audience. The host returned to the podium with a smile and tears in her eyes.

"Thank you, Deja," she said. "Thank you so much for sharing."

≈≈≈≈≈≈

The meeting lasted another forty minutes. The ladies talked about how to be a survivor by being a servant for the cause. When they dismissed, a handful of women wanted to congratulate Deja on her breakthrough. Tamara waited until they were all gone before she stepped forward.

"That was great, Deja. I'm really proud of you."

"Thanks."

The ladies headed for the exit together. Outside they were greeted by a beautiful, twilit sky and the smell of water from the nearby Trinity River. Deja's car was parked close to the entrance. Tamara lingered there rather than head for her own vehicle.

"What made you change your mind?" she asked. "I thought you didn't want to talk about it."

"I didn't," Deja said. "Me and my boyfriend broke up, and I want to leave a lot of the old me behind. I figured this is the best time to re-invent myself."

Tamara smiled. "Why'd y'all break up? It wasn't bad, was it?"

Deja shrugged. "Well, I caught him with a younger, skinnier and prettier girl. So it was kind of bad. But it's okay. We basically broke up eight months ago, when I told him I was pregnant. We've just been going through the motions since then."

"Younger and skinnier, *maybe*," Tamara said. "But I can't believe she was prettier than you."

That was an awesome compliment. But Deja didn't know how to feel about it, coming from a girl. "Than, thanks."

"So, do you have someone else?" Tamara asked, "in case you get scared or lonely at night?"

The question wasn't odd, but the way she asked it made Deja wonder about her new friend's sexual orientation. She pushed the thought away.

"No," she said. "There's no one else."

"You still have my card?" Tamara asked, digging in her purse.

"I still have it. I was going to call you pretty soon anyway, because I want your help setting up a neighborhood watch in my apartments."

Tamara's eyes brightened. "That's great! Anytime you want to get together, let me know." She gave Deja a warm smile and reached to squeeze her hand. "I gotta get going. I look forward to hearing from you."

"Okay. Bye," Deja said.

She got in her car and headed home to what she knew would be a dark, lonely apartment. The thought of the groping shadows in her bedroom gave her an unexpected fit of fright. Deja tried to draw strength from the encouraging words she gave the ladies tonight, but her speech didn't seem so encouraging anymore. She wondered if it ever really was.

CHAPTER ELEVEN
MALICE

At work the next day, more than half of Deja's patients returned home to their loving families. She hated to see them go, but it always warmed her heart when the owners showed up to reclaim their four-legged friends. There was nothing cuter than watching a dog lose complete control over its excitement.

At lunchtime Deja checked her cellphone, and she was surprised to see a missed call and voicemail from Jerome:

Hey, baby, I mean, Deja. I need to holler at you. Can you call me back? I'll be at lunch from twelve to one. If you can't call then, I'll call you back when I get off.

Deja figured there was foolishness involved in whatever he wanted, but she called Jerome back anyway – mainly because she didn't want him showing up at her job again. He answered on the first ring.

"Hello?"

"What do you want?"

"Oh, hey baby – I mean Deja. Damn. That's the second time I called you that. I think that's my brain trying to tell me something."

"It's not that hard to remember someone's name, asshole – I mean Jerome. Oops. Yeah, I guess it is kinda hard."

"Oh. You got jokes."

"Man, what do you want, the rest of my interview money?"

"You know something, I ain't cool with you making accusations like that, Deja. Why you think I got some of your interview money?"

"You saying you didn't?"

"No I did not. I gave you a check. How could I get anything from an un-cashed check?"

"You know I can find out, right?"

"You can, huh..."

"As a matter of fact, go ahead and give me their number."

"What number?"

"You said Channel Six called you, and you called them back and set up the interview. What's wrong, you don't remember your own lies?"

"Oh, *that* number. I don't have their number anymore."

Deja rolled her eyes. "How much did they give you, Jerome? I'm not going to call them. I don't even want any of it. I'm just curious."

"First of all, I didn't get any money for your interview," Jerome declared. "I mean, they did give me a little something for using my house, but that was totally separate. It didn't have anything to do with your money."

Deja shook her head. "How much?"

"That ain't, that ain't got nothing to do with you."

Deja knew that was as much as he was going to admit to, so she let it go. She knew that she was at fault for allowing Jerome to set up the interview in the first place.

"I gotta go back to work," she said. "Don't call me no more unless it's about Adrian."

"I want to come get my stuff," he said. "That's what I called for."

"What stuff?"

"I got some clothes and shit at your house."

"I'll pack it up for you," Deja said, glad to rid her place of his memory. "What time are you coming to get it?"

"At seven, but I want to pack it up myself."

"You must be out of your rabid mind, if you think you're going through *my* house."

"Come on, Deja. I know how this shit goes. You gon' dump a jug of bleach on it before you give it to me?"

121

"That's a good idea, Jerome – I mean *lying-ass asshole*. That's a real good idea."

"If you do that, I can sue you," he threatened.

"You really want to talk about someone getting sued, Jerome? You offered me $200 for child support when you know you make $2,500 a month. I looked it up. You're supposed to pay one-fourth of–"

"Alright, alright. I'll be there at seven."

"Fine," she said. "But I don't have any bleach. Can you bring me some?"

He hung up, and Deja felt something in her chest that she hadn't felt in a long time. It was a nice, warm feeling of – dare she say – *the upper hand*?

≈≈≈≈≈≈≈

Deja got home at 5:30. She immediately got started on packing up Jerome's stupid belongings. She didn't think there was very much there, considering he spent the night so infrequently. But Deja's apartment was a virtual treasure trove of Jerome artifacts. She was still working diligently an hour later.

Some of Jerome's property brought on a rough spell of nostalgia, and Deja gave up trying to fight it off. She uncovered a stuffed Tweety Bird in the closet that took her mind back to the first time Jerome took her to Six Flags. Back then he was the perfect boyfriend. They had their first French kiss in *Looney Tunes Land* after Jerome won the two foot Tweety in a ring toss game.

Deja found a set of ties she bought Jerome back when she thought religion would make him a better man. Jerome did go to church with her a couple of times, but only to shut her up. Deja caught him doodling whenever he was supposed to be taking notes, and when the new Xbox came out, it was over. Jerome continued to wake up early on Sunday mornings, but it was to play football rather than worship the Lord.

The most sentimental find was a Valentine's card Jerome gave her nine months ago. That was before she was pregnant, back when Jerome's love blazed hotter than a blue flame. Inside the card, Jerome felt Hallmark couldn't express his devotion as well as he could, so he wrote his own poem next to theirs. Despite everything that transpired between them since then, Deja got misty eyed while reading it:

Roses are red, like your sweet lips
Violets are blue like the shimmering sea
Let's go on a trip, like a cruise on a ship
Let's make exotic love on a white, sandy beach
I dreamt of an angel who would come from above
So soft and beautiful from her soul to her face
That angel was you, and I never knew love
Like this, have a happy Valentine's Day

Jerome

A knock at the door snapped Deja out of her reverie. She expected to see her ex-boyfriend through her peephole, but it was Shannon standing there. Deja let her in and then found a box of Kleenex to blow her nose. Shannon watched her with a hand on her hip.

"What you in here doing?"

"Packing up Jerome's stuff."

Shannon frowned. "What'd you find, some of his stanky-ass drawers? I know you ain't in here getting sentimental over that punk."

Deja chuckled while she wiped her eyes. "Thanks for coming. I was starting to get a little side-tracked."

"Hmph," Shannon said as she took a seat on the couch. Deja sat next to her.

"What you getting sappy about?" Shannon asked.

"Oh, I'll show you." Deja went back to the bedroom where she had one and a half trash bags filled with Jerome's things. There were still a handful of shirts and pants on hangers, but she didn't want to wrinkle those. She found the Valentine's card and brought it back to her friend.

"Here."

Shannon took it and read it slowly. "Who wrote this?" she asked after what felt like a long time.

"Jerome wrote that."

She smacked her lips. "Nuh-uhn."

"He did. I told you he had another side to him."

"I got another side of my ass he can kiss," Shannon said.

There was another knock on the door.

Deja's heart skipped a beat. "Damn. That's him. He's coming to get his stuff."

"So?" her friend asked with a sneer.

"You know y'all don't get along."

Shannon rolled her eyes. "Please. Ain't nobody stunting him."

Deja was still hesitant.

"Girl, answer the door. It'll be alright. I won't say nothing to him," Shannon promised.

Deja blew out a sigh as she got up. She opened the door to reveal Jerome standing stiffly with his arms folded over his chest. It was sunset and the fire was fading quickly from the western skies. Deja liked this time of day the best; when the horizon had the perfect mixture of red and orange.

"Hello," she said.

"Hey," Jerome replied. He had a suitcase with him.

"You won't need that," Deja said. "I already got most of your stuff in trash bags. The rest is on hangers."

"Oh, okay." Jerome set the suitcase down outside the door. He stared into Deja's eyes woefully and took a step inside. "Listen, I..." Whatever he was going to say got lost in a new emotion caused by Shannon's presence. Jerome's eyes narrowed when he saw her.

Deja thought trouble was brewing, but his features softened just as quickly. He was apparently resigned to the fact that he could no longer control Deja's company.

"Where my stuff at?"

"In the bedroom," Deja said and led him in that direction. There was another moment of tension when they passed the couch, but Jerome avoided Shannon's gaze. He didn't notice her sneering at him.

In the bedroom, Jerome stopped at the crib for a moment, but he didn't disturb the sleeping baby. He hefted his two bags

124

and headed to the car. When he was gone, Deja turned to her friend.

"What are you doing?"

"What?"

"Why you looking at him like that?"

"I'm just minding my business," Shannon said and looked down at her nails. "I said I wasn't gon' say nothing, and I haven't."

Deja shook her head. "You're full of crap."

A minute later, Jerome returned for his hangers. He headed straight for the bedroom with no small talk this time. When he reappeared with his slacks and collar shirts, Shannon could hold her piece no longer.

"You a sad sight of a man." Shannon's eyes never left the television (which was off), and she barely spoke above a mumble. But Jerome stopped in his tracks and gave her the attention she sought.

"What you say to me?"

He stood at the entrance of the hallway. Shannon was emboldened with twenty feet between them.

"I said you a sad sight of a man."

Deja couldn't believe it. She stared at Shannon with her mouth ajar. Jerome headed straight for his nemesis. Deja was quick to grab his arm.

"Hold on."

He yanked away easily. "I'm not gon' do nothing," he promised. "I just want to see what this he/she nigga got to say."

"Jerome, it's not even–"

"I'm not gon' do nothing," he said again. He spoke so calmly, Deja halfway believed him. Jerome stopped in the center of the room and looked down on Shannon.

She returned his mean glare with no fear.

"What'd you say to me?" Jerome asked.

Deja thought Shannon would back down. She didn't know her friend very well.

"You out of your mind, if you think I'm finna bite my tongue," Shannon informed him.

Deja stepped between the two.

"You cheated on Deja while she was pregnant," Shannon said. "That shit is not cool – especially after everything she put up with for you."

Jerome reached over Deja's shoulder and pointed a finger at Shannon's face. "You shut your mouth. You hear me?"

Shannon shook in mock terror. "*Ooh*! I guess I'm supposed to be scared of you? If you ever put your hands on me, I'm calling the *police*. I ain't finna fight no man."

"Shut up, faggot!"

Shannon rose to her feet and stood her ground. "You can call me whatever you want, but it's not going to change the fact that you a sorry ass nigga! You ain't shit, and you ain't never gon' be shit! Even your mama know you ain't shit!"

Deja knew that was the last straw. Jerome tossed his clothes and his ex-girlfriend aside, and he went after Shannon with his fists balled.

"Nigga, what you say about my mama?"

Deja took a few stumbling steps back before she regained her balance. "Stop! She didn't say nothing about your mama!"

Jerome wasn't listening. Or maybe he ignored her because he now had an excuse. There's an unwritten rule – especially among black people – that you must stop whatever you're doing and go into attack mode if someone says something about your mother. Sometimes it didn't have to be anything negative. Simply saying "Yo mama" in a sentence was enough.

Jerome charged like a pit bull that finally snapped his chain after months of taunting from the neighborhood kids. Shannon screamed and quickly decided defense was the best offense. She fell to her back and threw her arms and legs up in one swift motion.

She began to kick wildly, and she actually landed the first blow. An awkward ankle smacked hard against Jerome's cheek, and he was forced back for half a second. He put a hand to his face to inspect the damage before he went after her again.

"You dumb faggot!" He fell on top of Shannon with all of his weight and managed to trap her legs between them. He rained down punches like he was fighting a man. Shannon shrieked loudly, barely able to protect herself with her bony arms. She took a few blows to the dome, but by then Deja regained her balance.

"*STOP IT!*" she screamed. It was an unfamiliar roar that came from deep within her. In a split second she remembered the speech she gave at the WAAR meeting. She told the women they could do anything once they made the decision to stand up to a man, and she believed that was true.

She charged her ex-boyfriend and slammed into him like a linebacker. Deja didn't know to duck her head, but she did it, and she didn't know to take the majority of the impact on her shoulder, but she did that too. Their bodies collided with a sickening *crunch*, and Jerome surprised her with a loud grunt.

"*Oof*!"

Even better, he lost his balance, and they went flying to the floor. Deja landed on top. Jerome looked up at her with genuine shock.

"What you..."

Before he could mount another offense, Deja heard the wonderful sound of an unknown male voice.

"What the hell is going on?"

All eyes went to the front door, which was still partly open. Mr. Brezzell, Deja's neighbor from upstairs, stood watching them. Mr. Brezzell was in his seventies. If his potbelly and pencil legs didn't attest to his feebleness, the tufts of gray hair in his ears certainly did. But Deja didn't need him to be a tough guy. She just needed him to be there. Jerome had lost his mind, but he wasn't crazy enough to risk his teaching career over the likes of Shannon. He scrambled to his feet and scooped his clothes off the floor.

"Nothing's wrong," he said. "We was just playing." He headed for the door without a look back at the girls. Mr. Brezzell stepped aside to let him pass. The older man returned his attention to Deja when Jerome was out of sight.

"You want me to call the police?"

Deja considered it. She looked up at Shannon, who righted herself on the couch.

"That's alright," Shannon said. "I'm fine." She brushed her hair back with her hands and felt at least one contusion growing on her scalp.

Deja still thought Jerome should go to jail, especially after everything she learned at her meetings. She gingerly rose to her feet. "But that's the second time he went after you."

"I'm fine," Shannon said again. "Long as he gone, I'm good..."

Deja reluctantly told the Good Samaritan, "Thanks a lot, sir. I appreciate you coming down, but we're alright. I guess..."

"No problem," Mr. Brezzell said. He took a deep breath and farted loudly. He didn't acknowledge it, so no one else did.

≈ ≈ ≈ ≈ ≈ ≈

An hour later, the friends sat at the kitchen table with half a cheesecake and a multitude of opinions between them. Their saucers were scraped clean. Shannon held a bag of Birds Eye peas against her temple. Despite the viciousness of the attack, Jerome didn't land any punches on her pretty face.

Shannon acknowledged that she was *partly* responsible for the altercation, but that concession was nothing compared to her new revelation. Shannon was now 100 percent positive Jerome was the Sleeping Strangler. Deja struggled to keep up with her logic.

"Why do you keep saying that? Don't you know how serious that is?"

"I know it's serious," Shannon said. "As serious as me getting my ass whooped."

"We can still put him in jail for that," Deja reminded. "But just because he attacked you doesn't mean he tried to kill me."

"It shows a pattern," Shannon reasoned, "a pattern of violence."

"I'm glad you brought that up," Deja said, "because that's one of the major things missing from your theory: Jerome does not have a pattern of violence with me."

"What do you call that shit that just went down?"

"That's violence towards *you*, Shannon. If Jerome was going to strangle me, I think he would've tried to hit me at some point in our relationship. And what about the first four victims? Are you saying Jerome attacked all of them, too?"

"I think he tried to pull a DC Sniper," Shannon said definitively.

Deja frowned. "A what?"

"Don't you remember the DC Sniper? It was on the news for like, four months."

Deja did remember. "There were two guys, driving around shooting people at gas stations."

Shannon nodded. "They never got a real motive for the killings, but they did have a good theory. Do you remember what it was?"

Deja shook her head. She was all ears.

"That older guy wanted to kill his wife, so he could get custody of his kid," Shannon explained. "His plan was convoluted, but it was kinda good, too: At first they would kill a bunch of random people and get everybody scared of a serial killer. Then one day they'd kill his wife at a gas station, and everybody would think it was the serial killer that got her. Wouldn't nobody look at her husband, even though he was the serial killer all along."

Deja's jaw dropped. "I never heard that."

"That's because they wouldn't let them use it in court," Shannon said. "They didn't have enough evidence to support that theory."

"Then how do you know about it?"

"It was on a documentary they did about him."

Deja gave that notion some thought. "So you're saying Jerome strangled four people, just so he could kill me?"

"I know you don't believe me. But if you think about it, that is a good way to kill somebody. The police never questioned Jerome when you got attacked, did they? They automatically assumed it was the strangler."

Deja shook her head and ignored the fresh goose bumps sprouting on her arms.

"I don't believe Jerome would try to kill me," she decided. "And he definitely wouldn't kill four other people. He's not a psychopath."

"You didn't think he'd attack me in your living room," Shannon said. "You didn't think he would take money for your interview without telling you. You didn't think he was cheating on you.

"How many times does he have to keep doing stuff you never believed he'd do, before you finally realize he'll do damned near anything? Jerome didn't want that baby, girl. He knew Adrian was going to cost him a gang of money, for the next eighteen years. He knew it. He worried about it every day, until it ate him up inside."

129

Deja lowered her gaze and gave her friend's theory more thought. She sighed and shook her head again. "No. I just, I still don't believe it."

"Are you *positive*?" Shannon asked.

"How can I be positive?" Deja asked. "I guess anything's possible."

"That's it," Shannon said with a finger in the air. "That's what I want you to understand. *Anything is possible.* Just keep an open mind, Deja. That's all I'm saying."

CHAPTER TWELVE
NEIGHBORHOOD WATCH

Jerome called a few minutes after midnight. Shannon had just left, and Deja was still trying to wrap her mind around her friend's wild story. When she saw the number on the caller ID, Deja's eyes grew wide with fright. That was a terrible feeling, considering that (no matter what) Jerome was the father of her only child.

"Hel, hello?"

"Hey, Deja. You sleep?"

"What do you want, Jerome?"

"I just, um, I called to apologize – for what happened earlier. I didn't mean to go off like that. You know that ain't me."

"I don't know anything about you," Deja said. "You need help, Jerome. You really do."

"I, I know," he said. "My head's been all fucked up since we broke up. I'm stressed out. I know I made a mistake."

A part of Deja was glad to hear that. But Jerome was perpetually full of shit. This was no doubt another ploy.

"Is that all you want?"

"Uh, no. I also wanted to ask if you if y'all were going to, you know, call the police. I didn't mean no harm. I want to apologize – to Shannon too, but I don't have his number."

Deja rolled her eyes. "You are so full of it."

"I'm, uh... What you mean?"

"Everything you do. Everything you say." She shook her head. "I'm trying to figure out why you're calling me, and you make it so obvious. The only thing you care about is whether you're going to jail or not."

Jerome didn't respond. Deja decided to prolong his worries.

"Yes, we did call the police," she said. "I thought you were in jail already. I guess they'll come get you later."

"That's fucked up, Deja." All of Jerome's sweet talk was suddenly gone. "How you gon' call the police on me over that fag? I ain't never did nothing to you. I don't deserve that."

"I didn't call the police. Shannon did."

"You gave them a statement?"

"Of course I did. I was a witness." Deja hoped he couldn't hear her smile over the phone. She could certainly hear him fuming on his end.

"I better not get arrested," Jerome warned. His voice was cold, and dark. Deja knew she was pushing his buttons, but she couldn't stop.

"Is that a threat?"

"Call it what you want," he said and disconnected.

Deja lay there for a minute, wondering if she'd gone too far. She decided she hadn't gone far enough. Jerome should be in jail for what he did to her friend. If the worst thing that happened was his heart froze up every time he saw a cop for the next few months, then he should consider himself lucky.

As she fell asleep that night, Deja was grateful that she never gave her Jerome a copy of her new apartment key. She was 99 percent certain he wasn't the Sleeping Strangler, but that left one percent of doubt lingering in the back of her mind.

When the lights were off, that one percent felt a whole lot bigger.

≈ ≈ ≈ ≈ ≈ ≈

The next day passed without another word from her ex. By Friday Deja wasn't thinking about Jerome at all. She took a notepad to work with her that day and showed a couple of sketches to her co-worker Bea. During their shift, Bea converted Deja's notes into a flyer for her new neighborhood watch. When she got off work, Deja took the flyer to FedEx to make copies.

Tamara came over later that day to help with the exhaustive task of spreading the flyers throughout Deja's apartment complex. It was after seven when Tamara knocked on her door. By then the sun was on the decline, thankfully taking most of the scorching heat with it.

The friends set out on foot, handing flyers to residents personally or leaving them on the door of those who didn't answer. Both women wore shorts and tee-shirts for the venture. Deja toted Adrian in a carrier that draped over her shoulders like a backpack.

The majority of residents they encountered were receptive, especially to Tamara who was very outgoing and uncommonly stunning, even in casual wear.

"You'll probably end up with a night shift," Tamara said as they marched.

"Why do you say that?"

"Because *somebody* has to be awake in the wee hours of the morning, and you won't get many volunteers for that."

Deja shuddered. "That'll be fun."

"You have to rethink your perceptions about nighttime," Tamara advised. "If you want to be effective, you have to get used to the darkness; be comfortable in it. Nighttime is when everything goes down. It's a totally different world. You'll see people you never see when the sun is out, like they're vampires."

"What will these vampires be doing late at night?" Deja wondered.

"Everything," Tamara said. "Anything you can think of – most of it bad. Some things you'll turn a blind eye to. But some things have to be confronted."

"The police do the confronting, right?"

"You will become somewhat of an extension of the police department," Tamara said. "But your job is to *help* the officers, not overwhelm them with complaints. What's that over there?" Tamara pointed to a corner of the parking lot where three old school cars were parked. Parked *suspiciously*.

Six men, all of whom Deja would consider *hoodlums*, congregated around the vehicles.

"I don't know," she said. "Some knuckleheads..."

"What are they doing?" Tamara asked.

"How should I know? I assume selling drugs, bringing down the property value."

"Let's give them a flyer," Tamara said, and Deja was surprised to see her head in their direction.

"Wait." Deja followed hesitantly, with her baby dozing against her chest. "Where are you, what are you going to say to them?"

"I'm going to invite them to your meeting."

"But you don't know them."

"I don't know anyone over here."

"What if they don't want a neighborhood watch?"

Tamara stopped and regarded her oddly. "Are you really scared of them?"

Deja looked at the young men who were now watching her and Tamara. The tough guys ranged from 17 to 25 years old. They all looked violent and *evil*. One of them wore a Mets baseball jersey. It was unbuttoned, revealing a torso full of smooth, black muscles. A couple of them smoked cigars. They all had on the same color scheme; blue, black and white.

"They don't look scary to you?" Deja asked.

"Sure they do," Tamara said. "But this is what having a neighborhood watch is about. If you don't know who they are, you don't know if they're a threat, or if they can be of assistance."

"Yeah right."

"The only way to know is to talk to them," Tamara said and started walking again.

≈≈≈≈≈≈≈

The leader of the group was D Money. Deja knew his name because he was the one with his shirt open, and when they got closer, she saw his moniker tattooed boldly across his stomach. He stepped forward to meet the women.

"What y'all want?" D Money was dark like midnight and fairly handsome. His head was shaved completely bald. If Deja was alone, she would have retreated with her tail tucked between her legs. But Tamara showed no fear or hesitance.

"Hi," she said. "My name is Tamara, and this is my friend Deja. We're passing out flyers for a neighborhood watch we're starting up in these apartments. We're having a meeting this Sunday and wanted to know if any of you were interested in helping us out."

She offered him a flyer. D Money wouldn't take it. He folded his arms over his chest, and his minions tensed visibly. Deja almost took off running.

"Help you how?" he asked.

"I don't live here," Tamara said. "Deja's going to be in charge of this area."

She nodded at her friend, gesturing for her to speak up. Deja couldn't get any words to come out.

"Basically, we're just asking for support from the community," Tamara said when Deja didn't say anything. "I'm sure you know these apartments are not as safe as they could be. We had a violent attack on the premises not too long ago."

With those words, one of the other men stepped forward. He was a short, fair-skinned menace with dark, curly hair and big teeth. He looked at both women and finally focused his attention on Deja.

"I know you," he said. "You was on the news. You the one slept with that strangler nigga."

Deja was initially offended by his statement, but the introduction helped. His friends stared at her, and they too expressed recognition. Their leader unfolded his arms, and Deja felt safe around them for the first time.

"Say, that's some fucked up shit happened to you," D Money said. "If we woulda ever saw that fool creeping around, we woulda got him."

"Messed him up good," his curly-haired pawn agreed.

Deja was confused by this whole encounter, but she said, "Thanks."

"Ain't no man got the right to put his hands on no woman," D Money went on. "Especially if he trying to kill her. We ain't got no love for marks like that."

"No love," his hype man agreed. "No love at all."

"I'm glad to hear that," Tamara told them. "Now, are you going to take this flyer, or leave me hanging?"

D Money took the flyer, and Curly-Hair wanted one, too.

"Can I get one of those?"

"Sure."

"Me too," another one called and then another.

"I want one."

Deja handed out flyers as fast as she could.

135

"I hope all of y'all are coming," Tamara said with a smile. "Don't be wasting our flyers."

Curly-Hair smiled back at her, but D Money was still reserved.

"What's your deal?" Tamara asked him.

He shrugged. "Nothing. Just wondering what *else* y'all gon' be looking for over here. That strangler nigga already in jail..."

"You still have a lot of car thefts in the area," Tamara said, "and assaults and break-ins too. We just want to keep the residents here safe. People should be able to sleep at night without worrying about all that mess. Thanks for the help. We'll see you guys later."

She walked away, and Deja was glad to go with her.

"You think they selling drugs?" she asked when they were out of earshot.

"Of course they're selling drugs," Tamara said.

"So what do we do about them?" Deja wondered. "Call the police?"

"You're in charge over here," Tamara said. "That's going to be something you have to decide."

"I can decide right now."

Tamara grinned. "Don't be so quick to judge, grasshopper. Didn't you hear what they said about the strangler? They may be helpful one day down the road."

"No. I don't think so."

"Never turn down help," Tamara warned. "If you learn that now, it will save you a lot of time in the future."

≈≈≈≈≈≈

The ladies got all of their flyers passed out that evening. They had some leftover after touring Deja's apartments, so they took them to the neighboring complex as well as the one across the street. Tamara consistently wowed Deja with her outgoing nature and positive attitude about what Deja considered undesirables. Everyone responded in a positive manner. A lot of residents said they would attend the meeting at the manager's office on Sunday.

"I hope they have enough chairs in there," Deja said as they headed home.

Tamara laughed and placed a delicate hand on Deja's arm. "You don't think all of those people are really coming, do you?"

"Well..." Deja was confused. "They said they would."

"Half of them just said that to get me out of their face," Tamara explained. "How many flyers did you make?"

"Two-fifty."

"You'll be lucky to get a ten percent return."

"Really?"

"Yep," Tamara said. "That's the way it goes."

≈≈≈≈≈≈≈

Deja hoped her friend was wrong, but on Sunday afternoon Tamara's prediction came true. Deja's first guest arrived at 4:38, and the last one showed up at 5:15. The youngest enlistee was twelve years old. The oldest was 67. Deja counted heads as her guests arrived. The last head she counted was number 23.

For their dining pleasure, Deja brought cheese and crackers, little smokies with toothpicks sticking out of them, tea, coffee and lemonade. Most of the visitors snacked while waiting for the meeting to start, and Deja had time to evaluate her motley crew.

The youngest volunteer was a skinny sixth grader with long pigtails and wire rim glasses that wrapped around her ears. The oldest was Ms. Gladys from a building at the front of the complex. Ms. Gladys didn't talk much, but she paid attention to everything. Deja knew she would be an invaluable asset.

The rest of the posse was from all walks of life. Mostly females responded to Deja's invitation, but there were six guys there, too. The most handsome one was the community relations police officer who was the very last to arrive. He walked in wiping sweat from his brow, wearing shorts rather than long pants. He also wore gloves and a helmet, and Deja didn't have to look outside to know he had a ten speed bike leaning against the building. Only five percent of Overbrook Meadows' police department were bicycle officers, and surely they sent Deja the cream of the crop.

The policeman took off his helmet and looked around for someone's hand to shake. Deja rushed to greet him. His chest looked so big from across the room, she was eager to see if that was a vest or all him.

It was both, but mostly him.

"Hey," she said. "I'm Deja Franklin, the organizer for this neighborhood watch."

"Hi," the cop replied. "I'm Peter Rutledge." He was a few inches over six feet with 220 pounds of flesh and muscle stacked beautifully on his bones. "I'm sorry I'm late."

What can I do to get arrested? Deja wondered. "It's okay," she said. "Everybody's just hanging out, having a good time. Do you want something to eat or drink?"

"No," Peter said. "I ate not too long ago. Don't I... You look familiar."

"I've been on TV," Deja said. "I was—"

"When we gon' get this started?" The cranky voice came from the center of the room. They looked back and saw Ms. Gladys glaring at them.

"We're going to start right now," Deja told her. "Excuse me, Officer." She left his side and approached the front of the room. "Okay ladies and gentlemen, if y'all want to take a seat, we can begin. I think everybody that's coming is here by now."

≈≈≈≈≈≈

The meeting lasted a little less than an hour. After Deja wowed them with her personal story of survival, the liaison officer stepped forward and told them how helpful programs like this were to a community. He outlined the assistance the police department could offer and went into detail about what was expected of them.

The most important thing he stressed was that they not become a vigilante style *mob* and that they not put themselves in harms way. The list of things they could handle on their own was miniscule compared to the list of things they should call the police for.

After the policeman's spiel, Tamara assisted Deja in the most interesting part of the meeting; working with the volunteers. They got tee shirt sizes from everyone, so the landlord could get their matching "uniforms." And then they went over the possible shifts each team of two would work. Of course Deja was stuck with the worst shift, from four to six a.m., but she didn't mind.

"Thank you so much," she told her team before dismissing. "Y'all don't know how much I appreciate each and every one of you. I'll give you a call when the tee shirts are in. We should be ready to start in a couple of weeks. Don't hesitate to call me if you have a question about anything."

"You did a great job," Tamara said when the last watcher was gone.

"Thanks." Deja beamed. "I owe it all to you."

They stood there for a moment, watching each other. Deja felt like she should give Tamara a hug, so she did so. Their embrace was different than she expected. Rather than a casual squeeze, it was like the emotional hug of sisters (if not soul mates). Deja backed away with a hesitant smile parting her lips.

"Do you need me to help take these dishes back to your place?" Tamara asked.

"Yes," Deja said. "I would really appreciate that."

CHAPTER THIRTEEN
NIGHT PROWLERS

A week and a half passed before the landlord phoned to say she had their equipment. Deja got the call at work. She sat in the break room nibbling leftover lasagna. The news pleased her, but it also made her apprehensive.

"Time to get started," she told one of her coworkers.

"Get started with what?" Bea asked.

"They got the shirts and radios for our neighborhood watch. Looks like it's going down this weekend."

"You nervous?"

"A little bit," Deja admitted. "I've been going over the neighborhood crime reports and tweaking the schedules. I stayed up late a few nights and drove around, just to see what things are like when the moon comes out."

"What did you see?"

Deja shook her head in dismay. "It's like, a whole 'nother city. A sub culture. There are people in my neighborhood who are downright spooky. I got a new gun, but I don't have a license to carry it concealed. When I hit the streets, all I'll have is a flashlight, a radio, some pepper spray and a tee shirt that says I'm a snitch."

Bea laughed. "You having second thoughts?"

"No," Deja said. "This is something that definitely needs to happen. I'm just saying, my neighborhood is pretty rough. We have assaults almost every night – either in my apartments or the other two we expanded the watch to. There's break-ins and shootings, drugs and prostitutes."

"You'll be fine," Bea assured her. "You don't have to walk down the street with an arsenal to gain respect."

Deja hoped that was true, because it wasn't only her neck on the line. She had a whole crew of volunteers to look after.

≈ ≈ ≈ ≈ ≈ ≈ ≈

After work Deja picked Adrian up from her mother's house and got the supplies from the apartment manager. All Deja had to give her in return was a metal sign she could post outside of the office. The sign had "WARNING" at the top, a big eyeball in the middle, and at the bottom it read: "NEIGHBORHOOD WATCH" "WE LOOK OUT FOR EACH OTHER!" The manager was extremely grateful. She promised to display the sign proudly.

When she got home, Deja called her volunteers one by one to inform them of a new meeting on Friday night. Deja called Tamara, too, because she thought she needed a little more guidance before her friend stepped out of the picture.

"I'll come," Tamara said. "But you don't need me. You're a natural leader, Deja."

"What if I make a mistake?"

"Then apologize and learn from it," Tamara said. "No one expects you to be perfect."

"But you are coming, right?"

Tamara chuckled. "Of course, Deja. You can count on me. You know that."

≈ ≈ ≈ ≈ ≈ ≈ ≈

The meeting on Friday was initially nerve-racking because all of the volunteers were there by 7:15, but there was no sign of Tamara. Deja never had so many people depending on her. She feared she might lead them astray. She couldn't believe her friend abandoned her! Thankfully none of the volunteers knew what they hell they were doing either. Deja realized this when she heard two of her watchers talking amongst themselves.

"When do we get our guns?" Miss Gladys wanted to know. She was in her late sixties. When they first met, Deja thought she was a sweet, grandmotherly type. But it turned out Miss Gladys was one of the wildest in the bunch. "I'm ready to bust a cap in a nigga's ass!" the older woman declared.

Before Deja could point out all of the wrongs in that statement, the other volunteer said, "I thought we could only use non-lethal weapons, like bats and bricks."

"*Okay*," Deja said, holding back laughter. "I think we can go ahead and start the meeting now..."

≈≈≈≈≈≈

Before anyone got a radio, flashlight or a can of pepper spray, Deja had to go over the do's and don'ts for their community service. A lot of the stuff she thought was common sense turned out to be not so common for her eager band of do-gooders.

"Even if we had spike strips," she told Elaine, a mother of two, "we're definitely not qualified to use them."

"Can we throw bottles at their wheels?" Elaine asked instead.

"No," Deja said. "See, the thing I think you guys are having trouble with is the fact that we are not police officers. We're not deputies either. We're every day citizens, and we don't have any special powers."

Some of her volunteers were visibly upset about that. Deja hoped they wouldn't bail on her.

"What about a citizen's arrest?" someone called from the back of the room. It was Tamara. She was twenty minutes late, and this was the first thing she said since she got there.

"I'm not issuing anyone handcuffs," Deja said. "But technically it is legal to make a citizen's arrest. But, people, I would not recommend that – especially if we're talking about someone who's going to fight you back. If it's after five, my radio will be on the whole night. So call me and let me make that decision. The last thing we need is for someone to get hurt out there."

"Do we have to keep our radios on all night?" Kim Cheung asked. Kim owned a convenience store at the end of the block. He had a lot to gain from the neighborhood watch.

"Thanks for asking," Deja said. "The way it works is each of you will have a two hour shift. During that time, you *must* have your radios on. I recommend that you pair up with the other person on your shift. Henry and I are doing the last shift, from four to six am, and we're definitely going to stay together."

Henry was a freshman at Texas Lutheran. He was a thin, squirrely kid, one of few men on the watch. He nodded in agreement, and Deja kept talking.

"If some of you want to leave your radio on the whole time and help some of the other shifts, that's great. We should all watch whenever we can. When you take your kids to school in the morning, watch. When you go get the mail, look around. Take the long route to the mailboxes and *watch*. When you walk your dog, take the radio with you. Always have a notepad, so you can jot down license plates and descriptions. And never try to go at it alone."

"Can I tell my kids to watch, too?" Mrs. Farmer asked. She was a mocha colored woman with a beautiful smile.

"Yes," Deja said. "By all means, get the family involved. But make sure they don't confront anyone."

"I like to climb on the roof," Jasmine said. She was twelve years old, the youngest member of the team. "Can I watch from up there?"

"Um, I wouldn't recommend climbing any roofs," Deja said.

"Can I watch through people's windows?" Charles Simmons asked.

"Uh, no," Deja said. "That's called *peeping*. That's actually one of the things we want to look out for. If any of you see Charles looking through a window, feel free to report it."

Everyone laughed. Deja felt good about the way things were going. She locked eyes with Tamara in the back of the crowd. Her friend shot her a wink and a nod.

The meeting concluded with everyone getting a radio, a flashlight, a small canister of pepper spray, and their very own *West Side Neighborhood Watch* tee shirt. Deja even found a babysitter for her two hour shift. Ms. Gladys said she was always awake by four a.m., and she'd be delighted to look after Adrian while Deja did her patrolling.

≈≈≈≈≈≈

That night the team put all of their training into action. As the leader of the group, Deja had plenty of preparation. But that didn't matter when her alarm went off at 3:50 a.m.

Why would I do this? she wondered as she silenced the clock. *What the hell was I thinking?*

Deja forced herself out of bed and put a cup of instant coffee in the microwave. She threw on a pair of jeans and her neighborhood watch tee shirt. She spent another five minutes getting Adrian ready for the babysitter. Before she finished, she heard a strange voice on her radio.

"Huh, hello? Miss Deja? Over?"

She snatched it up and pressed the talk button. "Yeah, Henry. I'm up. Sorry. I had to... I'm up now."

"Hello?" a third voice said.

"Hi," Deja said. "Ms. Gladys, is that you?"

"Yes. It's me. Are you still coming?"

Deja was embarrassed to be the last one ready. "Yes, Ms. Gladys. I'm coming. I'm sorry I'm late, y'all. Henry, can you come to my apartment and walk with me to Ms. Gladys' house?"

"I'm already here," Henry said, and there was a knock at Deja's front door.

"Here I come," she said into the radio. "I'm sorry, y'all. Here I come."

≈≈≈≈≈≈≈

The night started rough, but things smoothed out once Deja shook the cobwebs from her head. Henry drove a brand new F-150. He wanted to do a little cruising during their shift, but Deja was in charge, and she preferred to walk. She knew she'd be too sleepy in the passenger seat of his truck, plus Tamara taught her to have a more personal approach. It was hard to scrutinize people from a passing car, and you couldn't get in the nooks and crannies like that, either.

They started in Deja's apartments and walked the whole parking lot, which conveniently made a circle around the complex. From there they crossed the street to Pilgrim Crest Apartments and did the same. Afterwards they walked to Kim's convenience store on the end of the block. From Kim's, they trekked to Falcon Ridge apartments, and then they headed home.

144

The whole trip took almost an hour, so they could only do it twice during their shift. There was plenty of time to talk and make observations. Not surprisingly, Henry wanted to hear more about Deja's encounter with the Sleeping Strangler. Deja was almost sick of telling the story. But she told it again, in great detail, hoping Henry would get his fill.

"Wow," he said when she was done talking. "You're amazing. You're an inspiration to all women."

"I'm just glad I survived," Deja said. "My only goal was to save my own life. But if I managed to inspire a lot of women in the process, I'm proud to do so."

≈≈≈≈≈≈

Deja learned a lot about her neighborhood that first night; the main thing being crack was everywhere, crack was deadly, and crack was the cause of almost every bad thing going on in the area. Deja and Henry counted seventeen drug addicts, prostitutes and vagrants wandering the streets. That wasn't a huge number, but they were only out for two hours, and there were different junkies on each shift.

Other than the addicts, Deja and Henry didn't witness or hear about any crimes being committed. They didn't have to talk to anyone, but Deja approached a familiar face she saw several times during their shift. The girl was in her early twenties. She was somewhat attractive and clearly selling her body on the lonely streets of Overbrook Meadows.

She tried to cross the street when Deja and Henry drew near, but she didn't run when Deja crossed the street with her.

"Hey! Hey, where are you going?"

"Whatchoo mean *where I'm going*?" The woman was fair-skinned, with curly braids of black and purple synthetic hair. She wore a tank top that ended just under her bra-less breasts and a pair of shorts that were no bigger than panties.

"I'm sorry," Deja said. "I didn't mean to get in your business. I've seen you out a few times tonight, and I was just curious..."

The girl looked Deja up and down with her sneer intact. She wore bright red lipstick and dark eye shadow that was starting to run. "Who is you?"

145

"I'm Deja. I'm the captain of a neighborhood watch we started today."

Henry came and stood beside her, and the girl's sneer intensified.

"Ain't you supposed to be watching from inside your house?" the woman of the night wanted to know.

"Probably," Deja said with a chuckle. "There's a lot I still don't know about this. What's your name?"

The girl looked around and over her shoulders. Deja didn't think she would say, but she finally mumbled, "Peaches."

Peaches had long, skinny legs, straight hips and a flat stomach. Even though she was young, she didn't look innocent at all. Peaches had old eyes that had seen a lot and remembered too much of it.

"I seen your papers," she said. "They be on the ground. Ain't nobody gon' join."

"Actually people have already joined," Deja said. "We have enough to watch the neighborhood twenty-four hours a day." She didn't mean to be confrontational, and thankfully Peaches didn't take it that way.

"So what you gon' be doing? Walking around all night?"

"Sometimes," Deja said. "What about you?"

"You know what I'm doing," Peaches said and rolled her eyes.

"No, I don't," Deja said.

"Then what you in my face for?"

Deja sensed she was losing her. "Listen, I'm not trying to upset you. I started this watch because I want to help. I was a victim of a violent attack not too long ago. Do you remember the Sleeping Strangler?"

Peaches' mouth fell open, and her attitude was immediately gone.

"Oh snap! That was you? I'm sorry. I didn't know that was you."

"It's okay," Deja said. "I don't walk around with a sign around my neck."

"That's why you doing this?"

Deja nodded. "I don't care what you're up to. We're just looking out for people. Everyone should feel safe in their own home."

146

"I respect that," Peaches said. "You cool with me. What you say your name was?"

"I'm Deja. This is Henry."

"Well, like I said, I'm Peaches. And I do be getting high. I don't want to, but I can't help it. If you gon' be out here every night, you gon' run into a whole bunch of crackheads. It's dealers everywhere. Mostly everybody mind they business, but people be getting desperate, you know? They'll prolly bust in somebody's car or something for a radio, or whatever change they got in the ash tray. Mostly people do right, though. When they don't have no more money, they'll go home."

Peaches was a virtual encyclopedia. Deja struggled to keep up.

"You know D Money?"

"Yeah," Peaches said. "He sell dope in Pine View – but he ain't about shit. Most people don't go to him, if they got twenty dollars or more. Big Moe got the good shit."

"Who's Big Moe?" Deja asked.

Peaches' eyes narrowed as she realized she was snitching. "Oh, naw, I can't be, I can't be talking about people's business like that. If you wanna know about somebody's house that got broke into, or somebody got mugged or something like that, I'll help you. But I can't talk about who be selling dope. Them dudes, they don't like that."

"Okay," Deja said. "Is there anything going on tonight that you *can* tell me about?"

"Maybe later," Peaches said and started walking again. "Ain't nobody's house got broke into lately."

Deja knew that wasn't true, but she didn't contradict her new contact. "Come on," she told Henry. "It's almost six o'clock. Let's go home."

"Do you, um, you wanna get some breakfast?" Henry asked.

"Uh, no, that's alright. Thanks though."

"What about lunch, later on?"

Deja stopped and gave her partner a good once-over. Henry was good-looking, but he was too skinny and definitely too young for her.

"How old are you?" she asked.

"Nineteen," he said with a goofy smile.

147

"I'm thirty-two," Deja informed him.

"That's okay."

She chuckled. "No, not really. Let's keep our relationship strictly on the business side. You're a cutie, but I'm not looking to date anyone right now. Okay?"

She stuck out a hand, and he shook it reluctantly.

"Alright."

"Once the girls at your school see you rolling around in that pretty truck," Deja said when they started walking again, "you won't have any trouble picking one up."

Henry grinned sheepishly. "You think so?"

"I *know* so. If you would've caught me ten years ago, I would've been the first one flagging you down."

Henry's chest swelled with pride. He was still grinning when they ended their shift five minutes later.

CHAPTER FOURTEEN
THE TRIAL OF GILBERT REYNOLDS

It took nearly a week for Deja to get adjusted to her new watch hours. Thankfully it wasn't all for naught. Within a month of the neighborhood watch's inception, the atmosphere in Deja's apartment complex changed. No longer would residents turn a blind eye to their neighbor's circumstances. When someone got into a domestic dispute, a neighbor called the police. When suspicious strangers strolled the parking lot, looking in random vehicles, a handful of watchers materialized, seemingly out of nowhere.

There was a different feel in the air. Almost everyone got caught up in a wave of caring and togetherness. The membership in Deja's watch blossomed from 23 to 56 volunteers. Some of those who didn't join still helped out by reporting crimes anonymously.

By the second month, burglaries and auto thefts in the area were down 75%. The watchers' radios were constantly abuzz. Deja used to get irritated with the endless chatter and daily false alarms, but now the banter of strange voices was welcome in her home. She lay in bed with Adrian sometimes, listening to her radio while they napped. Her volunteers couldn't have been a more hilarious bunch. They were also loyal and dedicated, and Deja was forever in their debt.

Things were going so well, Deja nearly forgot why she started the watch, until she got an unexpected call midway through June. Deja immediately recognized the voice on the other end of the line, and a chill scampered down her back.

"Hello?"

"Hi, Deja?"

"Yes."

"This is Detective Rudy Cervantes. I spoke with you a couple of times in March, after the, attack. I met with you at the hospital..."

The memory of Jackson Memorial brought with it images and emotions Deja was still struggling to forget about. Her hand moved to her throat subconsciously. She fingered her surgery scar.

"Hi," she said. "It's been a while."

"Yes, it has," Mr. Cervantes agreed. "I hope you've been well. I'm calling because it's getting close to that time."

That time could have referred to a number of events, but Deja knew what he was talking about right away. It was time to relive the absolute *worst* moment of her life in a courtroom full of strangers who would gawk and gasp, shudder and deliberate. And when it was all said and done, hopefully they would send the Sleeping Strangler to death row for his crimes against women.

"Okay," Deja said. "What do I need to do?"

"The prosecutor will call you soon," the detective said. "Her name is Denise Moffett. She wants to meet with you to go over your role in the trial."

"Okay," Deja said. Her voice was hushed. She felt like her intestines were twisting into knots.

"She'll probably call you sometime tomorrow. Hey, I hear you started a neighborhood watch."

"How'd you know that?"

"One of my co-workers told me. Officer Rutledge is a good friend of mine. You met with Peter, right?"

Deja was so distracted, she had to rack her brain to remember the handsome bicycle cop who came to her first watch meeting. "Yes," she said. "I remember him."

"That's a good thing you're doing for your community," the detective said. "You've already made a difference. Everyone's rooting for you."

≈≈≈≈≈≈≈

Deja got a call from Mrs. Moffett's secretary the following morning, and she agreed to go downtown for a meeting with the prosecutor. On Friday Deja showed up at the district attorney's office at 9 am. She sat anxiously in the waiting room for nearly fifteen minutes before a receptionist called her back.

"Miss Franklin, Mrs. Moffett will see you now."

The secretary led her to a huge office that had floor to ceiling windows on two walls and tall, library-style bookshelves against the others. The furniture in the office was solid oak. Sitting behind an L-shaped desk was a woman Deja had never seen before. She was tall and thin, with short, graying hair and no makeup. She had strong, intelligent eyes, a wide nose and full lips. The prosecutor wore a black pants suit that looked more expensive than anything in Deja's closet. She stood when Deja entered. Mrs. Moffett's handshake was unexpectedly strong.

"Hello. How are you doing today?"

"I'm fine," Deja said, taking in the majesty of the office and the woman it belonged to.

Mrs. Moffett had degrees mounted on the wall behind her and a picture of two smiling boys framed on her desk. She exuded confidence, which was to be expected as she was one of the most powerful women in Overbrook Meadows.

"Have a seat," she instructed. The receptionist stepped out of the office, and the district attorney took her seat as well. For a moment, she watched Deja over the files and piles of paper on her desk. "I read a lot about you," she said. "It's good to finally meet you."

"Thank you," Deja said. "I'm happy to finally move forward with the case."

Mrs. Moffett nodded. "Well, first off, do you have any questions to ask me? Did Mr. Cervantes talk to you about how we're going after your attacker?"

Deja shook her head. "No."

"That's fine," Mrs. Moffett said. "Gilbert Reynolds' trial starts on Wednesday, June 20th. We're going to prosecute him for the burglary and attempted murder at your residence. I know you might have thought the murder trials were coming first, but we've decided to hold off on those."

Before Deja could ask why, the prosecutor explained.

"The reason being," Mrs. Moffett said, "we want to use your case as the foundation for the others. You're the only living victim, so your trial has the best chances for success. Once we get a conviction, we can use it to tie Mr. Reynolds to the murders. Does that make sense to you?"

"Yes," Deja said. "But are you sure he'll be convicted for attacking me?"

"Well, we can never be *positive*," Mrs. Moffett acknowledged. "Mr. Reynolds did request a jury trial, and by nature juries are never one hundred percent dependable. But based on the evidence we'll present, I'm sure he will be found guilty."

Deja nodded, but it was clear she didn't possess the same confidence.

"You have doubts?"

"No. I mean... I never saw his face," Deja said.

"That's alright," the D.A. replied. "We never said you saw his face. And we never asked you to identify your attacker in a line-up. The testimony we need from you is regarding what he did at your home, rather than what he looked like."

"But they say he didn't have a pullover when he got arrested," Deja said. She always thought that was the strongest argument against Gilbert being her attacker.

"He didn't need one," the prosecutor countered. "The police apprehended Mr. Reynolds more than a mile away from your residence. That was twenty minutes after the 911 call, which means he had plenty of time to discard or destroy evidence. Mrs. Franklin, our case against Mr. Reynolds is strong. I assure you."

Deja didn't want to sound uncertain, but her talks with Shannon were still fresh on her mind. "What other evidence do you have?" she asked softly.

The prosecutor opened one of the folders on her desk. "Well, first of all we've got his lack of an alibi. Mr. Reynolds was drenched with sweat when the police apprehended him. He was heading away from your crime scene and could offer no explanation for what he was doing in the area at four in the morning.

"Mr. Reynolds had, what police refer to as, a burglary kit in his pocket at the time of his arrest. The detectives determined the kit was functional and could be used to break into your apartment with no sign of forced entry.

"We also found a footprint outside of your bedroom window. It's not a perfect print: We couldn't determine it's a 100 percent match for the suspect's shoes, but it could not be ruled out either.

"Mr. Reynolds fits the size, race and rough description you gave the police. And his criminal history will come up in trial once he's been convicted. He went to prison for rape – which he plead guilty to. While incarcerated, he attempted to murder one of his cellmates by strangulation.

"Once released from prison, Mr. Reynolds became well known to the prostitutes on the south side of town. He was known for his roughness and for a rape and sodomy incident that was never reported. That was a year and a half ago.

"We will also have testimony from the one woman Mr. Reynolds did manage to have a relationship with after he got out of prison. She will testify that Mr. Reynolds raped, sodomized, and choked her nearly to death on two separate occasions. She finally got her brothers to run him off. The strangler's first victim was killed less than a month after he and his girlfriend broke up.

"Psychologists will testify that Mr. Reynolds has a progressively worsening attitude towards women. We will also offer testimony from men Reynolds confided in during his incarceration for rape. Mr. Reynolds told them that the only thing he regretted about his crime was allowing the victim to live and tell her story.

"That's what he corrected, Deja. When Mr. Reynolds got out of prison, he made sure that none of his victims survived – until you. We don't need his fingerprints at your apartment, because the strangler left no fingerprints at any of the scenes. He never left semen or hair samples either. Because of you we know why.

"Mr. Reynolds' hair was kept neat and secure with the panty hose. And he never left semen because he didn't have sexual intercourse with the victims. The only clue Mr. Reynolds ever left was fibers from the same type of black pullover, and those fibers were found all over your bed.

"This office has never prosecuted the wrong man. We're not going to start now, Deja. All four of the strangler's victims were killed within a two year period. We haven't had one similar murder since Mr. Reynolds got arrested. Our evidence may sound circumstantial, but he's our man, and I'm going to prove it. Okay?"

Deja sighed and shuddered; finally at peace with the prosecutor's theory. If the jury consisted of rational and reasoning people, they would surely side with the D.A.'s office as well. And if Gilbert Reynolds was somehow *not* the Sleeping Strangler, he had a whole lot of explaining to do. He would need a defense team assembled by the late Johnny Cochran to weasel out of this.

"Okay," Deja said, the heavy weight of ambiguity lifted from her shoulders. "That's a lot more than I expected. I don't have any more doubt."

The meeting lasted another hour. Deja left the district attorney's office with enough knowledge of legal proceedings to write her own Perry Mason episode.

≈ ≈ ≈ ≈ ≈ ≈

On Wednesday, June 20th, Deja went downtown again. This time her destination was the Tarrant County Municipal building. Her goal was to do all she could to help convict a thief, pervert and psychopathic killer of women.

The media was back in droves, but they behaved a lot better at the courthouse than they did at Jackson Memorial. Things didn't get too pushy when Deja entered the building with her father flanking her right side and her sister on her left. She was nervous, but Deja wasn't the weak, fretful girl she used to be.

An ominous hush enveloped the crowd when the defendant staggered into the courtroom. Deja's throat caught, but she didn't scream or give in to a fit of nausea that had been bubbling in her gut all morning.

Gilbert Reynolds wore a bright orange jumpsuit and arm and leg shackles that rattled as he stepped. He looked bigger than he did at the pre-trial hearing. Beneath the new layer of fat, he was the same vile, disgusting creature. His eyes were low and shifty. His face was shaved clean. His nose was flat, and his lips were pursed. Deja thought he was attempting to hold back a grin or a sneer.

Gilbert hadn't had a haircut in a while. He wore a two-inch afro that was tangled and knotted and completely mashed down on one side, presumably the side he slept on the previous evening.

Deja thought the strangler was going to mount some kind of workable defense, but he wasn't starting off well. A bath and a suit would've gone a long way. Gilbert seemed resigned to his fate; resigned to look like he just crawled out of the gutter and was ready to jump on another woman at that very moment. The little old lady in the jury? Yes, Ma'am. Even you!

He looked around the courtroom and locked eyes with Deja for a second before he sat down. That was something Deja knew was coming. She hoped the stare-down would offer a moment of clarity. She thought she could use her eyes to ask, *Why did you do this*? and Gilbert could respond with a sigh or by looking away nervously. But none of that happened.

The strangler's expression was deadpan. He didn't offer any insight at all before he looked away and took a seat next to his defense attorney. Deja didn't have an opportunity to look him in the eyes again until she took the stand to testify a week later.

≈ ≈ ≈ ≈ ≈ ≈

The trial lasted two months. Gilbert's attorney was court-appointed, but he was highly skilled. He was a short, pudgy man named Gene Ackers. From day one, he made it clear that he wasn't about to sit idly by while the district attorney pulled the wool over everyone's eyes. Mr. Ackers argued about anything and everything. He fought hard against each piece of evidence the prosecution presented. He tried to discredit every witness the D.A. called to the stand.

For the prostitute who said Gilbert raped her, Mr. Ackers injected as much doubt as possible:

"Have you ever lied to the police?"

The woman looked around the courtroom and scratched behind her ear. "Ye, yes."

"Have you ever lied to a judge?"

"Um, yes."

"Have you ever lied to a boyfriend?"

"Yes."

"Have you ever lied on a lie detector test?"

155

"Uh, yes."

"Have you ever lied to a john?"

"Yes."

"Have you ever lied to your mother, sister, brother?"

"Objection, Your Honor."

Without batting an eye, the judge said the objection was, "Overruled."

"I probably lied to everybody at some point," the former prostitute conceded.

"Did you lie to the police when they questioned you about the defendant?"

"No, I did not."

"Yeah, of course you didn't."

"Objection!"

"That's fine. I'm done with her."

For Gilbert's ex-girlfriend, the defense attorney went after her motive.

"Did you and Mr. Reynolds have an amicable relationship?"

"What, what you mean?"

"Did you and Mr. Reynolds get along well? Did you like each other?"

"Yeah, when he wasn't trying to kill me."

"Yes, that's what I'm talking about; when he *wasn't* trying to kill you. Did Gilbert ever cheat on you?"

She looked confused before nodding. "Yes."

"Did he cheat on you multiple times?"

After another pause, she said, "Yes."

"Did he cheat on you with your very own sister?"

The witnesses' nostrils flared. "Yes."

"Did he steal your money?"

"Yes."

"Curse out your mom?"

"Excuse me?"

"Did the defendant ever curse out your mother?"

"Yes."

"And you swore you'd get him back, didn't you?"

"Objection."

"I'll rephrase: Did you ever make plans to get revenge for these bad things Mr. Reynolds did to you?"

"Um, no."

"Really? You never told anyone you wanted to pay Mr. Reynolds back?"

"I may have, um—"

"You may have, um, lied to this jury about him choking you? Isn't that right?"

"No! I would never do that."

"But wouldn't this be a great way to get your revenge?"

"No. I said I wouldn't do that."

"Sure you wouldn't."

"Objection!"

"Watch your step, Mr. Ackers. You're out of line, and you know it."

"Yes, Your Honor. I apologize."

Mr. Ackers watched his step, but he continued to pepper the prosecution's case with hole after hole: *How come the footprint the police found wasn't a definite match for my client? How come none of my client's DNA was found at the scene? How come Deja never saw this man stalking her previously? How come Deja couldn't identify Mr. Reynolds as her attacker – even now? How come there was no link between the victim's apartment and Mr. Reynolds? Couldn't the prosecution offer one witness who saw Mr. Reynolds on the premises?*

And where the hell is that pullover? If the strangler always wore a black pullover, then where's Mr. Reynolds' pullover? There was no pullover found at his home or on his person during the arrest. If my client was sweating profusely, then the pullover must have been covered with sweat. So why couldn't the dogs find it?

I'll tell you why they couldn't find it: Because they're trying to railroad this man. They have no evidence, yet they're trying to send him up the river. But not on my watch. No, sirree. Not in front of this intelligent jury, and not in front of God Almighty!

My client doesn't need an explanation for what he was doing out at four in the morning! The burden of proof lies heavily on the prosecution. And they haven't proved anything beyond a reasonable doubt! This is a travesty of justice. Someone should've intervened before this made it all the way to the courtroom!

But the intelligent jury members disagreed. They took less than six hours of deliberation to find Gilbert Reynolds guilty of all charges. They would convene again for sentencing in one week.

Deja knew he wouldn't get death or even a life sentence for her attack, but that was okay. The D.A. planned to indict Gilbert for Tawanda Murphy's murder in a matter of days. If he managed to dodge the death penalty for that case, they would charge him for Danielle Struthers' murder. And if the Sleeping Strangler still wasn't on death row by then, there were two more mourning families who were itching for their day in court.

≈≈≈≈≈≈

Deja left the courtroom with her father and sister doing their best to shield her from the reporters.

"Deja!"

"Deja! Over here!"

"How does it feel to finally have justice?"

"Do you feel safe now?"

"Deja!"

"Are you going to testify at the murder trials?"

Amidst the shouting, Deja thought she heard a familiar voice. She looked back and saw her good friend Tamara squeezing through the crowd.

"Deja! Congratulations!"

Deja broke away from her family and ran to her friend.

"Tamara! What are you doing here?"

"You know I wouldn't miss your trial!"

"I wish I could've–"

"Huh?"

They couldn't hear each other over the ruckus. Deja leaned close to her friend's ear. "Do you want to go somewhere?"

"Yeah!" Tamara yelled. She grabbed Deja's hand and pulled her past a barrier set up by the police. Deja looked back and waved goodbye to her dad, who was confused to see his little girl disappear with a woman he'd never met.

≈≈≈≈≈≈

Tamara took her to a coffee shop on the southwest side of town. It was after six by the time they got there. Deja thought Tamara was simply radiant today. She wore a white pants suit with black sandals that exposed her pretty toes. Her blouse had a low neckline that showed off just a little cleavage. Tamara's hair was down, her lipstick barely noticeable. Deja found herself in a daze as she watched her friend talk.

"When you took the stand," Tamara was saying, "I was so proud of you! You didn't let that lawyer phase you at all."

"Yes I did," Deja countered. "I was sweating bullets."

"I didn't notice," Tamara said with a smile.

The ladies sat in a booth next to a window. Other than them, there was only one customer and two employees in the shop. An hour crept by as the sun began its slow descent, leaving golden footprints across the sky. The quaint little shop smelled strongly of coffee beans and vanilla and other sweet flavors.

"Have you been going to the WAAR meetings?" Deja asked.

"Never miss them," Tamara said. "I notice you haven't been around."

"I've been doing better. I don't feel like I need it as much."

"We miss you," Tamara said. "I told my story again last Saturday. It was..." She sighed. "It never gets easy."

"I'm sorry," Deja said. She really felt bad for not being there for her friend. "You should've told me."

"It's alright. How's your watch been going?"

"Great," Deja said, but she didn't want to talk about the watch right then. "What is..." She cleared her throat. "What is your story, Tamara? I don't, I mean, you don't have to tell the whole thing..."

Tamara chuckled and looked away for a moment. "My story's pretty depressing. Haven't you heard enough sad stories?"

"Yes," Deja said. "I'm, I'm sorry I asked."

"I'll tell you," Tamara replied. "Just promise you won't get all sentimental on me."

"I won't," Deja said. "I promise."

"Yeah, we'll see," Tamara said with a slight grin. The smile faded just as quickly. "I'll give you the abridged version," she offered. "It happened six years ago. I remember the day very well because I just got my job at GM, and me and my friend went out to celebrate. We went to Razzoo's. We had one of those Gator bowls;

159

you know, the ones with all of that liquor in it. We drank it with two straws. It was romantic. My friend wanted to go back to my place, but I told her no. I had to get up early the next day for my first day at work. She got mad at me. I'll always remember, the way she got mad."

Deja tried to stay focused, but her mind was stuck on the word *she*.

"I had an alarm," Tamara went on. "But he disabled it. They said he did something to it from outside. The alarm I have now – you can't do that. If you manipulate any of the wires, the police will still call. But the old one... It was different. I didn't know he was in the house until he was in my bed. By then, it was too late. All I saw was his eyes and the knife."

Deja knew that feeling well. A heavy sorrow fell upon her. She reached across the table and squeezed her friend's hand. Tamara squeezed back and kept talking.

"I had never been with a man," she said. "So the penetration, that's something that will always stay with me. I don't like to say rape is different if you're straight versus if you're gay. But, it is different. When you've lived your life a certain way and someone comes along and takes that away from you, it's more than just rape. For me, I think it's a lot worse."

Deja put a hand to her mouth. "I'm so sorry."

"I didn't fight," Tamara said. "Back then I was always told not to fight back, just let him do his thing, and he'll leave. So that's what I did. But, but that turned out wrong for me. That's why I like you so much, Deja. You fought back. I would have too, especially if I had known my attacker was HIV positive. I didn't find that out until three months later, when the doctors told me I contracted the virus. I took the anti-retroviral pills, but I still got it."

Tamara wasn't crying, but Deja was. She couldn't help it. She never felt so badly for someone.

"Oh my God, Tamara. I'm so, so sorry."

"It's okay," Tamara said. "Things are a lot better now. All we can do is take what God gives us and keep moving forward."

Deja shook her head. "God didn't give you that. Some nasty rapist did that to you. You don't deserve it. You should never have to live with something like that."

"It's okay," Tamara said. "If I can get past it, so can you. Now straighten up there, missy." She plucked a few napkins from the dispenser. "How many of these you need? The whole thing?" She smiled. "Jeez, I talked to a high school class yesterday, and they held it together better than you."

Deja sniffled and chuckled and sniffled again. "Yeah. Give me the whole thing."

≈≈≈≈≈≈

The conversation never recovered from Tamara's bombshell. The ride home was quiet and tension-filled. Deja couldn't get over the fact that her friend's life was permanently altered because some disgusting pervert didn't jack-off one night.

Deja was overwhelmed with emotion, and she couldn't find the words to express what she felt. She feared Tamara would take her silence to mean Deja was repulsed by her story. Everything was so confusing now. Deja sat in the passenger seat and stared out of the window, unable to meet her friend's eyes.

When Tamara pulled to a stop in her apartment parking lot, Deja was crying again. She turned to face her friend but still couldn't find the words to express what she felt.

"Please stop crying," Tamara told her. "This is not–"

Before she could finish, Deja leaned in and kissed her. Her heart was thundering. The car felt like it was on fire. The kiss was nice and warm, slow and tender. Up close Tamara's perfume filled Deja's nostrils, making her head spin. Deja's eyes were closed. She felt more fireworks during the kiss than any boy or man ever gave her. She felt explosions in her chest, stomach and between her legs. When she opened her eyes, Tamara's eyes were still closed. Deja backed away with her chest rising and falling visibly.

Tamara opened her eyes and watched her friend curiously. "Wow. What, what was that for? It was awesome, but, what's the deal?"

"I love you," Deja blurted. Her face burned. It was the first thing she could think to say, but even better, it was true. Not since Jerome had Deja felt this way for someone. Her feelings for Tamara actually surpassed her feelings for any man she'd dated.

But Tamara shook her head. "You don't love me, Deja. Well, maybe you do. But we're friends. And you're not gay."

I am, Deja thought, but she couldn't get her mouth to speak. Instead she nodded.

"No, you're not," Tamara said. She smiled. "You've never been with a woman before. I'm probably the first girl you ever kissed."

It was much too hot in Tamara's car. Deja felt beads of sweat on her forehead.

"I remember the way you looked at that cop who came to your meeting," Tamara said. "Deja, you clearly like men. And there's nothing wrong with that. You're just confused right now. I've seen it happen at the WAAR meetings. Some girls have never experienced that much pain, and because of it, they turn against men completely. But what they don't understand is it isn't men who hurt them. It was that particular man. As for me, I've been gay my whole life. The only man I was ever with raped me. But you're different, Deja. You know you are."

Deja did know that. She started to cry again as her foolishness dawned on her. Tamara was quick to wipe her tears away.

"No. Please, stop crying. You're a beautiful woman, Deja. If you *were* gay, I would definitely take you up on your offer."

Deja looked up doubtfully. "Really?"

"Hell yeah," Tamara said with a grin. "I think you'd be the perfect girlfriend."

Deja chuckled. Tamara laughed with her.

"Now go on," Tamara said. "Try to get some sleep. I'll give you a call tomorrow."

"We, will we still hang out?"

"Sure," Tamara said. "But no kissing."

"Alright," Deja said and leaned over and gave her as big a hug as she could in the confined space of the car.

≈≈≈≈≈≈

Six months after his first trial, Gilbert Reynolds was dragged to court again to answer for the slaying of Tawanda Murphy. In less than five weeks, he was found guilty of murder. Given his track record with women, the jury easily voted for him to die by lethal injection.

Afterwards, the police tried to get Gilbert to confess to the murders of Danielle Struthers, Sheila Montgomery and Tracy Fielder. He continued to deny any involvement. They didn't prosecute him for those crimes, because it would have been a waste of time and tax-payer money. A man can only get executed once, and they could still stamp the other cases CLOSED without his confession.

There were no more Sleeping Strangler-style murders in the fair city of Overbrook Meadows, and by Christmastime, Gilbert Reynolds began to fade from everyone's memory. He took his place in the annals of American folklore, alongside boogeymen like Jeffrey Dahmer, Albert Fish and the morbidly zany John Wayne Gacy.

CHAPTER FIFTEEN
365

Deja loved the winter months.

Summertime in Texas was like roasting slowly on a spit with an apple crammed in your mouth. You could run the A.C., strip down to your skivvies and turn on every ceiling fan in the house. But at some point you'd have to go outside, and at that moment, you'd realize that you were, and always have been, nothing more than Mother Nature's bitch.

But winter was different.

When it got cold all you had to do was throw on a coat or jacket. You could light a log in the fireplace and make hot chocolate and cuddle with your significant other on a bearskin rug – or a shag carpet if you didn't get into dead bears. Deja didn't have a significant other or a fireplace, but she did have blankets and a cute, cuddly baby who loved to snuggle.

In February, Overbrook Meadows had its first (and only) ice day. Deja got to stay home from work while less fortunate commuters struggled to keep their cars from sliding off the slick streets. It iced over so infrequently in Texas, people didn't know what to do when their cars lost traction. They literally freaked out; jerking their wheel to and fro while the tires spun uselessly. Watching the news, Deja saw accident after accident – a lot of them live – and she didn't leave the house at all that day, not even for the café mocha she'd been craving.

By March things began to thaw, leaving behind lush greenery and bumblebees and all sorts of springtime beauty. March was the anniversary of Deja's attack by a certain Sleeping Strangler, but no one thought about that because March was also the birth month of a sweet little boy who almost didn't get to take his first breath. In his mother's eyes, this child was very lucky, so she gave him the middle name *Asad* so that he would always know how blessed his birthday was.

≈ ≈ ≈ ≈ ≈ ≈ ≈

To celebrate the 20th of March, Deja threw a barbecue in her apartment's recreation area. The party was technically for her son, but she invited all of the neighborhood watch members because she wanted to commemorate their success as well. The pools weren't open yet, but there was a sand volleyball court as well as a basketball court near the grill. There were picnic tables scattered throughout, and all of them were packed with people by six p.m.

Deja sat on a bench with her mom, nephews and sister while her father and brother cooked burgers and hotdogs for the guests. Deja asked the watch members to wear their tee shirts to the party, and most of them did. But the majority of people standing in line for a plate weren't part of the community project at all. Julie was against them getting a free meal, but Deja didn't discriminate – as long as they had enough to feed the volunteers first.

Deja wore her watch tee-shirt with canvas shorts that showed off her long legs but weren't tight enough to have guys staring at her booty all day. She held Adrian in her lap, but the child wouldn't sit still. He kept pushing with his pudgy legs until he reached a standing position with both feet on her thighs. Deja held his hands so he wouldn't fall backwards. Her mother looked on with a tear gleaming in her eye.

"He sho' is something. Put him down, Deja. I want to see him walk."

"That baby don't walk," Julie said.

"Yeah he does," Deja said. "He walks around the house, but he has to hold himself up on the furniture."

She sat him on the ground, and Adrian immediately struggled to get to his feet. He wouldn't have made it if he didn't have Deja's leg to pull himself up on. The baby turned and grinned at his grandma.

"Aww, he's so sweet," Shirley said. "Come here, Adrian. Can you make it over here?"

She bent and reached for him, wiggling her fingers. Adrian clucked and took a few wobbly steps towards her. When he got close enough, he reached for Grammy with both hands. That proved to be his undoing. He lost his balance and stumbled forward. He almost did a face plant in the soft grass, but Shirley caught him just in time. She lifted him over her head, and Adrian laughed hysterically.

"Who's that?" Julie asked. She was the only person at the party with a frown on her face. When Deja followed her gaze, she understood why.

"Oh, that's D Money, and... I don't know the short one's name. The short one's an idiot, but he has some pretty, curly hair. They're like Amos and Andy. Whatever D Money says, his friend has to be there to cosign."

The men in question were standing near the volleyball court, probably lusting over the bubble butt of one of the players. They were both munching on hamburgers Deja and the apartment manager paid their hard-earned money to provide for the watchers.

"*They* in the watch?" The way Julie asked made it clear that she most certainly hoped not.

"They're not volunteers," Deja said. She shook her head, but the smile remained on her face. "Those are the neighborhood dope men. They're members of a gang called the Hoova Land Crips. *Hoova Land* originated in Los Angeles. Neither D Money nor any of his crew have ever been to California, but that's the gang they claim. It's all pretty ridiculous."

Julie asked the obvious question: "If you know so much about them, why aren't they in jail?"

"Two reasons," Deja said. "For one, the tall one doesn't like men who prey on women – either sexually or to rob them. And two, they're not the big fish around here. They sell drugs, but taking them down wouldn't help this neighborhood at all. The dopeheads have too many other sources."

"Then you should take them all down, one at a time," Julie suggested. "Starting with *that* one."

Deja shook her head with a chuckle. "I used to think like that. My friend told me – ooh! There she is." Deja jumped from her seat. "Hold on. I'll be right back. I want y'all to meet her."

Tamara crossed the lawn twenty yards away. Deja went to greet her. Tamara wore a denim skirt that stopped above her knees with a short-sleeved pink blouse. Her hair was curled with auburn highlights that went well with her skin tone.

"Whassup!" Deja shouted. "Glad you could make it."

The ladies hugged like friends rather than lovers. Deja's smile was big and infectious. She and Tamara hadn't shared another kiss, but they were still close. After a little soul-searching, Deja came to understand that she was in fact *not* gay. Thankfully Tamara didn't hold the kiss against her. They never talked about it, even though they both knew the affection brought them closer in a spiritual way.

"Hey, hey," Tamara said. "Here. I brought this for Adrian." She handed over a gift bag with blue tissue paper sticking from the top. By the weight of it, Deja knew it was a toy rather than clothes.

"Thanks. Did you just get off work?"

"Yeah. How's your party going?"

"So far so good. I think we're going to run out of meat pretty soon, though."

"Did y'all sing to Adrian yet?"

"No. I was going to get his cake in a minute."

"What about his daddy? You still haven't heard from Jerome?"

Deja rolled her eyes at that. "Yeah, right. Hope I never do."

"I thought you'd hear from him today," Tamara said. "Even half-ass daddies show up for birthdays."

"If Jerome *was* a half-ass daddy, I could probably live with that. I don't even want to talk about him no more."

Deja wasn't upset, but the longer Jerome stayed on her mind, the worse her mood would become. She could understand a man not wanting a child. She could understand the reluctance of a man who was forced into the role of fatherhood. But what she couldn't understand was a man who could go months on end without wanting to see or even calling to check up on his baby.

"Hey, Deja. What y'all doing?"

Deja turned and laughed when she saw Shannon standing there. Ever since Deja told Shannon she kissed a girl (and liked it), Shannon was going crazy trying to find out who the mystery woman was. She knew it was someone named *Tamara*, but that was not nearly enough information to satisfy a gossip like her.

"Hi," Deja said. "Shannon, this is my friend Tamara. Tamara, this is Shannon."

"Hey," Tamara said.

"Oh, *hey*," Shannon said with barely concealed elation. She looked Deja's friend up and down and rolled her neck a little. "Hmph. *I'll say...*"

≈ ≈ ≈ ≈ ≈ ≈

By seven-thirty Deja started to wind things down, but one of the youngsters brought out a boom box and cranked things up again. There were a lot of middle age folks there, so they kept it respectful by playing the radio rather than their Lil Wayne CD's, but the radio still put a good number of party-goers in a time warp. Deja's mom, for instance, didn't know what a Soulja Boy was or what it meant for him to *turn his swag on*, and she took that as her cue to leave.

"Well, it's been fun," Shirley said, "but we're gonna go ahead and get out of here..."

"Hold on." Deja stood and motioned for her mom to remain seated. "We didn't sing Happy Birthday yet. Let me go get the cake. I'll be right back."

Shannon jumped up, too. "I'll go with you."

The girls headed off and soon noticed the apartment complex was sparsely populated for that time of day. All of the music and fun was behind them, and it looked like all of the residents were there, too. Deja didn't need help with the cake, and she had a pretty good idea why her friend wanted to go with her.

"So, that was Tamara..." Shannon said when they rounded the first corner.

"Yes, that was Tamara," Deja said. "And you know something, I'm glad you finally saw her. Now you can get over it, and we don't have to talk about that anymore."

"*Oh no*," Shannon said. "It ain't over. Now that I've seen her, I can visualize everything *perfectly*. So tell me," she said with a smack of her lips, "where were y'all hands when you kissed? Did you touch her on the side? Was your head tilted to the left or the right?"

"You're crazy if you think I'm going to tell you any more about that," Deja said. "I never should have told you anything to begin with. I don't know what I was think..."

Deja trailed off when a man descended the stairs of an adjacent building. He was of average height and build, dark-skinned with short hair and small eyes. Deja recognized him as someone she saw at the party earlier. He wasn't a member of the watch, and he wasn't a resident there, either. Deja thought she saw him with a couple of guys who lived in the complex across the street.

He looked up at Deja and smiled. She smiled back. He wasn't all that attractive, but it was the friendly thing to do. He stopped, still grinning.

"Hey," he said. "Are you, you're Deja, right?"

"Yeah," she said. "How do you know my name?"

"You're the one who threw the party," he said. "I was there with my friends. I had a couple of hot dogs."

"I remember you," Deja said.

"You started the neighborhood watch?"

"Yes."

"I was watching you," the stranger said, "a little bit. I was about to leave, but I wanted to talk to you first."

Deja blushed. "Talk to me about what?"

"Oh, I don't know." He looked down at his shoes. "I thought maybe you and me could, you know, get to know each other. Maybe go out one day..."

"Oh," Deja said.

The sun was starting to set, but there was still enough light to see the man clearly. He wore a white collar shirt that was long-sleeved and buttoned almost all the way to the top. His shirt was tucked into a pair of black slacks that were creased and neat.

"My name is Benton," he said.

"I'm, oh, you know my name."

Benton offered his hand, and Deja shook it.

His skin was soft and his grip was strong. Up close, Deja could smell his cologne. It was nice, but she couldn't tell what brand it was. Benton was clean-shaven with thin eyebrows and a somewhat pudgy nose. His lips were full. His teeth were near perfect.

"I think it's great what you've done with this neighborhood," he said. "For a woman to step up like this is really something. I don't even know you, but I already admire you."

Shannon hummed something in the background.

"Wow. That's nice," Deja said.

"So..." He rocked back on his heels. "Can I have your number?"

"Oh, um..." Deja dug her cellphone from her front pocket. "Why don't you give me your number, and maybe I'll call you?"

"Cool." Benton rattled off a number, and Deja punched it in. "I hope to hear from you," he said.

"Alright," Deja replied. She pointed a thumb behind her. "There's still more food. You don't want to get a hamburger or something to take with you?"

"Actually, no," he said. "I'm on my way to a friend's house. Thanks though. I'll, uh, I'll talk to you later, I hope..." He gave her one last smile and turned to walk away. Deja watched his butt until he was out of sight. It was nice; not too big, not too small, and thankfully not one of those high booties that start too far up people's backs.

"You like him?" Shannon asked as they entered Deja's apartment.

"I don't know. Maybe. What do you think about him?"

"He look alright," Shannon said. "He ain't *gorgeous* or nothing. But either way, you *know* you need to call him."

"How come?"

"You know why."

"No I don't."

Shannon sighed. "'Cause your bed is dustier than the OK Corral, Deja. It's been damned near a year since you got some."

"You don't know what you talking about," Deja said. The last time she got some was actually *more* than a year ago. Yesterday was the one-year anniversary of her and Jerome's final romp. But as Deja recalled, her ex-boyfriend couldn't maintain an erection that night, so that didn't count. And the time before that was – jeez. Just thinking about it made Deja's womanly parts cry out in displeasure.

"I don't know what I'm talking about?" Shannon asked.

"Even if you're right," Deja said, "that doesn't mean I should jump in bed with the first guy that comes along."

"Yes it does," Shannon countered. "That's why you kissed that girl, Deja. You can't neglect your sexuality like that. You're not meant to go that long without getting some dick."

"Okay, Dr. Ruth."

"My man came over last night," Shannon said. "He ran me a bath and lit some candles. He cut off all the lights and rubbed my shoulders while I sat in the tub. Girl, I closed my eyes and I was feeling *good* – you hear me? He kissed my neck and his hands was everywhere. I was like *good Gawd*! Mmm, mmm, mmm." She closed her eyes and got lost in the memory.

Deja frowned and looked away with a snort. "Come on and let's get this cake, girl. You pissing me off."

"Do you at least have a vibrator?"

"Yes, I have one!" Deja snapped. "Been buying batteries for that damned thing every other week!"

Dirty rotten scoundrels stealing
Backdoor burglarizing, peeling
Paint clean off the walls, 'cause healing
Comes from those who practice dealing
Death to those who're hooked. Appealing
Girls submit to constant drilling
Face down, ass up. The filthy feeling
Leaves when they meet those who're dealing
Death to the lives of squealing
Infants born in Sheol. Willing
Saps are caught up in the killing
Fields of those who practice dealing

CHAPTER SIXTEEN
PEACHES

Deja's alarm clock went off at 3:45, in what her mom would call the witching hour, and she shut it off within seconds. She was already awake – had been for ten minutes. Deja already had her coffee made and her baby changed, too.

This was a Thursday morning. She had to get ready for work right after her watch shift, but there were no red veins in the corner of Deja's eyes. Despite going to bed late because of the party, she felt very energetic. She lounged in the living room with her baby on her lap and her radio in hand.

Ms. Gladys and Mr. Cheung had her laughing so hard, Deja thought Adrian would wake up. But her little boy hardly ever stirred during this early morning ritual. Deja used to tell her mom Adrian must be part rooster, because no matter how much moving and shaking she did, he never opened his eyes until the sun came up.

"Most of them get the picture by now," Ms. Gladys croaked into the radio. "It's just every now and then you get the *ignant* ones." It took a lot to get on Ms. Gladys' bad side. Those who made the transition from ignorant to *ignant* were unlucky souls indeed.

"There are *a lot* of them like that," Kim Cheung piped in on his radio. "They steal all my candy!"

Ms. Gladys' watch shift was from three to four p.m. That was one of the safer shifts because of the broad daylight factor, but it was a different story down the block at Kim's 24 hour corner store.

"They get out of school, and come straight to my store," Mr. Cheung complained. "They know they don't have money. *I* know they don't have money! Just the *sticky finger*. They all got the sticky finger and take my stuff!"

Kim's exasperation was serious, and Deja wanted to empathize, but it was hard to keep a straight face when he was on one of his rants. His accent was so thick, and the Korean War was so long ago. Deja didn't think immigrants like him were still around.

"So what happened yesterday?" she asked.

"I caught me another one," Ms. Gladys said. Recently she made it her duty to walk down to Kim's store every afternoon to help keep the peace with the school kids. Already Deja was hearing stories about her (mostly unorthodox) tactics.

"He was a *fat one!*" Mr. Cheung exclaimed. "Stole all my Snicker bar!"

"He *was* big," Ms. Gladys agreed. "He had put the candy in his pockets, but his thighs was so fat, them Snickers was all squished up by the time I got 'em back. It was so nasty."

"How'd you get them back?" Deja was almost afraid to ask.

"I asked him if he was getting them for his mama to try to kick heroin."

"No you didn't."

"Yeah I did, girl. You know that lady, Karen, who stay in the building next to me?"

"Yeah."

"Well, you know she get high, don't you? She be snorting that stuff, the *brown* stuff, not the *white* stuff."

"Didn't know that," Deja said, no longer surprised by how Ms. Gladys found dirt on *everybody*.

"I told him, '*It's good if you want to help your mama get off them drugs, so she won't be bringing them different mens in the house all hours of the night. I know you don't like to hear them sex noises while you're trying to sleep.*'"

Deja's eyes widened. "You didn't tell him that."

"Yes I did, child."

"She got him good!" Mr. Cheung confirmed. He was working in his store at that moment, probably re-stocking the pilfered Snickers.

"What'd he do?" Deja asked.

"He looked around to see if people was listening," Ms. Gladys said. "And you know something, all of his friends just happened to be standing right there."

"They *just happened to be*, huh?" Deja asked.

"You know I don't like to put nobody's business in the street," the older woman explained.

"No," Deja agreed. "You'd never do that."

"He started crying!" Mr. Cheung said. "Fat boy cry big, *fat* tears. The girls all laugh at him. *Ha-ha! Your mama does the blow job!*"

"That's terrible," Deja said, and then she let go of the talk button so she could laugh.

"He give all my candy back," Mr. Cheung said. "It's all mashed, and I can't sell. But it still so funny! He ran out crying. The boys follow him. They say *Where your mama at! I got five dollar*. It so funny! Fat boy won't come back. I not see him no more."

Mr. Cheung might think that was a pretty good resolution, but Deja couldn't condone such ruthlessness. "Now you know you need to quit, Ms. Gladys. You're supposed to be at that store to *help* with the kids, not traumatize them. That boy will never forget what you said about his mama."

"That's right," Ms. Gladys said. "He'll never forget what happened that time he stole from Mr. Kim's store. Now, it's four o'clock. Are you coming or what?"

"Yeah," Deja said. "I'm working with the new girl tonight. She's probably still asleep. Bethany? You got you radio on?"

No one answered.

"She's still asleep," Ms. Gladys agreed.

"I'll drop Adrian off and then go get her," Deja said. "I'm on my way."

"How come you ain't working with a *man*?" Ms. Gladys asked. "You think it's okay to be out there by yourself?"

Deja thought that was a terrible question to ask. It was dark and ominous. If she was the superstitious type, it might be considered a warning of bad things to come.

"It's okay," she said. "You know I got a concealed handgun license."

"That's what I need," the older woman chirped.

The thought of Ms. Gladys marching down to Kim's corner store with a pistol in her purse made Deja's smile go away completely.

"No, you don't. If I ever hear about you with a gun, you're out of the watch," she threatened.

"Aww, you ain't no fun," Ms. Gladys pouted.

Deja left her apartment three minutes later with her baby dozing in her arms and a Colt .25 automatic strapped securely in her ankle holster. The hypocrisy of her carrying a pistol after condemning her volunteers from doing the same was completely lost on her, because Deja was a firm believer in the *Do as I say – not as I do* clause.

The police never gave her first gun back, and that was a shame. They were supposed to return it after the murder trial, but then they wanted to hang on to it for the appeal. Deja now understood that her 9mm might be stored in an evidence box *forever*.

Rather than wait it out, she bought two more pistols. The first was a black and chrome .25. It was small enough to fit in her front pocket, but she preferred to tote it properly in the ankle holster. Her second gun was the always faithful and forever powerful .357 magnum. That baby was all muscle, all bark *and* all bite. With so much firepower, some might ask themselves, *Do I really need so much weaponry?*

Deja wasn't one of those people. If she ever drew her gun, it wouldn't be for posturing. And if someone was bold enough to break into her home again, they deserved to lose the use of one or more limbs. Deja thought this was women empowerment to the fullest.

≈ ≈ ≈ ≈ ≈ ≈ ≈

She still didn't get a response from Bethany on the radio when she dropped Adrian off, so she headed to the newbie's unit at the front of the complex. Halfway there Deja encountered her first fight or flight moment of the night at the dumpster next to D Money's place.

The dumpster was enclosed on three sides by a concrete wall. Sometimes it wasn't only raccoons that crept in the small spaces around and behind it. Deja heard a human sound, possibly a cough, and she stopped suddenly, her muscles growing tense and blood-filled.

She had a flashlight and pepper spray canister latched onto her belt like Batman. She freed both of them without looking down. With one click, the whole dumpster was illuminated, but she didn't immediately see anyone. She cringed at the thought of a closer inspection, but she would do it, if need be.

"Hey," Deja tried instead. "I hear you over there. Come on out." She had no handcuffs or badge. But her voice was authoritative, and as Tamara once told her, most people will respond to just that.

A zombie stuck his dark, spooky face from behind the dumpster, and Deja's stomach tightened. She called them *zombies* because the drug addicts who prowled the streets at night would fit right into any *Night of the Dead* horror flick. They were disheveled and poor, walking the streets aimlessly (it would seem), staggering sometimes with slow, deliberate steps that were pulled by a yearning even they didn't understand.

But it was their eyes and vacant stares that mostly resembled the undead. The one behind the dumpster had that wide-eyed gaze. His jaw was slack and his confused expression was real. He was as high as a kite on crack cocaine. This was one of the ugliest things Deja had ever seen. Sadly, in the last nine months, she saw this state of psychosis more times than she could count or even cared to remember.

"Darren? Is that you?"

He nodded hesitantly. "Yes, yes, Miss Deja." His bottom lip hung and glistened with saliva. He kept his hands out of view, which would have made the average cop draw down on him. But Deja knew he was hiding a pipe rather than a weapon.

"How come you don't go home?" she asked. "You know you can't be doing that out here."

"I can't. I can't right now. Margaret, she mad at me." Darren was six feet even and a measly hundred and fifty pounds. He was a day-laborer, a father of four boys all under the age of ten. His common-law wife had a Section 8 apartment across the street. Margaret was once a smoker herself, but she'd been clean since she got their kids back from CPS last year.

Deja didn't want to know Darren's life story, but she ran into him almost every night. When sober, he was a talkative tramp.

"Where you coming from?" she asked.

"D Money."

"Why didn't you go to Grandma's?"

Grandma was a 56 year old woman who lived in Darren's complex. She boosted from department stores by day and hosted a smoke house by night, meaning for a cut of your narcotics, Grandma would let you get high in her apartment. That was always a better alternative to doing dope on the streets, or behind dumpsters.

"I didn't have enough, enough to give her," Darren explained.

Deja believed him. She also empathized with him. Him and his babies.

"I'm gonna go get my partner," she said. "I'll be back. You need to be gone when I get back."

"Okay," he said. "Thank you, Deja. Than, thank you." He returned to his spot behind the dumpster, and Deja continued on her way.

"God help him," she whispered into the soft and brutal night. And that wasn't some flippant comment coming from Deja. It was a heartfelt plea.

As expected, Bethany was sound asleep. She apologized profusely and scrambled to get dressed while Deja waited in the living room, admiring a collection of whatnots Bethany had on her coffee table and mantle. The little sculptures were all black folk, dressed in the rags of slaves and sharecroppers.

Bethany emerged from her bedroom wearing black jeans and tennis with her watch tee shirt. She was tall and big for a girl, dark-skinned with jet black hair and big, brown eyes. She was pretty, though right now she looked irritated and regretful of the neighborhood watch shift she signed up for. She struggled to carry her radio, flashlight and pepper spray in both hands.

"You can clip that radio on your belt," Deja suggested.

"I see you got everything on your belt," Bethany noticed.

"I like to have my hands free," Deja said.

≈≈≈≈≈≈≈

The girls started their shift twenty-five minutes late, but that was okay. Deja was now fully in control of four to six am. Nothing went on without her knowledge. She knew which junkies would steal, what they would steal, and from where they would steal it.

The things she didn't know about yet would be revealed sooner or later by one of her informants in the neighborhood. The people of the night had come to respect Deja and appreciate her. They never expected a reward for their tips and speculations. In return, Deja rarely condemned their loitering, prostitution and drug abuse.

"It's always interesting," she told the new recruit. "There's something new to learn every night."

The ladies were walking Deja's usual route from her complex, to the two across the street, and then down to Kim's corner store where they could get free coffee and doughnuts if they wanted. Deja was trying to allay her volunteer's worries, but Bethany looked more creeped out by the second.

"So, you actually get to know them?" Bethany spoke of the addicts like they were vermin you should exterminate rather than understand. By day she was a nurse's aide, so Deja thought she would be more sympathetic.

"Well, yes," she said. "This would be a pretty hard job if we didn't get to know them."

Bethany shook her head. "If they're living out here like that, they need to be in jail. I thought we were going to put them in jail."

"Alright," Deja said with a chuckle. "You can be the bad cop, and I'll be the good one."

The moon was unusually bright that night. The meteorologists expected a cloud cover most of the day with a 30 percent chance of rain, but Deja didn't think so. She didn't smell it in the air. Plus there wasn't a single cloud in the sky – which made it easier to spot her second troubled soul of the night.

Falcon Ridge apartments had a small playground in the northeast corner. As they approached, Deja thought she saw a familiar face huddled on one of the park benches. The vagrant got up and tried to cross the street when they got closer. Deja couldn't believe her eyes.

"Hey!" She took quick steps but didn't have to run to catch up. Rynesha Sheridan, better known as *Peaches*, could outrun most cops, but she stopped and waited for Deja.

"Huh, hi, Miss Deja."

Deja took the girl by the arm and looked her up and down, a hard knot of disappointment swelling in her gut. Peaches gained twenty pounds since the first time Deja saw her. And she wore pants and a golf shirt tonight, rather than her working outfit. But the truth was written all over her face, mainly in her big, bulging orbs. Peaches' pupils were so dilated, it looked like her whole iris was black. Her mouth was slack, her lips glistened with spittle.

Deja's eyes welled with tears. She knew there was no point in talking to her in that state, but she couldn't help it. Failure was a hard thing to accept.

"What are you doing here? Why aren't you in rehab?"

"I'm, I'm sorry, Miss Deja." Peaches gripped a pipe in one hand. Her other fist was clenched as well. Deja didn't need a crystal ball to know she was hiding crack. She could fight her for it, but that might be like taking a tiger cub from his mother.

"When did you leave?" Deja's face was hot and flustered. She felt like the relapse was her fault.

"Today," Peaches said. "I'm sorry. I, I tried to do it. I tried, Miss Deja. I really did."

This was Peaches' fourteenth fall off the wagon, but it was her first with Deja. It took months of nagging to get her back to a treatment center. Of all the crimes Deja thwarted in her time as the watch captain, she considered Peaches her most notable victory. Now she was her most notable failure.

Deja let go of her friend's arm, understanding that she had to start all over again. But she'd have to wait until Peaches was sober.

"Where'd you get it from?" she breathed.

Peaches squirmed under the moonlight. She wouldn't meet Deja's eyes. "You, you know I can't tell you."

"Okay," Deja said, learning all she needed to know from that. There was one dealer in close vicinity of the playground. "I'm taking Big Moe down," she vowed. "Starting today, he's at the top of my list."

"Don't, don't do that for me," Peaches pleaded.

"I'm not," Deja said. "I'm doing it for everybody."

"It won't solve nothing," Peaches said. The truth of her words pierced Deja's heart like a knife.

"Maybe not," she admitted, "but I have to at least try. If no one else cares about you, Peaches, *I* do. Remember that."

Peaches nodded, but it was not clear if she understood or truly believed what Deja was saying. Reasoning with a crackhead took a lot of time and patience. Fortunately Deja had a good deal of both.

"We'll talk tomorrow," she said and sent Peaches on her merry way.

"She's disgusting," Bethany said when they were alone again.

"Cancer wounds are disgusting, too," Deja said. "But we don't send those patients to jail. One day the world will realize addicts need rehab, not prison."

Even as she spoke, Deja didn't know if she truly believed that. She was putting a lot of faith in a world that was filled with hateful people.

"Come on," she told her new recruit. "Let's head back."

CHAPTER SEVENTEEN
DADDY'S HOME

Deja got an unexpected call at eight o'clock that morning. The sight of Jerome's name on the caller ID filled her with a myriad of emotions; mostly despise and disgust for everything they ever shared – except Adrian.

She sent his call to voicemail and didn't listen to it until she got to work:

Hey, Deja. It's me, Jerome. I'm sorry I didn't get in touch with you yesterday. I won't lie to you. I forgot it was Adrian's birthday. I just remembered it today. I know you did it big for him, though. I wish I could've been there. Anyway, give me a call back. I got something for my son.

Your son? Please. Deja deleted the message, wishing she could delete Jerome out of her life just as easily.

≈≈≈≈≈≈

At work Deja was able to forget about her baby-daddy, mainly because of a fat Maltese named Genie who came in for an emergent C-section. Dr. Fogerty got five puppies out, but one died within minutes and another was barely clinging to life. It was Deja's job to care for the ailing puppy. By noon it too had stopped breathing.

Deja usually found her job exciting and rewarding, but there was nothing pleasant about having a puppy die in her hands. At lunchtime she saw that she missed another call from Jerome.

She wasn't in the mood for him, so she didn't bother checking the new voicemail he left.

Deja knew that ignoring him would probably lead to something dramatic, so she wasn't surprised when Bea came to the break room to notify her of a visitor in the lobby.

"Who is it?" Deja brought tuna salad for lunch, and she was eager to dive into it.

"It's that man," Bea said. "Your ex-boyfriend."

"What does he want?"

"I don't know. You want me to call the police?"

"No." Deja put the lid on her Tupperware and pushed away from the table. "I might as well talk to his ass."

In the lobby, Jerome stood next to the front window, flipping through a rabies pamphlet. He turned when Deja emerged from the back, and a big smile spread across his face. His grin ebbed when Deja's expression remained hard and uninviting.

"What do you want?"

He chuckled. "You know, that's the exact same thing you said to me the last time I came up here. I'm starting to think you don't like me anymore."

Deja had so many smart remarks in reply to his comment, her tongue actually got tied.

"Do you want me to call the police?" Bea asked again. She went to her desk and reached for the phone.

Deja looked her ex up and down. Jerome was tall and muscular. He was handsome, but Deja saw a very ugly man standing before her. She despised him so much, her chest hurt.

"I don't know." She watched his eyes as she spoke. "Do we need to call the police?"

Jerome's smile went away completely, and he sighed in exasperation.

"Look, I just came to talk about my boy. If you want me to leave, that's fine. But we're going to have this discussion sooner or later."

Your boy? Do you even know what your son looks like? Did you know he has teeth now? Deja's blood boiled, but on the outside she remained poised. "What about him?"

Jerome shot Bea a look. "Can we, can't we talk about this in private, Deja? I mean, damn, why you wanna put our business out there like that?"

"She already knows everything about you," Deja replied coldly.

"I'll take you to lunch," Jerome offered. "Anywhere you want to go."

"I'm not going anywhere with you."

"Fine. Can we at least step outside for a second? Why you, you act like I'm gon' hurt you."

Deja found that amusing. If she wasn't afraid of unpredictable drug addicts at four in the morning, why in the world would she be afraid of a punk like Jerome? She sighed and looked to her friend. "I'm going to go outside. I'll be right back."

"Alright," Bea said. "But don't go too far."

"I won't," Deja promised. "I'll be right outside the door."

≈ ≈ ≈ ≈ ≈ ≈

The sun was bright, but not too warm that day. There were a few dark clouds in the sky, and Deja caught the scent of ozone in the atmosphere. She also noticed a new car in the clinic's parking lot. It was a silver Infiniti; brand new, still wearing the temporary dealer plates. Deja knew all eight of her co-workers, and it didn't belong to any of them. There were no customers there at that time.

Deja didn't venture too far from the main entrance. When she looked back, Bea was standing in the lobby watching them. You couldn't pay someone to care that much about you. Deja knew she was blessed to have such a friend in her life.

Jerome, on the other hand, was more like a curse. He took a few steps towards the parking lot and turned when he realized she wasn't following him.

"Oh yeah," he said. "I forgot you're scared to be around me nowadays. I don't know what that shit's about..."

Deja folded her arms. Her irritation was palpable. Later she would have to ask God to help take the anger away. But for now, she let it flow hot like lava.

"I don't owe you an explanation for anything," she spat. "You lost control over me a long time ago."

Jerome shook his head, grinning again. "You've been saying that a lot; how I controlled you so much. I was never controlling, Deja. I wish you would stop telling lies. You got these

183

people ready to call the law on me, and I never did anything to make you afraid of me."

"You attacked my friend in my house."

"That's between me and him," Jerome explained. "I'm talking about you. I never did anything to hurt *you*."

"You never hurt me?" That was so ludicrous, Deja almost cursed him out loudly, theatrically and royally. But this was her place of business, so she swallowed the bad words. "Your message said you wanted to talk about *Adrian*. If you got something to say, then say it. Otherwise, I'm going back to work. I don't have time for this."

"Aright," he said. "I, I wanted to apologize for not calling on his birthday. I really meant to call. I got the days mixed up, but I did mean to call. I'm sorry."

"First of all, I don't give a damn about your apology. And Adrian's too young to even care. So you can save it. Is that it?"

Jerome's whole face darkened for a second. He recovered quickly. "I want to see him. That's what I came to tell you. I want to apologize for the way I've been acting, and I want to be a part of my son's life now."

"Now?"

"Yes, now."

"It's been—"

"I know how long it's been, girl. I don't need you to be throwing that shit in my face."

"Excuse me?"

Jerome brought a hand to his head and rubbed his eye sockets. He sighed, his shoulders rising and falling like ships on a tide. "I'm sorry. I don't mean to get an attitude. It's just that, I call you, trying to be civil. You won't return my calls. I come over here and invite you to lunch, still trying to be nice to you. But all you want to do is point out my faults.

"I know it's been a long time, Deja. That's the one thing on my mind right now. That's the reason I almost didn't call – because the longer I waited, the harder it got. But I'm not doing this for you. I just want to make up lost time with my son. Are you going to let me see him or not?"

Deja wanted to turn him down, but she thought about explaining this conversation to Adrian one day, when he got old

184

enough to ask about his father. Even worse, how would Jerome describe it when he got a chance to tell his side of the story?

I tried to be there for you, Adrian. I went to your mom's job and got down on my knees. I remember it like it was yesterday. I begged her to let me be a part of your life. She looked me right in the eyes and said No. So that's why I haven't been around, son. It's not my fault. Ask your mama.

Deja rolled her eyes. She took a deep breath and released some of her tension when she exhaled.

"Alright, Jerome. You can see him – at my house. If you want to take him somewhere, you need to put yourself on child support and get a visitation schedule."

Jerome's face lit up. "Really? You'll let me see him?"

"Yes. You can visit him *at my house.*"

"That's cool," he said. Jerome clapped his hands and rubbed them together. "When can I come, Deja? I got something I want to give him for his birthday."

"Whenever. Just give me advance notice."

"Can I come tonight?"

She knew he was going to say that. Her eyebrows knitted together, but she didn't go back on her word. "That's fine, Jerome. What time?"

"Seven," he said. "Or seven-thirty. Soon as I leave work."

"You got a new car?" Deja asked.

The question threw him off guard. Jerome looked back at his clean machine and couldn't help but smile. "Yeah."

"You couldn't think of anything else to spend four hundred a month on?"

"Huh?"

Deja turned and headed back inside. "Don't worry about it big-timer. I'll see you later."

≈≈≈≈≈≈

When she got home, Deja made chicken and macaroni for dinner. She didn't intentionally cook enough for Jerome. But she was distracted, and she kept dipping more poultry in the batter. When she was done, she had enough to serve three adults.

Jerome smelled the good cooking as soon as he walked in at a quarter after seven.

"Dang it smells good in here. What'd you make, chicken?"

"Yeah."

"Did you make enough for me to get a plate?'

"I guess."

"Why you looking so upset, girl? Where the baby at?"

"He's sleep. Do you want to see him now or after you eat?"

"I guess I could eat first, if he's sleep." Jerome patted his flat belly. "I sure miss your cooking, Deja."

She headed for the kitchen, and he followed.

"Did you make some greens?"

"Macaroni."

"That's good, too," Jerome said. "You're a great cook, Deja. You could put Luby's out of business, if you set your mind to it."

"Why are you trying to sweet talk me?" she asked. "I already said you could see Adrian. What more do you want?"

"Just for you to eat dinner with me. Have you eaten yet? Do you have time to sit with me?"

"What do you want, Jerome? Spit it out. I can tell you right now, I'm not giving you any money."

He laughed. "I don't want no money. I just want to eat dinner with you and see my boy. Come on, now. I haven't seen you in damned near six months. I miss your company, and I like talking to you. Can't we be friends?"

Deja served Jerome a big, manly plate and sat across from him while he wolfed it down. Jerome had to provide the bulk of the dinner conversation, and Deja couldn't deny that she did miss him a little. Jerome told her about some of his new students. He talked about his school's basketball team and eventually moved the conversation to his dating status.

Jerome said he only dated one girl since they broke up, and that he and Melinda didn't last very long. He said he'd been single for the past four months. Deja didn't respond or particularly believe him. She wondered why he felt the need to divulge.

After dinner she brought Adrian to the living room, and Jerome got down to the serious business of being a wannabe dad. Deja sat on the love seat and paid close attention to every move he made. She expected him to do something ridiculous like pick Adrian up by the ankle or try to kidnap him, but Jerome was a surprisingly skillful father that day.

The baby was awake and a little fussy. Jerome didn't get frustrated. He took the crying like a man. Eventually Adrian stopped complaining long enough to stare at the strange man holding him. Their son wasn't fearful of Jerome, like Deja expected. After fifteen minutes, Deja was surprised to see Adrian smiling at Jerome's silly talk.

The birthday gift he brought was a huge, stuffed kitten that performed a series of actions when you pressed the buttons on its paws or ears. Jerome didn't get a chance to teach these buttons to Adrian, because they were having a ball with no props at all. When it was time for him to leave, Deja was confused and guardedly pleased with the new Jerome.

"That looked like fun." She went and scooped Adrian from his father's lap. Jerome stood with a hearty grin.

"That *was* fun." He leaned down and kissed the baby on the top of the head. "I couldn't play with him too much when he was little, but now he's not so fragile. I don't have to worry about his big head rolling around on that little neck."

"Yeah, he is a lot bigger now," Deja agreed. "You ready?"

Jerome patted the wrinkles out of his pants and looked for his keys.

"You throwing me out?"

"It was a nice visit," Deja said. "But I have to get ready for bed now. Your keys are in the kitchen."

"Oh." Jerome disappeared in that direction and came back with his key chain jingling in his hand. By then Deja was standing next to the open front door. "Dang," Jerome said. "You really want me out of here, don't you?"

"I have to go to bed early," she reiterated. "I'm tired."

Jerome stepped outside but stalled under the porch light.

"What about my next visit. When can I see my boy again?"

"I don't know," Deja said. "I think we should go to court and get that settled by a judge. Then you'll have set days and times, and there won't be any confusion."

"We don't need all that," Jerome said. "I thought we could work this out between you and me."

Deja shook her head. "No, I think it would be better with a judge."

Jerome chuckled. "We don't need a judge, Deja. We're better than that. As a matter of fact, I don't think we need *any* space between us."

He stepped forward until he was flagrantly inside Deja's safety zone. She took a step back inside her home.

"Uh, no. We do need that space."

"You got me thinking about something," Jerome said and tried to close the distance between them again.

Deja thought that was a clear sign of disrespect. But she wasn't frightened. If Jerome pursued her inside her home after she made it clear that she wanted him to leave, she had the right to shoot him. She didn't want to kill her baby-daddy, but she wouldn't mind busting a cap in his arm or leg.

"I liked eating with you," he said. "I had fun kicking it with you and the baby."

"Um, it was alright."

"It was more than alright," Jerome insisted. "It felt like home. It felt right to me."

He reached and put a hand on her side. His caress was an unexpected fire. No man had touched her there in over a year. Deja couldn't control her body's response or deny her yearnings. She needed a man. She wanted to be held and kissed and loved.

But no way was she this desperate. Casual sex was fine and good, but not with Jerome. Never with Jerome. Deja slowly, yet forcefully, removed his hand from her side.

"Don't ever touch me like that."

"Why not?"

"I don't know you, Jerome. I don't know you, and I don't trust you. I have no idea what you've been up to since we broke up. You think just because you come over and play with your son for a little while, you can try to push up on me? Negro please. You didn't want me when I was fat, so you shouldn't want me now."

"Deja, that was different. I made a mistake. I told you I was wrong."

"You might want to back up a couple of feet."

"Huh?"

Deja took a step back herself and slammed the door closed. Jerome wasn't completely out of the way. He had to jump back at the last second to avoid a plywood sandwich. Deja knew it was a cold move, but she didn't care. Jerome was the cause of the worst pain she'd ever felt.

And she did give him fair warning to get out of the way.

"You wrong for that," Jerome shouted from the other side of the door.

Deja didn't respond. She fastened the deadbolt and checked the peephole. Jerome was already walking away.

"Yeah, you wrong for that," he said before he rounded the corner and was out of sight.

CHAPTER EIGHTEEN
LADDERS OF HOPE

It was nine-thirty by the time Jerome hit the old, dusty trail. That was the perfect time for Deja to go to sleep and wake up fresh for her watch shift, but she didn't feel like going to bed right then. Her mind was still on Jerome's advances, and gradually she began to feel depressed about her love life in general.

How could she go a whole year without sex? And how come Jerome was the only man hitting on her? Was she ugly? Still fat? Maybe she was getting stagnant in her routine. All she did was go to work and come home. Her only recreational activity was the neighborhood watch, and she certainly wasn't going to find a good man on the streets at four o'clock in the morning.

Deja warmed leftover macaroni for Adrian, and then it struck her. There was a man out there who liked her. He wasn't the best-looking guy in the world, but he wasn't bad-looking, either. He was a snappy dresser, and he smelled good and Deja was fond of dark, chocolate brothers.

She fetched her cell phone from her purse and found his number in her contacts. He answered after three rings.

"Hello?"

"Hi," Deja said. "Is this Benton?"

"Yeah. Who's this?"

"My name is Deja. I'm the captain of the neighborhood watch in Pine View Apartments. I met you a few days ago."

"I remember. I was hoping to hear from you. I didn't think you'd call."

"I almost didn't," Deja admitted.

"How come?"

"'Cause I don't know you. A girl's got to be careful."

"You're right. There are a lot of weirdos out there."

"You have no idea," Deja said. "Were you busy?"

"No, just watching TV."

"I can't talk long," Deja said. "I have to get up early to do some patrolling. I just wanted to call and say hi."

"I'm glad you did. How's your neighborhood watch going? You meet a lot of interesting people doing that?"

"Interesting is one word for them."

"How does it work?" Benton asked. "Do you get people to stare out of their windows all day?"

"Some of them do. But most of us leave the house."

"Really?"

"The only thing you're going to see is what's going on outside of your window, if that's the only place you look," Deja explained.

"That's awesome," Benton said. "I admire people like you; activists, community organizers."

"I'm not an activist."

"Don't be afraid to be important. Your leadership skills is something that attracted me to you."

"Thanks," Deja said, blushing a little. "So, what about you? What do you do for a living?"

"I manage a Great Western overnight," Benton said. "It's boring. I read a lot."

"What do you read?"

"The encyclopedia mostly. I know something about almost every subject. My friends say I should go on Jeopardy. What about you? What do you do – other than look for creepazoids at night?"

Deja was impressed that he was a manager, and she was intrigued by his intelligence. "I work at an animal clinic. Do you really just pick up the encyclopedia and read?"

"Yeah."

"Like, from front to back?"

"Malcolm X read the dictionary front to back, but I can't read an encyclopedia? Ask me something."

"Something like what?"

He chuckled. "Something like anything."

191

Deja wasn't aware that her mouth hung open. "What's the lion's worst enemy?"

"Technically *man* is the lion's worst enemy," Benton said. "But since you said *what* instead of *who*, I suppose you're referring to the hyena."

"You're right. I got another one: What's the largest spider in the world?"

"Another animal question?"

"That's what I do," Deja said. "I have to ask about something I know."

"Fair enough. The largest spider in the world is the Goliath Birdeater, from the rainforests of South America."

"Amazing."

"I'm a Trivial Pursuit king," Benton boasted. "There's nothing better than learning."

"That's awesome."

"What are your special talents?" he asked.

Deja felt very inadequate all of a sudden. "I don't know. I don't have anything that impressive."

"You're being modest," Benton guessed. "What about the stuff you do on the streets? You've got to have some pretty good people skills to start a neighborhood watch."

"Yeah. I guess so."

"And you're a lot braver than me," he said. "There's no way I'm patrolling the streets at night. If I hear a noise in my place, I turn off the TV and crawl under the sheets."

Deja giggled. "You're kidding."

"No, I'm serious. The darkness is creepy. I've seen enough horror movies to know to stay inside. The ones who go outside, to *check things out,* are always the ones who get stabbed and sliced up. I'm like, *man,* it's not rocket science, people. Keep your brave tail in the house! They killing folks out there!"

Deja laughed. "And animals. I'm good with animals, too."

"That's another thing I can't do," Benton confided. "I like dogs, but if I got one and it crapped all over my floor, I'd take his butt to the pound."

"And when you leave, they'll probably kill him," Deja said. "The pound is one of the worst places you could take a dog."

"Nice," Benton said. "I like your passion. I can feel it."

"I'm sorry." Deja giggled. "I'm over here getting upset about a hypothetical dog."

"Do you have a pet?"

"No. My last dog was Roscoe. But he got killed, about a year and a half ago."

"How'd that happen?"

Deja sighed. "I didn't keep him in a kennel when I went to work, because Roscoe was a good dog. He didn't tear up the furniture or mess up the carpet. Plus I wasn't going to leave my baby in a cage for nine hours a day. I know a lot of people do that, but I didn't have the heart.

"Anyway, they had a leak in the apartment above mine, and they had to come in to see if I had any water damage. As soon as the maintenance guy opened my door, Roscoe shot between his legs. He was just running around, playing really, but the more they went after him, the more he ran.

"Out of all the streets he could've got killed on, I ended up finding him myself on the way home from work. Roscoe was just lying on the side of the road, already in rigor. Hardly any blood. Nobody cared enough to get my baby off the street."

"That's a real sad story."

"Yeah," Deja said and wiped her eyes with the back of her hand. She never talked about Roscoe for this very reason.

"You decided not to get another dog?"

"Not until I get a house," Deja said. "When I go to work, I don't want to leave a dog in a stuffy apartment. They would have a better time in the backyard, where they can run around and get some sun and chase squirrels and eat bugs. I think all Roscoe wanted was a little fresh air. Who can blame him?"

≈≈≈≈≈≈≈

They talked for almost an hour. Staying up past ten was a big No-No, but Deja wasn't tired when she woke up at a quarter till four. She didn't even need coffee. The conversation with Benton was still on her mind, and she felt excited and energized.

Deja met a lot of men in her lifetime, but none who immediately impressed her as much as Benton. Usually it was physical attraction that drove her desires. Deja thought it was much nicer to be attracted to someone's brain for a change.

≈ ≈ ≈ ≈ ≈ ≈ ≈

Her patrol with Bethany that morning went smoothly and quickly, without any major incidents to mar Deja's good mood. They took a few surveillance notes on Big Moe's operation, but it would be a while before they had enough evidence to turn over to the police.

Peaches was out and about again, but Deja didn't confront her or nag about going back to rehab. There would come a time in Peaches' life when she'd be sick and tired of feeling sick and tired. At that moment, Deja could try again.

She forgot to get her mail yesterday, so Deja checked her box at the end of their shift. Among the usual bills, she had a letter from Huntsman, Texas. She used to get letters from prison all the time when her brother was locked up, so Deja was familiar with the address. But Vincent was currently free, and this letter didn't come from an inmate. It came from a prison official.

Deja was so curious, she couldn't wait until she got home. She tore the letter open and read it slowly under the fluorescent light in her apartment's mailroom.

Dear Deja Franklin:

My name is Hubert Freeman. I'm a social worker for the Texas Department of Corrections. I'm currently stationed at the Piedmont unit in Huntsman, but I also work at the Terrell, Stiles, Duncan and Elmwood units. I'm writing with hopes that you would like to take part in a victim-offender reconciliation program called Ladders of Hope. The offender in your case is 36 year old Gilbert Reynolds. I've spoken with Mr. Reynolds personally on more than a dozen occasions, and he would very much like to meet with you to personally express his grief and remorse for the attack against your person. Mr. Reynolds is currently on Death Row awaiting an execution date years from now. He would like to make amends before the state takes his life away.

The Ladders of Hope victim-offender reconciliation program was initiated in 1984 by the Office for Prisoner and Community Justice of Methodist Charities. The program is designed to provide victims with an opportunity to meet with their offenders in a safe and structured setting for the purpose of dialogue, negotiation and problem solving. We've had much success with this program in Texas as well as prisons in Arizona, Minnesota, Louisiana and California. Offenders who participated in this program were less likely to commit violent crimes (in cases where they were released), and victims were significantly more likely to view the system as fair compared to victims who did not participate.

What I would like to know, Ms. Franklin, is if you believe this program is something you would like to participate in. I understand you may be angry with your offender, or you might be upset because the trial did not go the way you planned. These feelings are understandable. All we ask is for your consideration. Giving Mr. Reynolds an opportunity to unburden his guilt will do wonders to help his state of mind as he counts down his last days on earth, and getting an apology from him directly may help your understanding and overall satisfaction with the legal system.

I look forward to hearing from you. Thank you for your time and consideration.

Hubert Freeman

Deja read the letter a second time, still not believing what they were requesting. The thought of being in a room with Gilbert Reynolds sent chills through her entire body.

She took the letter to work but didn't have time to call the prison until lunchtime. Hubert Freeman was out of the office, but Deja got to speak to a prison chaplain who was familiar with the Ladders of Hope program. He introduced himself as Chuck Pearsons. His voice was gruff, with a strong southern twang.

"It's actually a beautiful thing," he told her. "Some of the offenders here, well, they were not very nice people out on the streets. Some didn't have a family, a religion, and they didn't give a darn about anyone they hurt.

"But, for some, things are different when they're in prison. They restore relationships with their family and start going to church. They have a lot of time to think about the bad things they did and the people they hurt.

"I've seen the worst of the worst, big, 300 pound men cry uncontrollably when they finally get the chance to apologize to their victim. The majority of the ones who participate in this program don't commit more violent crimes after they're paroled. Some do, but most don't."

"That's fine," Deja said. "But who came up with this idea? Did the social worker ask him to do it? Because I remember Gilbert didn't have anything to say to me in court."

"Mr. Reynolds heard about the program through other inmates," Chuck said. "He approached us with the idea. Gilbert is never going to be eligible for parole, so he has no motive to lie to us or you. I've spoken with him myself, and I do believe he is truly regretful and repentant. He's on death row. He knows he's going to die. He wants to get right with God, and he believes this is a necessary step in that process."

"Why should I help him get right with God?"

"Well, as a pastor I'm obligated to tell you that forgiveness is something God expects of you, Deja. I'm not saying you have to come here, but I do believe you should find a way to forgive Mr. Reynolds for what he did to you. He is going to die. There's no if ands or buts about it. It's possible that you need closure as much as he does."

Deja hadn't forgiven Gilbert for what he did to her. She didn't think she was ready to do that. "How do I know I'll be safe?"

"Well, the meeting would take place here at the prison. Mr. Reynolds will be brought in wearing arm and leg shackles. Four guards will remain in the room the whole time. It would be virtually impossible for Mr. Reynolds to harm you or even touch you during this encounter."

"Let me give it some thought," Deja said.

"Okay. I'll let Mr. Freeman know you called. God bless you, Ms. Franklin. You have a nice day."

Deja called her brother after that. She wasn't surprised Vincent was still asleep.

"Hello?" His voice was muffled and grumpy.

"Good morning," Deja said. "I didn't expect you to answer. Did your girlfriend have to go to work to keep a roof over your head?"

"Who is this?"

"This is your sister, fool."

"Call you back. I'm sleep."

"Boy, wake up! It's after twelve."

Deja listened to her brother humph and grunt as he rolled over and presumably sat up in bed.

"What's going on, Deja?"

"I got a letter from prison. They want me to go down there and meet with the strangler."

"Meet with him? What for?"

"It's a program they have," Deja said. "He wants to apologize, and it's supposed to make us both feel better. Or something."

"Fuck that nigga. Tell them to go to hell."

"I'm not doing that," Deja said with a nervous chuckle. "I'm gonna go. I wanted to know if you would go with me."

"Where, prison?"

"The same one you were in."

"I'm not going back there. I told them fools I would die before they saw my face again."

"This is different," Deja said. "You'll be a guest, and you can tell everybody to kiss your ass on the way out."

Vincent considered that. "That'd be cool. Okay. I guess I'll go. When is it?"

"I don't know. I gotta tell them I'll do it first."

"Alright."

"Hey," Deja said before he hung up. "What ever happened to that assault I bailed you out of jail for?"

"Dude dropped the charges after he found out I ain't got no money for him to sue for."

Deja laughed. "Wow. Being an unemployed freeloader finally paid off."

"I ain't no freeloader," Vincent said. "My girl know what she getting. She ain't never got to complain about this dick game I'm—"

"Eww!" Deja couldn't hang up on him quickly enough.

CHAPTER NINETEEN
ROAD TRIP

Deja called the prison back, and they scheduled her Ladders of Hope meeting for next Saturday – which gave her a little more than a week to think and dread and consider cancelling on a daily basis. She wasn't worried about her safety at the prison. But the idea of sitting across from the man who tried to choke the life from her made Deja apprehensive.

There was no denying Gilbert Reynolds was a dark and creepy individual. If Deja went to the prison, he would look her dead in the eyes with his sinister, shadowy orbs. He'd speak directly to her for the first time since the assault. And though his words would be apologetic, Deja would watch his mouth and remember the way his lips were flattened behind the panty hose. She would remember him threatening to harm her and her unborn child.

I'll kill you and the baby! If you scream again, I'll stab your stomach!

But even with these ominous thoughts, Deja didn't cancel the meeting. Deep down, she knew there was nothing to fear but fear itself. Gilbert Reynolds was the most notorious killer Overbrook Meadows had ever known. But he was locked up, and there was no way he was getting out.

He wouldn't waste his only opportunity to apologize with idle threats that would get him tazed by the prison guards. Deja believed he would behave like a perfect gentleman, because Gilbert knew this was his only shot to get it right. The fate of his eternal soul might be on the line. He would not squander his last chance to make amends.

≈≈≈≈≈≈≈

On Saturday, March 30th, Deja woke up at 3:45 a.m. and went about her regular routine of defending the neighborhood from the clutches of evil. When she got home, she had time to shower and iron her clothes before she got a telephone call from a new friend who had become quite endearing as of late.

"Hello?"

"Morning, Officer Deja," Benton said.

Deja grinned and checked the clock on her nightstand. It was 7:45.

"Hi."

"You busy? You're going to the prison today, right? Are you still nervous?"

Deja lay back in bed smiling pleasantly. Benton was always caring and interested in whatever was going on in her life.

"Yes, I'm going. And I'm still nervous. I don't know why. I don't feel like he'll try to hurt me, but I feel *something*. In the back of my mind, something's telling me not to go. Like something bad is gonna happen."

"I wouldn't go, if I felt like that."

"But I'm not good with premonitions," Deja said. "Every time I feel like something bad is *definitely* going to happen, nothing does."

"I never heard of women's intuition on the fritz."

"Me neither." Deja thought about the night she woke up and thought it was Jerome in her bed. "That's actually a bad thing, if you think about it."

"I'll bet it is," Benton agreed. "So, what are you going to tell this guy at the prison?"

"I was hoping he'd do most of the talking."

"Are you going to forgive him?"

"I don't know. I want to, but honestly, I don't know if I can. I'm still upset about it. I still have a lot of anger."

"Wouldn't it be cool if you don't forgive him, and then he goes to hell?"

"Nothing I do has any power over where he's going when he dies. God alone will make that decision."

"You're a good person to give him the opportunity to make it right," Benton said.

"Thanks. I try to be."

"But you're not a prude, right?"

"A prude?"

"I was wondering if you'd bring a chaperone when we go out."

Deja giggled. "*When* we go out? Don't you mean *if*?"

"I... Well, I, I guess I thought we..."

"Why would you think that? You never asked me out."

"Oh, but, you know, I tried."

"When?"

"Right now," Benton said. "I'm trying to ask you out right now. *Jeez.*"

"I'm just giving you a hard time," Deja said with a chuckle. "You're usually as cool as a cucumber. I've never seen you flustered before."

"You think I'm cool?"

"As a cucumber. Where do you want to go for our date?"

"Have you been to Kabash?"

"Never even heard of it."

"It's a Moroccan place on Hemphill. Do you like Moroccan food?"

Deja couldn't even find Morocco on a globe. "I never had it."

"Then you *got* to go," Benton said. "A first date with a new guy – you should have new food."

"Sounds great. When?"

"We can go tonight, if you want. Are you doing anything else today besides your meeting at the prison?"

"No, that's it. I should be back by five."

"You're not going to be stressed afterwards?"

Deja was wondering the same thing. "I should be alright."

"Okay. I'll call you around six."

"That's fine."

"What does, what's up with this guy you're meeting?" Benton asked. "What did he do, steal your car or something? When are you going to tell me about him? You're being so secretive."

"I don't mean to be secretive," Deja said. "I'll tell you all about him tonight. This is the kind of story that needs to be told in person."

"Okay. I look forward to it. Have a nice day, Deja."

"Thanks. You too."

She disconnected and called her brother.

"Hello?" It was his girlfriend.

"Hey," Deja said. "Is my brother there?"

"Yes, but he's still asleep."

"Can you get him up?"

"Sure."

The woman put the phone down. After an eternity, Vincent picked it up.

"Hello?" He was as groggy as usual.

"Wake up, boy."

"I'm woke. What's going on?"

"We're going to the prison today. You didn't forget, did you?"

"Naw. I'm good. What time are we going?"

"I'll pick you up at nine."

"What time is it?"

"It's eight."

"Alright. I'ma take me a quick nap. I'll be up by the time you get here."

≈≈≈≈≈≈≈

Vincent was not up by the time Deja got there. She waited in the living room, flipping through a hair style magazine, while her brother threw on some clothes.

"I'm almost ready," he called from the bedroom. "What time we gotta leave?"

"It takes four hours to get there," Deja told him. "We should've left at nine. It's already a quarter after."

"It's cool," Vincent yelled back. "Everybody there is waiting on us. It's not like they can have the meeting without you."

Deja subdued her irritation, because anytime she had dealings with Vincent it came with a *What did you expect?* clause.

Twenty minutes later they finally hit the road. Their destination was Huntsman, Texas, better known as far, far away. Deja didn't want to do all of the driving, but Vincent was dozing in the passenger seat by the time they passed the city limits.

Luckily Deja had a nice rotation of music in her CD changer, so she didn't get too bored with the endless lanes of highway. As the sun continued to rise in the eastern sky, her Sentra ate up mile after mile of interstate. She'd been to the prison a few times when her brother was locked up, and it never failed to impress her how big and beautiful Texas was. Most of the land was free of urban decay; just hills and trees and bluebonnets as far as the eye could see.

Vincent slept the whole 200 miles. He didn't stir until they got to Huntsman. Deja watched him sit up and wipe the sleep from his eyes. Huntsman was a small town that reminded her of the Andy Griffith Show. The prison was the biggest and most profitable business in the county.

"We already here?"

Deja turned down the radio. "Yeah, just about."

"I can tell," Vincent said. "I recognize this city."

"How?" Deja asked. "You only passed through here once on your way to prison, and one more time on your way out."

"If you'd ever been locked up, you'd understand."

"I guess..."

Vincent rubbed the hair under his chin and then nibbled his fingernail; something Deja rarely saw him do.

"People never forget their first bus ride to prison," he said. "They take you from county jail and put you on the road for hours, headed in this direction. Some of them dudes on the bus with me was veterans. They fell asleep as soon as we got on. But I couldn't sleep. I was scared to death. I wanted to know where I was, in case I wanted to escape."

"Escape?"

"That's all I was thinking about at the time."

"What happened to that plan?"

"Shit, I got to prison," Vincent said. "That's when I found out you *can't* escape from that motherfucker."

"What's prison like?"

Vincent shook his head. "It's like hell, lil sis. Imagine the biggest, meanest, stankiest and ugliest men you know, all locked

203

up together, eating together, going to the rec, taking showers together. Everybody's disappointed about what happened to their life or how nobody in the free world is supporting them. They feel like don't nobody care anymore. That anger makes them want to take it out on somebody, and nobody fights fair. If somebody fucks with you, you have to fight back. But then you might get jumped. But if you *don't* fight back, shit gets even worse. They'll take your money and snacks and shit for the rest of the time you're there. If somebody thinks you're cute, they might take even more than that.

"And you still got the guards to deal with. Them motherfuckers can make your time go by real slow. They used to make us cut the whole lawn with a hoe – in hundred degree heat. They had lawnmowers in the shed, but we had to use a hoe. The guards can make you strip naked, bend over and cough whenever they feel like it. They be beating on niggas, too; sending them to the infirmary with missing teeth and shit."

"If it's so bad, why do people go right back?"

"'Cause prison trains you to be a criminal," Vincent said. "You put a nigga in a cage with some more niggas that's been in there for ten, fifteen, sometimes twenty years. What you expect gon' happen?"

Vincent kept talking before Deja could offer her guess.

"He gon' turn into an animal, just like the rest of them," he said. "And then you parole that animal to the streets – to the very same block you arrested him on. Only now he got a felony on his record, so even if he wanted a job, he can't get one. What you expect him to do then?"

"Buckle down and try harder?" Deja ventured.

Vincent grinned at her. "That's the problem right there, sis. Some niggas don't know *how* to buckle down and try harder. If they was responsible, they never would've went to prison in the first place. Everybody knows prison fucks people up way worse than they were before they got there. But the white man gotta keep us under his thumb some kinda way."

Deja knew *the white man* was going to be the ultimate culprit in her brother's story. She didn't doubt what he was saying, but if you know the truth and still allow yourself to be a pawn in the white man's game, then how could you continue to blame anyone but yourself?

They drove for another fifteen miles, and finally Deja saw the prison looming in the horizon. The Piedmont unit was colossal. It was a fortress made of bricks, steel, concrete and bulletproof glass. The perimeter walls were topped with not one, not two, but three rows of razor wire that glistened in the sunlight.

Outside of the perimeter walls, there were three rows of chain-link fence that looked to be over twenty feet tall. Each fence was topped with barbed wire, and there was more skin-slicing razor wire coiled on the ground between them. If an escapee did manage to get past all of that, they also had guard towers with bored gunmen who would brag for months if they actually got a chance to shoot someone.

Deja shook her head and gave her brother a sideways look. "I can't believe you'd try to escape from here."

"I said I *thought* about it," Vincent said. "I never said I was dumb enough to try it."

≈≈≈≈≈≈≈

Deja found a parking spot, and they made it inside the prison twenty minutes late for her meeting. A guard at the information desk directed them to the chaplain's office where Deja met up with the man who wrote her Ladders of Hope letter. Hubert Freeman was tall and red-headed. He jumped from his desk and went around to shake Deja's hand.

"Well, hello! I didn't think you were going to make it." Hubert had rosy cheeks and a baby face.

"I'm sorry," Deja said. "I would've been here on time, if it wasn't for this knucklehead." She gestured towards Vincent, and the chaplain stared at him for a second.

"I know you," Hubert said. "I never forget a face, and I know yours. Have we met before?"

"Naw," Vincent said. "I don't know you."

"Are you sure?" Hubert narrowed his eyes. "I *never* forget a face." He was too polite to ask if Vincent had ever been locked up, and Vincent was too much of an asshole to disclose the information.

"Nope," he said again. "Never met you."

"Oh. Okay," the social worker said. "You must have a twin somewhere." He leaned back on his heels, smiling with his hands in his pockets. "Oh, well, I guess we'd better get started." He motioned for them to exit the way they came. "Right this way."

Hubert led them to another room that was a lot smaller and less cheery than his office. Rather than a couch and desk, there was only a table and chairs in there. On one side of the table were two wooden chairs with padding in the seats. On the other side was one metal chair that was bolted to the floor. It didn't have any padding, and it didn't look comfortable at all.

The side with the metal chair also had rings on the floor and table, presumably to chain down the human animals they were confining in the back. The walls in the room were completely white. There were no windows.

"If you guys want to take a seat on that side," Hubert said, "I'll go and fetch Gilbert for you. When we get back, we're going to enter through this door. Gilbert will have four guards with him. They'll shackle him down to the table and floor, and they will remain in the room throughout the meeting. I will, too.

"If you should feel stressed or uncomfortable at any point, and you would like to end the meeting, simply rise from your seat and approach me. We'll remove Gilbert from the room first, and then you can leave – but I'm sure that won't be necessary. Do you have any questions?"

Deja didn't, and neither did Vincent.

"Alright. You two take a seat. I'll be right back."

Hubert left the room with a pep in his step, and Deja and her brother took their places. While he was gone, Vincent tried to lighten the mood with humorous stories about his stay at the prison, but Deja told him to be quiet after a while. Getting her to laugh or even smile was impossible. She had a strong inclination to run, *right now*, as far away from the prison as she could. Who cared if Gilbert found Jesus and finally saw the error of his ways? Deja couldn't come up with one single reason why this was a good idea. What the hell was she thinking?

Not too many sounds made it to their little white room. Deja grew more tense with each second that passed. Her heart knocked, and her breathing became shallow.

Vincent noticed her distress. "Calm down," he said. "Ain't nothing gon' happen."

But he was wrong about that, and Deja knew it.

By the time they heard the distinct rattle of chains – a sound Deja still remembered from the pre-trial hearing – fourteen minutes had passed. Deja drew in a sharp breath when the room's only door swung open. The social worker stepped in first. Behind him was a crowd of men. Four of them wore black uniforms. One of them wore a bright orange jumpsuit.

Gilbert Reynolds looked the same as Deja remembered. But at the same time, he was completely different. He was in the big house now, and they didn't allow afros or beards. This was the first time Deja had seen him with short hair and no facial stubble. The minor change made him look ten times more presentable.

Deja also thought his skin tone was lighter than she remembered it. She knew that a full year with little sunshine could do that to a person. Gilbert's nose was wide and flat, his eyes small and beady. His thick lips were set in an expression Deja hadn't seen on his face before. For the first time ever, she thought he looked frightened and timid, unsure but hopeful. He locked eyes with Deja in the doorway and she became his only focal point from that moment on.

The strangler's wrists were cuffed together in front of his body. The manacles had a chain that was fastened to a leather belt that fit over his jumpsuit. More chains snaked from the belt down to his feet, where another set of shackles limited his movements to a shuffle.

Gilbert brought the smell of *prison* in with him. It was faint, but you couldn't miss it. It was the smell of sweat, urine, body odor and blood. He smelled like linen that needed to be burned rather than laundered. The scent was so acrid, Deja thought it singed the hairs in her nostrils. Breathing through her mouth offered some relief, but then Deja felt like she could *taste* his stink. Her mouth filled with saliva, and she fought to keep the contents of her stomach down.

The guards led Gilbert to the table. Deja had tunnel vision by then. She couldn't say whether the guards were black or white, fat or skinny. Her eyes were transfixed on the inmate's, just as his were fixed on her. When he sat down, Deja began to push away from the table unconsciously. Her chair made a loud *SCRUURR* sound as it scraped on the floor. Vincent looked over and saw the terror in her eyes. He saw her chest rising and falling at uneven intervals. He reached into Deja's lap and held her hand. She didn't notice the gesture. Suddenly her mouth was completely dry. She felt a dusty *CLICK* in her throat when she tried to swallow. It felt like her hyoid bone was still broken.

Gilbert broke eye contact and looked around nervously as they fastened his chains to the table and floor. Two guards stood on either side of him. They worked diligently and watched the prisoner carefully, lest he try something stupid. Hubert Freeman stood at the head of the table with a self-satisfied grin.

Only Deja was watching the killer's eyes. What she saw made a soft wail float up her windpipe and rattle in her voice box. What she saw was not a look of remorse or the look of someone who wanted to ask for forgiveness. Gilbert's eyes were low and furtive. Deja's whole body became frigid and numb.

She opened her mouth to tell them she no longer wanted to do this, she didn't give a damn about Gilbert's ladder of hope, but it was too late. The guards secured the last locks and stepped away from the table. Hubert sauntered forward to start the meeting, and that's when Gilbert made his move.

He rose from his seat. The chains went taut before he could stand fully, but that was all the lift he needed. He leaned over the table so quickly, all they saw was an orange blur. His wrist shackles prevented him from breaching the halfway point of the table, but he managed to thrust his face within two feet of Deja's. All of this happened in the split second it took her to inhale sharply. As the guards rushed to him, Gilbert began to scream.

"I DIDN'T DO NOTHING TO YOU, DEJA FRANKLIN! *I DON'T KNOW YOU!* **YOU GOT TO TELL THEM IT WASN'T ME! THEY'RE GOING TO KILL ME FOR** *NOTHING!* **YOU KNOW IT WASN'T ME!** *YOU KNOW IT WASN'T!***"**

His breath smelled like fish and peanut butter. A few flecks of spittle flew from his mouth and landed on Deja's cheek and forehead. She recoiled like it was acid. By the time a scream escaped her lips, the guards had the strangler by the arms, and Vincent rose to his feet with fire in his eyes.

Vincent swung only once. His arm and shoulder rose and fell so smoothly, Deja wasn't sure if he actually moved. His punch connected perfectly with the strangler's chin, and the lights in Gilbert Reynolds' brain went out instantly, like someone flipped a switch.

The strangler fell forward, his head rolling loosely on his thick neck. He would've fallen face first onto the table, but the guards pulled him back against the metal chair. Gilbert's shoulders slumped. His chin came to a bumpy rest between his clavicles.

Outside of TV, Deja had never seen a man knocked out cold with one punch. She really didn't see it then, because she was too busy screaming. She pushed away from the table so forcefully, her chair rocked and fell backwards. Her legs flew into the air. Her arm's flailed like helicopter blades as she tried to regain her balance. Before she hit the floor, Deja had time to understand that she was going to die. Everything in the prison was hard and brutal, and when her head impacted the hard floor, soft things would come out.

But Vincent grabbed her arm, and Deja held onto him for dear life. The chair continued to fall out from under her. It crashed loudly on the concrete, but Deja staggered to her feet before hitting the floor herself. She continued to scramble away from the table until she encountered an unyielding wall. Her pulse thumped so hard, she felt every single blood cell rushing through her veins. Vincent threw his arms around her and obstructed her view of the table and the unconscious killer still bound to it.

"*Get that motherfucker out of here!*" he shouted over his shoulder. "*What kind of shit y'all got going in here*?!"

The guards were just as jumbled as everyone else. They were unaccustomed to taking orders from civilians, but they quickly undid the strangler's restraints and drug him from the room with his chains and lifeless legs trailing behind him. The social worker didn't break his paralysis until they were almost gone.

"*Oh my God, Deja.*" He ran to them with his mouth hanging open. He was completely pale. "I am so sorry! *Oh, oh, dear Lord. I am so sorry!*"

CHAPTER TWENTY
PRETTY RED DRESS

Deja didn't think they would ever get out of there.

From her vantage point, the unfortunate incident looked like an open and shut case of cause and effect: The Sleeping Strangler caused a commotion, which in effect brought about physical violence. Deja didn't expect her brother to hit him. She didn't condone it either, but what was done was done. If anyone was going to get punished for the ordeal, she thought it should be Gilbert Reynolds.

But Gilbert wasn't around anymore. He got dragged away to somewhere far from the little white room with no windows. He was probably still snoring, with a contusion growing on his jaw and bloody saliva bubbles bursting between his teeth.

And while all of that was regretful, Deja thought she and her brother should be able to go on about their business. Unfortunately that's not how things worked down at the Piedmont unit. They had rules and procedures. Things had to be documented when there were *incidents of violence* – especially when they involved a civilian.

Hubert, the cherry-cheeked social worker, tried to allay Deja's irritation. He apologized profusely and asked her to return to her seat, but she wouldn't.

"I wanna go home."

"Okay, Deja. We're going to let you go as soon as we can. The assistant warden is on his way down. He wants to take care of a few paperwork issues first."

"Fuck your paperwork!" Vincent spat. He lunged forward and put his finger in the chaplain's face. "You brought us down

210

here for some bullshit! Man, we finna go." He grabbed Deja's wrist and pulled her towards the exit. But the doorway was blocked by one of the guards. "Move!" Vincent ordered. "Get out the way, man."

"Sir, could y'all please go back to your seats?" The guard was tall and chubby, with dark hair and gray eyes.

"We ain't gotta sit down," Vincent barked. "You can't make me. You done let this man come up in here and yell at my sister like that. You know y'all wrong. *Move*!"

The guard folded his arms defiantly. "Sir, you assaulted one of our inmates—"

"He jumped in my sister's face!"

"He was not a threat to her at any time."

"He looked like a threat to me! We didn't know what he was gon' do. Move, man! You can't hem us up like this!"

"Sir, we are not hemming you up. The assistant-warden's on his way down. He wants to hear your side of the story. We need to fill out a report—"

"Forget your report!"

"This is my last time asking." The guard spoke calmly. "Would you please take your seat, until the warden gets here?"

"This some bullshit!"

"Let's just wait," Deja said.

"Naw, Deja. Fuck these people!"

"Oh dear," the chaplain bawled. "Oh, please stop. *Please*. Oh, oh, oh dear."

≈ ≈ ≈ ≈ ≈ ≈

Things went a lot smoother when the assistant-warden got there, but Deja understood her brother's aggravation. All she wanted was to go home. Every second she was not allowed to do so made her feel like she had somehow become an inmate at the prison.

"I don't see why y'all are blaming us," she explained. "He yelled at me and lunged at me. Everybody saw him."

"I didn't say we were blaming you," the warden said. He was short and stocky with deep, blue eyes. "I just want to hear what happened, get your side of the story, get you guys to sign a few papers, and then you're free to leave. I don't want Mr.

Reynolds to wake up and sue me, and I don't want y'all to take me to court either. We need to get everything settled right now, before you two leave."

Deja thought that sounded more like a threat than a compromise.

"We don't have to sign shit," Vincent growled.

"I don't want to argue anymore," Deja told him. She was exasperated. The stress was clearly taking a toll on her. "Let's just get this over with. I wanna go home."

Vincent relented and allowed the assistant-warden to take care of his business.

By the time everyone got their stories told and their papers signed, forty-five minutes had passed. Deja felt like she got paroled, when she finally walked out of the prison.

"We shouldn't have signed them papers," Vincent said when they got in the car. "I didn't even read that shit. Did you?"

"Yeah." Deja fastened her seat belt and started the car at the same time. "Basically we don't hold the prison responsible for anything negative that happened."

"Man, I knew we shouldn't have signed. Now we can't sue."

"I don't care about suing," Deja said. "It's not even worth it. I just wanted to *leave*. I hope you never get locked up again, because I'm not coming back here, Vincent. You hear me?"

He laughed. "Don't worry. I ain't never getting locked up again."

Given his explosive temper, Deja had a hard time believing that. She let out a huge sigh of relief as she piloted her Sentra through the prison's main gates. She wanted to speed away but was afraid a hillbilly cop might arrest her and send them back to the prison.

"That strangler was crazy, wasn't he?" Vincent asked. "What'd you think about that shit he was saying?"

"It gives me chills," Deja said. "I'm freaking out right now, just thinking about it."

"Why? You believe him?"

"No, but you got to take a minute to at least consider it, right?"

"If you say so."

"You don't think so?"

Vincent shook his head. "I don't see no point in that."

"What about the way he sounded, the look in his eyes? He didn't sound like he was lying. I'm, I really don't know if he was."

"That wasn't nothing but acting," Vincent declared. "You have to remember, there hasn't been *one* person killed since that fool got arrested. If he wasn't the strangler, then who is? And how come they haven't killed nobody else?"

"Shannon thinks Jerome is the strangler."

"*Jerome?*"

Deja explained her friend's theory.

When she was done, Vincent shook his head. "Uh-uhn. I don't see that. A clean cut nigga like Jerome committing all them murders?"

"There's something else," Deja said. "I didn't think about this until I bought my new pistols. Whoever attacked me that night took off before I got my gun out. I jumped out of bed and headed for my dresser. By the time I turned around, they were gone. Jerome was, like, the only person who knew where I kept my gun."

"That was a hunch," Vincent said matter-of-factly. "Most everybody keeps their gun in a nightstand, somewhere close to the bed. That's weird you think Jerome would do that to you. He a dumb ass, but he got a coward's heart."

"I didn't say I thought he did it," Deja clarified. "That's Shannon's idea."

"So, what do you think?" Vincent asked. "You think they got the right one, or do you think you put an innocent man in jail?"

Asked in that format, Deja had to go with the option that didn't make her look like a fool. "I think they got the right guy. But the way he acted, it just makes me think, is all I'm saying."

"Don't even worry about it," Vincent advised. "That fool is crazy." He slumped in his seat and closed his eyes. "Say, didn't you have some Rick James on earlier?"

"Yeah."

"Play that shit. Are we gon' stop somewhere to eat?"

"I'm going out to dinner when I get back."

"With who?"

"This guy I met."

Vincent looked over at her and smiled. "Good. It's about time. Well, can you stop to get *me* something to eat then?"

213

Before Deja could respond, he told her, "I don't have no money."

Deja rolled her eyes and put in the CD he requested. As she drove, she was quiet and contemplative. Stamping Gilbert Reynolds as CRAZY was one way to put this behind her, but was it the truth? Other than the murders, he never seemed crazy before. Even his defense attorneys never tried to avoid the death penalty by playing the insanity card.

The fact that Deja had doubts beforehand made Gilbert's outburst that much worse. The social worker said Gilbert initiated the Ladders of Hope conversations. Why would he want her to come all the way to prison for a three second rant? Were these the actions of a crazy man who deserved to die but would try his best to avoid it? Or was this the last-ditch effort of an innocent man who had exhausted all other avenues and could not bear to die for crimes he did not commit?

Deja couldn't live with herself if she caused an innocent man to die. Rather than drive herself crazy with *what ifs*, she let it go for now. They had seventeen months before Gilbert was scheduled to be executed. If they were wrong, she was sure more clues would come to light by then.

≈≈≈≈≈≈≈

When she got home, Deja picked up her son from Ms. Gladys and took a long, hot shower while Adrian bounced in his baby walker. It felt good to get the prison funk off her skin and out of her hair. But when she got out, it occurred to her that she could still smell Gilbert's fishy peanut butter breath. The thought made her gag.

She thought she should cancel her plans for the evening, but Benton sounded so hopeful when he called at six.

"Hello?"

"Hello! Glad you're back. How'd it go?"

"It went terrible."

"Really? What happened?"

"He didn't apologize," Deja explained. "I don't think he ever wanted to. He just started yelling at me."

"Yelling? About what?"

"He said he didn't do it. He wanted me to tell the truth, so he could get out."

There was a pause on the other end of the line.

"That's crazy," Benton said. "Wha, what was that all about?"

"I don't know," Deja said. "It was scary. My brother got in a fight with him."

"No..."

"Well, he hit him. It wasn't really a fight."

"Why would that guy go through all this trouble?" Benton asked. "I thought he was already sentenced. Is he up for appeal, or something? When is he getting out?"

"He's not getting out," Deja moaned. "He's on death row – because of me."

"*For what?*" Benton sounded appalled.

"I told you, we can talk about it when I see you."

"But, are you, are we still going out tonight? You sound like you should take it easy."

"No, I don't mind going," Deja said. "I don't want to sit at home by myself, thinking about all of this mess."

"Are you sure?"

"Yes," she said. "I would still like to go out with you tonight."

"Okay. Alright." Benton sighed. "If you're sure. What time do you want to have dinner?"

"We can go at seven, but I need to be back by nine-thirty."

"That's fine. Do you want me to pick you up, or–"

"I'll meet you," Deja said. "Give me directions to the restaurant."

≈ ≈ ≈ ≈ ≈ ≈

Benton gave her directions, and Deja realized she was familiar with the area. When they got off the phone, she put on an outfit that had been marinating in her closet for much too long.

The dress was chili pepper red with a V-neckline and an empire waist. It wasn't tight, but it tied in the back and accentuated her breasts and hips. She admired herself in the mirror and stepped into a pair of open-toed sandals. She couldn't remember the last time she felt genuinely sexy. It was a great feeling.

Deja dropped her son off with her mom and arrived at the restaurant a few minutes after seven. The place was small, about the size of a two story house. Deja thought it had actually been converted from a residence. Out front, they had a huge business sign with lettering Deja recognized as Arabic. Under the foreign letters, the word *KABASH* was printed in beautiful calligraphy.

The parking lot was less than half full, so Deja parked close to the entrance. When she got out of her car, someone exited another vehicle three spots down. It was Benton. Deja's heart smiled at the sight of him.

"Hey, Dej– oh my goodness." A big smile lit his face as he approached. Benton wore a collar shirt tucked into khaki slacks. His shoes were shiny and hard-soled. His dark skin glowed under the fading sunlight. "Wow. I didn't know I was going out with a princess," he said.

Deja's grin was so big her dimples showed. "Oh, go on."

"Go on? Okay." Benton grinned, too. "That red makes you look very sexy. You got legs for days. Your hair is beautiful. Your eyes are captivating. Your–"

"Okay, that's enough," Deja said with a giggle.

"Are you sure? I really could go on for days."

"Maybe later," Deja said. She took a deep breath. The air was cool and refreshing in her hot lungs. "I never had Moroccan food before."

"I'll help you pick a meal." He held the door open for her and wolfed her down with his eyes as she passed through. "My, my, my..." he said and followed her inside.

Deja knew she was attractive, but it had been a while since someone made her feel this special. Benton was growing on her by the minute.

The restaurant was quiet and dimly lit. There weren't a lot of customers, so Benton had no problem getting them a secluded booth near the back. Romance was definitely in the air. Deja had never heard of anything on the menu. Benton made good on his promise to order for her.

For an appetizer, they had grape leaves – which turned out to be real grape leaves stuffed with rice, tomatoes, mint and parsley. For her entrée, Deja had *chicken brochette*. Benton had *tangine of lamb.* Deja had never tried lamb before, so she sampled a little of his. She found it delightful. Her meal was delicious as well.

After eating, Deja finally told her new friend why she went to the prison and the sordid story that led up to the visit. Benton was positively floored – so much so, Deja wondered if he would accept her afterwards. He remained silent while she described Gilbert's antics during today's meeting.

"I talked to my brother on the way home," she said. "He thinks it was a trick. He says you can't believe anything a man on death row says."

Benton nodded vaguely. "Yeah, that, that's probably right."

Deja cocked her head. "What's wrong? That was a lot, right?"

He nodded. "Yes. It was, that was a, um, quite a story." He shook his head and sighed. "You, my God, Deja. You've been through a lot."

"It's not so bad," she said. "I feel like I'm a stronger person because of it. The way I stood up to him, a lot of people admire me because of that. And because of the neighborhood watch, I'm not afraid of the dark anymore. You should've seen me before all of this happened. I used to be so weak."

Benton smiled. "Weak is the last word I would use to describe you."

Deja smiled, too. "Thanks. That really means a lot to me."

He looked away for a second. "So, what happens now? I, I really don't know what to say about your, situation. I mean, I admire you. But..."

Deja's heart sank. "But what?"

"But, that's such an awful thing to go through. I don't have the words to express my sympathy."

"Do you still want to talk to me?"

"Well, yeah." Benton looked like this was common sense. "Of course I do."

"Then you don't have to say anything about the strangler," Deja said. "We don't have to talk about him again. I don't want you to feel sorry for me. That's my past, and I want to leave it in the past."

Her date grinned. "Okay. If that's how you want it."

"It is," Deja said. "Now it's your turn."

217

"My turn to what?"

"Tell me a story about you."

Benton put his elbows on the table and rested his chin on his fists. "You know, you have such pretty lips."

"Why thank you," she said and licked them subconsciously.

≈≈≈≈≈≈

At nine o'clock Deja checked her watch and was not happy to see that it was time to go. Benton walked her to her car like a proper gentleman. Unfortunately he did not attempt the hug and kiss Deja had been longing for.

"I had a good time," he said instead. "I hope to see you again."

"Me too," Deja replied. "I'll talk to you later."

Sometimes my nightmares be stalking
Up out of my bed I'm sleepwalking
Cries filled with dread
Just like my life
But I keep my head up regardless
Cause the enemy's looking to take my head off
If I'm weak in this slaughter
The enemy's looking to make me backslide
If I slip in this water

CHAPTER TWENTY-ONE
JUSTICE FOR GILBERT REYNOLDS

Deja woke up at 2:32 a.m.

She woke up completely.

The cause of her stirring was not immediately clear. But she sat up in bed and listened, and then she heard it again. Something went *bump* in the night. It was faint, but it was real. It sounded like it came from somewhere in the house.

Deja was immediately alert. Her heart grew icy, but her mind wasn't filled with panic or overwhelming fear. If someone was breaking in, that was a problem, but every problem had a solution. The solution to this one would be a gravely wounded crackhead if Deja caught a prowler inside her home. It would be a hard lesson learned for some unlucky sap, but the lesson wasn't just for him. It was also for the next guy who might consider following in the intruder's footsteps.

Deja looked to the crib as the hairs stood on her arms and legs. Her eyes adjusted to the darkness, and she saw her son fast asleep, lying on his side. Last month she thought about getting a bigger apartment, so the baby could have his own room. Now she was grateful she didn't follow through with the plan. It would drive her crazy if Adrian wasn't within eyesight at a time like this.

With her son's safety confirmed, Deja's next move was for her pistol. She slid out of bed as quietly as she could while listening for more sounds. She kept her eyes on the bedroom door, moving slowly, so the intruder wouldn't be alerted to the fact that she was alerted to him.

She made it to the floor and crouched on the balls of her feet. She crept to the nightstand and pulled it open. Once the .357 was in her hand, everything changed. The playing field was not just equal, but the advantage had shifted. Even if the intruder had a weapon, Deja had home field advantage. And he probably wasn't expecting his victim to ambush him.

Once outside the bedroom, Deja heard the sound again. This time she recognized it as a *scrape* rather than a bump or bang. It definitely came from the kitchen, and she was pretty sure it originated at the back door. She took a deep breath and the fear began to rise again. She pulled the hammer back on her firearm, and that made it subside.

Deja looked back inside her bedroom and spied her radio on the dresser. She could go for it now and alert whoever was on patrol at that time. That would be Lupe and Ana, a boyfriend/girlfriend crew of interminable insomniacs. The only problem with that was Deja would have to speak above a whisper, and her crew would respond on the squawky radio. The burglar would no doubt hear them.

So she ignored the radio and headed for the kitchen. The hallway was carpeted, so her footsteps made no sound. She kept her gun pointed in front of her, with her head low and her eyes wide. She reached a bathroom on her right. The door was half open, and it was very dark in there.

Deja was positive the noise she heard came from beyond this point, but she had to check. Allowing someone to get behind her was not an option. She pushed the door in as slowly as possible, but the rusty hinges betrayed her. They emitted a loud *SCRUUEEEK* that sounded like a scream in the quiet apartment. Deja winced and froze and craned her ear towards the kitchen.

There were no sounds.

"Dammit," she whispered. She swung her gun briefly into the restroom and did a quick search. She left her shower curtain open – thank God for small favors – and was able to see the room was empty. She trained her gun down the hallway again but sensed her window of opportunity had closed. If the bathroom door was as loud as she thought it was, the intruder would be long gone by now.

With that in mind, Deja picked up the pace while remaining cautious and observant. She didn't find an intruder in the kitchen. She backed into the refrigerator and scanned every corner. There was nothing. She hurried to the living room and did another sweep. Again she came up empty.

Deja rounded the couch and reentered the kitchen from the dining room. She checked the backdoor and found it secure. She lifted one of the blinds on the small window. Again, nothing. Still not believing she was crazy, Deja undid the deadbolt and stepped out into the shadowy night. She looked to the right and to the left. Her building's exterior lights were as bright as ever. She saw no human or non-human forms lurking amidst the dark shrubs and bone colored trees.

She lowered her gun and walked a quick lap around her building. When she got back to her apartment, her hopes were dashed, but her confidence was soaring. She didn't know if she chased the intruder away, or if he was never there to begin with. But she did know that she could hold her own, which was almost as good as catching the bastard.

She couldn't get back to sleep when she got inside, so Deja got on the radio to check on her two a.m. team.

"Hey, Lupe, you there?"

After a few moments he responded. "Hel, hello? Miss Deja? Is that you?" There was giggling in the background.

"Yeah, it's me."

"What are you doing up so early?"

"I thought I heard somebody at my door. Do you mind coming over, to check around the building for a minute?"

"Yeah, we'll be right there." More giggling.

"What's going on?" Deja asked. "Where are you now?"

"I'm at home," Lupe said. "Me and Ana – stop."

"Are you too busy to do your patrolling?" Deja asked, slightly perturbed.

"No," Lupe said. "Why you say that?"

"Because someone could be screaming for help out there, while you and Ana are playing kissy-face."

After a pause, Lupe said, "Alright. We're on our way."

≈≈≈≈≈≈≈

The couple knocked on her door twenty minutes later. Deja invited them inside for coffee and teacakes. Afterwards, the three of them did some real patrolling. They didn't find anyone suspicious hanging around Deja's building or evidence that anyone had ever been there.

Deja checked again when it was time for her watch shift at four. She and Bethany had the same results. It was windy that morning, so Deja conceded that she might have heard the branches of nearby trees scraping together as they swayed in the breeze.

At six am she picked up her baby from Miss Gladys and went home to catch the early bird news. They were running a new story about a guy named Gilbert Reynolds. Deja was immediately glued to her television.

Channel Six anchorman Chad Collins sat alone behind the news desk. Deja couldn't tell if he was upset because he had to wake up at such an hour, or if it was the solemn news he was delivering that made him appear gloomy. Either way, Deja's expression soon matched his somberness.

She sat on the edge of the couch with her baby napping on the cushion next to her. She brought a hand to her mouth and subconsciously gnawed on her longest manicured nail. Deja thought she had 17 months to get to the bottom of Gilbert Reynolds' outburst. But as fate would have it, she actually had less than 17 hours.

"Alright folks," Chad was saying, "if you're just joining us, we're bringing you breaking news on Overbrook Meadows' most notorious serial killer: Gilbert Reynolds, AKA *the Sleeping Strangler*, is dead."

In case anyone misheard, a huge crawler began to scroll across the bottom of the screen: **SLEEPING STRANGLER GILBERT REYNOLDS FOUND DEAD... SLEEPING STRANGLER GILBERT REYNOLDS FOUND DEAD... SLEEPING STRANGLER...**

"Early reports from the prison," Chad said, "indicate the strangler committed suicide sometime between Saturday evening and Sunday morning. Autopsy results are pending, but according to information provided by the prison, guards found Gilbert Reynolds alone in his cell. He was unresponsive, and he had torn sheets fastened into a noose that was wrapped around his neck."

Chad wore a light-gray button-down with a dark tie. His hair was perfect. His eyes were a chilling blue.

"For more information on this story," Chad said, "let's go to Jessica Serrano, who is on the scene. Jessica, what can you tell us about Mr. Reynolds' death?"

The view switched from a solo shot of Chad to a split screen of him and a pretty reporter Deja recognized from her own interview on Channel Six News.

"Hi, Chad," Jessica said and the view changed to a shot of only her. "I'm standing outside of the warden's office at Texas Department of Corrections Piedmont Unit in Huntsman."

Deja was surprised to see a hallway she recognized. She was even more shocked to see the assistant warden she and her brother argued with yesterday. He was wearing black slacks with a white shirt and tie. He looked downright sociable, but it was the same good old boy who refused to let Deja and her brother leave the prison until they signed a form that stated no one was at fault for their troubling incident.

"I'm here with assistant-warden Charles Matheson," Jessica said. "Mr. Matheson, what can you tell us about what happened?"

"Well, ain't much to tell," the warden said. "Mr. Reynolds had been upset for quite a while, ever since they brought him to death row, really. He didn't eat much, and he didn't talk much. But we never had any indication that he required suicide precautions. We didn't get no warning like that from the courts, and we didn't get it from his lawyers neither." The cowboy gave the camera a smug and self-satisfied nod.

"In any event," he said, "we kept him pretty safe up there, like we do for all our inmates on death row. But some things can't be avoided. We can't take his clothes and sheets from him, 'cause that's unconstitutional. We do make sure they don't have anywhere up high to tie their sheet or garments onto, but sometimes that ain't enough. If a man wants to kill hisself, I reckon he can find a way to do it.

"From what I understand, Mr. Reynolds rigged his sheet on the sink somehow and wrapped it around his neck. He just sat there and slumped or leaned away from it. His butt was on the ground the whole time."

"How long would something like that take?" the reporter asked.

"Sorry, but I ain't no doctor," the warden said.

Newsflash, Deja thought.

"But I guess it wouldn't take too long," he continued. "Once you cut off your circulation and pass out, the brain will die within a few minutes, if it don't get no oxygen. I can't say that's exactly how it happened with this one, but that's what we're figuring."

"Were there any incidents recently?" Jessica asked. "Did anything happen that might have upset Mr. Reynolds last night?"

Deja's mouth fell open, and she held her breath until he answered.

"Naw," Mr. Matheson said. He stared right at the camera with the coldest blue eyes Deja had ever seen. "Things like this, if the inmate is serious, we won't get no warning, because they know we'll stop 'em. This is a private thing a man keeps to hisself, until it's time to do the do. I reckon the only person he told about it was God, and God told him to go on and do it."

His response was so callous, it even gave the reporter pause.

"Al, alright," she said and turned back to the camera. "Chad, it looks like we aren't going to get any more information until an autopsy is completed – which I'm told will not take place until later on today. The guards searched Mr. Reynolds' cell from top to bottom. If they found more evidence, they are not saying at this time."

"Thanks, Jessica. You do good work," Chad told her and the view switched back to him in the newsroom. "Alright, if you're just joining us, we're reporting on the death of convicted serial killer Gilbert Reynolds, better known to Overbrook Meadows as the Sleeping Strangler. For those of you not familiar with the case, here is a recap of his capture, capital murder trial and death sentence just one year ago..."

224

The station launched into a pre-recorded segment, and Deja's phone rang. She jumped at the sound and reached back for it with her eyes glued to the screen.

"Hello?"

"Baby?" It was her mother.

"Hi, Mama."

"Child, what are you doing? Are you watching the news?"

"Yes," Deja said. A cold numbness rolled down her chest and through all of her limbs. "I'm watching it right now."

"Girl, ain't that a mess," Shirley said. "Didn't you just go see him yesterday?"

"Yeah," Deja said, wondering if it was her visit that sparked Gilbert's suicidal ideation.

"How you taking it?" Shirley asked. "Are you there by yourself?"

"Yes, just me and the baby."

"Why don't you come over here," her mom asked. "You know those reporters will be back. Everybody is gonna want to know how you feel about it."

As if that was a premonition, Deja's phone vibrated against her ear. She checked the display and saw Tamara's name on the caller ID.

"Hey, Mama, let me call you right back."

"Alright, baby. Are you going to come over here? You can come after church. I'll make a big dinner and invite everybody. Ain't nothing better than to be around family."

"Alright," Deja said. "I'll come after church. I'll call you back in a few minutes."

"Okay. Bye, sugar."

"Bye, Mama." Deja disconnected and took the new call. "Hello?"

"Hey," Tamara said. "What are you doing?"

"Watching the news." As Deja spoke, she saw her own image appear on the television screen. The old her was sitting on Jerome's couch, her face still chubby with fat from the pregnancy. Jessica Serrano asked what happened on the night in question, and Deja watched herself take a deep breath before beginning her story.

"What are you thinking about?" Tamara asked. "How you feeling?"

"I, I don't know how to feel," Deja admitted.

"Didn't you see him this weekend?"

"I did," Deja confirmed. "But it didn't go like it was supposed to. He didn't apologize. He just, he started screaming. He said it wasn't him that attacked me, and I needed to tell the truth. He said they were going to kill him for nothing, and it was my fault." The room became blurry. Deja was surprised to find tears welling in her eyes.

"I'm sorry that happened," Tamara said. She spoke softly. Her words were nurturing. "But you know people will say anything when it comes down to the wire, like it was for him."

"I know," Deja said with a sniffle. "But I never saw him, Tamara. I never saw his face."

"I know you didn't, Deja. And I also know you weren't the prosecutor, and you weren't on the jury. It wasn't your fault he got convicted. All you did was tell them what happened to you. You never said it was him that did it."

"I know," Deja said. "But it *was* because of me. Everything that happened to him was because of me. He nev, he never would've been arrested."

"He got arrested because he was prowling the streets at three in the morning with a burglary kit in his pocket," Tamara countered. "Don't forget that man raped women before. He went to prison for rape, and he tried to kill someone in there. And you weren't the only woman who testified, Deja. What about the girls who said he choked them after he did his time for rape?"

"But what if he didn't attack *me*?"

"First of all, he did," Tamara assured her. "The police worked hard on your case, and they put the right man behind bars. But *if* he didn't..." There was a pause. "Deja, even if he was innocent of *your* assault, he still did a lot of other bad things. He abused those prostitutes. He was out late that night, trying to break into *someone's* home. He was going to rape again, so I don't have any remorse over his death. I'm glad he killed himself," she declared. "There's no telling how much money tax payers would've wasted on him over the next year and a half, with all of his appeals and stuff."

Given the nature of Tamara's own attack and the death sentence her rapist left her with, Deja understood her reaction. But she wasn't in agreement.

"Why don't you come back to the meetings?" Tamara asked. "I don't think you should've stopped going."

Deja shook her head, her eyes still fixed on the television. "I don't want to go back. All those stories... Those little girls and their fathers, uncles... I can, I can take the adults sometimes. But the little ones..."

"Then let's get some coffee," Tamara suggested. "What are you doing today? Do you want to meet at Starbucks?"

"I'm going to go to church," Deja said. "After that, I'm supposed to go to my mama's house."

"Well, give me a call back," Tamara said. "I really want to see you, Deja. I can help you get through this."

"Thanks. You're a good friend."

"I'm always here for you," Tamara said. "Call me later."

Deja left for church at nine-thirty. As she pulled out of the parking lot, she saw a news van from Channel Six pulling in. There wasn't a big mystery as to where they were going, but Deja did a U-turn and followed them anyway.

The van stopped close to her building. Deja watched until she saw Jessica Serrano emerge from the passenger seat. The reporter had on the same outfit she wore during her prison interview that morning, and Deja guessed they came straight from the Piedmont Unit.

It felt wrong to let them make the long trip for nothing, but Deja didn't feel like being on television that day. She couldn't face the reporter's hard stare and answer questions when she wasn't sure about things herself. She eased off the brakes and drove away slowly, without calling attention to herself.

≈≈≈≈≈≈

The folks at church were either too polite to bring up Deja's troubles, or they didn't watch the early morning news. Not one person at Emmanuel Baptist said a word about Gilbert Reynolds. Deja didn't get there in time for early prayer, but she stepped forward at the end of the sermon when the pastor made his altar call.

Deja dropped to her knees and asked God for understanding of things she was confused about and forgiveness for any part she played in Gilbert's suicide. She asked the Lord to tell her the *true* identity of her attacker, but she understood if that request took a while to answer – or if it was never answered at all. She knew that God was not a Magic 8 Ball. Sometimes He only gives you what you need to get by. Deja was grateful that He loved her at all.

Dinner at her mother's house brightened Deja's mood considerably. Her mom made spaghetti with garlic bread, mixed vegetables and apple cobbler. The strangler was the topic of discussion, and all of Deja's relatives had the same opinion. They said Deja was in no way responsible for Gilbert's death, and he was surely lying when he professed his innocence during their meeting yesterday. Because he saw Gilbert's outburst firsthand, Vincent was the biggest spokesman:

"That nigga was lying, y'all. He just wanted to scare Deja. That's why I had to put these paws on him. He know he killed them women, and he know he was gon' burn in hell. I'm glad he dead, but I think he got off too easy. I wish they would've let us stone him or something..."

≈ ≈ ≈ ≈ ≈ ≈ ≈

Deja didn't make it home until 3 pm. She had totally forgotten about the reporters by then, and that proved to be a big mistake. She fished her keys from her purse as she approached her apartment. When she looked up, she noticed an unfamiliar man loitering near her door. They locked eyes for a second, and Deja made a quick right, as if she meant to go that way all along.

"Uh, excuse me," the gentleman called.

Deja half turned, hoping he wouldn't recognize her with all of the baby weight gone. "Yeah?"

"Do you know the woman who lives here?" he asked. "Uh, Deja Franklin?..." The man wore a golf shirt tucked into black slacks that were too tight around the waist.

"Nope," Deja said. "Don't know her."

"I'm from Channel Nine News," the stranger said. He pulled a card from his pocket. "If you happen to see–"

"I told you, I don't know her." Deja kept walking. She casually peered over her shoulder as she rounded the next corner. The stranger was watching her, but he didn't follow.

Once out of sight, Deja sped up and made it to Shannon's apartment with sweat glistening on her brow. It took her friend two agonizingly long minutes before she answered the door.

"Girl, what are you doing?" Deja asked.

Shannon yawned and stretched like a tomcat. She rubbed sleep from her eyes but had trouble getting them to open all the way.

"Nothing," she said. "Sleeping. I didn't get home 'til six this morning."

"*Six?*"

"I was clubbing," Shannon said and a wicked smile parted her lips. "I drunk so many shots, I don't know *who* took me home last night. He was cute though, I think..."

Deja's pastor spoke about the sinful club scene this morning, but she wasn't the type to cast stones. "Can I come in?" she asked. "There are reporters hanging around my apartment."

Shannon's face scrunched up. "Reporters? Why?"

"The strangler killed himself last night."

"Hmph. Good for him. What's in that bowl?" She eyed the Tupperware container Deja toted.

"My mama made some spaghetti."

Shannon's face lit up. "Ooh, girl, come on in. Can I have some?" She reached for the food, and Deja handed it over like it was a toll.

Seven minutes later the ladies sat at Shannon's kitchen table. Shannon slurped down the spaghetti while Deja fed her son broccoli and carrots.

"I told you it was Jerome," Shannon said. "I told you that a long time ago, but you didn't listen."

"I still don't want to hear that," Deja said. "Just because Gilbert killed himself doesn't mean he was innocent."

"I don't know," Shannon said. "It sure makes him *look* innocent, especially after what happened on your visit."

Deja was already half-convinced Gilbert wasn't the strangler, but she remained optimistic.

"That stuff he pulled at the prison just shows how deceptive he was. He was mad at me, and he knew that was the only way he could get me back."

"*Or...*" Shannon held a finger in the air. "Or maybe he was so distraught, so *desperate*, that he would try anything. Can you imagine if you were found guilty of a crime you didn't commit? Everybody's telling you to just tell the truth, and they'll find you innocent. But you do that, and they don't. You end up on death row when you didn't do nothing but take a walk in the middle of the night."

"Whatever."

"So you call the victim," Shannon went on. "You ask her to come down to prison, because she is the only one who knows it wasn't you who attacked her. You bare your soul and beg her to tell the truth. But when she rejects you, it's over. You don't have nothing else to live for. You know you're going to die, so you take yourself out."

"I'm not going to argue with you," Deja said. "You have no idea why Gilbert killed himself. And Jerome is not a killer. You've been saying that for over a year, and it still doesn't hold water."

"Then why'd Gilbert kill himself?"

"How should I know?" Deja said. "He still had appeals left. It wasn't like yesterday was his last day or even his last year. He had a lot more fighting he could've done."

"Then what made him say, fuck it?" Shannon asked.

"He knew he was guilty."

"Or he knew he was innocent."

Deja's phone beeped. She dug it from her purse and smiled for the first time that day when she saw her new text message.

Hi. U busy?

She texted Benton back. No

"Who's that?" Shannon asked.

"It's that guy I met," Deja said, just as her phone began to ring.

"You hit it yet?"

Deja shook her head and said, "Hello?" into the cellular.

"Hey," Benton said. "Whatcha doing? I saw you on the news this morning. Did you know that guy who attacked you is dead?"

"Yeah. I know."

"What do you, how's that affecting you?" he asked.

"I'm alright. But I've been talking about that man all day. I'm kinda burnt out on him."

"Okay," Benton said. "We can talk about something else, like your pretty face. I'll bet you're looking beautiful today..."

"I'm *okay*," Deja said with a dopey grin. She scooped her baby up and headed for the privacy of the living room.

"Where you going?" Shannon asked.

"To the sofa."

"You can talk right here," Shannon said. "Don't be getting all high school on me, just 'cause you got a man now."

Deja thought about that and decided she liked the way it sounded. It felt good to almost, sort of, somewhat have a man – a real man for a change.

"What about you?" she asked Benton as she plopped down on the sofa. "What's going on with you today?"

CHAPTER TWENTY-TWO
THE LITTLEST INDIAN

It took nearly a week for the reporters to leave Deja alone. She stopped trying to avoid them. Instead she yelled, "No comment!" whenever a stranger approached and started firing questions at her.

Luckily the Chase bank downtown was robbed on Wednesday, and all local media were sent there. That story, along with the subsequent manhunt for the suspects (who wounded two policemen during their getaway), took the media attention away from Deja completely. By Friday no one cared how she felt about the strangler's suicide, and her life became relatively normal again.

On Saturday, April 6th, Deja had her second date with Benton planned, and she didn't leave anything to chance this time. The mission that night was to get past second base, and she wasn't at all ashamed about it. It had been over a year since a man loved her, kissed her or passionately explored her erogenous zones – with his hands or anything else he chose to explore with. Deja didn't know if it was Jerome, the baby or the attack that put her in a rut, but...

"It's a damned shame," Shannon said. Deja thought that summed things up perfectly. She stepped out of the bathroom with a towel wrapped around her body and a curling iron in hand.

"What's a damned shame?"

"These perverts," Shannon said. She sat on Deja's sofa watching more bleak news on the boob tube.

Deja went and stood next to her. Adrian crawled on the floor behind them, playing with his alphabet blocks. Deja was sure he couldn't spell *on purpose*, but sometimes he put together letter combinations that made her do a double take.

"Somebody snatched a little girl," Shannon said. "Don't nobody care when a black girl come up missing, but the whole city be looking if it's a white girl."

"That's not true," Deja said, knowing it was sort of true.

On TV a young mother wept openly. Deja's heart went out to her.

"How long has her daughter been missing?"

"Since she got out of school yesterday," Shannon reported. "You know they gon' find her dead."

Deja cringed. Shannon's cold-heartedness put a bad taste in her mouth. "You told me you wanted to get married one day and adopt some kids..."

"And?"

"I hope your daughter doesn't come up missing."

Shannon's eyes widened. "Take that back."

The news went to a commercial, and Deja went back to the bathroom to finish her hair. "Take what back?"

Shannon got up and followed her. "Take back what you said about my future daughter. Why you gon' put a curse on me like that?"

"I didn't put a curse on you," Deja said with a chuckle. "I'm just saying; karma is real, and it is a bitch."

"Fuck karma," Shannon said. She sat on the sink and watched Deja in the mirror. "Just take it back."

"Alright," Deja said. "I take it back. *Dang*. I didn't know I had the power to curse your future life. But if it makes you feel better..."

"It does," Shannon said, and her smile came back.

"What are you doing tonight?" Deja asked. "You're not going to have company, are you? I don't want Adrian there if you're making out with somebody."

"Ain't nobody coming over my house tonight," Shannon said. "What's wrong, you don't trust me to watch your baby?"

"I trust you," Deja said. "I just—"

"You don't want him to see two *mans* kissing," Shannon guessed. "You wrong for that."

"Bitch, I didn't even say that."

233

Shannon grinned. "I was just playing. So tell me, Miss Deja, how is your new boyfriend in bed? Them chocolate niggas are always packing."

"Mmmm. I wish I knew," Deja moaned. "But he's not my boyfriend. This is only our second date. We haven't kissed or nothing."

"Damn, girl. You be taking it slow."

"What? Are you saying we should've had sex on the first date? You're crazy."

"No, you're still living in the old days," Shannon said. "What you gon' do, take a chaperone with you tonight? Hey, after you get back from your *old-timey* date, do you think you can show me where the Underground Railroad is, so I can gets free?"

Deja laughed.

"*Swing low*," Shannon sang.

"Alright, Anita *Faker*. You know you don't need to be singing."

"Girl, whatever. I can blow."

"I'm not talking about your freaky bedroom skills," Deja said. "I'm talking about your singing."

"Oh, ha ha. You got jokes."

"No, I'm just tripping. Girl, you know I'm trying to push this relationship a little quicker. I usually wait five dates, but tonight—"

"*Five dates?*"

"At least."

"Damn. No wonder you could hold out this long."

"Yeah, but I'm reaching my breaking point," Deja confided. She put the curling iron down and stared at her reflection. She had her hair down in loose curls. She got caramel-colored highlights at the beauty shop a few days ago. She thought her 'do was gorgeous. "What do you think?"

"You look good," Shannon said. "You know you do." She looked away wistfully, and Deja was reminded of her friend's self-imposed shortcomings. Shannon's wealthy father would give her anything she wanted – *except* the money she needed for hormone therapy or gender-reassignment surgery. Shannon's only recourse was to get a job and save her own money (that was laughable), or find a rich sugar daddy. Every weekend she hit the clubs, hoping for the latter.

"What are you gonna wear?" Shannon asked.

"Ooh, let me show you."

Deja slipped into her bedroom and reappeared a few minutes later wearing the best freakum dress she had in her closet. It was purple and sleeveless, with spaghetti straps and a V-neckline that continued *way* down her chest, revealing a good two inches of cleavage. The dress fit snugly around her waist and hips. It was the kind you'd have to be constantly aware of when you sat, stood, bent or did anything else that required the slightest movements.

"Girl, you got some nice hips," Shannon noticed. "You look good, Deja. If he don't give you no dick tonight, he's gay."

Deja still wasn't sure she wanted to go *all the way*, but Shannon was right. If Benton didn't want her in this outfit, then something was definitely wrong.

≈ ≈ ≈ ≈ ≈ ≈

For their date that night, Benton took her back to the quaint Moroccan restaurant called Kabash. Deja didn't think her meal there was *outstanding* the first time around, and she would've liked to mix it up a little. But Benton really liked the place, and she liked him, so she didn't balk at his request.

Since she didn't have to drop her son off with her mother, Deja let Benton pick her up and drive her to the restaurant. He showed up at seven pm sharp wearing khaki slacks with a black button down. He did a double take when Deja answered the door. She watched his eyes bug, just like a cartoon.

"Oh, my. You are something else."

"Thanks." Deja beamed. She couldn't have asked for a better reaction. "You look nice yourself."

"No." Benton shook his head. "Compared to you, I look like a beggar. I'm, to be honest, I'm almost embarrassed to be seen with you. You're like a goddess, Deja. I am not worthy."

She blushed. "You sure know how to sweet talk."

"Maybe so," Benton said. "But I promise I have never fed you a line. You take my breath away, woman. You truly are a queen."

"Oh, you make me feel so special." She stepped out of the doorway and threw her arms around him. Benton stiffened for a

235

moment, and then he put his hands on her waist. The delight of being in a man's arms filled Deja with powerful emotions. She inhaled the scent of his cologne mixed with his natural pheromones. She felt blood rush between her legs, making her clitoris harden. That was the first time she ever felt that from just a hug.

She backed away and kissed him softly on the lips. Benton wasn't expecting it, and he barely had time to pucker, but it was still nice. Deja liked his confusion and nervousness.

"Wh, wow. What was that for?"

"For nothing," Deja said and unhanded him. She turned and locked her door. When she turned back, Benton looked up from her tailbone and regained eye contact. *No, this one's definitely not gay*, Deja thought. "You ready?"

"Uh, yeah..."

"Or we could stay here, and I can cook you something," she offered.

"We, you uh..."

"I'm just kidding," she said. "Come on. Let's go." She started down the sidewalk, and he followed.

"You got my head all messed up," he said. "Did you say you wanted to cook instead?"

"Maybe next time." Deja glowed under the fluorescent lights around her building. "I got dressed up, so we might as well go out."

"That's cool, too," her date replied. "Whatever you want, Deja. Your wish is my command."

≈ ≈ ≈ ≈ ≈ ≈

Benton drove a two year old Chrysler 300. It was all black with no upgrades on the factory wheels or interior. Last year Deja thought about getting a 300 herself. The cruise in Benton's sedan revitalized that dream. Benton's ride had a built-in GPS, parking assistance and an awesome audio system – a must for any serious lover of music. They drove to the restaurant listening to the Isley Brothers. The mellow tunes and sultry lyrics soothed Deja's heart and mind. She was pleased with everything Benton had offered her thus far.

For dinner, Deja had *tfaya*, which was chicken breast baked in cinnamon and saffron. Benton ordered *rabat* for himself. That turned out to be skewers of beef tips marinated in spices. Deja thought her meal was perfect. She was equally impressed with Benton's when he gave her a taste.

Per Deja's request, the dinner conversation ranged from anything and everything *not* involving a certain Sleeping Strangler. Instead Benton told her more about his humble childhood on the east side of Overbrook Meadows. Deja knew that was a rough part of town, but Benton's story about a hot summer day and a near-fatal plum expedition had her on the edge of her seat.

"We were really hungry that day," he was saying. "I was twelve, and my brother had just turned thirteen. Summer was always a bad time for us, because our mom worked long hours, and we were left pretty much unsupervised from sun up to dinnertime."

"How come she didn't put you in daycare?"

"Couldn't afford it," Benton said. "My dad took off when I was three. My mama only made eight-fifty an hour at the bus station. We usually went to the Boys Club, because they had a free daycare program, but Mama signed up late that year, and they were full."

"I would've made you stay in the house."

"Yeah right. Me and my brother, we feared Mama, but we also had a lot of street smarts. We knew she was gone when we woke up, and she wouldn't be back until it was time for dinner. It didn't take long to figure out we could do whatever the hell we wanted, as long as we made it home by five."

"She didn't leave enough food?"

"That was always the problem," Benton said. "Our mom was a good mom. She did the best she could, but usually there wasn't any dinner leftover. Our refrigerator stayed empty. We didn't even have condiments most of the time. We used to get government cheese and eat it with bread and mayonnaise. When the cheese ran out, we ate just bread and mayonnaise. When the bread ran out..." He brought a hand to his chin and ran a finger across his dark lips. "When the bread ran out, that's when we started stealing."

Deja shook her head slightly.

237

Benton shrugged. "It is what it is. But as I was saying, we started to become a menace in our neighborhood. We stole from the main grocery store up on Berry, and we stole from all of the corner stores, too. The corner stores figured us out real quick. And pretty soon the folks at the big store caught us, too.

"We started stealing bikes when kids left them in the front yard. We couldn't keep them 'cause mama would kill us, so we sold them to some of our friends. It was a small neighborhood, so it caught up with us pretty soon. Our friends had to give the bikes back, and then they'd come to us, asking for their money, but we already spent it."

"They didn't tell your mom?"

"Towards the end, she found out. But it wasn't her who put an end to me and my brother's thievery. It all came to a head when we jumped in Mr. Milner's backyard one day."

"Mr. Milner?"

"He was an old guy who lived close to our school. We always passed his house when we walked home, and we knew there was a plum tree in his backyard. It only bore fruit in the summertime, and each year we waited for it. We'd check on it a lot. When the plums got big enough to fall off by themselves, that's when we'd make our move."

Deja shook her head again.

Benton chuckled. "We'd jump back there and pluck as many as we could haul off. Except that day – that *last* day, all of the bad stuff we did that summer caught up to us."

"I'm afraid to hear the rest of this."

"It's okay," Benton said. "This is a childhood story, so nobody got killed."

"There was a dead guy in your other childhood story."

He laughed. "Yeah, there was. Anyway, me and my brother were on our usual walk that day, looking for something to steal. When we saw that Mr. Milner's plums were ready, we jumped the fence and crouched under the tree, so he couldn't see us through the window. We started stuffing our pockets, and we held our shirts out like a basket and stuffed that, too.

"We were almost done when my brother stopped me. His eyes were as big as quarters. He pointed at the house and said, *'Ain't that Mr. Milner right there?'* I looked up and damn if it

238

wasn't. Him and his wife were sitting on the back porch, had been there the whole time."

"Oh no."

"Yeah," Benton said. "That's what I thought. I turned back to my brother to tell him to run, and this fool's already leaping back over the fence. I was mad that he left me, but I looked back at the porch before I took off, and that's when I saw Mr. Milner get out of his seat. He went inside his house, and I knew he was going to call the police.

"I turned and tried to get over the gate myself, but the plums were a hindrance. I couldn't move too fast while holding my shirt, and my pockets started squishing. I felt plum juice running down my legs. It was a sticky mess, but I wouldn't leave my load. I eventually made it over the fence, but it was too late. As soon as my feet hit the ground, I heard someone yell, '*Stop right there!*' I turned around slowly, and that's when I realized Mr. Milner didn't go call the police. He went to get his pistol."

Deja couldn't believe it. "He pointed a gun at you?"

"Right at my chest."

"And you were thirteen?"

"I was twelve. My brother was thirteen."

"But..."

"I know," Benton said. "I didn't think he would shoot, but, like I said, I was twelve. I had no idea what he would do."

"What happened?"

Benton chuckled. "I started crying, of course. I dropped those plums and went to shivering and snotting. I pleaded with that man not to shoot me. I begged for my life, literally. I'm sure I was a sight. I wish somebody had recorded it."

"He let you go?"

"Well, sure he did. The way I was bawling and sniveling, with that plum juice staining my pants like I went to the bathroom on myself, he probably figured I suffered enough."

Deja chuckled. "I couldn't imagine something like that happening to me."

"It wasn't that bad," Benton said. "I definitely learned my lesson. That was the last time I stole from anybody. It was all fun and games at first, but to find out I could actually get *killed* for taking people's stuff... That was it for me, me and my cowardly brother."

Deja smiled. "Did you get mad at your brother for leaving you?"

Benton frowned. "Yep. I whooped his little butt, as soon as I found him. I still get on him about that. Sometimes when we meet for the holidays, I sneak up behind him and slap the back of his neck. When he turns around, ready to fight, I tell him, 'That's for leaving me at Mr. Milner's house!' We'll laugh."

"Okay," Deja said. "You were right. I did like that story."

"Yeah. It's a lot better than that tear-jerker you told about your dog."

"Oh..." Deja's smile went away. "I miss my Roscoe."

≈≈≈≈≈≈

They left the restaurant at nine-thirty.

Benton tried to pull his gentleman routine when they got back to Deja's complex, but she wasn't having it.

"I'll see you later," he said. "I had a really good time."

"Me too," Deja said. "Are you going to walk me to the door?"

"Of course."

Benton got out and went around to open the door for her. He didn't put his arm around her on the way to her apartment, and Deja knew she'd have to do most of the work.

"Why don't you come in for a drink?" she asked when they got to her doormat.

Benton smiled nervously. "I, I have to work later tonight."

Deja unlocked her door and turned back to him. "Why don't you come in for dessert?"

"I, uh..." He cleared his throat. "I'm still full from the, um...."

Deja sighed and rolled her eyes wistfully. "Why don't you just come in then?"

"You mean..."

"Yes." Deja's smile was devilish and sensual. "That's what I mean." She pulled him inside by the belt buckle, so there would be no doubts about her intentions.

≈≈≈≈≈≈

For someone who didn't want to stay for drinks, Benton was a surprisingly good kisser. Deja pushed him against the door as soon as she closed it. She pressed her body close to his. She thrust her tongue into his mouth the moment their lips touched. Benton sucked it like a peppermint stick, and Deja moaned softly through her nose. She flicked her tongue and placed her hands on his chest. She rubbed his pecs through his shirt, loving how hard and powerful he felt.

Benton's arms remained at his side, however. Deja didn't like that at all. She reached for his right hand and brought it to her hip. His mitt was hot and a bit moist. He didn't immediately grab onto her. She backed away from his lips and moved to suck his earlobe.

"Baby, you can touch me." Her breath was hot and sweet on his neck. Her voice was more seductive than any sex chat operator.

She knew Benton wouldn't be able to resist, and she was right. His hand sprang to life on her hip. He squeezed like he was looking for a ripe melon. His left hand shot forward, and it was like fire on Deja's skin. Her legs tingled. She felt moisture between her second set of lips. Her hot kisses skated from his neck back to his lips. Her tongue swam between his teeth and his between hers.

His hands went from squeezing to caressing. They slowly claimed more real estate, until he gripped her ass firmly, a cheek in each hand. He pulled her closer and grinded against her hips. His hands soon moved at an unfettered pace, and Deja felt her little dress rising. When Benton caressed her bare cheeks, he inhaled sharply, and Deja felt him shudder against her. She wore a G string, but Benton may have thought she bypassed her panties altogether tonight. His touch made her nipples and clitoris hard and sensitive. He ran his hands across every inch of her ass, squeezing and pawing like a blind man finding booty for the first time.

"Let's go to the bedroom," Deja whispered. She backed away and took his hand to lead the way. But Benton's back remained glued to the door. He shook his head and a desperate, almost pained expression took over his features.

Deja couldn't believe she was being rejected this late in the game. She thought it was a joke. "Come on." She grinned, but the smile slipped from her face when she reached between his legs. Benton was fully erect, but it didn't feel like he had a dick down there. She looked up at him in confusion. Benton looked more sullen than she had ever seen him. He pushed her hand away.

"Stop. Don't do that."

"What's wrong?" Deja asked, still not believing what she felt. She reached again and gave him a good squeeze this time. His body parts were all there: She felt two balls and a penis. But the size of his apparatus was like some freakish joke. Benton's testicles were of average size, but his penis was definitely smaller than her pinkie. To make matters worse, it was rock hard.

He brushed her hand away again. Actually he slapped it away this time, so quickly there was a slight *clap* at impact.

"I said *no!*" he said. "Don't, don't touch me."

Deja was already perplexed by the size of his pigmy penis, but the expression on his face was even more confusing. Benton looked dark and angry now, like he might strike her if she reached for his manhood again. But then his features softened, and the pain was back.

"It's okay," Deja said, "we can, we can..." She trailed off because she had no idea what they could do. Benton's dick was shorter and thinner than a pack of Lifesavers. She didn't know there were black men around who were so small. She didn't think there were *any* men so depraved.

Benton sneered at her. The malevolence flashed in his eyes again. "Yeah, that's what I thought." He turned and fumbled with the deadbolt.

"Wait," Deja said, but he swung the door open and disappeared into the night.

≈ ≈ ≈ ≈ ≈ ≈ ≈

Deja called him three times to apologize. She left a message on his voicemail the last time:

"Hey. I'm sorry about what happened. I didn't want you to leave. I still like you, and, and we can work this out. Just, call me back."

She stayed up until midnight, but Benton did not return her call.

CHAPTER TWENTY-THREE
BAD VIBES

The next morning, Deja thought she was stuck in an episode of The Twilight Zone. She watched the Channel Six News at daybreak every day when she got back from her four to six am patrolling. Sunday was no exception, except Deja was surprised to see award-winning anchorman Chad Collins in the studio.

Chad never worked the weekends – unless there was big news. Upon seeing him, Deja knew something bad had happened. But she had no idea the story would involve her yet again.

"This is becoming quite a saga," Chad said. "Most of us thought it was over with Gilbert Reynolds' suicide last week. But it seems the tale of the Sleeping Strangler has not reached its conclusion." He wore a black suit with a black shirt and tie that morning. Deja thought his attire was fitting, considering the macabre story he was bringing the viewers.

"We've got Jessica Serrano on the scene," Chad said. "Jessica, what can you tell us about the terrible development this morning?"

The view cut to a side-by-side shot of Chad in the newsroom and Jessica standing under a street lamp in a neighborhood Deja didn't recognize. Behind the reporter, Deja saw several police cars and crime scene tape encircling an area out of view to the right.

"Hi, Chad," Jessica said. "I'm standing on the 5700 block of Oakmont Avenue. As you said, this is a tragedy *no one* expected – especially after the suicide of Gilbert Reynolds, who was convicted of the Sleeping Strangler murders."

The view changed to a shot of only Jessica. Deja sat up on the couch. She had her .25 automatic out of the ankle holster, lying on the cushion next to her. She trembled and bounced her knee uncontrollably. She looked down at the gun for the eighth time in less than a minute. It was still there. All she needed to do was cock it, point it and shoot at whatever she wanted dead.

"The police have just released the victim's identity," Jessica said, looking down at her notes. "Her name is Violet McNairn, and she lived alone. She was 28 years old, a bus driver for the Overbrook Meadows Transit Authority.

"According to reports, a neighbor heard screams from the McNairn residents at approximately 2:30 am. But this neighbor is elderly, and she does not have a working telephone in her home.

"We're told she got dressed and went to another neighbor's house to call 911. By then more than twenty minutes had passed. The police indicate they got the call at 2:52, and a unit arrived at Ms. McNairn's home at three am. They found the backdoor closed but not locked. When an officer entered the residence, he found Ms. McNairn in the bedroom, dead from an apparent strangulation."

The view went back to a split screen of the two reporters. Chad looked genuinely forlorn.

"Jessica, you've done a lot of work on the Sleeping Strangler murders. Could you give the viewers a quick recap, leading up to this point?"

"It all started with the murder of Tawanda Murphy," Jessica said. "She was a 24 year old prostitute and drug addict found strangled in a south side motel. The police didn't realize we had a serious problem until a second body – that of Danielle Struthers – was found less than a month later. Danielle was also a prostitute, and the police found multiple links between hers and Tawanda's murder. At that point the media realized there was a serial killer on the south side of town, and we began calling him the *South Side Strangler.*

"But then the killer changed tactics, no longer preying on prostitutes. The body of Sheila Montgomery was found inside her house, and Tracy Fielder was killed inside her west side home. The police still had no idea who they were looking for, until the strangler's fifth victim, Deja Franklin, survived a brutal attack at her west side apartment. It was Deja who gave the police their first insight into the killer's M.O., which included him lying in bed with his victims, for possibly up to two hours. At that point, the media began to refer to him as the *Sleeping Strangler*.

"Like Violet McNairn, all of the victims were African-American females. A convicted rapist by the name of Gilbert Reynolds was arrested and subsequently convicted for Deja's attack and Tawanda's murder. Mr. Reynolds was sentenced to die for his crimes."

"And he killed himself last week," Chad said.

"He did," Jessica agreed. "A lot of people were glad to see him go. It looked like we could finally put the senseless killings behind us. But now the police aren't so sure anymore."

"What are they saying?" Chad asked. "What makes them think the murder of Violet McNairn is related?"

"Well," Jessica said, "I spoke to one officer, who does not want his identity revealed because he is not authorized to give a statement on this matter, and he said this new crime is virtually identical to the four previous murders. At this point he would not say exactly what similarities are involved, but he said the connection is strong. He is sure DNA evidence will provide a definitive link."

"He did acknowledge–"

"What about a copycat murder?"

"That's right, Chad. The officer I spoke to did acknowledge that this might be a copycat murder. But it's too early in the investigation to say for sure."

"Wow," Chad said. "That would be awful, if it's not a copycat killing. I mean, either way this is very tragic, but..."

"You're right," Jessica said. "Talking with the police, I almost get the sense they would prefer this was a copycat killing. Because if it's not, that would mean this is the work of the same individual who killed the first four women, which would mean the man convicted of those crimes, Mr. Gilbert Reynolds, was innocent all along. Obviously there is no way to absolve him at this point, because Mr. Reynolds has already taken his own life."

"Oh my God," Deja whispered. Her heart sank deep into her belly, and her head swam.

Her phone rang. She reached for it with numb fingers.

"Hello?"

"Baby?" It was her mom.

"Hey."

"What are you, are you watching the news?"

"Yeah, Mama."

"Oh, child, this is something else, ain't it?"

"Mama, this is the worst thing in the world. I feel so bad..."

"Baby, it's okay."

"*No*," Deja cried. "Mama, it's not okay. That man is dead. I put him in prison, and now he's *dead*. There's no way to make that right."

"This may be a copycat, Deja, like they said. Even if it's not, that man took his own life. You didn't make him do that."

"And there's still a killer out there," Deja cried. "The police haven't even been looking for him because of me."

"Deja, you can't be thinking like that. None of this is your fault. Just be glad you made it through your situation. Thank God this weirdo didn't come looking for *you* last night."

"I just..." Deja trailed off as that thought sank in. The killer didn't come looking for her last night, but why not? Out of all of his victims, Deja was the only one who survived. That was reason enough to finish what he started. It wasn't like she was making it difficult for him to find her. So convinced they caught the right man, Deja didn't even move to a different apartment. Why did the killer choose Violet McNairn last night instead of her?

That thought was followed by another, more sinister one. This time the blood chilled in Deja's veins and she felt weak allover. She remembered how she awakened from a sound sleep a few days ago. She could've sworn she heard someone trying to get in through her back door. What if that was the killer?

"Oh my God," she whispered.

"What, what's wrong?"

"Mama, I gotta go." Deja looked around fretfully. It was after six, but the sun wasn't fully up yet. She could only see darkness beyond the curtains in the living room.

"Where are you going, baby? What happened?"

"I'm going to my friend's house," Deja said. "If the same person who killed the first four girls is still out there, he knows where I live, Mama."

"Call the police," Shirley advised. "Deja, don't go out there. Just call the police."

"I'm just going a few buildings over, Mama. I'll get somebody from the watch to go with me."

"Somebody from the watch? Deja, I don't know those people! You need to call the police."

"*I* know them, Mama. It'll be alright. I'll call you back in a few minutes."

≈≈≈≈≈≈≈

Deja got off the phone and picked up her gun. She checked the magazine. It was full, like always. She didn't cock it because only a fool (or a Plaxico Burress) would walk around with a cocked gun in his pocket. But she did take the weapon off safety, just in case.

She got on the radio and called the 6:00-7:00 am patrol shift, which consisted of Cassandra Tucker and Roland Mitchell. The couple didn't know each other prior to the neighborhood watch, but Deja heard that a relationship had blossomed since then.

Neither Roland nor Cassandra asked why Deja wanted an escort to another apartment building. They arrived five minutes later. By then Deja had her baby ready and her biggest diaper bag packed with things she might need for a day away from home.

There was another stressful moment when Shannon didn't answer her door after five knocks, but she eventually opened up, sporting baggy, bloodshot eyes that said more about her Saturday night escapades than her mouth could have.

"Can I come in?" Deja asked. "I need to leave my apartment for a while."

Shannon stepped aside and let her in with no questions. She was used to her friend's interesting life by now.

"If anyone asks where I am," Deja told Cassandra and Roland, "*especially if it's a reporter*, don't tell them. You know what, even if it's not a reporter, still don't tell them."

"Why would reporters be looking for you, Miss Deja?" Roland asked.

"Watch the news when you get home," Deja instructed. "You'll see."

≈≈≈≈≈≈≈

247

The day at Shannon's house was mostly uneventful due to the fact that Shannon slept all morning. She didn't emerge from her bedroom until two pm. In the meantime Deja made herself at home, watching the news, feeding her son, and talking to well-wishers who saw the story and wanted to give their theories on Gilbert's suicide and the new murder.

The one person Deja didn't think to call was the detective who originally worked her case. She was surprised when he called her at nine o'clock.

"Hello?"

"Hi, Deja?"

"Who, who's calling?"

"My name is Rudy Cervantes. I'm a homicide detective."

Deja sighed, her mind temporarily overwhelmed with the fear, pain and weakness she felt at Jackson Memorial.

"It's been a long time."

"It has," he agreed. "How have you been doing?"

"Not too good," Deja admitted. "I had to leave my house today."

"How come?"

She chuckled nervously. "I know *you've* seen the news."

"I have," the detective said. "That's why I'm calling. They're saying some pretty outrageous things on Channel Six, and I was worried you might buy into it."

"What do you mean?"

"Well," Mr. Cervantes said, "I'm working the new murder, the McNairn case. I was at her residence this morning. The reporters say some *unidentified cop* told them there's a strong resemblance to this new murder and the strangler's first four victims."

"I heard that," Deja said.

"That's what I want to talk about," Mr. Cervantes said. "I didn't want you to start thinking the *real* killer of the first four women is still out there, that Mr. Reynolds was convicted of crimes he didn't commit."

Deja was totally confused. "I, I did think that."

"That's a bunch of bull," Mr. Cervantes said. "You don't have anything to worry about, Deja. I don't know what cop they're talking about on the news, but if I find him, I'll kick his ass personally. Gilbert Reynolds *did* kill the first four women. This new murder is not related to the Sleeping Strangler murders *at all.*"

Deja's relief couldn't be measured, but, "How, how do you know?"

"Well, this is an ongoing murder investigation, so anything I tell you must be kept confidential. Do you understand?"

"Yes. Yes, of course I do."

"This new murder," the detective said, "it's a lot more disorganized. There are very few similarities between McNairn and the other victims. It's so different, I wouldn't even categorize it as a copycat. It's simply a totally different murder."

Deja didn't want to come off like she was a better detective than he, but her life was at stake, so she had to ask, "What are the differences?"

"There's no pullover," Mr. Cervantes said. "This new guy wasn't wearing the same outfit as the Sleeping Strangler. And he made no attempt to tie her up, like with the others. The victim put up a hell of a fight, and for the first time we actually have skin samples under her fingernails. It looks like we'll get DNA from those. But even if we don't, we have something better: There's *semen* at the new crime scene. The Sleeping Strangler would have never been so sloppy and left so much evidence. The only similarity we have is the fact that he choked the victim to death.

"So you don't need to worry about Gilbert Reynolds being the wrong guy. He was convicted by a jury of his peers, and he did the world a favor by taking his own life. This new murder is in no way related to the crimes he committed."

Deja was so happy, she almost cried. Her own personal safety aside, she was mostly relieved that she didn't play a part in Gilbert Reynolds' unnecessary incarceration. He killed himself because he knew he was guilty, just as everyone had been telling her.

"Thank you for calling," she told the detective. "You don't know how bad I needed to hear that."

≈ ≈ ≈ ≈ ≈ ≈ ≈

Deja was ready to go home by the time Shannon staggered out of the bedroom, but she didn't want to be alone.

"Morning," she told her friend. "Glad to see you made it back to the world of the living."

Shannon frowned and shaded her eyes from the afternoon sunlight streaking through the blinds. She wore a long, white tee shirt. Deja hoped there were undergarments beneath it, but with Shannon, you could never be sure.

"What you doing here?"

"You let me in, goofball."

"Why?"

"Because I was in need, and it was the most Christian thing to do."

"That don't sound like me."

"Well, you did it. It's too late to take it back now. I made you some breakfast earlier, but it's already after lunchtime."

"What'd you make?"

"Sausage, eggs, buttermilk biscuits..."

A smile grew in the corner of Shannon's mouth. "I'll still eat it. You brought all of that from home?"

"No. You had it in your refrigerator."

That was an even bigger surprise. "*I* had groceries?"

Deja shook her head. "Go take a shower. I'll heat it up for you."

Shannon returned twenty minutes later wearing cargo shorts with a V-neck blouse and a silk wrap around her head. She wolfed down the food while Deja updated her on the latest happenings. When she was done, it was three o'clock, and Deja was still not ready to return to the comfort of her own home.

"It's the reporters I'm mainly worried about," she said. "I don't want to run into them, if they're over there."

"Why would they care about you, if it's a different killer?" Shannon asked.

"They don't know it's a different killer," Deja explained. "The police told me, but they haven't held a press conference yet. Until then, everybody's guessing and speculating."

"That's why I don't watch the news," Shannon said. "They don't never know what they talking about."

"That's ridiculous," Deja said. "But anyway, I don't even know for sure if they're at my house. Can you go check for me?"

Shannon rolled her eyes and sighed. *"I guess."* She pushed away from the table reluctantly. "I'ma curse 'em out, too, if it's some over there."

"Feel free," Deja said. "They're no friends of mine."

≈ ≈ ≈ ≈ ≈ ≈ ≈

Deja waited nearly fifteen minutes for her friend to return. Her nerves were nearly shot by then, but Shannon walked in with a cheesy grin.

"Where you been?"

"Down there, talking to them reporters." She took a seat on the couch and crossed her legs daintily.

"Talking to them?" Deja sat next to her. "You were supposed to come back and tell me if they were there – *that's all."*

"I was," Shannon said. "But they stopped me. Byron Charles was there. You know, that beautiful, dark chocolate thing from Channel 11."

Deja had seen the reporter on television. "You know he's straight, right?"

"Hmph," Shannon said. "He wasn't acting like it. He gave me his number and everything."

"Let me see."

Shannon pulled a card from her pocket. Deja took it and saw that it was his business card for the station.

"Why'd he give you this?"

"I'm supposed to call him if I hear anything about where you are. He said he'll make it worth my while."

Deja shook her head. "They get on my nerves. I'll bet that's how they got Jerome. *We'll make it worth your while."*

"You know I got your back," Shannon said. "I told them you moved out and ain't nobody seen you in a month."

"Thanks."

"Byron Charles is cute though. I think you should do an interview with him. Maybe you can get him to come to my apartment. I'll take him to the back to do his, uh, makeup."

"Yeah. I'm sure he'll like that – him and his wife and three kids."

Shannon plucked the card from Deja's fingers.

"Maybe he's not all that happy in his marriage."

251

"Keep dreaming."

"I will," Shannon said. "'Cause that's one thing your pessimistic ass can't take from me. What about your love life? How'd your date go last night?"

The question changed Deja's whole demeanor. "That was, it was, something..."

Shannon chuckled. "What happened?"

"I think I messed it up," Deja said. "Actually *he* messed it up with his little dick. But I messed it up too, the way I reacted."

Shannon's mouth fell open. "Y'all did something?"

"I tried," Deja said with a sigh. "The date was perfect up to that point. He took me out to eat, and we were digging each other the whole night. I asked him to come in when he dropped me off, but he didn't want to. I knew something was up, but I pushed it." She frowned. "I found out why he was reluctant."

"Was it *real* little?" Shannon asked. "You saw it?"

"I felt it through his pants," Deja said. "It was little, girl. *Real* little. I would say *freakishly* little. *Embarrassingly* little. *Ridiculously* little. Teeny-weenie."

"Maybe he wasn't hard. Some men–"

"He was hard," Deja said. "That's the worst thing about it. That little thing was as hard as it could be."

Shannon looked down and shook her head. "That's messed up."

"It really is," Deja said. "I thought it was about to go down."

"Why didn't you try?"

Deja shrugged. "I guess, I don't know. It was kind of a surprise to me, when I felt it. I couldn't help but look surprised and disappointed. And he saw the way I looked. He got mad and left. I tried to call him, like three times. He didn't call back."

"I wouldn't call you back either," Shannon said. "You probably hurt his feelings."

"I definitely hurt his feelings."

"That's wrong," Shannon decided. She was the very last person Deja expected to hear that from.

"Excuse me?"

"If you liked him, why you flip out just because he was little?"

"Maybe if I was married," Deja said, "and my husband's dick got cut off in some weird accident, I would stay with him. But me and Benton aren't that close."

"That man is thirty-something years old," Shannon said. "You don't think he know he got a little dick?"

"I'm pretty sure he does know."

"And don't you think he done found some ways around it? I'm pretty sure he could make you cum just like anybody else."

"Explain."

"Haven't you ever heard of vibrators, nipple clamps, strap-ons, Ben Wa balls, Viagra, *oral sex*, dick pumps, anal plugs, clit suct—"

"Yeah, let me stop you right there," Deja said. "I don't even know what half that stuff is."

"I thought you was one of them *progressive* chicks," Shannon said. "A big dick can only get you so far, Deja. I wouldn't stay with a man just because of that."

"I wouldn't either," Deja said. "I'm not some sex fiend. But I don't think you understand what I'm telling you. This man's dick was *abnormal*. Either way, I knew I was wrong for the way I reacted. I called to apologize, but he won't call back."

"He'll call back," Shannon predicted. "He just needs some time to cool off."

Deja sighed. "To be honest, even if he does call, I don't think I can work with that dick of his."

"Girl, how small was it?"

"It's smaller than my pinkie!" Deja held up the digit as a reference.

Shannon stared at her finger and frowned and then shook her head. "It was all the way hard?"

"As a rock," Deja said, glad she was finally getting through to her.

"So, *did it* get chopped off in some weird accident?"

Deja couldn't stop from cracking up. "Girl, I'm too scared to ask him!"

CHAPTER TWENTY-FOUR
THE FINAL CHAPTER
CONNECT THE DOTS

The police didn't hold a press conference until 5:30 pm. Not until then did they break the news that the McNairn murder was committed by someone other than the Sleeping Strangler. They explained how the victim was not bound, the manner of break-in was completely different, and there was semen collected at the scene. They said the McNairn's murder wasn't even similar enough to be considered a copycat killing. The police chief assured the public that his detectives were hot on the new killer's trail.

What he didn't say was there was no need for the media to get a comment from someone like Deja Franklin, as this had nothing at all to do with her. Deja wished he would've included that, but the reporters got the picture. In the next few stories they aired about the McNairn murder, the Sleeping Strangler was mentioned only as a side note. They didn't mention Deja at all, and when she sent Shannon to check on her apartment at seven, there were no reporters hanging around for a scoop.

"I guess they through with you," Shannon said and took a seat on her sofa.

"Cool," Deja said. She yawned and stretched lazily. "I'm about ready to go home. I've been here for twelve hours."

"You should get another apartment," Shannon advised her. "Too many creepies know where you stay."

"I know," Deja said. "I don't want those reporters coming back to me every time somebody gets killed."

"The unit across from me is vacant."

"When I move, I want a house," Deja told her.

"You gotta save up a long time for that."

"I have been saving. I got about seven thousand so far."

"*Seven thousand*?"

"And I did that without child support," Deja said with a slight sense of pride.

"Speaking of Jerome..."

"Oh, drop it."

"You can at least call him and ask where he was last night."

"Drop it, Shannon. For real. Jerome didn't kill anyone, and he never tried to hurt me. Your theory is bogus."

"You won't think it's bogus if you wake up dead."

"If I wake up dead, I'll come and apologize to you," Deja said.

"I'm not opening my door for no ghost," Shannon said and Deja laughed.

≈≈≈≈≈≈≈

The next hour took on a more somber tone when Deja got ready to leave. Shannon hovered over her while she packed her diaper bag.

"Why don't you stay here?" Shannon offered. "You can spend the night and get another apartment in the morning."

"Girl, I already told you I don't want to move into another apartment."

"Well, why don't you stay, just for tonight?" Shannon asked. "Until all of this blows over?"

"It has blown over," Deja said. "The reporters are gone, Gilbert Reynolds is dead and the police said it was a totally different killer this time. What's the problem?"

"There's still *somebody* out there," Shannon said. "They haven't caught whoever killed that lady today. I would feel better if you had a man at home with you."

"I'm sorry, but that position is still vacant," Deja said. Her cellphone rang. Her eyes brightened when she saw the incoming number. "Hey, it's Benton."

Shannon's eyes brightened, too. "Are you going to give him another chance?"

"I don't know," Deja said. "He's probably still mad at me."

"Answer it."

"I'm trying to, if you shut up." Deja sat down so she could give him her full attention. "Hello?"

"Hi, Deja?"

"Yeah, it's me."

"I, uh..." He sounded tired. His voice was a lot more gruff than usual. "I'm sorry for leaving like that yesterday. I got your message, and I should've called back. I was um, I was too embarrassed."

"I'm sorry too," Deja said. "I didn't mean to react that way. I was, it just caught me off guard."

Benton sighed. "I want to see you. I want to talk about things, if that's okay."

"Yeah, that's fine," Deja said. "When?"

"Tonight. I can be there in fifteen minutes."

Deja put a hand over the phone and whispered to her friend. "He wants to see me tonight."

"Do it," Shannon hissed back. "Tell him to come over here first, so he can walk you to your apartment."

"Okay," Deja said into the phone. "But I'm at my friend's house. Can you come over here, and then we can go to my place? It's been a real weird day."

"Yeah," he said. "What's the apartment number?"

Deja gave it to him, and he said he'd be there soon.

"When is he coming?" Shannon asked when she got off the phone.

"About fifteen minutes."

"Is he going to spend the night?"

"I don't think so," Deja said. "I think he just wants to talk."

"I got one word for you," Shannon said. "*Cunnilingus.* If he can't stick it, he *gots* to be good at licking it."

Deja didn't respond, but she thought licking it without sticking it was like a ham and cheese sandwich with no mayo. Who the hell would want that?

≈ ≈ ≈ ≈ ≈ ≈

Benton showed up twelve minutes later wearing blue jeans and sneakers with a collar shirt that wasn't tucked in. This was the

256

most casual Deja had ever seen him, but it was fine because she still had on jeans with the neighborhood watch tee shirt she put on early this morning.

But her attire didn't matter, because this was not a date. It was a different kind of encounter. Deja saw it in Benton's eyes as soon as she opened the door. He still wore the look of defeat and shame she saw the last time they were together. Deja was embarrassed as well. She had as much trouble making eye contact as he did.

"Hi," she said. "Let me get my baby, and I'm ready to go." She turned and hefted her diaper bag. Benton took a hesitant step inside.

"Here, I'll carry that for you."

"Thanks." Deja handed it over and scooped up her baby. Adrian was fast asleep. He didn't stir when she picked him up. "Okay, I'll see you later," Deja said to Shannon.

Shannon nodded, watching them closely from the loveseat. "Alright, girl. You take it easy. Give me a call later on."

"Thanks for letting me stay for so long," Deja said and then turned to her pitifully endowed beau. "Okay, I'm ready."

Once outside, Deja saw that the sun had completely set. As usual, the night prowlers were out and about. It was almost eight-thirty. Deja was usually getting ready for bed at that hour, and she'd forgotten how active her neighborhood could be. She heard the shouts of excited children who should've been inside an hour ago as well as the *boom-boom-clap* of subwoofers knocking in one of the dope dealers' cars.

Benton walked a couple of steps ahead of her. Deja admired the trapezius muscles on his back. He didn't have a bodybuilder's physique, but Benton had nice definition in certain places. It was clear he hit the gym regularly. Deja was reminded that there were so many good things about this man. Surely she could get past his one little–

"Hey, Miss Deja."

Peaches appeared, as if out of a dream. Deja looked up in surprise.

"Girl, where'd you come from? You scared me."

"I'm sorry, Miss Deja. I was coming from D Money and them. I didn't have nowhere to go. I was just, over there…"

Peaches pointed to a secluded area behind a row of tall shrubs. Deja sighed as she took in the junkie's appearance.

She hadn't seen Peaches very much since their failed attempt at rehab. Word on the street was Peaches was avoiding Deja purposefully, out of shame. But Deja thought she might have gone to jail for a while. Tonight Peaches wore a short dress that was sleeveless and skin-tight. It was barely long enough to cover her genitalia. She could flash the whole neighborhood simply by raising her arms. Deja knew Peaches was raising a lot more than *arms* on the dirty streets of Overbrook Meadows.

Peaches was high and nervous. She was too skinny, and her hair was unkempt. She was still beautiful, but you'd have to love her to notice.

"Why don't you go home?" Deja advised her.

Peaches shook her head. "I ain't got nowhere to go." She was talking to Deja, but she was looking at Benton. Deja found that odd, so she followed her gaze and saw that Benton was staring back at the prostitute. His eyes were dark and cold, and Peaches looked away. She looked at Deja and then down at the sidewalk.

"I gotta go, Miss Deja." She walked away quickly. Deja watched until she was out of sight.

"You know every dopefiend out here, don't you?" Benton asked, and they got moving again.

"Yeah," Deja said vaguely and turned to follow him.

Inside her apartment, Deja took Adrian to his crib while Benton took a seat on the sofa. Deja checked her appearance in the mirror over her dresser and spritzed a little perfume on her neck and wrists before returning to her guest. She entered the living room and saw Benton seated with his hands in his lap. He was staring deeply at a television that wasn't on. Deja sat next to him, knowing this would be a hard talk.

She cleared her throat and got things started. "Look, I'm really sorry for the way I acted last night. Really, I don't know what came over me. That's not me at all."

Benton nodded. The lamp in Deja's living room only had a 60 watt bulb, but it was bright enough for her to see something strange as she studied his expression. Benton's hair was not combed. It wasn't all that noticeable, because he kept it short, but it was the first time Deja had seen it out of place.

As she considered that, Deja caught the distinct odor of alcohol emanating from his person. Benton was not a heavy drinker. He told her so on the phone, and he proved it by only having half a glass of wine when they went out. But now, if Deja didn't know any better, she'd swear he was fully drunk. Looking closer, she saw that his eyes were nearly bloodshot.

It pained Deja to see him this way, knowing that she was the cause of his sorrow. Apparently Benton spent the whole night drinking and crying because of her rejection. But there was something else.

"Wha, what's that?"

Benton turned towards her, and Deja could see the bruise more clearly. There was a scratch on his cheek. It wasn't deep, but it was nearly two inches long, and—

"I cut myself shaving."

Deja had only half a second to digest that before her cell phone rang. She watched Benton as she dug it from her pocket. He watched her, too. His dark stare and cold eyes were starting to give her chills, and Deja thought about her nickel-plated pistol in Adrian's diaper bag. She didn't know why she thought about the gun, but it was the first thing that crossed her mind.

"Hello?"

"Deja?"

The voice was not immediately recognizable. In over a year of watching the neighborhood together, this was the first time Deja got a call from Ms. Gladys on her cellular.

"Yeah..."

"This is Ms. Gladys," the older woman said. "Is you still there with that man?"

The question caused Deja's eyebrows to bunch together. Ms. Gladys knew absolutely nothing about her love life. How could she know that Benton was at her apartment? Deja watched his eyes, and Benton's head tilted slowly to the side. A slight frown grew on the right side of his face.

"I got this girl Peaches here," Ms. Gladys said. "She say she need to talk to you. Are you somewhere where you can talk?"

"Um, hold on," Deja said. She pushed off the couch and backed away from her friend. "I'll be right back," she told Benton and headed for the bathroom. Halfway there Deja frowned and blew hot air from her nose. She already knew what Peaches wanted to tell her – she saw in the junkie's eyes when she and Benton stared at each other a few moments ago.

Peaches only knew three types of men on the streets; they were either dope dealers, dopefiends or johns. Benton wasn't a dealer or a user, so that meant he must've propositioned Peaches for a date one day. Deja felt like a fool! She couldn't believe she was about to forgive this man and maybe have sex with his dickless, perverted ass, and all the while he'd been picking up nasty prostitutes.

Deja closed the bathroom door behind herself and flipped on the light. She stared at her angry reflection in the mirror and kept her voice low.

"Alright, put her on."

Peaches came to the line a second later. "Miss, Miss Deja?"

"Yeah. It's me."

"You, you gotta get away from that man," Peaches said. Her voice was almost a whisper. It gave Deja a deep chill, all the way down to her bones.

"What?"

"That's the *bad* man," Peaches said. Terror made the junkie's voice childlike. Deja was even more freaked out. "He took my friend," Peaches said. "She, she never came back. He tried to take me, too. I saw him..." She sniffled. "I saw him in the apartments, Miss Deja. Two, three times. He walked off when, when he saw me."

Deja's eyes flashed open, wider than they'd ever been. Her heart started to knock in her chest, hard and persistent. The fresh blood flowing to her brain jumbled things up at first, but then everything got placed into perfect order. She felt like an idiot for not seeing it before.

Where had Benton come from? He said he was visiting a friend in the apartments, but Deja never saw him there before the barbecue. She knew she hadn't gone crazy when she heard a noise at her door that night, and why was Benton so insistent they go to that quaint little restaurant where there were no customers – and get a secluded booth in the back?

Deja remembered the look on his face when she touched him last night, the fury in his eyes when he stormed out of her apartment. She remembered what the police said about Violet McNairn: Her crime scene was not like the others, because it was *rushed* and sloppy. There was skin under Violet's nails, and a scratch on Benton's face.

"Open up, Deja!"

There was a huge *BOOM!* on the bathroom door. Deja shrieked. She dropped her cellphone, and it impacted the floor with a vicious *SMAK!* She saw that the screen cracked as it bounced and landed next to her bathroom scale.

Deja ignored the phone and spun towards the flimsy door. She had two guns in the house. One was in the bedroom with her sleeping baby. The other was in the diaper bag at the foot of the couch. Deja looked around for another weapon, but there was nothing useful in the small bathroom, just deodorants, pill bottles and cheap leg razors she got from Family Dollar.

There was another loud *BOOM!* and then he tried the door. It was locked. He kicked it. Deja watched in horror as the whole bottom portion of the door pushed in before settling back in place.

"*Open the door, Deja!*" he yelled. "I got your baby out here with me. *Don't forget about your baby.*"

"*No!*" Deja cried. "*Please! Please, just go.*"

"I'm not leaving," Benton said. He hit the door again, with his shoulder this time. There was a mighty *THOMP!* followed by a *SCREEENN* sound of wood separating from nails. The whole doorframe buckled. Paint chips flew at Deja's face. The door held, but there were big gaps between the frame and the wall now. The gaps were so big, Deja saw nails protruding, struggling to hold it together.

"*Stop it! The police are on the way!*"

"*I don't care!*"

He kicked next to the knob this time. The door came flying in so fast, Deja had to back against the sink to avoid the collision. It swung all the way to the opposite wall and slammed into the stopper so viciously the whole apartment shook. Deja screamed again as the doorway was filled with a dark and terrible figure she didn't recognize anymore.

Benton's face was set in a snarl. His chest heaved. His hands were at his sides. One fist was balled around nothing. The other was wrapped around his own pistol. It was all black, a .380 from the looks of it. But it was hard to tell because the barrel was soon pointed squarely at Deja's nose. She tried to back away, but the sink dug into her hindquarters. She reached around the basin

261

for something, *anything*, but everything she touched was weak and flimsy. She sent combs and toothbrushes flying to the floor. Benton took a step inside the bathroom and brought the gun within six inches of her face.

"*You'd better stop!*"

"*Oh, God! Please, don't do this!*"

"*Shut up!*"

"*Please, Benton! Please stop!*"

"*Shut the fuck up! You're gonna die!*"

"*The police are coming!*"

"*I don't give a damn about the police!*" he bellowed. "*Do you think I care about that now? They're going to get me anyway, Deja! Because of you! It's all because of you!*"

"*I didn't do anything!*" Tears rolled down her face. Her whole body was cold and numb. She felt completely frigid.

"Do you think I don't know what I'm doing?" Benton asked. "Do you think I don't know?"

"*I don't know! Oh, my God...*" Deja squirmed but couldn't stop the urine from spilling from her. She barely noticed.

"*I had a plan!*" Benton shouted. He reached down with his free hand and jerked his pants down. Deja didn't want to look, but her eyes were compelled to follow. What she saw almost made her pass out.

She realized her initial assessment of Benton's package was right on the money. He was fully hard now, all one-and-a-half inches of him. But that wasn't what made Deja gag on her own hot tears and vomit. Even worse than his pinkie penis was the condom Benton had rolled over it. The condom was small, but it was much too big for his deformed genitals. He used two black rubber bands to hold it snugly at the base. The rest of the condom hung off his meat like an elephant's snout.

"*Oh, Jesus.*"

"*I always cum!*" he growled. "But they never find it, because I'm not *stupid*, Deja. *I don't leave semen, because I'm careful!*"

Deja looked away from his privates. She threw up in her mouth and forced it back down. Benton pulled his pants up and smiled. It was an awful smile that showed almost all of his near-perfect teeth but never made it up to his eyes.

"You don't like that do you?" he asked. "You don't like to see that because you're a *slut*, just like the rest of them. I knew—" He winced and rubbed his eyes with his free hand. "I knew I shouldn't have played around with you. I should've just killed you. I had you so many times. You have no idea how bad I..." He shuddered. Deja was surprised to see tears sprout in his eyes. He wiped his face again, and his smile turned completely upside down, like a clown's.

"I didn't want to do it again," he moaned. Deja knew he was talking about Violet McNairn. "*But you laughed at me,*" he cried. "*You laughed at me.* Just like, they always laugh at me!" He sobbed openly, his big shoulders bobbing like fishing floats.

"No I didn't," Deja said. "*Please don't do this, Benton.*"

"It got all messed up," he said. He hiccupped and gasped for air, his face set in a wretched scowl. "I didn't plan. I wasn't ready, and it got messed up. She, she scratched me. I nev, I *never* go in unprepared. But, you, you made me..."

"I didn't do it, Benton. *I didn't do nothing...*"

He took a few deep breaths and then stared at her with calmer eyes. He suddenly had the resolve of a man who just made the most important decision of his life. He shook his head roughly, as if trying to break free of the demons that haunted him. "I'm not going to prison Deja."

"No, please...."

"*You ruined everything*! So now, we both gotta go. First you, then me."

"*No!*"

"*Shut up*! I'll let the baby live."

There was a knock at the front door.

All eyes moved in that direction. Both predator and prey held their breaths.

"Deja?" a shrill, female voice called after a few seconds. "You alright in there?" It was Ms. Gladys.

With Benton momentarily distracted, his gun wavered an inch off target. Deja only had half a second to make her move.

She dove to the right and landed hard on the floor mat in front of the toilet. Her shoulder slammed against the glistening bowl, and she cried out unexpectedly. Benton turned back to her and squeezed off the first round.

BLAK!

The gun erupted loudly in the small bathroom, like a cherry bomb in a mayonnaise jar. The bullet sped through space Deja was no longer occupying and slammed into her vanity mirror with the force of twenty sledgehammers.

Glass rained down like a hailstorm, but Benton and Deja were both on the move again. Benton moved the gun downwards, towards Deja's new position on the floor. She sat up and reached back blindly for the lid of the toilet bowl tank. She got her hands on it and hefted it, but it was a lot heavier than she thought. In the moment it took her arms to compensate for the weight, Benton fired again.

BLAK!

This time, his shot was true. Deja felt something like a fiery piano fall into her lap. She screamed and used the fear and shock to strengthen her body for one last defensive measure. Benton brought the gun up towards her head as Deja pulled the heavy lid off the toilet bowl tank. She hurled it at him with all of the hope and faith David must've had against Goliath, knowing that if she missed, it was over. Benton would kill her. Maybe he'd be true to his word and let the baby live before he killed himself.

Maybe he wouldn't.

But God's grace was still upon her. The 20 pound lid hit Benton perfectly in the middle of his forehead. There was a soft *CLUNK*!, and he dropped the gun. Both of his hands flew to his face. He staggered backwards and fell to a sitting position. Still anesthetized by a rush of adrenaline, Deja didn't feel the pain in her hip. She dove forward and fell upon Benton, kicking and screaming.

He rolled to his back, and Deja mounted him. She saw the toilet lid lying next to his shoulder, and she grabbed it with both hands. Screaming wildly, she lifted it over her head and brought it down on his face with all the momentum she could muster. It connected with another *CLUNK*! that was both hard and squishy. The second time it was more squishy than hard, and on the third blow the lid cracked in two upon impact.

Gasping for air, Deja looked first to the heavens and then down at the mess she made. It was odd to see a man's face rearranged in such a way. Benton's forehead was split so wide, you could lay a quarter flat in the wound. His nose was twisted and mangled. His lips were cracked like a dropped watermelon. A couple of teeth rolled out of the corner of his mouth. Blood oozed from his head like a sprinkler with very little water pressure. Deja gagged, and she could no longer hold her gorge.

She vomited fully and loudly. The contents of her stomach fell directly onto what was left of Benton's face. The sight of it caused a second wave of puke to explode from her.

When she no longer had the energy to support herself, Deja rolled off of him and found that her panties were completely wet. She looked down and saw that it was blood. *Her blood.* That realization brought with it a tremendous pain that rolled down her legs like an 18-wheeler. Deja fell to her side and pawed at an unseen hole on the left side of her pelvis. She grunted, as if in the throes of labor, thrashing her head to and fro like she was possessed. Sweat beaded on her forehead and ran down her face in rivulets.

"Oh, God! Please..."

The pain was worse than anything she ever experienced. In the distance, Deja heard her baby crying. She wanted to go to him, but by then her legs were completely numb and useless. She couldn't move from that spot if her life depended upon it.

She was still awake and in agony eight minutes later when a policeman kicked in her front door. The moment he knelt and touched her shoulder, everything faded to black.

EPILOGUE
JACKSON MEMORIAL HOSPITAL
FIVE WEEKS LATER

April was always a rainy month in Overbrook Meadows, but Deja loved that time of year. She liked the smell of the earth after a long night of thunderstorms. She liked to hear the new birds of the season chirp in the trees while busy bees darted to and fro, pollinating gorgeous flowers that were fresh and sweet, as colorful as the rainbows and the beautiful dresses and suits of Easter.

Deja loved to be a witness to the wonders of spring, but that year she had to do most of her observing from a hospital window. Her recovery took days that piled into weeks and weeks that piled into a month. It wasn't until the second week of May that her doctors deemed her well enough to leave the hospital.

By then May was just as nice as April, in Deja's eyes, and she couldn't wait to get out into the mid-ninety degree weather. She sat on the side of her hospital bed wearing jeans and a tee shirt. She looked like a student waiting for the last bell while her nurse went over her discharge orders.

"You need to take those pain pills twice a day, or as needed. I gave you the OxyContins, right?"

The nurse looked down at his chart, and Deja looked over at her bag of personal belongings on the bed. The bag was stuffed to the brim, as was the suitcase her brother toted and the duffle bag her father had draped over his shoulder. Her mom made a move for the bag on the bed before Deja could get to it. She looked through it for a second and came up with a white pill bottle.

"Yeah, we got them," Shirley said.

Deja's nurse looked down at her. "Good. Doctor Ogden already spoke with you about your ongoing physical therapy…?"

Deja nodded. "I have to go three times a week for-*ever*."

Her nurse chuckled. He was fair-skinned with a nice, friendly smile. His name was Kevin. Deja's daily interactions with him over the last five weeks were the only thing she thought she might miss about the hospital. Kevin was only thirty one, but he already had six years of experience on the rehab floor. He wore his hair short and had wire-rimmed glasses that made him look a little nerdy.

"I'm pretty sure you don't have to do rehab *forever*," he said.

"It already feels like I've been here forever," Deja replied.

"Aw, hush girl," her mother said. Shirley wore a big smile and a bright sun dress that afternoon. "You need to be happy you're getting out of here at all. Not too many people take a bullet and live to tell about it."

"For real," Vincent said. "I got this one friend who got shot in the back of the neck. He lived, but he can't walk or talk or *nothing*."

Deja shook her head, wondering why her family felt the need to embarrass her in front of her handsome nurse friend. But Kevin grinned politely.

"Well, I guess that's it." He cradled her chart in his arms and rocked back on his heels. "I'll call transport, and they'll take you downstairs. Are you sure you don't want to take that walker?"

"I'm not taking that walker," Deja told him for the umpteenth time. She eyed the folded, metal contraption with disdain.

"Well, you're going to take your cane at least, right?"

"Yes, I'll take the cane," Deja said. She really didn't want that either, because it wasn't one of the cool, pimp daddy canes. It looked like a nursing home cane, complete with four stubby legs on the bottom.

"I think you should take the walker," her sister said. Julie stood in the doorway with Deja's son in her arms.

"Don't worry about it," Kevin said. "She's not going to take it. I know when Deja has her mind made up. That's fine. The

267

more she walks without it, the sooner she'll be independent again. And that's what we all want."

"Amen," Deja said and got a few chuckles from her relatives.

Her one gunshot wound entered her groin area on the left side and proceeded to slice through everything in its path until it hit her pelvis. Deja had to undergo her second surgery at Jackson Memorial to remove the slug from her ilium. Fortunately there was no major damage. Her orthopedic doctor said she wouldn't even have a limp by Halloween. Rehab was the hardest part. Dr. Ogden said she'd need a lot of will power and determination. These were two qualities Deja had in abundance.

"Okay, well, I'll go call transport," Kevin said. "Deja, it was an honor working with you. I wish all of my patients were as delightful." He stuck out a hand and Deja shook it. "You guys take it easy," the nurse said. He waved goodbye to the rest of the family and exited the room.

"That's a shame," Shirley said when he was out of sight.

"What's that?" Deja asked.

"I could've swore that boy was going to ask for your phone number, the way he's been grinning at you for the past few weeks."

"He was just being nice," Deja said, though inwardly she'd been thinking the same.

"I'll go get the car ready," her father said. "You coming with me?" he asked Vincent.

"Yeah, I'm coming," Vincent said and followed him out.

A moment later someone knocked on the open door. A tall, Hispanic man stuck his head in and smiled. "Can I come in?"

It was Rudy Cervantes. Deja hadn't seen him since he took her statement when she first got to the hospital.

"Sure," she said. "But I'm about to leave. They already called transport."

"Good. I'm glad I caught you. Wanted to let you know that our guy finally talked last night. I've been up with him since three this morning."

By *our guy*, he was referring to Benton Howard. Deja was surprised. After the punishment she inflicted on him, no one thought he would ever be coherent again. But Benton was a strong man. He made it out of ICU three weeks after his bout with a toilet tank lid. He suffered skull fractures, *extensive* facial fractures, and more cuts and bruises than a no-legged rooster after a cock fight. Benton would never look anything like the man he was before the fight. His left eye would never look in the same direction as the right one. He would never be able to speak without having a hand towel handy to catch the drool leaking from his misshapen mouth.

"What'd he say?" Deja asked. She was somber now. Despite it all, she felt pity for Benton, rather than hatred.

The detective looked from Deja to her mother and sister.

"This is still confidential," he said. "We haven't given any of this to the press yet."

"They won't say anything," Deja assured him.

"I promise I won't," her sister agreed.

"Scouts honor," Shirley said. Deja was pretty sure her mother knew nothing about the Boy Scouts codes and ethics, but she didn't say anything.

The detective took a seat on the bed next to Deja. She could tell he was excited. "Okay, so you were right. He confessed to the first four murders."

Deja nodded. The police were reluctant to accept that when they initially questioned her.

"And that means you were right about Gilbert Reynolds being innocent the whole time," Mr. Cervantes said. "But it's not your fault he got convicted. He put himself in a bad spot. We still don't know what he was doing out there the night he got arrested-"

"It's okay," Deja said.

The detective stared at her. He knew how strongly she felt about Gilbert's suicide. "Are you sure?"

"I'm not *great*," she said. "But I did a lot of thinking and praying since I've been here, and I don't blame myself for that anymore. I never said he was the one who attacked me. If he would have kept believing and kept praying, he'd be free by now. He made the decision to take his own life, not me."

"That's good," Mr. Cervantes said with a nod. "That's exactly right, Deja. I'm glad you feel that way."

"Did Benton say why he came back for me?"

"Yes. But first off, you have to understand that this guy's crazy. I mean, I've met some loonies in my time, but this one takes the cake."

Deja didn't like to hear that because she really liked Benton up until the moment he tried to kill her. She wondered how he could act so normal if he was so crazy. Or was she so desperate, she didn't notice he had issues. "What did he say?"

"He said a lot." The detective stretched his legs out and crossed them. "I guess it all started for him around puberty. Growing up, Benton didn't know he was different, until around the sixth grade. He was using a urinal next to one of his classmates, and he says he looked over and saw a *big discrepancy* between what he had compared to the other kid. He says it hurt his feelings, but at the time he didn't think anything of it. He thought he would, you know, grow out of it. Things didn't start to get bad for him until a couple of years later, when he got his first girlfriend in the eighth grade."

Deja nodded. She had already mapped most of this out in her head, based on what Benton told her during the attack.

"To make a long story short," Mr. Cervantes said, "that first girl kicked off a spiral of relationships that all went downhill, one after another. Benton quickly realized it was his small manhood that was to blame. He's not just a small man. He's actually got some type of deformity.

"He didn't think he could change it, so he began to resent the girls who rejected him. He went through a lot. He gave me a laundry list of incidents that hurt him in high school, things they used to say about him. He still remembers the name of every girl who teased him when he was younger. I'm talking fifty or more people. He knows their first and last names, where the incidents occurred, what the girls were wearing. Everything."

Julie squeezed Deja's baby tighter.

"Of course that's no reason to kill people," the detective said. "But somewhere in Benton's twisted mind, that's what he decided to do. That, to him, was the only way he could get back at the people who hurt him."

"Why didn't he go after the ones he was mad at?" Deja wondered.

"Because once he got older," Mr. Cervantes said, "they all looked and acted the same to him. He didn't have to find his girlfriend from the eighth grade because all black women were hateful in his eyes. They were all superficial and mean – in his

270

eyes. No one wanted to give him a chance and find out what kind of man he could be."

That hurt Deja because she thought she tried to do just that. She sighed. "So, how many did he kill?"

"The first four for sure," the cop said. "And Violet McNairn. He claims to have killed two more in Texas before Tawanda Murphy and another two in Louisiana and Oklahoma while Gilbert Reynolds was in jail. We have to do a lot more talking before we can verify the others, but, yeah, I believe him."

Deja believed him, too.

"And as far as coming back for you, things simply got personal. Benton had been killing for so long, he began to think he was invincible – especially when someone else got convicted for his crimes. He didn't think we would ever catch him. And you were a thorn in his side, because you were the only one who got away.

"You were like a curiosity to him. He watched you on the news. He says he wanted to get to know you, to lull you into a false sense of security before he, um...."

"Before he got his butt kicked," Shirley said. "He picked on the wrong one, didn't he baby?"

Deja was starting to feel tense, but she smiled at that. "Yeah, Mama. I guess so."

"The weird thing is," the policeman said, "Benton saved up enough money for some type of penis enlargement surgery. He actually had a surgery date scheduled. It would've been a couple of weeks after he shot you."

Deja was startled by that. "If he would've waited, he would've been normal?"

"Well, he would've been *physically* normal. That's what I mean about him being bitter and crazy. It wasn't about him being normal or abnormal anymore. It was about punishing women."

The room went quiet while everyone let that sink in.

"Hey, uh, y'all ready?"

They looked up and saw a burly teenager standing in the doorway. He pushed a wheelchair ahead of him. Deja knew that was her ride to freedom.

"Yes, I am." She tried to stand, but there was still a lot of soreness. She reached for her cane. The detective jumped to his feet and helped her up.

"Thank you." Deja's movements were stiff, but she was glad to finally get out of there. You couldn't wipe the smile off her face with sandpaper.

The policeman helped her into the chair and said, "I'll walk out with you, if you like. They got the reporters sectioned off this time, but it still might be a hassle."

"I appreciate that," Deja told him.

"Are you going to do another interview?" her sister asked as they exited the room.

"Yeah, but not with no funky *Channel Six*," her mom said.

"With who then?" Julie asked.

"Oh, I thought I told you," Deja said. "Oprah called."

Julie's jaw dropped. "Get outta here."

"I guess if you survive a serial killer *twice*, your story's kind of a big deal," Deja said.

"My baby in the big leagues!" Shirley squealed.

"Ain't that something," Julie said. "Oprah's my hero. You gotta let me meet her!"

Halfway down the hallway, they ran into Deja's nurse, who appeared to be loitering for no good reason.

"Hey," he said. "I thought you were gone already."

"How would we get by without you seeing us?" Shirley asked. "This is the only way out."

"Oh," Kevin said. "Well, uh, if you have any other questions, Deja, don't hesitate to call. I only work three days a week; Tuesday, Wednesday and Thursday. But if you leave a message for me–"

"Why don't you give her your number?" Shirley butted in.

Kevin blushed and grinned sheepishly. "I was, um, I'm trying to..."

Julie laughed. Deja was so flattered, she could only smile.

"So, how about it?" the nurse asked her. "Think you'd ever like to see me outside of the hospital?"

Before Deja could answer, her mom butted in again.

"You haven't killed nobody, have you?"

"My sister had some bad luck with men," Julie chipped in.

Deja's mouth fell open. *Oh, my God!*

"No, I haven't killed anyone," Kevin said to Shirley. "And if you give me a chance," he told Deja, "you'll see that I'm not like those other guys."

"Okay," she said. This was so embarrassing, but also endearing. Deja didn't think she looked cute right then, and over the past five weeks Kevin saw her looking worse than that. If he was still interested, it had to be deeper than a physical level.

He scribbled his number on a Post-it and handed it to her.

"I'll talk to you later," he said and backed away.

"Alright," she replied and giggled, and the transporter got them moving again. Deja didn't get her breathing under control until they got on the elevator.

THE END
BY KEITH THOMAS WALKER

ABOUT THE AUTHOR

Keith Thomas Walker, known as the Master of Romantic Suspense and Urban Fiction, is the author of more than a dozen novels, including *Fixin' Tyrone*, *Dripping Chocolate* and *The Realest Ever*. Keith enjoys reading, poetry and music of all genres. Originally from Fort Worth, he is a graduate of Texas Wesleyan University. Keith was nominated for an Emma Award in 2010 for Debut Author of the Year. In 2012 Keith was the recipient of a BRAB Book Club Award for Male Author of the Year (for Harlot) as well as a SORMAG Award for Fiction Author of the Year. In 2013 Keith was the recipient of a BRAB Book Club Award for Male Author of the Year (for Dripping Chocolate). Visit him at www.keithwalkerbooks.com.

CPSIA information can be obtained at www.ICGtesting.com
Printed in the USA
LVOW10s0921160214

373874LV00002B/5/P

9 780988 218031